A vast dread lodged itself in l
Somewhere a boundary had
of alien intrusion was no less imn
would have been if Osobei had pu
But which boundary? She began n
encampment, rising slightly on her toes as though that would really help her see better. Osobei fell into step beside her, his expression more curious than concerned.

Then they heard the first scream.

She broke into a stumbling run. The scream was immediately joined by others. They came from near the warriors' *gers*. She smelled plenty of roasting meat, horse-sweat and *qumis*, but the rising scent of vampire blood quickly threatened to overwhelm them all.

From the campfire protruded the lower half of someone Deverra was sure she should recognize. Qarakh stood in the center of a knot of his Cainite soldiers. Long earth-colored claws extended from the tips of his hands and also from his feet, shredding through his soft leather boots. As she watched, he bodily picked one Cainite up and threw him a good ten yards. Another he seized by the throat, then he snapped the man's spine over his knee and began to drink lustily from the outstretched neck.

Copyright © 2004 by White Wolf Publishing
ISBN 978-1-950565-61-0
All rights reserved. No part of this book may be used or reproduced in any manner whatsoever without written permission except in the case of brief quotations embodied in critical articles and reviews
For information address Crossroad Press at 141 Brayden Dr., Hertford, NC 27944
A Mystique Press Production - Mystique Press is an imprint of Crossroad Press.
www.crossroadpress.com

Crossroad Press Trade Edition

Vampire: The Dark Ages

CLAN NOVEL
TREMERE

BY SARAH ROARK

WHITE WOLF

Dark Ages Tremere

ARBITRIUM VINCIT OMNIA

Sarah Roark

AD 1231-1232
Eleventh of the Dark Ages Clan Novels

For Brett, for too many reasons to name.

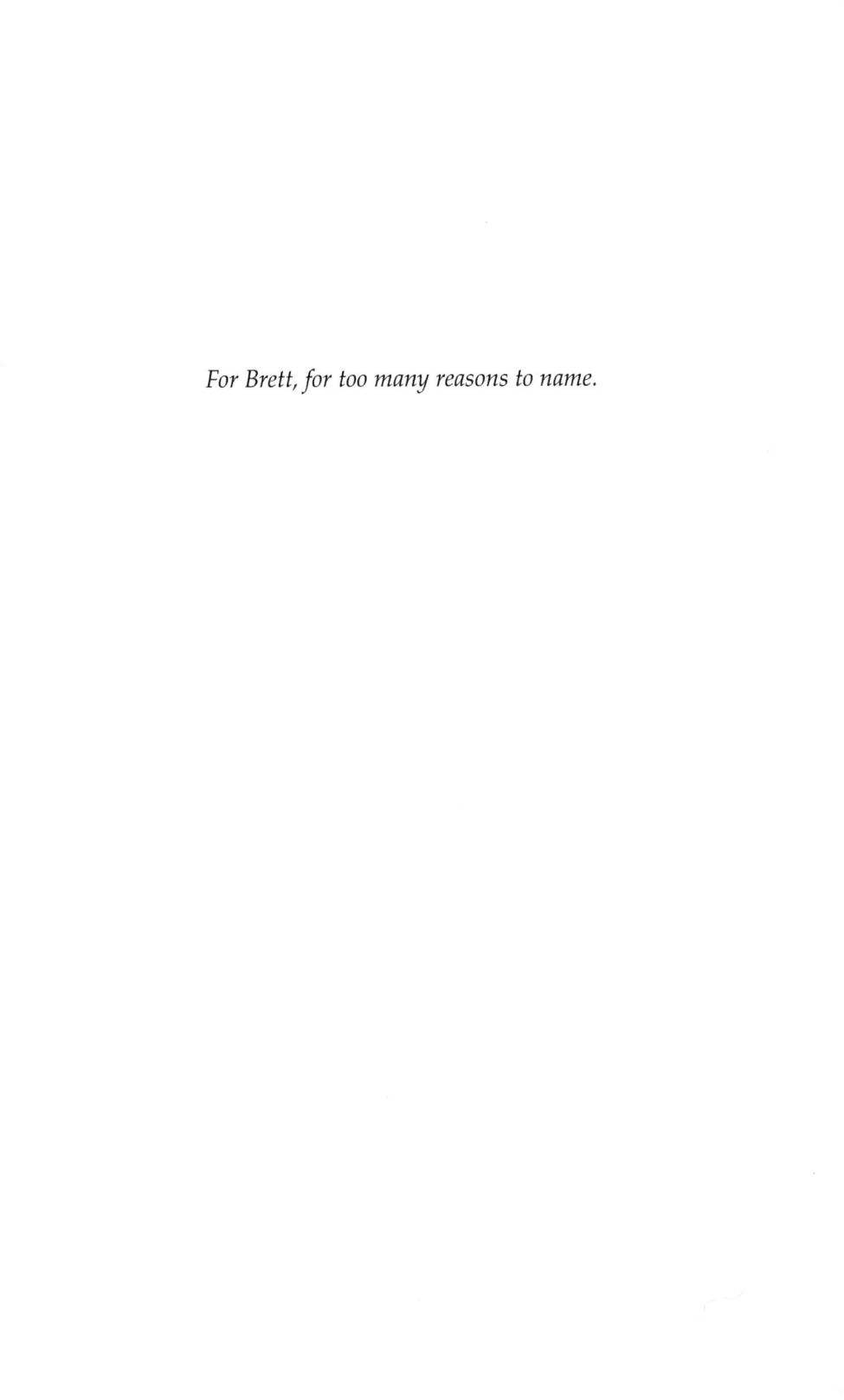

What Has Come Before

It is the year 1232, and decades of warfare and intrigue continue among the living and the dead. The Teutonic Knights and Sword-Brothers have embarked on campaigns to conquer and convert pagan Prussia and Livonia, spreading the crusading zeal into new lands. Bloodshed has, as always, followed in its wake.

Away from the eyes of the living, in the shadowy world of the undead, these crusades have dark echoes. The powerful Saxon vampire Jürgen of Magdeburg shares the Teutons' zeal and leads the so-called Brotherhood of the Black Cross, a secret order within both the Teutonic Knights and Livonian Sword-Brothers. He is determined to expand his domain into Livonia, using the banner of Christianity to increase his holdings. Last year he sent his guest-cum-rival Alexander to lead the conquest on his behalf, but that mighty vampire fell before the vampiric chieftain Qarakh, who leads a band of pagan blood-drinkers in alliance with Deverra, a blood sorceress and unliving priestess of the pagan god Telyavel. Qarakh's might in battle and Deverra's witchery together brought ancient Alexander low. Jürgen is rid of a rival, but his plans of conquest seem in a shambles.

Existing in the midst of this chaos is Jervais bani Tremere, a vampire and wizard who wishes to establish good relations between Jürgen and his superiors in the Tremere order. Unfortunately, Jürgen is not inclined to trust Jervais (who once schemed to deceive him) or any Tremere (whom he considers interlopers among the undead). Jervais attempted to make himself useful by conveying the warning that Qarakh had sorcerous aid. Now he must deal with the evident fact that his warning was either insufficient or went undelivered.

And hope that it doesn't cost him his head…

Prologue

*H*e knew he was dreaming, but that did not help.

It was a room he could remember being in a long time ago, a library in which he and his master had once spent a few months. Bookshelves covered each wall from floor to ceiling, some holding codices, some with ancient moldering scrolls that threatened to spill out onto the floor. They towered over him, silently judging him a child and a fool. He moved through the cavernous chamber, filled with dread. He listened but heard only the sound of his own footfalls. Perhaps it was watching him, matching his pace. He could not hear it breathe. But it didn't always breathe.

Across the room, a pile of books and maps suddenly tumbled to the floor. He stared at it in a panic, and for one searing moment tried to will himself to believe that it had simply been overbalanced. Then he saw the blood spattered across the pages. He ran.

Now he could hear it quite clearly, footsteps ringing like marble on marble and furniture flying in all directions behind him. Eight doors led out of the library, but most of them lay back toward the Thing. He chose a door from those before him, yanked on the handle several times before it gave way at last, then dashed through.

And so it began. The next room he also recognized, but it didn't belong to the same building. That hardly mattered. It had six doors leading out. He tried to remember which one he'd chosen last time. The one on the left, he thought. This time he went right. Still the Thing came hot on his heels.

The chase seemed to last for hours. Every door he opened led only to a room with more doors, and though he tried at first to keep his bearings, he soon lost all concept of direction and distance past a vague horror that somehow his path was being bent in upon itself—that he was being herded.

He also found that while the first rooms he'd wound through had had six, eight, twelve, four-and-twenty doors, the later ones had only two or three. His choices were narrowing. And though he still couldn't hear the Thing behind him breathe, he could hear the devastation it wrought in its wake. Whatever it was, it was enormous. He had no idea how it was fitting through the doors. Yet somehow or other it gradually gained on him. He ran faster, chose his doors with diminishing care. He was sure he was making mistakes. Mistakes he might have avoided if he'd only been able to pause, think, consider. But he also knew with the absolute certainty of dreaming that if he stopped or even slowed down for an instant, he would die in its teeth.

In another part of his mind, in a parallel reverie to this frantic scrambling, he was aware of his body tossing in its daytime slumber. He longed to wake himself up, but that would take his attention away from the maze for that one fatal instant. During other instances of this nightmare he'd imagined that she came to him, as she had come to him once (and only once) in reality, and laid her soft cool hand across his sweating forehead. Just now he could not conjure even the imagination of her. He was all alone, immured in stone. Sometimes the master heard echoes of the torment, but even he could do nothing.

And then there were the others that also heard—some locked within their own torpid bodies, some with no bodies at all. They heard and laughed, taunting him with the truth they all knew: that even immortals could only run so far and so fast for so long before that final slip, that brief hesitation that was all the Thing would need...

Chapter One

Lady Rosamund moved the last of her pieces off the board. "I didn't think the magi of Tremere were taught always to let a lady win," she remarked.

Jervais bani Tremere tilted his head to the side in a slight gesture of acknowledgment and began to reset the board again. It bought him time to consider his response. "I can't speak for the rest of my brethren, milady," he answered, "but for my part, I was taught always to give a lady precisely the sport she requires, neither more nor less. Why do you mention it?"

"Well," she said lightly, "wizards are supposed to be clever, are they not? I hardly expected to defeat one so handily twice in a row. I'm forced to wonder if you're playing to win at all."

"I always play to win, milady."

"I detect a note of irony."

"Milady has a fine ear for music."

"Ah, we must be embarking on the obligatory chain of political metaphors now."

"Good God, I hope not," he exclaimed—and was rewarded with her first genuine, though small, smile of the evening. "Surely we haven't run out of actual conversation just yet."

The smile vanished quickly at that. He immediately regretted his words. He'd thrown her off rhythm, and while that was often a worthwhile goal in diplomacy, tonight he needed just the opposite. No doubt this was already difficult enough for her, even if one would never know it. But she quickly recovered herself and gave him another smile. It was pretty, warm, invitational and not half so captivating as the real thing now that he'd seen the difference.

"Do they not play tables in the sorcerers' towers, Master Tremere?"

"There's little time for such pursuits, I fear."

"Such frivolous pursuits, is that what you were going to say?"

"I would certainly never say that, milady."

Her head remained bent over the board, but her hazel-green eyes flashed upward. "But someone else would?"

It was necessary, he reminded himself. It was the price of admission, or rather of re-admission. She would be satisfied when she believed she'd obtained more than he'd meant to give. Things could always be worse. It could be Prince Jürgen the Sword-Bearer himself putting him through the paces, rather than Jürgen's beauteous mistress. Still, Jervais did not have to force much reluctance into his voice.

"That is what is taught to our apprentices, yes. If they have time to play, then they must have time to study more, work harder. No doubt there are floors that could use a scrubbing, at the very least."

"They don't even play chess, then?" She shook her head. "That has, as you know, a special significance to certain bloods. It is also widely extolled as a thing that sharpens the mind, teaches the art of the stratagem. The game of princes."

"I know of but one Tremere prince, milady," he returned mildly.

"There is something to be said for standing behind the throne, I suppose."

"Or at the side of it. That isn't the argument, however. Why waste one's time toying with men and Cainites and governments when the levers that move the very world are waiting there to be discovered and mastered? Conquer them, and you conquer everything."

She knocked a blot of his onto the bar. "Ah. You don't seem to agree, however. You play. You must have been a very stubborn apprentice."

"I have been accused of it, milady. But is it stubbornness to realize that not everyone cares about the virtues of onyx or the exact shape of the wards on Solomon's key, and that while one is shut up in one's little room learning Creation's secrets, Creation itself rolls by outside?"

"I suppose I shouldn't be surprised to hear such a widely traveled man utter such sentiments," she said wryly. "I must have assumed it was a matter of duty and not pleasure. The others of your clan I've spoken to—who, I admit, are few enough—all seemed to hate the world as much as any anchorite."

"Many do. I've never understood it myself. There's far too much to see."

"Even in Magdeburg?"

"Especially in Magdeburg," he chuckled. "Far more to see here than in the very clearest crystal."

"And at Ceoris?" she prompted.

That drew him up short. "At Ceoris—at Ceoris what?"

Her eyebrow flickered a bit, noting his reaction. He inwardly cursed himself once again. "Is there much to see?"

"Ah."

"Ceoris *is* in Hungary, is it not?"

"Yes, of course, milady."

"Of all that country I only know what I've read in soldiers' letters from the battle front, which, as you can imagine, are short on detail." She sighed. "I'm not one of those ladies who needs to be entertained with long soliloquies on pine and lake and mist and moonlight in foreign lands, Master Tremere, but for those of us who must wait at home with the distaff, there's always that desire to know more of what those dear to us saw and suffered."

"What they suffer even now," he said. He couched it as a polite murmur, obligatory courtesy, but he did want to see what she made of it.

She nodded solemnly and cast her gaze downward for a moment. "Yes. But alas, unlike Hungary, you have not seen Livonia with your own eyes. Or so you said the last time we met."

A quick parry, then. Interesting. "No, milady." Since they were treading so closely to the real content of their meeting already, he dared continue a little further along the path. "I do trust the information I gathered on the subject of Livonia has proved useful to his Highness, however."

"That would be something you'd have to ask his Highness, of course."

"Then I hope to have opportunity to do so."

"We all have our hopes, Master Tremere." Her slim hand reached out, fast as a striking adder, to catch a die that tumbled off the table from her overly enthusiastic roll. "I am sure that for its part, Ceoris hopes for a better issue from your endeavors this time around."

He accepted his punishment without complaint. It was his own fault. She had tried to approach the subject gracefully, from the perspective of the worried grass widow, and he'd insisted on turning it into a foray into what was clearly uncomfortable territory. It was so hard to shut down that instinct, but he had to remember his real purpose here. *Stop sparring*, he told himself. *Perhaps you should even let yourself be a bit bewitched in earnest.*

"Ceoris is more convinced than ever, milady, that Prince Jürgen's interests and those of House and Clan Tremere coincide so closely that they simply must ally for both their sakes… as soon as possible."

"If you mean that should the Black Cross fall, Ceoris will have that much less standing between it and the wrath of the *voivode*," she said archly, "I would tend to agree. Are you telling me that the war goes badly for your brethren there?"

"No, not badly, milady. Petty harassment and scattered raids."

"Then why this urgency?"

"Milady, clearly we've all been rather hoping Rustovitch's forces would simply fall apart in the wake of the truce, and just as clearly, that hasn't happened. Perhaps it'll help if I explain that petty harassment and scattered raids are precisely the *voivode's* favorite tactic for keeping his enemies occupied while he rebuilds his strength and whips any faltering allies back into compliance. When he has truly given up, we will know it."

"Oh? How?"

"Because it won't look like anything we've ever seen before," he answered in the most serious tone he could command. "Milady, we have weathered him and the rest of the Tzimisce storm for nigh on two centuries now. I can assure you from personal experience that giving up is not in his nature. He'll take time, when it's given him, to rest and replenish. Then, just as that eye of calm begins to pass..."

She stared at him, game piece in her fingers, momentarily forgotten. "You think Rustovitch is waiting to see the issue of the fighting in Livonia, then."

"I think the treaty between Rustovitch and Prince Jürgen might as well have been signed in Qarakh's blood, because he's its only guarantor. The truce is a handy excuse for Rustovitch to recover himself while he watches to see how badly his Highness can be damaged by the campaign against the Balts. Nothing more."

"You seem to be assuming his Highness will in fact be damaged." She made her move and regarded him with a defiance that she no longer tried to disguise under flirtation. "What if he triumphs instead?"

"He *must* triumph, milady," he exclaimed. "My masters' only desire is to ensure that."

"And your own desire, Master Tremere? Is it the same as your masters'?"

An expected line of questioning, but unwelcome nonetheless. "Mademoiselle Rosamund...I was, as I've told you, quite firmly corrected by my superiors for my earlier mistake. However, that doesn't change the fact that I was pursuing their goal to the best of my ability, which was and is friendship between our clan and Prince Jürgen's court."

"They don't appear to have appreciated your efforts on their behalf any more than his Highness did," she noted dryly.

He did his best to submerge his growing irritation. "No, milady." He let the pause afterward speak for him.

She gave him a consoling look. "It simply makes me wonder why it's *you* that's here once again, Master Tremere—instead of some other representative. Surely that would have been more comfortable for all concerned?"

Jervais seized an opportunity to knock her onto the bar just as she was about to begin bearing off. He sat back, trying to school the look of relief on his face into something less earnest. The two concurrent games had nothing to do with each other really, yet it was odd how even the smallest victory in one helped his resolve in the other. Now he could marshal his thoughts. He *had* to give her something. The more the reasoning part of his mind repeated this, the more badly the rest of him wanted to give her nothing, nothing at all, not even the courtesy of a refusal. Under the table, one hand clenched in his lap, bearing the burden for all the rest of his body.

"Comfort is not a priority for my masters, milady," he said at last. "Particularly not my comfort. They have generously proffered me one—and only one—opportunity to clean up the mess I made of things. This is how I've chosen to make that attempt... bearing in mind the rules as they have now been explained to me."

"I see." She leaned forward. Her voice lowered. Could it be actual sympathy? The damned bitch. "And if you should fail?"

The laugh that bubbled up from his throat was a good deal more bitter than anything he'd meant to give voice to. "Failure is not among the choices before me, milady."

There. Will you be satisfied at last? May I pass on to my next torment now, hellcat?

"I see," she said again. She began bearing off her pieces. "You are hardly the only one in Magdeburg laboring under that constraint, Master Tremere."

He frowned. It was a hint, certainly. The question was whether it was meant to help him or mislead him. Then again, if she really wanted to frustrate his plans, all she had to do was go on ignoring his existence just as she had for the last several months. Hopefully, the fact that he was here tonight at all meant she felt a need to test the waters, which meant that Jürgen felt a need to test the waters...which must mean that he was worried.

"Your turn," she informed him.

"Actually, since your ladyship has clearly won already, I'm happy to concede the game."

She laughed, a perfect bell-like laugh. He relaxed. They were back on their original footing. Perhaps he'd passed the test. Or perhaps they were only on to a new one now, since she followed up the laugh with: "Very well. I'll let you concede, if you'll show me a bit of magic instead."

"A bit of magic?" he repeated.

"Unless you've suddenly become like those other wizards you were speaking of earlier, who say they're students of the great secrets and not street-conjurors performing for coin," she teased him.

"Not at all, not at all," he said, feeling absurd. "It should be my honor to amuse such a beautiful and noble lady. Let me see, let me think. Ah. May I use a scrap from that sewing basket?"

"Certainly."

He retrieved one and selected a short length of silk cord from within. "And may I impose again and borrow the ring on milady's left hand?"

She smiled, slipped it off and passed it over. He knotted the ring onto the string, then closed his hand over it.

"*Phorba phorba askei kataski!*" he cried out, gesturing with his free hand. A spark of blue radiance flashed out from between his closed fingers. He opened his fist to show the cord, now unknotted and missing the ring. Then he rubbed his hands together, to emphasize their emptiness, and extracted the ring from the dice-cup.

She laughed again and clapped. "Lovely."

"But..." he supplied.

"But..." She hesitated, then shrugged. "Well, the truth is I once saw a juggler do almost exactly the same trick, only without that flash of light."

He chuckled. "I'm sure it *was* the same trick, except for the flash of light which, I admit, I added for pure show."

"Then—I see, you've been having me on."

"Never having you on, milady. After all, I confessed the truth to you right away. But once I did it for a fellow-wizard, and do you know, he pestered me about it for the rest of my visit. Was it this spell, was it that spell, was it a variation on Celorb's dispersal perhaps?"

"And yet it wasn't a spell at all..."

He polished her ring on the shoulder of his *bliaut* and handed it back. "If you can't tell the difference, what difference does it make?"

"If you can't tell the difference." She looked the ring over.

He felt a jolt of embarrassment as he realized she was trying to ascertain that he'd indeed returned the genuine article.

"Milady, surely you don't think—"

"No, Master Tremere, I can see that it's mine. Even you could hardly know to copy the inscription on the inside of a band that hasn't left my hand since it was first put on, could you? And as you said…at least you confessed the truth to me right away this time," she went on in a more serious tone. "It's better for the future, I think, that we clearly understand each other. You are a wizard, yes, but you also believe in practicality."

He recovered himself as quickly as he could. "Yes, milady. It is in itself a kind of wizardry to know when to use magic, and when some other method will serve just as well or better—"

She held up a warning hand. He stopped, irritation melting into apprehension as it became clear that she was genuinely listening for something. One of her handmaidens appeared in the doorway.

"Mademoiselle, forgive me," the woman said. "But your brother—"

"Yes, yes, of course," Rosamund interrupted. "See him in."

The woman dropped a hurried but graceful curtsey and backed out again. Jervais heard the soft chink of spurs and the slap of leather on wood, which was shortly followed by the entrance of Sir Josselin de Poitiers, Rosamund's brother-in-Blood.

"*Petite*," he began, "you must—ah." He stopped short, looking down his slim handsome nose at Jervais. His glare rippled violently through the warlock. Those of Josselin's blood often had that ability, to send the passions of their humors through the very air. Though Jervais had grown more used to it over time, it still caught him unprepared now and again. His teeth gritted under the onslaught.

It seemed to catch the knight himself unprepared too, after a fashion. At least he hastily reined himself in, the aura of demigod's pique disappearing as though it had never been, and turned instead to Rosamund. "Blanche might have told me you were still with…your company."

She waved this off. "Josselin, not now."

"No, not now," he agreed at once.

"Is there news?"

"Yes. You must come at once. You've been asked for. Forgive us, Master Tremere," he added.

Why is it I'm never granted my own name? "Not at all, messire," Jervais replied in his best tone of empathetic concern. "I certainly would not wish to keep her ladyship from anything important. Indeed, if it's that serious, perhaps I should go myself."

"I don't recall your being appointed one of his Highness's advisers," Sir Josselin returned. Then he seemed to realize that he was giving away too much in his eagerness to insult, and he fell silent.

"Of course, and I should hardly presume, messire," Jervais said. "But if his Highness is indeed summoning his advisers, then he may soon require the assistance of his humbler servants as well. And I would far rather arrive to find my services unwelcome than hear later that I was asked for and nowhere to be found."

The two nobles exchanged glances.

"In that case, I suppose we should all ride together," Josselin said. "We wouldn't want anything to happen to you on the road."

"You do me too much honor, messire." Jervais stood and made a low, unctuous bow.

Chapter Two

The ride to St. Paul's was short and silent but filthy. The streets and roads were plagued with muck that three days' worth of drizzle had dampened but not washed away. At first Jervais tried vainly to hitch up his fine long *bliaut* so that it wouldn't be spattered, then he decided it might be to his advantage to give the appearance of having hurried pell-mell to his host's aid. It was important to remember what sort of Cainite Jürgen was, and his monk-knight lieutenants in the Black Cross order as well. The preciosities that other courts thrived on they considered despicable, indulgent. A little mud no doubt conveyed sincerity.

A pair of groomsmen took the bridles of their steaming horses almost before they'd stopped, and a young squire was waiting nearby to usher them inside.

"Lady Rosamund," he blurted. "Sir Josselin." He stopped and stared at Jervais.

"And Jervais bani Tremere of Ceoris," Jervais supplied richly. "Your august lord knows the name, I assure you."

The lad opened his mouth to speak, glanced at Rosamund and Sir Josselin (who offered no help or hindrance whatever), then shut it again and nodded. "Very well. Come, please."

He conducted them across the grounds into the guesthouse of the fortified priory. A fire leapt on high in a hearth at one end of the room—a huge hearth, meant to warm a room filled with dozens of human folk, perhaps cook them some soup at the same time. With a bare handful of wax-pale Cainites there now, the enormous blaze looked more menacing than cheering. Indeed, as Jervais used his blood-strength to sharpen the weak eyesight a mocking God had given him, he could see that they all stood a safe distance away from it. Rosamund and Josselin were let inside without a murmur, but the door-guard's spear came down at an angle before Jervais, stopping him at the threshold. The squire leaned up on tiptoe to whisper into the guard's ear. Jervais could have sharpened his hearing as well and heard the precise words, but there was hardly a need. The guard leaned his head slightly inside the door to hiss at someone just within. Further words were exchanged. A few moments later Jervais heard a murmur arise at the far side of the room. The voice of Prince Jürgen soared over it.

"I don't care. Let the man in. *Let him in!*" he repeated for the benefit of the mortal man at the door. Jervais smiled as the spear moved aside again. But he hastily composed himself into what he hoped was the right purposeful, slightly worried manner before he went in.

"Meister Tremere. Hurry along there," Prince Jürgen called out. "Don't bother making all the legs, just come."

Jervais halted in mid-bow and did as he was told, bustling up to the front. "Your Highness," he said, touching knee to stone as quickly as could be done. Jürgen immediately motioned him up.

Next to Jürgen stood a thin Cainite in a priest's cassock—Father Erasmus, Jürgen's confessor—and another one Jervais didn't recognize, dressed as most of the Black Cross knights dressed, in the garb of the mortal Teutonic Order. Brother Christof, Jürgen's second in command, stood brooding off to one side, hand straying reflexively to sword hilt. It took Jervais a little longer to find the last person in the room because he was the only one sitting down. He was a Cainite with hair tonsured in the knights' usual style and wearing an emblazoned habit, huddled in a chair in Jürgen's substantial shadow. A blanket covered his legs. One leg seemed to be little wider than a broomstick, and Jervais could just imagine the sight that lay beneath. A vampire could recover even lost limbs, given time and blood enough to heal, but the process of re-growing bone and muscle and re-stringing sinew, was slow and arduous. The firelight threw the lines of pain in his face into harsh relief.

"Very well. Now that we're all here…" Jürgen nodded at a human squire, who ran off. "Lady Ambassador, Herr Josselin, Meister Tremere. I think Herr Josselin is the only one of you to have met Brother Eckard before."

"Of course, on campaign in Hungary," Josselin nodded, bowing. "I am sorry to see you injured, brother."

The wounded man bowed in turn from the waist. "Herr Josselin. I remember you with great respect."

"Brother Eckard rode all the way from the Livonian front despite his wound to carry us the news," Jürgen said brusquely, glancing at Josselin and then at Rosamund, who stood frozen. "I'm afraid it's very bad. I thought that you should be the first to know, *meine Dame*."

He turned to the squire, who'd returned with a bit of folded cloth that he transferred into Jürgen's hands. The prince let it fall open. Framed in his powerful arms it seemed very small indeed, sized more for a slip of a boy than a man—which wasn't far from the truth. It was a surcoat of fine white cloth, now bloodied and streaked with dirt. Still visible through the blotches of red were the black embroidered "tails" of the ermine pattern and the purple stripe that ran vertically down the middle with a circlet of leaves embroidered atop that in gold thread.

A choking sound echoed in the room. Jervais glanced up, startled. It was the only graceless noise he'd ever heard emerge from the Lady Rosamund's swanlike throat. With utmost gravity Jürgen brought the cloth over to her, offering it. She hesitated but then took it. A moment later her skirt wobbled and she began to sink toward the floor. Sir Josselin caught her elbow and bore her up until she recovered her usual proud posture.

"*Vair, on a pale purpure, a laurel wreath or,*" he murmured, gazing at it in shock. Rosamund tried to blink back the film of red in her eyes.

The arms of Alexander, sometime Prince of Paris, now liege-lord to Lady Rosamund and general in service to his far younger clansman Jürgen the Sword-Bearer; recently sent to Livonia to subdue the upstart pagans. As every other heart in the room either sank or quailed, Jervais felt his rise and expand, unshackled at last.

"How…how is it possible?" Josselin managed at last. "One of such age, such power…"

"But no faith, I fear," Brother Eckard finished. The prince frowned but said nothing. "Forgive me, milord. Milord Alexander showed great courage and gallantry in the face of the enemy, and I pray nightly for his soul. But he would not humble himself before the Lord, even though it was the Lord's work we sought to do. I fear our enterprise suffered for it in the end. Perhaps…perhaps the rest of us failed in spirit somehow as well. I must do penance."

Father Erasmus laid a hand on his shoulder.

"There must have been treachery of some kind," Christof broke in. "Heathen sorcery." His quick dark eyes darted over to Jervais.

Jürgen looked at Jervais as well. "Yes, sorcery…I'm afraid there likely was that."

Jervais simply nodded, not knowing if a response was expected.

"The Tartar *was* like one possessed—whether by sorcery or some other foulness I don't know," Eckard mused. "He went bareheaded and barefoot, and moved more like a beast than a man. It was so swift, the fighting, that the eye could barely follow it except when they locked each other immobile for a brief moment. Yet for all the swiftness, it seemed to take hours… and then I was drowned and saw no more."

"Could no one intervene?" Rosamund asked desperately.

"*Meine Dame*, it seems a mire quite suddenly opened up under the battlefield, trapping everyone, or nearly everyone, except for Qarakh himself and your lord," Jürgen answered.

"Who *is* this Qarakh?" Josselin wanted to know. "Are we any closer to finding that out?"

"We have a little information… Thanks, in part, to the Tremere of Ceoris," the prince said.

A public acknowledgment of my assistance? What next?

"And now," he went on, "Brother Eckard and the two other brothers who've made it back so far have a little more that they've told us."

"We must call a council," Christof urged.

"We *will* call a council, but not tonight," Jürgen assured him. "Herr Josselin, your lady sister needs to be seen home."

"Of course, your Highness."

"After that, we must request that you do us the great kindness of conveying the news of Lord Alexander's death back to his childe in Paris."

Jervais valiantly suppressed a smirk. That would be Geoffrey, *current* Prince of Paris—at his lord sire the former prince's expense. He wondered whether there would be the pretense of grief, or not.

Josselin absorbed this with obvious difficulty. "Your Highness." He bowed again. "It is my honor to serve, so long as milady gives her permission of course."

Rosamund nodded faintly.

"Good. Then go at once with my earnest thanks, *mein Herr*. You may go as well, Meister Tremere, but I think we must have a talk sometime soon. I will call for you."

"Of course, your Highness." Jervais made a deep obeisance but decided not to append any courtly words to it. No doubt they'd only be taken as a jab or an expression of unseemly pleasure. He followed Josselin and Rosamund out and all but ran for his horse. Thank Great Tremere, the house that Jürgen's seneschal had chosen for him in town was quite close to Lady Rosamund's abode. He didn't have much time. Jürgen had said, "Go at once," and Sir Josselin was, if nothing else, a man to follow orders.

"Stop looking at me like that," Jürgen muttered.

Christof turned his grim face away, but the reproach in the air remained.

"There's no choice anymore," he went on. "Clearly we went in missing vital facts. Either this squat-legged savage is a lot older than we gave him credit for, or he does indeed have the aid of some demonic power. Alexander is *dead*, my friends."

"With all due respect, *Hochmeister*," Brother Meinhard put in, "better him than you. If the Lady Rosamund had not, so to speak, volunteered him…"

"And if he hadn't agreed to go, for her sake no doubt."

"And for his own," Meinhard reminded him hastily. "In any case, not for the right reasons. I must agree with Brother Eckard fully on that."

"Yes, but even if he went in with the worst reasons in the world, he should still have been able to defeat such ragamuffins handily." Jürgen paced over to a chair, whirled it around and sat. "Clearly we need help. They've offered it. I intend to take them up on it."

"The Tremere have shown their treachery to you once before, milord," Christof said, in a voice close to a growl. "And the stories you yourself brought back from Hungary, about the ambitions the Usurpers cherish that have *not* yet been exposed to the princes of the West."

"Stories from Rustovitch's lickspittles and attendants," Jürgen returned. "Hardly an unbiased source. I'm sure they were ordered to sound me out about the possibility of colluding with their master against the Tremere. I think Rustovitch would gladly take the hand even of my sire, if it meant the wizards' destruction. And just as gladly the wizards seek to take *my* hand in a mutual pledge to destroy Rustovitch—or if I won't accede to that right away, to a pledge to destroy Qarakh in Livonia so that Rustovitch may be next. And neither Rustovitch nor the Tremere are truly my friends, whatever agreements we make to the contrary. We all wish each other gone from Hungary—indeed from all the East. It's only a question of what temporary alliances will form on the way to utter annihilation. Be sure I'm well aware of all of this, Brother Christof, but unfortunately it changes nothing."

"If I may, milord." Father Erasmus spoke up hesitantly. "Surely the answer to nigromancy is not more nigromancy."

The prince brushed wearily at his mustache with a thumb and forefinger. "Father, do you realize that the bulk of the troops the Sword-Brothers are using in Livonia are in fact Letts and Livs? Natives, whose devotion to Christianity consists almost solely of the yearly tithe they pay. The only hymns they sing are songs of delight in the plunder they capture from their ancestral enemies. Let's be honest in this room. An entire nation doesn't convert overnight, not in its heart. But the outward observances come little by little to be matched by inward belief. That's the hope we all cherish. Until the time comes when they serve the Lord in truth, however, the Sword-Brothers are happy to let them serve the order instead. A spear doesn't care what sort of hand let it fly. If it's worthy of the Sword-Brothers to let pagans kill pagans in the name of killing paganism, then what is there to object to in letting sorcerers kill sorcerers?"

"I don't pretend to understand the methods of the Sword-Brothers, Highness."

"Very well, then, milord—write to Ceoris," Christof interrupted, wisely heading off any debate on the virtues, or lack thereof, of the Teutonic Order's Livonian counterpart. "But not *this* Tremere. That they have the unmitigated gall to even send him back here insults us and speaks ill of them. You could at least demand, as a token of their sincerity, that they dispatch some other messenger."

"Not gall but guile, I'd wager," Jürgen mused.

"Exactly. *Hochmeister*, we're speaking here of a man—of a Cainite—who was willing to steal a Toreador bauble and replace it with an elaborately crafted forgery, then *pretend* to discover the deception in open court, and all for what? A moment of political embarrassment for some far-off queen who never was among your stauncher or stronger allies anyway? Do you honestly believe that such a man even says 'Good evening' without meaning something else by it?"

"At least it's a well-balanced bauble." He patted the gilded pommel of the sword at his side. "Well, perhaps I'll ask him that. I'm sure I'll get an interesting answer. I'm curious, in any case, to see what he has to say about it all now that the years have intervened. The Lady Rosamund assures me that he's apologized most satisfactorily to her..."

"It's *you* he should apologize to," Christof grumbled.

"Yes, he should. And we shall see how satisfactory that apology is," he said with a keen smile. "What do you think, Akuji? Akuji? Surely she's here."

"Yes, your Highness." The voice was, as always, a marvel: smooth, faintly husky, yet despite its huskiness unmistakably, alluringly female, tinged with a hint of foreign spice.

The other Cainites in the room edged minutely away, except for Christof, who grimaced in private amusement. Akuji—whose form, draped and veiled in dilapidated linen, was no match for her voice—stepped forward.

"What do you think, old friend?" Jürgen asked her. "Ignore the Tremere completely, write to Ceoris or treat with Meister Jervais?"

"A difficult choice indeed, your Highness." She paused. She had an exquisite sense of when and how long to pause, to make her audience bend to hear the next word. "Perhaps, however, it is worth pointing out that of the three possibilities, two are not mutually exclusive."

"Here, Josselin, please."

"What do you want me to do with it, *petite*?"

"I don't know." She drew her raw lower lip into her mouth again. "I don't know what to do. I don't know what I *should* do."

He gazed at the length of bloody, sliced cloth with only slightly less than complete revulsion. "Myself, I'd fling it into the fire. I know you don't like to hear things like that, but I can't help it."

"I know, I know." She gazed at it as well. Part of her, too, wanted it gone completely, destroyed, like some heathen idol—as though doing that could banish Alexander and all thought of him from past, present and future forever. Just as much of her was terrified to do it for that exact reason. Perhaps some idols still had the power to revenge themselves on their desecrators. The reach of the ancient boy-prince, junior in blood only to the Eldest himself, had been long.

"What is it?" He knelt by her side. "Rosamund, don't. *Please* don't cry. Don't dignify it. I beg you."

"Forgive me," she said in a small, weak voice. She wiped away the tears, but new ones took their place.

"He doesn't deserve your mourning. He doesn't deserve a single one of your tears, unless it's a tear of joy. After what he did…"

"And what do I deserve, Josselin?" she blurted. A sob escaped on the heels of this question. She stood up.

"You deserve to be free. And you are free, now." His passion heated his words, made them fairly glow.

She shook her head. "You heard what Jürgen said. Sorcery. Heathen sorcery! Josselin, it *is* my fault."

"*Petite*, it's not."

"My doing, then. That much is true. Don't argue with me, my brother. I am not the little girl you once knew in Chartres. I know what I've done when I've done it. I simply—I simply have to make peace with it, that's all."

"Rosamund." He followed her as she paced away. "Make confession, then, if you feel you must. We can get you a priest! But don't keep it, no matter what. It'll only eat away at you, and I can't bear watching any more of that. He's had long enough to make you suffer. It must finish now."

"I can't. I can't burn it. Don't ask me to, Josselin."

"I'll burn it for you."

"No!" She cried out and reached toward him, even though he made no move toward the fire as yet. He stepped forward and put his arm around her.

"Will you at least let me take it with me and offer it to Geoffrey?" he murmured into the flame-colored cloud of her hair. "He has the strongest claim on it, anyway, and it would be well within the bounds of custom to bring it to him as proof. Then it would be out of our sight at least. Will that suffice?"

She hesitated for a long moment, then nodded. As she nodded he could feel some of the tension drain out of her frame.

"Good. Then that's what I'll do."

Just as he thought to pull away, she began sobbing. He tossed the surcoat to the floor as though it were so much rubbish and comforted her.

"Sh, shh. You only did what you had to, *petite*. To save yourself—to save all of us. It's over now."

It has to be, he thought. *Dear God and Our Lady, let it be.*

But on a night when God's favor rested inexplicably with a wild-eyed blasphemer in the dark swamps of Livonia, it might be wise to retain a certain prudent caution in one's heart regardless.

"Don't be such a whiner, Fidus," Jervais hissed. "It's quite simple. They've never seen you before, so there's no *danger* at all."

Fidus stood without shivering, despite the raindrops running down the length of his white nose and tumbling off. "But, master, I...look at me. I can't pass for ali—for a mortal anymore."

"Ridiculous." The older Tremere waved this off. "It's easy. All you need to do is bring the color up into your cheeks and remember to breathe. Trust me, they're all far too distracted right now to go worrying about you. You tell them you have some message from me."

"What message?"

"I don't know—surely you can think of something! A request for another meeting, perhaps. That way you'll be sent out of their presence to wait for an answer, and if you do a little wandering about the house while you wait and aren't too clumsy about it, no one will much mind. Look, I'm not even asking you to actually lay hands on the thing—although for Tremere's sake, if the chance falls to you, take it—but if you can even find out where it's being kept or what they're planning to do with it, that alone may be enough. Now do you think you can manage it or not?"

"I'll do my best, master." Fidus brushed his hair out of his eyes and made for the gate behind the house, trying to remember what it felt like to blush. He thought of the time several years ago when Jervais had sent him out to dig up toadstools and neglected to mention that he'd be entertaining women in the house that night—all so that when Fidus came back road-beaten and covered with soil Jervais could send the little trollops into gales of laughter with a mocking remark. Yes, that did well enough.

A few bursts of hammering on the gate brought a harried-looking, middle-aged man to open it. He had something wadded up under his woolen cloak to keep it out of the wet.

"Yes?"

"A message for your lady from my master Jervais," Fidus said, and coughed for verisimilitude. He let his cloak fall open to show he was unarmed.

The man looked even less patient at that, but he stepped

aside. "All right, come in. You may just have to give it to Peter to give to them. I don't know if they're receiving any more messengers tonight."

"Thank you." He dutifully followed the man, who stopped at the stables en route to the house itself. Evidently Fidus had caught him halfway through the process of loading saddlebags. Fidus turned his body away as the man stuffed the wadded-up bundle inside the bag, feigning disinterest, but glanced over sidewise at the last moment. There, a flash of bloodied and ripped cloth. Good—it was packed away in the saddlebags already then, doubtless in preparation for a hasty departure the next evening. Far easier to get at than if it had remained in the house.

Surely one more small rip in a garment so woebegone would never be noticed. Jervais had taken pains to teach Fidus that the minutest loss to one person could represent the most bountiful gain to another. And to a wizard of Tremere, for whom blood fueled unprecedented wonders, even a tiny dried stain of ancient's essence could prove useful in ways few other Cainites would ever suspect.

Chapter Three

"You do as you like, Meister Tremere, but I hope you won't mind if I speak very plainly to you." This first volley was out of the sling before Jervais had even finished his bow.

"Not at all, Highness," he replied smoothly. "I am simply grateful to have a personal audience with your Highness at long last."

And *that* was no exaggeration. Evidently Jürgen was not a man to be hurried by even the most terrible news. Despite his warning that he'd call for Jervais "sometime soon," a solid two months had gone by before the summons finally came.

"Even though the last words we exchanged at any length were hardly friendly?"

"Especially for that reason, your Highness. I fear I've never had opportunity to convey fully my regrets, my humblest apologies for the conduct of my childe Alexia in the matter of your sword all those years ago."

"You could have said so at the time."

Plain speaking, eh. Well, perhaps it wouldn't hurt to try some. "I did make some poor effort in that direction, Highness, but as I recall, your Highness was understandably too angry with me to entertain that effort at the moment, and dismissed me instead."

"Did I? I suppose I did." Jürgen, Prince of Cainites for Magdeburg, Overlord of Saxony, Thuringia and Brandenburg, and Lord Protector of Acre, sat in the room's single chair. That there should be only one chair in Jürgen's antechamber was a bit odd—no doubt orchestrated, so that Jervais could be forced to stand without making it seem like a deliberate rudeness on the prince's part.

Jürgen studied him minutely, un-apologetically for a little while. Jervais wondered what the matter was: whether he looked too much the wizard, or not enough. Usually it didn't do to make too open a display. That was something a lot of other magi, who came to court wearing whatever musty, antimony-smelling old robe they'd been working in that night, didn't quite understand. When folk were already hard at work conjuring scenes of child sacrifice or demons leering out of smoke pillars every time they so much as *looked* at a Tremere, there was little enough need to remind them. There were certainly other times, however, when sorcery was the one asset of interest, and on such occasions Jervais troubled himself to look the part. Tonight he'd been unsure of himself on the whole matter, so he'd chosen a long, plain, dark-blue velvet scholar's robe with some discreet but distinctly occult-looking jewelry. Even that much had drawn chilly looks from the mortal and Cainite brethren who'd shown him through the successive portals.

"So, you return to my court after all this time to, what, tender those long-neglected regrets?"

"Not that only, Highness. I've made no secret, or I don't think I have, of the fact that the House and Clan still earnestly hopes to win your goodwill. I believe that an alliance between your forces and ours could alter the entire *mappa mundi* of Cainite relations—alter it to your Highness's very great benefit."

"And to the House and Clan's."

"Naturally, your Highness. But our ambitions aren't the same as princely interests, so there need be no strife in that regard."

"Yes, I've heard that this is the usual Tremere homily. 'We're not rulers, but scholars. We seek inward not outward power, and wish only the liberty to do so.' But that's not entirely true, is it, Meister? For if it were, then why do you stay in Hungary, defying those who've tried to exterminate you for centuries? Wouldn't it be just as easy to conjure in…oh, England, say, or Paris?"

He was naming the places deliberately, demonstrating his knowledge. Jervais shifted his not insubstantial weight from one foot to the other. "Milord, it's true that the land that cradled us, no less than it did the Tzimisce, remains dear to us. There is power in place, but it's not the sort of power immortals of your Highness's rank concern themselves with. It's not found in crops or taxes or pilgrim's coins or even in the throngs of mortal denizens. It is something more elemental, if you will."

Jürgen only grunted. "I daresay Hungary's hardly the only place with such power."

"Not the only place, no."

"And where stands Livonia on the list?" As Jervais struggled to formulate an answer that would sound neither ominous nor patently untrue, the prince continued. "I couldn't help noticing that the information you so kindly provided us a few years ago was rather specific. Specific enough to show some study had been made of the subject. Am I wrong in thinking your kind rarely studies anything in vain?"

"No, Highness. Not wrong in the slightest," Jervais agreed, relieved not to have to answer after all.

"Then why?"

"Your Highness, I was ordered…" He paused, reconsidered the wording, but decided in the end not to change it. "Ordered to do whatever was necessary to regain your trust. And you've made it perfectly plain just what sort of man you are. Words will not suffice, only deeds. Am I wrong in thinking that?"

"No," Jürgen said, acknowledging the echo of his words with a wry look.

"No. Good. And I knew that Livonia might prove a, a troubling spot to your Highness, and so it seemed to me prudent to gather as much as I could on Qarakh and his compatriots. Indeed with your Highness's permission, I'm prepared to go further yet. That is, if your Highness is not quite done in Livonia."

He faded to a halt. The room seemed to tighten inexplicably around them, an oppressive squeezing. Even Jürgen bent his back under its force, leaning his elbows on his knees.

"No," Jürgen said at last. "No, I am not quite done in Livonia."

Jervais smiled. "I'm glad to hear it, Highness."

Jürgen sat up again. "I must assume, then," he said, "that this offer of alliance which you've spoken of to Lady Rosamund, and now to me, is officially on the table."

"Yes, Highness," he said eagerly. "Indeed it is. You need but say the word…"

The prince held up a hand at that. "I'm quite convinced of your enthusiasm, Meister Tremere. But if enthusiasm alone were enough for conquest, we should have had it by now. What makes you think that the Tremere can stand against this Qarakh? After all, he's now slain an ancient, one of the eldest forebears of my clan."

"Yes, but he could not have done so without aid, milord, as your own lieutenant pointed out."

"So you agree that there *was* sorcerous aid."

Jervais blinked, surprised. What was afoot now? "Of course, Highness," he replied cautiously. "Remove that aid, and you can break the very back of his little kingdom."

"And that's what you are proposing—to remove the aid."

"Of course."

"One is forced to wonder what gives you such confidence in your ability to do so." A sour note of suspicion had crept back into Jürgen's voice—the last thing Jervais wanted.

Perhaps, then, it was time to name a name of his own. "Your Highness, Deverra is a sorceress of some power, and may have truck with spirits of even greater power, but—"

"Deverra?"

"Yes, milord. We've learned her name, and several other noteworthy things about her, since I spoke with the Lady Rosamund during your Hungarian campaign." A lie, of course. He'd known Deverra's name himself for over a century now, and others in the House and Clan had known it for even longer, but he'd decided to hold the fact in reserve until it might be needed. Now seemed a good moment.

"Oh, really. And yet you didn't think it necessary to mention at that time that there *was* a sorceress in the first place?" Jürgen turned a sudden glare on him.

Oh.

Jervais felt as though he'd been splashed with ice-water. His mouth of its own accord sought to form itself into a startled little *o*, which he tried to smooth out before Jürgen saw. Damnation—if he'd only caught it a moment earlier, he could have not said anything, could have gone to her afterward and—

"Meister Tremere." Jürgen's voice had gone rock-hard now. "Answer me. What the devil has taken your famous tongue?"

"I…" Was there some way to salvage the blackmail potential of the thing? No time to calculate it through. He attempted to sense the instinct of his soul. It seemed to say *no*. All he could do now was use the truth to play upon the man's emotions. Still, he had to thank the Lady Rosamund for providing even that much. "I… I'm sorry, milord, I'm feeling a bit—confused. I…" He hesitated, judiciously.

"Speak!" the Ventrue demanded, and then underscored it with the coercive power of his august blood. "*Speak!*"

"Yes, your Highness. I don't know what exactly to say. I—I *did* mention there was a sorcerer, or sorcerers, aiding Qarakh. I told her what little I could at the time about it. I assumed that meant you'd been told as well. Forgive me."

There was an uncomfortable pause. Jürgen moved his feet, as though to stand, then didn't.

"Perhaps she didn't quite catch that part," he said at last. "She's a lady of court, not a general…" But it didn't sound as though he were even convincing himself.

"Quite possibly, quite possibly I didn't impress upon her enough how significant it was." He let that hang. "After all, her grief at Alexander's death was…quite apparent for all to see."

Enough. Yes, that was good. Jürgen was in that terrible half-state between outright confidence and outright suspicion. Leave him there. It could only make the Tremere look better by comparison.

"You were saying about this Deverra."

"Yes, your Highness. She leads a cabal of sorcerers. A large one by now, I'd fancy, for they've been bringing natives of the region into the blood. They have a magic that's not unlike that of the Tzimisce."

"But I take it they aren't Tzimisce."

"It's possible they may be…a sort of offshoot of that blood,"

Jervais replied. There, one of the finest shadings of truth he'd managed for years.

"But you're not sure."

"One would have to get closer to examine them better. But that's all right. It'll certainly be necessary to get closer to destroy them, in any case."

The corner of Jürgen's mouth twitched. "You are a cheerful man when it comes to the business at hand, Meister. I'm sure the Tremere would rather there were no other sorcerers in the world, Tzimisce or otherwise."

"These sorcerers are a threat, your Highness. Not only to the Black Cross and the mortal knightly orders, but also to the entire cause of Christianity in the region."

"Come. What do the Tremere care for the cause of Christianity?"

Now *there* was a question, with only one simple answer among the many possible ones. "For better or for worse, milord, we've cast our lot with those who care quite passionately. Their welfare is our welfare. *Your* welfare, to be frank, is our welfare."

"And Ceoris, it would seem, agrees with your assessment."

"Yes, Highness, it does." Jervais nodded. Then something struck him about the way Jürgen had said that. "I beg your Highness's pardon?"

"I hope you'll excuse an old man's wariness," Jürgen began, suspiciously amiable. "You see, it's not as if we don't have a history, you and I. Or rather, your childe Alexia and I, as I suppose you'd have it."

Jervais frowned, trying not to let show his annoyance at having that particular diplomatic evasion thrown back in his face so casually. "I take full sire's responsibility for my childe's mistakes, Highness."

"Of course. In any case, since Alexander's death I've begun seriously reconsidering the question of my relations with the House and Clan. And so I thought it meet to write Ceoris and confirm with them that you were indeed their designated envoy, and did in fact have license to make and seal such bargains on their behalf. You'll be pleased, I'm sure, to know that they fully endorse you." Jürgen got up, strode over to a side table, picked up a parchment letter and brought it over. "They were impressed with your initiative. In fact, your master Etrius expresses such confidence in your good faith and ability in this instance that he agrees completely with my idea of the best disposal of the matter—and at my urging has appointed you chief, leader and director of the entire expedition."

He handed the parchment to Jervais, who examined it bewilderedly. The secretarial hand looked familiar, and the seal was indeed Etrius's seal. Jervais would not insult the prince by testing it here and now, but the likelihood of anyone in Magdeburg successfully faking the careful angles and intricate filigrees, even given a genuine model to work from, was rather low.

"Expedition, Highness?" The letter had made ridiculously good time, then. Perhaps Ceoris had sent the reply by gargoyle. Damnation.

"Yes. To Livonia, to take care of this Deverra and whatever other magicians Qarakh may have attracted to his banner. The advance wizard's guard, if you will. That *is* more or less what you had in mind, isn't it?"

Jervais had grown quite used to the taste of bile over the years. He knew when it was time to swallow another dose and smile. "More or less, your Highness. Yes."

"Good. Then I shall look forward to the tale of your success. If you wish, I can offer you the services of Brother Hermann, one of my lieutenants, good man to the core, along with a reasonable portion of my order's forces. They may be of some use to you—not only in Livonia but also on the journey there, which you doubtless already know to be a hard one." He picked up another folded parchment from the same table. "Oh. And this letter came along as well. It's for you."

Jervais took it without making a move to open it. He fancied he already knew the contents anyway.

"And allow me to be the first to offer my congratulations." Jürgen no longer bothered to hide the pleasure this was giving him, though he tried to soften it by clapping a manly hand to Jervais's shoulder on the way out.

"Thank you, Highness."

"The hairy, flaxen, *petit-noble*, thundering son of a Bratovitch brood-bitch *flanked me!*"

Fidus silently handed Jervais a bronze goblet, and Jervais flung it across the room. It bounced off the wall plaster, knocking a chip out. He peered at it as it spun to a stop on the floor.

"There was nothing in that," he accused his apprentice.

Fidus shook his scrawny head. Sometimes it wasn't at all flattering to be known too well.

"Well, how about *putting* something in it?"

The younger Tremere collected it obediently, then went over to a little ewer with a silver band of hieratic engravings and a jade stopper. He poured out its contents into the goblet, which he carried back to Jervais. He sloshed the remainder around within the ewer. "Not much left, master. Shall I fetch more?"

"No, don't. I'll make a visit downstairs later. There are some nights…some nights when you need to bring down the stag and not just have it served to you on a spit."

Fidus nodded and went back to scrubbing down the ritual sickle with salt.

Jervais took a swallow of the blood, lukewarm and kept *almost* tolerably fresh by the spell on the ewer, and continued disgustedly, "Don't nod as though you had an inkling. My idea. My work! Two years of spy-mongering; three years of crawling through the diplomatic mud. I *knew* that Livonia would be next. The very moment I heard the Teutons were going into Prussia, I knew it would come to this and I started preparing for it. Did Etrius direct me? No. In fact, how much would you like to bet that if I'd mentioned it he would have told me not to be a fool? And now that the idea turns out to be *worthwhile*, suddenly the great toad wants it for himself and connives with the blasted Saxons to steal it out from under my very nose!"

"Master… No, never mind."

"What is it? Bonisagus's beard, Fidus, either finish a thought or don't start it in the first place."

"Well, if you'll forgive me, master, not exactly stolen. You are in charge of the thing, aren't you?"

"Oh, I'm in charge of the thing all right," Jervais grumbled. "Right up in the general's saddle, where everyone can get the clearest shot. You do not seem to grasp the magnitude of the reversal here, Fidus. I was brokering the most sage and immortal Councilor's services. Now the Councilor is brokering my services, and by the way, bear in mind that that means you're going to Livonia too."

"I know, master."

"With a prior stop at Ceoris itself."

That stopped the fledgling vampire cold. He looked up at his master. "Ceoris?" he repeated, in what Jervais was gratified to note as precisely the right tone of apprehension.

"Yes," Jervais returned grimly.

"But, but Ceoris, that's not on the way to Livonia, is it?"

"No, it's not even close to on the way." Jervais picked up the letter Jürgen had handed him and waved it. "But evidently it's necessary to further remind me of my place before I embark on this little venture. I am to report to the High Chantry immediately to discuss plans and collect my informers—forgive me, I mean my assistants—for the mission."

Fidus returned to his chore, his face carefully neutral, but the older Tremere could easily let his slightly blurred eyesight unfocus just a bit further, revealing the array of soul-colors skittering uneasily in a tight halo around his apprentice's body. Fidus hadn't yet been to the High Chantry, had never delved the chambers of the clan's cold stone heart. He was afraid. He frightened easily sometimes.

But Jervais, for his part, was glad no one was there to see his own colors.

Chapter Four

"All right, all right," Brother Hermann shouted, "that's what this training is for. Quickly, rope!"

The rider who'd just plunged mount and all into the ice looked like a slight lad of perhaps twenty, although to be fair he was armored. Jervais, who was a bit barrel-shaped himself—he would have placed the middle of that barrel in his chest, though some observers wouldn't have been nearly so charitable—drew his horse up sharply even though he was well removed from the crack. Around him, squires and knights, mortals and Cainites alike rushed forward.

"Remember, biggest of you to the back. If any more get pulled in, it'll be up to you. And—heave! Heave!"

The Cainite himself soon scrambled out with minimal help, though his skin had gone even whiter from the water's intense cold. The beast's struggles, however, almost took a few of the men into the hole with it. Its horrible noises echoed from the walls of the streambed for what would have been more than sufficient time to chant many charms.

"And *that's* why you don't want to ride too near the edge, as I said before," Hermann called out once the horse was out, the rest were calmed, and relative order had prevailed again. "Or... you see over there, at that inlet, where the water is moving more swiftly underneath? That's where the ice is thinnest. Wipe those looks off your faces. If the Sword-Brothers can march across a frozen sea to kill the Osilian pirates, you can manage this. We're about to journey to a land of mire and muck, gentlemen, death to horses and horsemen, especially in battle! And so the iced-over rivers must be our highways and the snow our paving.

And God Almighty above, as always, will be our conductor." He raised a hand halfway, toward the moonlit sky.

"*This* time," came a sour mutter from among the knights. Plainly the tale of Alexander's disaster had spread within the order.

"I was rather hoping for more earthly help along the route," Jervais said dryly.

"Don't worry. We'll provide the earthly help and leave the unearthly to you." Hermann frowned and ran a gloved hand through his dark hair, cut in a short, rather bristly tonsure. "Are you sure you didn't make the ice a bit thin?"

"I hadn't thought so, but no doubt it's gotten at least a bit thinner over the past few hours. Not nearly cold enough out."

"Hm. Well, I suppose there's only so much even a wizard can do with a few magic words."

Jervais said nothing and concentrated on not wavering in his saddle. Fidus had better have the larder restocked when he got back in. A few magic words, indeed.

"That ash-wand, must you always use it for your enchantments?"

"No, only for some."

"Good." At the Tremere's questioning look, Hermann went on. "I'd hate to have you turn out to be like one of those sorcerers in the old tales, where all one need do is steal his staff or his talisman or the box that holds his heart, in order to render him useless."

Jervais changed the subject. "*Are* there any of your brotherhood left in Hungary? If so, I assume that'll affect the route."

"There are a few there that still serve the *Hochmeister*." He looked away a moment after that and called out, "All right, men, that's enough! Back onto the banks, we're going home." Then he said to Jervais, "Why, don't the Tremere have some sure path of their own through that country?"

"East of Buda?" Jervais snorted. "Nothing's sure after that."

"I'm not sure I see the wisdom of this diversion in the first place. But since your masters demand it."

"And they do demand it. It'll just be us and your little mortal squadron through Hungary then—is that right—while the rest of the company proceeds east from Saxony along the coast?"

"Yes."

"And then we meet them—where? Thorn?"

"No. I don't want to wait 'til Thorn to be sure I have an army, thank you," Hermann returned. Even though he clearly didn't mean it at all humorously, Jervais could not help an appreciative quirk of the lips. "No, we'll meet them in Stettin."

"Oh! Then we could sail out of the gulf up to Riga, try to recruit a little support there, and then come southward to meet the enemy."

"No, it'll be too late in the year by then, too stormy. You'll never get the mortals on board..."

He trailed off. The image came to Jervais very powerfully then, almost as though it had journeyed directly from Hermann's mind to his: a crash, a creaking splinter of wood, and while the mortals buoyed—at least for a little while—to the surface, the vampires would spiral down and down into the inky murk. Frozen from the water's chill and soon empty of blood, wasted down to the bone, perhaps unable even to move, drifting aimlessly with the leviathans...

"Yes, no doubt you're right about that. No help from Riga, then?"

"Oh, we'll have help from Riga if there's any there to be had. Once we've made Stettin I'll try to send a scout up north to see. Perhaps we could even squeeze the pagans from both directions, but right now even his Highness isn't sure what remains of Cainite Christianity out there."

They urged their horses up onto the road, eager to get back now that they were on less treacherous ground. Jervais glanced wistfully at his creation, a sheet of ice winding through a trough of green grasses and wildflowers, pleased with its very unnaturalness. A short-lived but eloquent testament to his skill. Though no one besides Hermann had mentioned it so far (much less thanked him), he felt it wise to make little demonstrations here and there so that the knights would feel able to rely on him by the time they engaged the enemy. Costly, though. His eyes ached to droop closed, yet he could also feel the dry thirst convulsing in the core of his body, throat to belly. The smell of his horse suddenly seemed overpowering.

"As for the Hungary leg, we should go through Prague," Hermann continued. "And Brno, and then south to Bratislava."

"No," Jervais managed. "Vienna."

"Vienna? Oh yes, I suppose it does make sense to stop in Vienna instead. That way, should anything happen to us, your brothers will at least know we got that far. Dare I hope—"

At that moment a loud toneless fluttering started up in Jervais's ear, as though an insect had flown into it. His hand involuntarily rose to cover it over, but he restrained it. "I'm sorry, *mein Herr*. What was that?"

Hermann looked at him oddly. "Where did I lose you? I was asking whether your brothers would come looking for you right away if you went missing."

The scrabbling sensation in his ear canal grew from a tickle to a wide, frantic wobble. "Yes, yes," Jervais assured him hastily. "Pardon me, *mein Herr*—you won't mind if I ride on ahead? I just—just remembered something."

The knight nodded tersely. "If you must, certainly. Be careful. You may be under his Highness's official protection, but the rogue Cainites and wolf-demons lurking hereabouts won't likely ask."

"Thank you. *Gute Nacht*," Jervais called as he spurred his horse into a brisk canter. The jogging motion made the sensation even worse. He hunched over the saddle and tried to blink his watering eyes clear. Luckily neither enemy vampires nor werewolves appeared, and his mount knew its own way back home once they were back inside the town.

Fidus hurriedly rose from his book and inkpot as Jervais pushed aside the invisible curtain of the ward on the house and stumbled in.

"Master?"

"Chalk bounding circle," Jervais said hoarsely. "Hurry." He fairly ran over to the brazier and set it on the floor, then got its coals going with a bit of kindling from the hearth. He set the lumps of dragon's-blood incense in it and dribbled several drops of blood from the pad of his thumb onto it.

"Where in hell did you put the *moucheron*?"

"It's on the second shelf, master."

Reaching the second shelf required straightening up, but he managed to fish the little silver device down without knocking anything off or injuring himself. "Fidus, the Saxons have already bled me half dry tonight. I'll need..."

"Yes, master."

"I tell you, whatever it is, it'd better be bloody important. That Hermann must think I'm mad."

They quickly drew and fortified the circle and Jervais censed the quarters. He settled himself inside the circle and did his best to descend quickly into trance. In this his fatigue actually aided him. Soon the insect that seemed to have taken up residence in his head grew smaller but louder, becoming a low humming that vibrated his entire skull. When the humming had steadied somewhat, he took the *moucheron*—the "stinging gnat"—in his left hand, gourd-end in his fist and shunt-end pointed into the white flesh of his inner arm. Its true name wasn't *moucheron*. That was simply what Jervais called it because the blood it stole was irretrievably devoured, boiled away by the wine-red carbuncle hidden inside the crucible of the gourd. With a deep breath he squeezed his fist and bent his wrist so that the shunt entered deep into his skin. Then he arranged his arm by his side so that the blood's own weight would conduct it into the gourd. Once the gem got going it would need no further help. Like a vampire itself, it would draw on him hungrily and swiftly.

In his hand the silver gourd began to grow warm. A nauseating heat invaded first his body and then the space within the circle. Even the ground itself gave up a faint steam that drowned out all sight of the room without.

"*Cruor cruorem evocat redditque vocem cruor. Loquere et intra, si amicus es genusve,*" he intoned. "*Aliter abi damnatus a quoque ex Septem Nominibus.*" *Blood calls to blood, and blood returns the call. Speak and enter in, if you be friend and kin; otherwise begone and be damned by each of the Seven Names.*

Kin, at the very least, was the dry response. *And I hope I am still friend, but like many an old man with a grandson who wanders far from home, I find myself waiting rather long between messages.*

Ah. Well, that explained the forcefulness of the summons. He should have known better than to expect some Ceoris lackey. Jervais quickly girded his mind as best he could, drawing in all extraneous reaction like a man drawing a cloak close about himself. In the inexorable intimacy of spirit-contact, the lesser wizard often found far too much of himself laid bare before the greater—a chief reason why this method of making report had never become as popular as certain ranking Tremere would have liked. "Grandsire. It has indeed been a long time. My apologies. I hope you're well in Paris?"

I am well, if that is the way to put it. And the clime in Saxony? Am I to understand you find it milder in these nights than formerly?

"There's little mildness in Jürgen Sword-Bearer, I fear, but he's now found someone to hate far more fiercely than myself. That must suffice."

The impression Goratrix made in person benefited considerably from his handsome face: slim, eternally set in clean patrician lines, eyes amber-brown and keenly lit from within. But the rite of the Thousand-League Whisper stripped away those softening ornaments and left only the starkness of the archmagus's soul, the insistent, hammering drumbeat of his thought, which pressed around Jervais, ensnaring him.

Indeed, it usually must for our kind. But the Sword-Bearer has so many enemies. Who could it be this time?

A ridiculous charade. The old schemer would never go to this kind of effort if he didn't already have some idea. "The warlord in Livonia, milord."

Ah, the beast-blooded one. Jürgen means to avenge himself, then, for the death of our late Alexander.

"I see Sir Josselin did reach the Grand Court, then. How was the news received?"

With relief, I think, overdyed in various shades from shame to satisfaction. The specter of Alexander's possible return never really did leave anyone's mind, particularly not Geoffrey's. Myself, I think the Sword-Bearer owes that barbarian chief a debt of gratitude for eliminating his most dangerous houseguest. But I suppose he can't be blamed for not seeing it that way. Tell me, what part do you play in all this?

"I'm not sure why your lordship assumes that I must have a part to play."

Come, Jervais. It wouldn't be like you to just sit by while someone's starting a war. Besides, what else would you be doing in Magdeburg? There must be a dozen other courts where you could have started fresh and had a more pleasant time of it. In any case, that Sir Josselin is quite a talkative sort. Even I didn't find it at all difficult to get him started on the subject of you. He doesn't seem to remember you too fondly.

"Well, naturally I've pledged the House and Clan's assistance to the endeavor."

My understanding is that you were already pledging the House and Clan's assistance to Jürgen before word even came back about Alexander. But perhaps his Highness is taking that offer more seriously, now that the Telyavs have demonstrated their power.

"Yes."

I must assume that you haven't gotten around to mentioning anything to his Highness about our particular relationship to the Telyavs.

"No, not yet."

Not yet? The tone was cool, reserved—too cool and reserved.

"It may at some point become unavoidable."

Hm. Would that not be as unfortunate for us as for them? After all, everyone knows the Tremere stand absolutely united. Our allies depend on that fact, and our enemies also tread more carefully because of it.

"Which is exactly why the Telyavs must be made an example of, grandsire. Indeed, presuming we succeed, having the truth about them come out would only gain us *more* awe, since it would demonstrate once and for all just how we deal with traitors. As far as I can tell, I have little to fear from exposure… this time."

Now we come to it. Jervais, you surely must understand the delicacies of my position. If you had succeeded in your little plot—

"I see. Now it's *my* little plot."

—Again, if you had succeeded, then things would have been very different all around. As it was, how do you think it would have looked if I'd petitioned to have you transferred to France and to my jurisdiction,

so soon after such a debacle? Would it not have incriminated you beyond the shame you'd already suffered?

"I must thank my grandsire for his concern. Since you express such interest in my welfare, I should report that I too am in a rather delicate position these nights."

Yes, I know. He'll never stop trying to make you suffer, and it's all on my account, I fear. He pours upon you the contempt that distance and terror prevent him from pouring upon me.

"Well, whoever's account it's on, I'm the one that must deal with the consequences."

Perhaps not forever, though, my son.

Aha, Jervais thought grimly. "What do you mean, grandsire?"

Perhaps enough time has passed, I mean, that I could send for you without it being taken the wrong way.

"That's very kind of you, but it's a bit too late now, isn't it? I'm going to Livonia."

Ah, so you are going to Livonia yourself then. Palpable satisfaction.

"Yes."

But I'm thinking of after you come back. After all, should you satisfy Etrius that the Telyavs are destroyed, then you'll be in a far better position, will you not, to ask for a different placement?

"If I satisfy *Etrius* that they're destroyed?"

He will require some sort of proof, naturally. He is not that great a fool.

So that was the game. The rumors must be true, then: that Goratrix had a running correspondence with the Telyavs despite—or because of—their shaky standing with Ceoris. Certainly it would please Goratrix to keep such a thorn pressed into Etrius's side for as long as possible. Anything that distracted or inconvenienced his old archrival pleased him.

"I see. You're saying, then, that if I do satisfy Etrius on this matter…"

You remember when we spoke just before your first journey to Magdeburg? "A Frenchman always longs for his France," you said. You talked of gentle rolling hills, of fragrant vineyards and primroses, of fair maids...I thought it all needlessly sentimental at the time, but lately I've come to appreciate the truth of what you said. Ceoris will always contain some part of my soul, as all one's creations must, but this land is indeed home. To be honest, I had forgotten what it felt like.

Sickening, to hear his own words returned to him so polluted with insincerity. Jervais silently vowed never again to speak from the heart with Goratrix, not even in the cause of persuading him.

"You are saying, grandsire," he began again patiently, "that if I satisfy Etrius, you will definitely secure my transfer?"

I don't see what could possibly prevent it.

And yet something would no doubt come up after the fact. How many times did Goratrix really think he could be made to dance to this same tune?

He forced a smile through his exhaustion and anger. The archmagus wouldn't see the smile, but it would color Jervais's thought-words in the right way. "I am glad indeed to hear you say so, grandsire. Shall I contact you, then, when I've reached Livonia?"

Yes, do that. Tell me what you find, and I shall be able to better instruct you.

"As you wish."

Good. Then I won't keep you longer. A safe journey to you, my son.

"Farewell, grandsire." And not a moment too soon. The *moucheron* slipped out of Jervais's weakening fingers and fell to the floor; at once the feeling of Goratrix' presence evaporated and the room reappeared. Jervais started to rise, dismissing the circle with a gesture of his ritual knife, then fell forward onto his hands.

Fidus, who stood guard over a haggard young mortal lying on the floor bound in irons, rushed forward immediately.

"Master." With a grunt of effort Fidus lifted Jervais up onto his knees, supporting him as he half crawled across the room. The terrified lad bucked and tried to squirm away.

"Hold him, Fidus. Hold him..."

Fidus straddled the mortal's legs and held his upper body

still enough for Jervais to find purchase in the hollow of the neck. Jervais latched on greedily. His arms encircled the lad and squeezed, as though to speed the blood even more quickly on its way. Sometimes he thought he could discern flavors in it, traces of whatever the mortal had eaten or drunk, echoes of humors and feelings. Right now, however, taste was entirely secondary to need. This lad was sick from lack of sunlight, from close confinement, but he'd been fed well at least. Jervais insisted on that. The blood was thick and potent. Very quickly he went from feeling complete emptiness—worse than emptiness, an aching void that would never be sated—to the absolute contentment of an infant at mother's breast. It honestly did not occur to him that the stream of nourishment could stop until it did stop, slowing to a trickle and then finally running dry. A little moan of disappointment escaped him as he let the body slip free of his teeth. But the sight of it, of the boy's lightless eyes, brought him out of his inner realms of pleasure and back into the practical world.

"Get off," he ordered his apprentice. He looked over his robe. There was one spatter on the end of the sleeve. Damnation. "I'm all right now. Hands off of me. You said there was more where this one came from, didn't you?"

"The man said he was quite accustomed to acquiring youths of both sexes for noblemen and merchants with peculiar tastes, master."

"I should speak with this person. The pickings are so lean hereabouts. Hand me the sickle."

"Yes, master."

Jervais took it. "Now let's see. Pay attention, Fidus. The uses of the harlot. Tongue, if I recall, is good for enchantments to reveal a falsehood. Eyes and heart for love-charms, the liver for curses…"

Chapter Five

"Pleasant," was Hermann's laconic comment.

Jervais surveyed the hills before them. Not in order to take in the scenery but to search for evidence of raiding parties—still, in the process, he couldn't help agreeing with Hermann. After all, unlike either of his companions, he remembered what the place had looked like upon his last visit. They were in the Carpathians now, and even the relative lowlands were less clement than the fields of the Ile-de-France or even Saxony. This ground had once been green and wooded with fir, stretching all the way up to the tree line. And here, at their feet, had run a beautiful if ice-cold little stream that emptied into a mountain lake not far away. Every so often one could look down from a chantry parapet and spy a shepherd leading his flock along the streambed—during the day, at any rate. When he'd left for the final time, Jervais's eyes hadn't gazed on a sunlit sky for many years, but he knew the herds still passed through occasionally because he found the cropped grass in their wake.

"It looks as though there's been a forest fire." Hermann picked up a handful of soil, smelled it and wrinkled his nose in disgust. "Foul…"

Jervais did likewise, sniffing carefully at the little clod of earth.

"Salted," he said at last. "Scorched and then salted."

The stream still flowed, but weakly. It had silted up, choked with islands of ash and blocked with charred fallen trees. It also bore a thin rime of ice around the edges, a warning of winter's swift approach.

"Tzimisce?" Hermann asked grimly.

"Perhaps," Jervais temporized. But even as he said it, he knew it was a lie. Much of the reason the Tzimisce tried again and again to take this region was because they held it sacred. The ancient blood-drinkers didn't graze herds or grow crops, but their magic, their very blood-strength was rooted in the earth's power. These mountains, where ground and sky touched, were especially holy to their pagan creed, and their fertility made them holier yet. He supposed it was always possible that the Fiends' war-lust had blazed so high that they'd decided to lay waste to the area rather than let the Tremere enjoy it unspoiled... but it wouldn't be like them.

It would, however, be perfectly in *Tremere* character to do such a purely practical thing: denying the enemy all cover from spell or sun, clearing the land of any spirits of wood, soil or water that the Tzimisce *koldun*-priests might summon for aid. As long as the ley line still flowed between the hills to soak Ceoris's stone foundations—and by letting his vision slip off-center from the waking world just a bit, he could see that it did, a blue-white river of radiance that dulled and changed color as it passed through the barrens but remained as thick and swift as ever—the House and Clan had all it truly needed from the earth. Sheep, and grass for them to gorge on, were pleasant but ultimately unnecessary.

"Well, which way now? Toward the highest and most forbidding peak, I fancy."

"Which one is it, Fidus?" Jervais prompted his apprentice, who, to his credit, was already fishing out a little lead plumb on a string. He held it loosely in his thumb and forefinger, letting it swing until it found the correct axis. Those who could not directly *see* the ley line could still dowse it fairly quickly, it ran so strong here.

"The middle one," he reported glumly.

"Good lad. Exactly right."

"As I said," Hermann grumbled. "Can you even *get* a horse up there?"

"Yes. That is, a Cainite can usually get his horse up," Jervais answered. "But you see now why I thought it best to leave the men in the village and do the last leg alone. It's only a few miles, but it's a few nearly vertical miles. Besides, they can cover our backs. This is the only known way in. Or at least I hope it still is."

Fidus laid a hand on his horse's flank, trying to coax her on. The beast could find no sure footing, and she tossed her head back fearfully.

"Come, Sirene. You're all right, I promise. Come! Look...this is what you want, isn't it?" He bit into his wrist, tearing it open, and showed her the gleaming bead of vitae that welled up. Her large, floppy lips closed around the wound, nipping at it.

"Yes. Trust me now? That's a good girl." He wiped the saliva off on the side of his gown with a grimace. She went far more willingly now. At first it wasn't clear whether she'd really regained her courage or was just hoping to get at his arm again, but soon she began to nudge up behind the monk-warrior's big gelding, who refused to move one whit faster.

"They're spooked," Hermann muttered. "Something's not right up ahead."

"That may be what their noses tell them, but I'm telling you we're no safer below than above," Jervais called back. "I've been nearly murdered two or three times down in the foothills. Keep moving."

"Magog knows his own footing. Fidus! Restrain that animal of yours."

"I'm—I'm trying." But the mare, newly braced with unnatural nourishment, was determined to push ahead. She bumped up against Magog and then tried to edge up alongside him. The gelding, who had also fed on blood earlier that evening, jostled her away, perilously close to the edge. Hermann pulled hard on the halter.

"Magog! No, lad."

"Sirene! Back! Come away! Leave him alone."

"Easy, lad. Let it be. Fidus, boy, for the love of God!"

"What in *hell's* name is going on?" Jervais stopped and leaned around his own mount's substantial bulk, looking back. "No room up here for playing king of beasts—"

Even as he said it the two horses turned and reared against

each other. Sirene snapped at Magog, who responded by falling heavily against her neck. She staggered and put her hoof down awkwardly upon the snow, which slid away to reveal a patch of loose rocks. A moment later she was straddled across the steep edge of the trail. Fidus seized hold of her, his ropy muscles straining taut enough to pop. Hermann forced Magog away from the edge and forward.

"Fidus!" shouted Jervais. "Let her go, you stupid boy, you'll fall."

"Master, help! The equipment!"

"I said let her go. Hermann!" Jervais fairly yelped as the mare's left rear leg slid over the edge, taking most of the rest of her with it, dragging Fidus—who still clutched her front leg—right up to the brink. But the knight made no move other than to keep restraining his horse. Jervais pushed past him and squatted down to lock his arms around Fidus's torso.

"Fidus," he spoke calmly into the young Tremere's ear. "I can get a new horse and new equipment far more easily than a new apprentice. Now *let her go* before she takes us both over. I promise I won't be angry."

He braced his feet against the slick rock as best he could, just in case his worst-case scenario began coming true. But then the horse's leg slipped through Fidus's fingers, as though by accident rather than design. With a piercing cry the animal disappeared into the chasm.

They both sat there for the space of several deep mortal breaths, absorbing what had happened and what could have happened. Jervais flung an unfriendly look up at Hermann, who regarded them both impassively.

"Well? Are you all right?" the knight asked after a moment. "Can you continue?"

"Of course, Brother." Jervais hauled Fidus to his feet. Despite the promise otherwise, the apprentice cringed in clear expectation of a blow that didn't come. In truth, Jervais could feel his anger rising now that the danger was over. No alchemist's apparatus! He'd have to acquire a new one from the chantry before they left. That meant he would have to ask, no, beg for it from someone. But he said nothing as they got back into single file and continued upward. A thin fog seemed to descend as they went, though perhaps they were simply passing through a layer of it from beneath.

"How much further?" Hermann wanted to know.

"I'm not sure. We should be almost there."

"This mist, is it natural?"

"How should I know? What difference does it make?"

Jervais sighed as they came up to what he'd thought for certain was the final bend and saw a massive gray ridge rise up on their left.

"And what *is* that smell?"

Jervais ground his teeth together, willing them not to lengthen any further.

Behind them, Fidus's disheartened steps slowed to a stop. He'd been running his hand along the ridge, more out of habit and for something to do with his empty fingers than for support.

"This isn't..." he murmured. He felt at the edge of a rocky projection. His fingertips slipped off the pebbly surface and plunged into sudden, fragile softness. He snatched them away, viscerally repulsed. "Master, this isn't stone."

Jervais and Hermann, too, had turned toward the ridge, identifying the direction of the smell at last if not its nature. Hermann took out his dagger and picked at it. "No," he said, lip wrinkling in disgust. "It's flesh."

They stood back as far as the mountain edge would allow. The thing was enormous, easily the size of a respectable fishing boat's hull laid along its side. The hide was leathery, stretched tight over the armoring bone-spurs of what looked like the spine, but it had decayed in places or been eaten away, leaving half-hollowed tunnels of rotting meat.

Jervais walked around the hulk, getting a view in the round. The two others followed uneasily.

"What is it?" Fidus quavered. On this side, by what had once been the softer underbelly of the thing, the stench was far more noticeable, although the fact that it could be borne at all testified to its age and state of decay. Most of the actual innards had already rotted away, and the rest was frozen through.

"A trebuchet," his master answered.

"A what?" Hermann gave him an incredulous look.

Jervais gestured at the long arm that straggled outward from the wreck of the ribcage. It was about as thick as a pine tree's trunk and ended in a three-pointed—hand? foot?—with the tattered remnants of pouchy webbing between the points. "Here's the sling, you see. I'll bet this arm could rotate freely in a near-perfect circle; it would have simply reached back and thrown forward, and sent boulders each a good yard across flying at whatever you liked. It was a living, breathing siege engine."

"But how could it see what it was aiming at? Where the devil is the head?"

"There doesn't appear to have been a separate head, which makes sense enough, as there wouldn't have been much need for it. I'd guess the eyes were set somewhere in this region, atop the torso. I've seen others built that way."

"If you're saying this is the work of the Tzimisce flesh-twisters, then I too have seen such beasts. But even they were not quite this…bizarre." Hermann bent over the place where the head should have been, as if unable to believe that it could possibly have been omitted.

"Bizarre is the Fiends' stock in trade, I fear," Jervais said dryly. "We can only hope they never figure out how to make the infamous things reproduce."

"God above forbid!" Fidus interrupted in an uncharacteristically devout tone, and raised his hand as though to cross himself. Jervais made a silent note to correct the boy later.

"Anyway, this is what they charmingly call a *vozhd*, their king of monstrosities," Jervais went on. "The *voivodes* sometimes capture whole villages of men, women and children to provide the raw material for such creations."

His horse (whose only name so far was "my horse") shied and strained at the halter. He turned away to calm it and suddenly noticed that they were not alone.

"Well, hallo there," he said. The other two vampires turned to glance at him, wondering why his voice had richened and sweetened all at once. Standing at a respectful, or wary, distance was a boy of about eight years.

"Are you going upstairs?" the little boy asked with startling gravitas.

"Yes. In fact, we were just going to do that now."

"Upstairs?" The knight finally tore himself away from the massive, incomprehensible corpse for long enough to take in what lay beyond it. Less than an arrow-shot's distance from the *vozhd*, upon the small plateau-shelf on which they now found themselves, stood a long half-collapsed stone wall about five yards high, through the gaps of which they could spy the thatched roofs of a cluster of dispirited little stone houses. A narrow wedge that looked as though it had been carved directly out of a spur of mountain-rock sprung out from behind the wall like some fairy-tale beanstalk. It was terraced into what must have been several hundred stairs, thrusting up into the peak's continuing heights.

"That's where they put the keep." As they passed between the houses, many of which bore holes and gouges in their walls, or black scorch-marks licking along their sides, the residents came out to gaze at them.

"And what are these people? Your…stair guard?"

"No, they raise the food for the mortal staff that live up in the chantry."

"They do, eh?" Hermann pointedly swept his gaze from left to right, surveying the war-pocked ground of the plateau, upon which precious little visibly grew or grazed at the moment.

"Well, they did." Jervais laid an easy hand on the little boy's shoulder. One of the women in the crowd that was slowly gathering broke away from it and ran up to him, jabbering in a rapid pidgin of Magyar and Latin.

"What's she saying?"

"Nothing important."

"Don't give me that, warlock." Hermann turned to the woman and repeated in slow Magyar. "What are you saying?"

The woman stared at him. "Please…you must talk to the lords above. The evil magic, it doesn't go away."

She seized the boy away from Jervais and bodily turned him around, peeling back his shirt to reveal an ugly, purplish boil partially scabbed over. "Look. He went to play in the stream and came back stricken."

"Then I wouldn't let him play there again, if I were you," Jervais said. "Those Tzimisce curses hang on."

"My niece is the same. And another boy..."

"How long since the battle?" Hermann asked her. "The battle? When?"

She took a moment to digest his accent, then nodded her head sharply. "Yes...summer."

"That stinking leviathan has been lying there since *summer*? Hellfire, that must have been a treat for their lungs. Surprised these people haven't all keeled over with plague," Hermann muttered. "Come to that, some of them don't look far off from it."

"They don't look so deathly ill that they couldn't have at least started rebuilding the damned wall," Jervais answered. "I think I will have to speak to the 'lords' at that."

"These are your clan's own villeins, Meister Tremere," the knight began with a frown. "You're their protectors."

This from the man who's meant to fight Fiends and Lupines for us if need be, but couldn't be bothered to stop poor Fidus from plummeting off a mountainside. Well, I suppose Magog is more useful to the Black Cross than my apprentice.

"I'll mention it when we get in, Brother."

Two men-at-arms stood nominal guard at the foot of the stair. Jervais took the hand of one of the men and made a certain signal into his palm. The guard nodded and waved them up. Tied to his belt were two little bells, one with a red handle and one with a white handle. He unhooked the white one and gave it a ring. It was a gentle, barely audible shimmer of sound, but to Jervais's wizardly senses the very air seemed to ripple around it in response. The other guard took their horses. Hermann released Magog only with the greatest reluctance— clearly whatever stabling once existed in this village was going to be much the worse for wear. They slung their saddlebags over their shoulders and began the long climb.

Jervais had discovered long ago that it was best to stare straight ahead at the next steps and move quickly, because something in the pattern of the mountain rock tended to give one the sudden impossible conviction that the stair was listing to one side. (The sensation could make even a vampire woozy.) As they neared the halfway point, he spied a large shale-colored lump that blended in perfectly with the stair stone. It uncurled and stretched like a cat waking from an afternoon nap, then separated from the rock, spreading bat-wings a good six yards wide. If it had chosen to, it could easily have swooped down and knocked them off balance one by one—a prime reason why enemies found this invasion route so difficult. Instead it only circled them, keening, several times then flew up toward the top. Hermann drew his sword but, seeing Jervais march on unconcerned, made no further complaints. The fog grew denser again, rolling past them in visible billows. It got under the clothes and turned the little hairs on Jervais's arm damp.

"Stop it," he murmured. It didn't do any good—the tendrils continued to reach, probe, register.

By the time they reached the top, the mist had so thickened that they didn't see the keep until they were practically on the threshold. The enormous portcullis of what Jervais still thought of as the "new" gatehouse rose up out of obscurity. A figure robed in dark green satin stood holding a lantern and gazing out at them from behind the grating, one white hand resting lightly on a horizontal rail. As Jervais reached it, the figure doffed its hood. The face was young and unfamiliar, the hair and beard white-blond.

"You must be our wandering *vis*-master," the strange Cainite said. "I'm told things are not the same here since you left. I don't know if that's meant precisely as a compliment, but I thought you might take it as one regardless. My name is Torgeir. Welcome to the eyrie, my friends."

Chapter Six

"His Lordship the Councilor is expecting you," Torgeir said as he pattered through the Great Hall. His pace was just slightly quicker than plausible, and whisper-quiet on the flagstones, causing Jervais to privately imagine him ever after as a species of rodent.

Jervais's strongest memory of this chamber was of his initiation into the Second Circle of Mystery. A world ago, easily. He'd still honestly believed House Tremere to be the axis of all power and grandeur in the world, and the Great Hall had strengthened that impression, lined as it was with rows of tall stone stalls like a massive choir. Statues of history's great sages and wizards stared down from the pillar capitals. A knife-thin, glittering floor tracery of inlaid silver outlined a ritual circle of such exquisite construction that one could work in it all night without headache or fatigue. Harmonized with the very fundamentals of the *vis* energy that wound through the Southern Carpathians, all one had to do to ignite it into liquid fire was to strike the bell at hall's end and chant a perfect fifth above it. The circle's adornments still drew their reverently calculated geometry of vesicae, gnomonic spirals and Golden progressions across the floor, but the stalls had been allowed to fall into terrible disrepair. And despite the standing candelabras and chandeliers, the hall overall seemed dingier, gloomier than Jervais could remember it being even in the longest mortal nights.

Looking up, he stopped and gave a little involuntary noise of dismay. The others stopped too, quizzically following his gaze.

"What happened?" he exclaimed.

Torgeir peered up into the black reaches of the upper arches.

"Ah…yes. There was stained glass in the windows once, wasn't there?"

"Stained glass! There were depictions of the founders of the twelve Houses along with the signs of the zodiac, starting with Bonisagus and ending with Tremere. As day or night passed, the light would cast the different portraits upon the wall…" He stuttered to a halt, remembering his audience, who stared at him as if he had suddenly sprouted horns.

"Yes, well, we had an especially nasty siege a few years back, and it was decided that it just wasn't worth the risk. Besides, it isn't as though there are any mortal magi to complain of the dark anymore, is it?"

"No." He didn't expect Fidus to understand, and certainly not Hermann, but the casual tone of the other magus galled him. He gazed up forlornly at the stone window frames, hastily bricked up with blobs of stray cement drooping down from the joints, and streaked from end to end with rough incantations in…hard to tell from this distance even with senses honed, but doubtless dried blood.

"Well," he said at last. "We mustn't keep his worship in suspense. Lead on, Torgeir. Let's find some pleasant corner for Brother Hermann to wait in."

If there is a pleasant corner left in this basilisk's den.

The thought itself seemed to wing naked up into the darkness, meeting with a sour reception. Jervais would not have retracted it, however, even if he could. Anything that might hear him no doubt knew the truth of the sentiment at least as well as he did.

"If milord is busy with his magic, I can certainly come back later tonight," Jervais murmured, not straightening from his bow.

"Don't be dense, Jervais. What do you think this is all for?"

Jervais rose and surveyed the room, noting the rather malodorous assortment of things scattered across the counter. He knew some of their uses individually but had no inkling of their effect in combination.

"I have no idea, milord," he replied, wishing he didn't still have it in him to feel foolish when Etrius disparaged him.

"For you, of course. Or perhaps you thought I had you come all the way out east just to have the pleasure of your insincere abasement once again?" There was a great crunching noise as the Councilor crushed something in a little handheld press. Thin brown legs stuck out at crazy angles from the edges. Spiders or scorpions, probably.

"Of course not, milord. But…what exactly…" Jervais eyed the contents of one particular jar with special distaste, but there could be no argument. As Etrius's direct subordinate, not only his labor and his talents but his very body were at the archmagus's complete disposal. No sacrifice was supposed to be too great for the sake of the Art, and to quail at participating in a necessary spell, however ominous, was one of the greatest dishonors a Tremere could suffer.

"I'm not about to let you wander into the midst of the Telyav cult without some protections. And certainly not without helpers."

Jervais nodded hopefully. "Yes, I was assuming it would take several of us to have even a chance against Deverra."

"Indeed, I'd strive for a full *sodalicium*, if I were you," the Councilor agreed.

Strive? "I see. Then there aren't six already waiting for me here?"

"I'm afraid I don't *have* six spare Tremere, Jervais. They don't exactly grow on trees, and as you must have noticed, Rustovitch hasn't forgotten us on this lonely rock even with all his other pressing engagements. I did call Master Antal back from the Bistritz front for you—he should be arriving any night now. He's quite the war-wizard. I don't doubt his talents will prove invaluable. Surely you can also convince your sire to let at least one of her juniors go with you?" Something dankly amused in his tone suggested he knew quite well how unlikely that was. "As for the rest: I will write you a letter of credit to take with you to the chantries along the way, directly authorizing you to recruit as you see fit for the enterprise. It's, what, three hundred leagues to Livonia? You should be able to fill out your *sodalicium* by then."

"Doubtless, milord."

"Oh, and you may wish to take a gargoyle or two. They don't scout as well as they fight, but there's nothing quite like a bird's-eye view." The Councilor studied Jervais for a moment— his tired, jowly face and the dark smudges under his eyes contrasted sharply, as always, with the alertness of his keen blue gaze. Then his long-nailed fingers reached for the pestle and picked it up, and he turned his black-robed, bulky back on the younger magus. "You didn't ever meet Deverra, did you?"

"No, milord."

Etrius was silent for several moments. "*Dea de verra...* 'goddess of strife.' That was what her old master called her when he was cross with her, and the other apprentices nicknamed her *Deverra* for sport. When she became full maga she took the name he'd saddled her with, but with a different meaning, *de vera*, 'of truth.' She had a way of doing that, of taking what was meant as an insult and turning it into a mark of pride."

Jervais said nothing. When elders cast their minds back into the past like that, they had a way of dredging up the most interesting details, and he didn't want to break the reverie.

"But I'm afraid even she couldn't manage what comes so easily to you: to be proud of what your grandsire's 'experiment' turned us into. She asked to be sent away from Ceoris, to study the witchery of the Tzimisce and see whether we could adapt it. That's what she told me. Evidently she thought I wouldn't approve of her true purpose." Was that a note of injury? "She told those she tried to entice along, however, that her homeland held formidable powers, vital spirits of nature that might be able to restore the walking dead to true life again." He shook his head. "You find that droll, I'm sure."

"No, milord. Certainly I believe that 'true life' is often overrated by those who never got much of it, or those who prefer nostalgia to accurate recollection. But there are some gifts only true life provides, that can't be denied."

"I wonder which gifts *you're* thinking of," Etrius said dryly. "At any rate, she and her cohorts sent regular word of their discoveries for a time. She mentioned in one letter that they'd set themselves up as a sort of priesthood for a god named Telyavel, and were accepting blood libations from the people in that guise. I should have taken warning at that right away. That sort of thing is fit only for hedge-wizards and idolaters—not for those who study the wonders of the one transcendent Logos. I thought she'd left the petty gods of her pagan childhood far behind, just as I abandoned mine long ago, but it seems they have reclaimed her."

He turned. His eyes were downcast, almost closed. "Which means she is lost to us."

"Master." Jervais rarely used the term of address with Etrius. It felt familiar, and they both despised anything that smacked of closeness between them. But the turn in the conversation was alarming him now. "Are you sure you…want me to destroy her? Them?"

Etrius's eyes snapped back open at that.

"You insolent little *maggot*," he said in a strangled tone. "You dare worm into my thoughts? You think to unlock my heart, the hearts of all your betters and learn our secrets like spells you'll invoke at your later pleasure?"

"Not at all, milord—"

"You haven't even been back an hour! Doesn't common decency prescribe some kind of grace period?" The archmagus's teeth gnashed, but it wasn't his teeth Jervais watched with dread: it was his deft hands, to see if they were shaping themselves for some terrible curse. *"Look at me!* Do you believe this is the *first* time I have had to order the death of someone I once counted a magus of quality. Do you honestly believe that?"

"No, milord! I, I beg your lordship's pardon." He hated himself even as he said it, but he knew that the word *beg* was the fastest way to signal complete submission. Unlike Goratrix, who'd always seemed to think a great warlock never showed anything past polite contempt or contemptuous amusement to inferiors (and he plainly counted nearly everyone in the world, with the possible exception of Great Tremere himself, his inferior), Etrius didn't trouble to hide his hurts. In fact, he wore them almost as badges of honor. But that didn't make him an idiot or unsubtle. He knew quite well that Jervais wouldn't forget this outburst. Jervais never forgot an unguarded word anyone spoke. There was nothing Jervais could do about that now. All he could do was try to present as insignificant and meek a target as possible.

"I've had almost a century to think about the Telyavs, Jervais, and they've had just as long. In fact they have had multiple warnings, which they've chosen to ignore. Rest assured, the requisite agonizing has been done. Nor do I seek *your* moral guidance on who is and isn't a loyal scion of the House and Clan. I am telling you what you need to know to perform your duty. That is all."

"I understand, milord." Jervais bowed low, hoping this would be the end of the tirade, but it wasn't. His superior's sluggish movements had taken on a decided spark of animation now, as though his own anger warmed and limbered him.

"I'd think a man in your position would deem it wiser to keep his mouth shut. The question of your own loyalty isn't on the firmest ground as far as I'm concerned. There must be some reason you haven't found time to come home and do your job in over a decade. They left you to hang, didn't they—your sire and grandsire? A fine reward for your long years of conniving on their behalf. I cannot believe you still don't grasp how much they despise you. How much they've always despised you."

The elder Tremere smiled unpleasantly. He took a hissing snake out of the round blown-glass globe that held it, expertly hooked its fangs over the lip of a small vial, squeezed its head to milk out the venom, then broke its body open and poured the blood in as well. He took the mortar full of pungent crushed herbs and dumped both it and the vial into a pan of sludge sitting in the coals of a little brazier. He picked up the pan carefully with a pair of tongs and tilted it around to let the contents mix.

"You never were the cloth out of which Tremere are cut. You're not one of their kind, or mine. You barely had the skill to be a myopic *grog* scribe in the Paris chantry basement. And don't think they don't know it. They're happy to lead you on, of course, because they know your envy makes you a fine tool. It makes of you a well-balanced dagger to twist into others' backs. But you will never be a true wizard, Jervais. Despite whatever lies they told you, the blood can't give you that. I know you don't believe me now, but the centuries will teach you the bitter truth." He dusted off his hands. "Assuming you survive."

It was still so easy for the old ruin. He must have been

keeping in practice all this time, at some other luckless soul's expense. The shame was awful, sickening, pestilential. It was also the only thing that kept Jervais from dashing forward to try to tear that scornful throat open, or lay hold of that pale, blubbery arm and set the cold blood in it boiling—which would have given Etrius great delight, no doubt, in addition to a fine excuse for a sorcerous drubbing. Still, he hoped the hate and not the pain was what showed on his face. He'd heard these charitable sentiments before, of course, but never all in a string...

All at once he realized that the Councilor's gaze was not just figuratively but literally going through him. He turned. Fidus (whose presence in the chamber he'd completely forgotten about) stood there frozen with eyes open wide to catch every nuance of the scene before him.

Little pitchers have big ears.

"Fidus, why don't you go see if our quarters are in shape for the day's sleep?"

The lad scampered off immediately, still goggling.

"Laying groundwork for the future, milord?" he said bitterly.

"Rubbish, Jervais." Etrius took the pan out of the brazier, holding it by the tongs, and stuck a mop-ended brush into the potion. "I'm sure the boy has long since formed his opinion of you. After all, he has the joy of your nightly company. A few candid words of mine won't cancel that out, will they?"

No, they'll just let him know to whom he can run crying if he ever feels especially ill used.

The Councilor smiled again as though he'd heard this thought (quite conceivably he had), and, still holding the pan, he proceeded to chant softly. He snapped his fingers in the air just inches short of Jervais's skin to prick his halo, the protruding edge of his soul-body, awake. He smoothed it in some places and drew it out in others, shaping it easily with gestures of his free hand. Jervais had always loathed the touch of Etrius's spellcraft. Not that it was painful or cruel, as his words had just been. In fact, just the opposite. It was effortless, light as a butterfly's wing, artful as its flight, pleasant and even inspiring to experience, a masterpiece of efficiency...

A true wizard's touch.

Even the Swede's derelict face seemed alight with something like a soul when he was at his work. He'd likely never known a day without the magic. Possibly a night, though. Possibly those first nights lashed awake each sunset by the hunger of the Blood, before the Tremere learned to adapt the old sorcery to their new, unbreathing bodies. How he must have suffered, how they all must have, at the thought that they might never practice the Art again. And even now, perhaps, at the nagging knowledge that what they had now was not, could never again be, what they'd once possessed. Their flight toward Heaven had ended like Icarus's had, in drowned prayers and wings scorched beyond healing.

Let him suffer. Let them all suffer. And let them sneer, too, at their brothers who never knew the oh-so-transcendent joys of the "natural" gift. At those who have only this *life, this half-life, in which to taste whatever measure of infinity they can. At me.*

Etrius took his brush then and slopped it across Jervais's face. The foul, stinging stuff stuck reasonably well but did drip onto his robe. Jervais didn't flinch. He would not give Etrius the gratification of a flinch. As the old vampire continued to work the dweomer whose purpose he had not, would not and saw no obligation to explain, he paused once in his chanting to snort ironically. "I see your colors, Jervais, not a pretty sight. Keep at it. This is exactly what the charm needs. I knew the chief serpent of my snake den would not disappoint me."

I am not *your serpent to milk or crush,* Jervais promised himself while he endured stroke after stroke of decorative filth. *I'm not a true wizard either, but I will show you in time just what it is that I am. And long after you're gone and your precious mortal magic is the stuff of nursemaids' tales, I will have taken what is truly there to be taken and known what there truly is to know.*

It was a vague enough oath, but it carried him through that moment on its sheer vehemence, and that was all he required of it for now.

He carried a candle that glowed with a little spark of cool, flameless light. It was necessary to see at all in the cave-black rooms, but even with benefit of starlight he would have wanted something to sweep the gloom from the corners. The Ceoris keep held something like two dozen blood-wizards and even more servants and vessels, but one would never have known it just now, in the gritty violet predawn. A constant, distant dripping was the only noise, and it seemed to follow him around, always just off to his left. In his old quarters, cobwebbed and neglected like the tomb of an especially disliked uncle, trunks and reasonably fresh bed linens awaited him, but no apprentice. (He also noticed that someone had long since broken the enchanted lock on the wardrobe where he'd once kept his stores of *vis*.) He frowned, continued through the corridor and hurried down the stairs.

"Fidus?"

No answer. His spell-light sputtered and crackled, dancing on the wick. He felt a surge of rage and struck the cold wall with the flat of his hand.

"None of this nonsense..."

He ran through the second and ground floors, the abandoned dining room and the near-abandoned chantry kitchen, calling. When that proved fruitless, he started to spiral down into the first basement, but a sudden suspicious instinct came to him and he ran back to the ground floor, into a little chamber that had once been the robing room for the Great Hall. It had been a necessary precaution, of course, back when the occasional mortal guest magus had still walked Ceoris's halls. No doubt Etrius still preferred that not every magus of the Blood know the location... Yes, there—a sharp, damp, moldy smell and a hunk of wall that had missed coming back into its original position by a fraction of an inch. Jervais touched his tongue to the correct block of stone then felt his way down the cramped tunnel that the block and its neighbors swung aside to reveal.

Even the candle couldn't penetrate this wormhole. Extending his senses, he heard the croupy, labored breathing of the larder inmates in the hollow on the other side of the tunnel wall, and that maddening ghostly drip again, and a low muttering. How far had the idiot *gotten*? Jervais stumbled forward in a near panic.

"Fidus!" he shouted, then even more frantically, *"Fidus!"*

The boy stood before a very old ward, carved directly into the tunnel rock and then re-articulated with powdered emerald in a binding agent: emerald, enemy of black magic, here in the very Olympus of black magic. Embedded in the rock above the ward was a skull with its mouth fixed open and a small vial set within—no doubt containing the tongue of whatever poor devil's head had been evicted from its grave to serve as guard and alarm here. Fidus was tracing the contours of the ward with a finger now smeared in blue-green. At the sound of Jervais's voice he paused in his tracing, but the muttering went on. Jervais came up beside him.

"Mars in the eighth house and in opposition with Mercury... and when Jupiter is in Capricorn again, how shall I come back then? Ah, I see..."

"*Jorge.*" To his relief, the young Tremere's birth name was shock enough to startle him out of his daze. Fidus jolted. "What— just *what* do you think you're doing?" Jervais demanded.

"I thought I was in bed," Fidus whispered.

"You *ought* to be in bed."

"I was in the library of Alexandria...there was a book I had to find. It was hidden in a secret room, and if I could only unlock it, I would have the answer to everything. There was a voice explaining how." His eyes strayed yearningly to the ward again. Jervais shook him so hard his teeth clacked shut.

"The chantry library is upstairs," Jervais growled. "I will show you tomorrow. There's nothing down here for apprentices, do you hear? *Nothing.*"

"I've never heard such a voice, master."

"I have. Was it just slightly lower pitched than most men's, in an accent impossible to define, calm and unyielding as marble?"

The lad frowned. "Yes—yes, it was. It was so wise, so assuring...but master, how, I mean when—"

"Hush. Never you mind."

"Master, you're shaking."

"*I said hush.* You mustn't listen to anything that may speak to you in this place, Fidus. Listen to me—listen *only* to me. Believe me when I tell you I am your only path out of here." When his words alone didn't produce immediate movement, Jervais seized Fidus's arm and dragged him up out of the tunnel and back to their bedchamber, where he set Fidus to reciting the first chapter of Marbode's lapidary just to chase all dangerous thought out of the boy's head.

Nothing is mine here, he thought fiercely as Fidus droned on, simultaneously helping his master undress for bed. *Even my own student whom I've poured all my labor and wisdom into. Etrius sees there only one more heart to turn against me, and the* other...*well, the other sees fresh blood, and innocence...*

He made himself quiet his own mind. "That's enough, Fidus. To bed."

Now clad only in his nightshirt, he slid into bed. At least someone on staff had remembered his tastes, and supplied him with good sheets and a rich wine-red coverlet stuffed with goose down—precious little good to him when he lacked breathing company in bed, as his own torpid body gave off no warmth for the goose down to catch. Still, it was comfortable and soft. He snuggled down and waited for sweet oblivion.

Then he began to hear the voices from elsewhere on the floor. They started out as disturbing murmurs, which he had to prick his ears to decipher, but quickly grew too loud to ignore.

"*You can't do anything wrong, can you, Curaferrum, as long as you have His Porcine Majesty's robes to run underneath? And now no one else who licks his arse on a regular basis can do any wrong either—*"

"The robes you *could* always quite literally be found under aren't here anymore, milady. That is the only reason you complain of my position now."

"*Your position! You see, you still dare not say milord's name even as you cast vile aspersions on him, you lap-dog!*"

"And you, you will not pronounce the name of mine, lest he hear—"

"*Oh, won't I? Etrius! Etrius Worm-spine!*"

Jervais turned onto his other side, as though that would help. Not a peep from Fidus, but Jervais could fairly taste the lad's avid attention. Wasn't the sun up yet? Surely it was up already. It had been a long trip, a long torture session with the Councilor...surely he would fall asleep quickly now...

"I'll thank you to keep a civil tongue in your head when you speak of this chantry's master, milady!"

"A master indeed! Can he not even control the brats sucking at his teat? Or is this Torgeir doing his dirty work for him? Once upon a time, your precious master at least had the courage to do his own whining and plotting and sneaking. That was, of course, before he deliberately started drinking from only the most wine-besotted wretches in the larder."

"Too many of us are reduced to that too often, milady, since we can depend on you to drain the best vessels dry right away!"

"Ah, ah, look, you see! You are trying to change the subject yet again, which is the outright breach of the Code committed by your little spy—"

You mustn't listen to anything that may speak to you in this place... Why couldn't he follow his own damned advice? He wondered if Etrius heard as well. Of course Etrius heard. If he, Jervais, could not block it out, then certainly the great archmagus was perfectly aware. He pictured mighty Etrius also lying on his side in a chilly room, perhaps also futilely curled away from the source of the sound, pretending to be asleep. That image did not comfort as much as it might have.

"Well, now your own little spy is back, whom I doubt could even recite the Code in proper Latin much less follow it, so I suppose fair will be fair from now on, won't it?"

He *needed* to sleep. He could feel it grinding in his very bones, the exhaustion. Every moment he lay here as though bewitched to stay awake was another drop of recovery lost to perdition. He didn't want any part of this; didn't want to hear anyone's honest opinion of himself or Etrius or anyone else right now. He didn't want to know what the people who dictated his existence were screaming at each other lately in the dead, tired hours of the dawn.

He stared out into the dark, imagining grain after grain slipping through the desk hourglass. Somewhere out in the true world the sun roused itself for one more bright roll across the dome, and still the arguing went on for what might only have been an hour but seemed like four, and Jervais did not sleep.

The next evening, he turned from unpacking to find Malgorzata breaking upon him like a wave. Her chestnut hair was piled on her head in regal undulations, plaited and coiled together with gold thread; her eyebrows elegantly tilted and plucked; her lips dark red and just slightly blubbed, almost raw, especially compared to the ghostly pallor of her sculpted cheek. She reached out to him. He reached back without even thinking. She kissed him on the cheek and then stepped back to glance over him.

"You look well." This was always her little joke whenever they reunited, ever since they'd both become vampires. It embarrassed and pleased him at the same time. He couldn't help thinking of his bald pate, his eyes puckered and prematurely crow's-footed from peering, his body rather too mountainous to qualify as handsome, but she never seemed to mind. She touched his face, ran her hand along the bottom of his beard from jaw to chin, then let it come to rest on his shoulder. It smelled of sandalwood and jasmine, the oriental scent that had turned his head like wine as a young man. On her fingers sat a minor constellation of rings, the most prominent of which was topped with a cabochon caged in gold. Within the ring, unless she'd been neglecting to refill it, was her emergency store of a poison that would kill a mortal within a day and send the Cainite who fed off such a mortal into several hours' unconsciousness.

"And you, milady sire, look far better than merely well. As always." Damn. What was the matter with him? Could he conjure no finer flattery than that? Her face fell very slightly, but then she smiled. "Ah, I can always count on you, Jervais. I've missed you. You have no idea what I've suffered since you left."

Oh, I have some idea, he thought. *In fact I think half the chantry must, unless they're deaf.*

"You were always my pillar. These...children, they're no help at all." She shrugged ruefully. "And His Porcine Majesty has taken advantage of the situation to fill out his stable of toadies, of course."

"Yes, so I've seen."

"Yes. Can you believe it? He's gotten even less subtle with age. He sends his lackeys to spy on me, and they don't even have the decency to pretend they're doing something else anymore! Jervais, I caught one of them, that little albino rat, in my very *laboratory* just last night."

He was supposed to be astounded and infuriated, he knew. Plainly she had no idea how their voices had carried, or else she was deliberately oblivious. And to intrude on a magician's sacred privacy, there were few graver (or more common) violations of custom or Code. He nodded as fervently as he could make himself.

"That one! Yes, I wouldn't put it past him at all."

She looked even more distraught. A hint of menace entered her smooth voice. "*No*, Jervais—my heart, you don't understand. There is *no way* the little pestilence could possibly manage to get past my ward without direct help from Etrius himself, or Curaferrum at the very least. Curaferrum most likely." She pronounced his name in the same tones most Tremere reserved for *Rustovitch*. "After all, he's the one protecting the brat now. I caught him red-handed, mind you. Red-handed, and that... functionary has the gall to say he has only my word to go on. *Only my word!* I sit in the High Chantry council chamber on our lord Goratrix's behalf! And yet do you think I will see a moment's justice for any of it in this tower of iniquity?"

She was rigid with outrage, staring at him. He remembered—or thought he remembered—towering rages, fits worthy of the maenads, which left him gasping. At the moment all he could think of was how much shorter she was than himself, and how had he failed to notice something that obvious for that long? He turned back toward his trunk: a mistake, he knew, but not as great a mistake as continuing to stand there staring back at her blankly.

"I don't seem to recall your ladyship ever waiting for anyone to serve justice on your behalf," he said.

"How right you are, my heart." Her voice grew silky again at that. "Yes...thank you for bringing me back to myself."

Yourself? he thought whirlingly. *Where is it? Where are you?*

The next moment, arms delicate as herb-roots were twining around his chest. Once again he knew what was supposed to happen. He was to fold himself around her now and wait in agony for the slightest taste of her blood, so enticingly forbidden by the Code they'd both sworn to. He was to promise to do any tomfool thing to ease her burdens and earn her smile. He, who hated nothing more than to subject his will to another, ached to want that now. He couldn' t recall ever *not* wanting it with Malgorzata. It had been his temptation and his guilty pleasure. Now he just felt at a loss. However she might play the part now, she was not the helpless female, she had spells he didn't even know about, and if she determined that she was reaching out toward something that was simply, inexplicably no longer *there* it could be very dangerous for him indeed.

"Don't—don't risk your position, madame. Don't lower yourself, please," he said, and at least he didn't have to struggle to make his voice husky.

"You would have me endure such insults?"

"No! No, of course not. I'll take care of it for you, madame, that is what I meant."

"Ah, my heart. I can't have you risk yourself so soon after your return. Etrius will be looking for the first excuse to hurt you, hurt us both, and you know it."

He could not believe in her feint at concern. It was excruciating not to, but he couldn't force himself.

"Besides, what would you do?" she asked quietly.

I don't know yet, madame. But it's bound to be better than whatever overcomplicated scheme you were cooking up to involve me in.

"You'll see," he answered, kissing her hand reverently.

"Ah. I do enjoy it when you surprise me. *I* always believe in you, Jervais, even when others are too foolish to see. I knew the Paris master was wrong the very moment I met you. And time proved me right, did it not? No, you. You proved me right." She laid her head on his shoulder. He could hear that she was smiling. He used to feel so proud when she said such things. He implored her in his mind to leave.

"Well, I won't keep you from your settling in," she said after a moment. "But come and see me afterward. I have some very interesting research to show you—research which, thankfully, the rat did not manage to ferret out."

"Of course, madame." And her light footsteps padded out,

leaving him alone once again with only her perfume lingering.

He tried to concentrate on re-assembling his orrery. He found himself blinking rather more than usual.

Chapter Seven

"You have to be gentle with her. She's very sensitive." Lady Virstania hitched up her diaphanous robe and frowned thunderously at Fidus, who'd just tendered the knobby gargoyle looming over him a peace offering of fresh rabbit and nearly gotten his fingers bitten off along with it.

"Just back up slowly and don't look away," Jervais advised him with a half-smothered smile. "Oh, and raise your shoulders with arms akimbo, you'll look bigger."

"*Maître* Jervais thinks he's a gargoyle expert. Rixatrix is a female, Fidus."

"It is?" Fidus stammered, transfixed by the hand-sized yellow eyes blinking at him from scant inches away. They were level with his only because their owner had bent nearly double to put them there; nor did he seem to appreciate the courtesy of that gesture.

"She is." Virstania dimpled her plump cheeks at the creature, patted its haunch and began to carefully clean its talons out with an iron pick. It submitted to her with a lamb's patience. "And that means the *last* thing you want to do is look bigger than her mate."

"No danger of that, I'm sure," Jervais scoffed, but then he stared at the creature that swooped in from the heights in back of the cave. It wasn't quite Jervais's size in the body, and its wings looked barely wide enough to carry it. It landed with room to spare on Rixatrix' craggy shoulder and hunched its back into a hump.

"What is this, a bantam rooster?"

Virstania left off her polyglot cooing over the big female. In an instant, her voice changed from beatifically maternal to cool as the surrounding cavern air. "I was told, *maître*, that you required two of my adult flock for scouting and fighting. Dear Falco is an excellent spy, and I've never seen my sweetheart lose a battle yet. They're a mated pair. They all but dream in concert. They will gladly die for each other and even more gladly die for you." Clearly she had her doubts as to whether Jervais, or anyone else, was worthy of such an honor. "I trust that will be satisfactory."

Jervais nodded gamely.

"They mustn't be made to fly for more than three hours in a row," she went on. "Falco has a quirky gut, and shouldn't hunt game alone. Rixatrix will see to his proper diet if she is with him. If she's not, then you must make sure he stays clear of horses and deer, or indeed any large herbivores. *Why* is your boy not taking this down?"

Fidus jumped as if struck and immediately picked up the little wax tablet that hung from his belt.

"Quirky gut, no game alone, no big herbivores…"

Virstania glared at him. Rixatrix, the perfect weathervane for her mistress's mood, growled. It sounded like an avalanche in progress.

"Sh, sweetheart. You're scaring your love. He'll think he's done something wrong again."

Falco chittered and nibbled at his mate's stony ear. Rixatrix gave an angry moan and swatted idly at him.

"It's also very important to clean their claws after any real fighting, because they're prone to split if kept wet…"

"What, can't the miraculous creatures clean their own claws?" Jervais prodded her.

"They're gargoyles, *maître*," she said heavily. "Not cats."

"Rix want cat. Little rabbit gone in one drink."

"Not just now, dearest. Mother hasn't got any cats to hand. We can get you both a nice juicy man though. I seem to recall one of Epistatia's raiders offended her recently. Wouldn't that be yummy?"

"What about our Ventrue friend?" Jervais asked. "How do we keep them from eating him, and the other Ventrue and their mortals?"

"You'll have to introduce them, of course," Virstania answered. "Let them get a scent of everyone in the company, one by one. A few times if you can manage it."

"Well, that'll be entertaining to watch at least."

A mortal apprentice scuttled into the room. He fairly staggered back, eyes wide, as three white vampire faces turned to stare at him and a cave full of gargoyles stirred.

"Your pardon, masters, but I was told Master Jervais would be here."

"Yes? What is it? Hurry up."

"Master Jervais, you're wanted upstairs. Master Antal has arrived from Bistritz."

"Very well. That means we'll be leaving, Lady Virstania. Are these beasts ready to travel?"

"I'm sure they're in at least as good a shape for that as you are, *maître*," Virstania assured him.

"Excellent. Thank you, milady." Jervais was not about to let to a cutting remark keep him from making the fastest possible exit.

"You, boy." Halfway up the tunnel Jervais put a hand on the shoulder of the mortal apprentice and stopped him. Without further ado he gouged his fangs into the lad's wrist. The apprentice leaned against the tunnel wall for support until it was over.

"That's better," said Jervais. "So much easier to face the vultures on a full stomach. Well, lead on."

"Yes, master."

The boy conducted them to the great main library, where Etrius usually received magi who were neither as disfavored as Jervais nor of especially exalted rank. Over centuries of acquisition and only the most occasional reorganizing, the room— originally designed in a spacious Roman aesthetic—had become a rat's warren of rough-hewn bookcases and stacks of multicolored books nearly as tall as a man. Every so often a reading desk or chair would randomly and maliciously appear in one's path, necessitating a winding detour. Jervais, who generally preferred cleanliness and luxury and had long since come to hate nearly every cubic inch of Ceoris, had nevertheless fallen in love with the library the moment he'd set foot in it. Especially the scent of the musty old leather and parchment. He felt like the richest man in the world when he smelled it, never mind that none of the books truly belonged to him.

But the sound, unlike the scent, was troubling. There were too many voices in here...not shouting, but still overlapping one another in a way that suggested argument.

"I *demand* that something be done, milord Councilor." Malgorzata's voice. So much for not lowering herself and waiting for him to think of a plan.

"Ah, Jervais," Etrius said as Jervais rounded the corner. For once, he seemed less than utterly disgusted to see him—glad more of the interruption than of Jervais himself, doubtless. "There you are. This *was* to have been the occasion of presenting you and Master Antal to each other. Master Jervais, Master Antal Garaboncias of Bistritz; Master Antal, our *vis*-master, Master Jervais *fils de* Malgorzata..."

Etrius laid his hand on the shoulder of a dour, dark-bearded, rather monkish magus who wore robes of mulberry broadcloth with singe marks on the sleeves. Something in his look suggested that if Etrius were to let go of him for one instant he would shake himself out like a wet cat and then bolt for the door.

"Master Antal." Jervais bowed in response to Antal's grudging courtesy. "I've heard stories of your heroic struggle against the Fiends."

"Yes," Antal replied. His Latin was heavily inflected by the Magyar accent. "The most august Councilor has informed me that we in Bistritz have many long-distance admirers. It is most heartening, of course."

"And now Master Jervais can admire your work up close," Etrius said amiably. "I have promised him he shall find your assistance invaluable. I know that you won't disappoint him, or me."

So Antal needed reminding of who was in charge. Well, at least Etrius himself was undertaking to perform that duty. Jervais couldn't quite find it in himself to feel grateful, but he did make note. It was a hopeful sign that perhaps he truly was intended to succeed and not to die—though he was quite sure

Etrius would make the best of either outcome.

"Milord Councilor." Jervais turned, instinctively, toward Malgorzata's voice as it cut in. Only then did he notice what stood behind her—Torgeir, the "albino rat." (Now that Jervais got his first good look at the Dane's eyes, he realized that Malgorzata hadn't been exaggerating at all. The irises appeared somewhat pinkish in the library light, and they jumped oddly about.) Torgeir attempted to edge toward the friendlier clime of his master's shadow. Malgorzata prevented him with a swift, venomous glance. "All these pleasantries aside, you still have not said—"

"But milady, these pleasantries are of great and pressing importance to the clan," Etrius interrupted. "Surely you don't begrudge our champions against the Telyavs a chance to seal their alliance with a courteous introduction before they leave us with tomorrow's first darkening?"

"You still have not said, milord," she persisted, "when you will even agree to hear the case. What good does it do us to campaign against the Telyavs for whatever wrongs you suppose them to have done you, if justice within Ceoris's own walls is no longer in order?"

"Bonisagus, milady!" No one in Ceoris had the otherwise common Tremere habit of swearing by Great Tremere or even his Seven Names. The long-vanished Bonisagus, founder of the Hermetic Order, was far safer. "The case will be heard when such cases are *usually* heard, especially since you've written half of the magi in this part of Europe requesting their attendance, and not all of them can fly."

"By which time he'll have gotten up to who knows what other mischief, and we still have no idea who's helping him, milord. I should think you should wish to discover the intrigue in your own wing."

"I'll submit him to an oath in the meantime, then," Etrius said wearily. "With a suitable hex if he disobeys."

"Was he not submitted to the great Oath of Tremere, the same as all our initiates? If he dares those eternal consequences without fear, milord, how shall he fear a simple hex even from his own powerful teacher?"

"I presume your ladyship already has some other suggestion in mind for keeping him out of trouble."

"Well, there *is* always the dungeon, of course," she said, putting a finger to her jaw and making a thoroughly transparent pretense of deliberating. "And the manacles my sire devised for its prisoners of the Blood. It's only for a month after all."

"Hmm. As you pointed out, much can happen in such a span. And those manacles were designed to hold Fiends."

Keeping him out of trouble...

"If I may, my most august, sage and immortal Councilor, my revered lady sire," Jervais spoke up.

Etrius scowled. "Yes?"

"Is it not tradition that the accused in such a case may offer to undergo an ordeal to prove his loyalty to the House and Clan, in lieu of a trial, on the occasion of the first offense?"

Torgeir gave him a look of thorough alarm.

"Yes, it certainly is," the Councilor answered slowly, "but as young Master Torgeir has expressed no such interest, why would you mention it?"

"Because it occurs to me, milord, that joining me in my expedition against the traitors would serve as an excellent test of his loyalty. Put him under my command, and I will very quickly determine out of what stuff he's made."

Etrius's eyebrows rose so high they seemed in grave danger of disappearing into his hairline. "Yes. Yes, I'm sure you would, Jervais...and you would be one step closer to your full *sodalicium* as well."

To Jervais's relief, Malgorzata's face lit with pleasure. Torgeir under Jervais's authority—where he could be declared a traitor on Jervais's say-so, sent to his death at leisure, rendered desperately beholden to their faction or at the very least humbled to within an inch of his existence—was clearly an even more delightful thought than Torgeir subjected to Goratrix's Iron Torment. Just as clearly, she took Etrius to be flummoxed and embarrassed at this turn of events, and not merely astounded at what Jervais knew was the gift he had just tossed into the old archmagus's lap.

He was, after all, *volunteering* to take along a confirmed spy, and thus spare Etrius the labor of a trial which Malgorzata had obviously meant to make as big an embarrassment as possible.

"Well, Torgeir. It is your right to request such an ordeal…if you wish." Etrius grimaced. "Ordeal it'll certainly be, if Master Jervais has aught to do with it. But it may still be preferable to letting milady have her way."

Torgeir stared. His lips flopped minutely open and shut a couple of times as though to protest, but it didn't take much spy-craft to tell where his master's will lay. He brushed nervous hands down the front of his robe. "Yes, master—most august lord Councilor. It would please me greatly to be given this chance to clear my name."

"Then so be it. Go pack. As of this moment, your obedience is to Master Jervais, and I'd better not hear otherwise. Master Antal, let me see you to your quarters. We must talk before you depart."

"My heart," Malgorzata whispered, excitedly slipping her arm into Jervais's as they walked out, "why on earth didn't you mention you'd come up with such a marvelous plan? I would never have written all those silly letters."

"I wanted it to seem spontaneous, milady," he smiled.

"But you could have told *me*, my heart."

"You said you enjoyed my surprises. You did look quite convincingly surprised."

"Did I?" She laughed. "Well, good. Better the old bat doesn't suspect so much. Perhaps he'll even start to think you've gone over to his side. But listen, I already know how we can make the best of this Torgeir while you've got him. Now this may seem a little complicated, but you'll see the sense of it in a moment."

He didn't want to listen at all, but he had to know what he was supposed to do if he was going to figure out later how to prove tragically incapable of it.

Chapter Eight

*O*ne...

Himself, of course. For his own strand he selected a bit of green silk, requisitioned from Ceoris's stores just before their departure. It was deceptively soft and luxurious, but of great tensile strength, capable even of catching arrowheads. He knotted it onto a wire framework of his wizard's sigil and set it out to catch the light of Scorpio, his birth sign, for three nights in a row. Then he unknotted it again and ran it through a lodestone with a hole in the middle while chanting the proper formulae.

Two...

Antal. Jervais didn't know much about Master Antal, and certainly there wasn't sufficient trust between them for Jervais to ask for his blood or his sigil. But Jervais could fairly see and smell the blood-soaked battlefield spreading just behind Antal's grim flat eyes, so he selected a length of sackcloth thread for the Hungarian's strand. First he dragged it through the ashes of a dead child which he dug up in a churchyard as they headed north through the Saxon country, then he passed it through a cloud of burning sulfur while performing the spoken enchantments.

Three...

Torgeir. At least since he had clear seniority over Torgeir—not to mention sole discretion in the matter of Torgeir's ordeal—he could reasonably demand a few drops of blood with which to anoint Torgeir's strand. He had Fidus rouse a dyer's family in Culus in the middle of the night for a length of undyed wool yarn and some good lye to bleach it with. (Fidus reported the dyer's comment afterward: "If one must choose between accepting the devil's silver or the devil's curse, the former is preferable by far.") Seized with a whim inspired by his sire's words and his own first impressions, he then bound the pale cord around a rat he'd caught and waited until it had starved. Then he unwrapped it from the desiccated little body and proceeded to make the same incantations as he had with the other threads.

Four...

"Of course, I would leap to assist his most august lordship in any way I possibly could," Regent Karolus said, setting the parchment down rather dangerously near a brazier, "but I'm afraid I simply can't spare anyone right now."

"Oh. I'm sorry to hear that." Jervais made a little moue of concern. "Are the Fiends' depredations heavy of late?"

"No, no, it's not so much that, Master Jervais," the regent replied uneasily. "It's that I'm in the crucial stage of a project of great importance to House and Clan."

"So I'd heard."

"You'd heard?" Immediately the man's voice sharpened. "Heard from whom?"

"Why, from your brother regent in Szatmar-Nemeti."

"He's not my brother," Karolus snapped. He picked the parchment back up.

"He isn't?" Jervais returned with an expression of surprise. "He gave me to understand that you'd served apprenticeship together. In any case, we're all brothers in the Blood…"

"Yes, yes. I mean that he has never behaved as a brother should to *me*. I'm sure he had a lot of pretty tales for you, though."

"Oh, no, not really."

"Ah, you see, he never changes. What did he say?"

"Just petty little things. Nothing worth your concern."

The more he demurred, the more agitated Karolus became.

"Tell me what he said about the project. Come, Master Jervais, you're absolutely transparent. He said something, didn't he?"

"Well." Jervais rubbed at his beard. "Well, to be honest, he did try to convince me to bring some of his 'concerns' about it to Ceoris. His most serious charge was that in forty years, your research hasn't produced a single innovation of clear, immediate and practical use to either the blood war or the clan at large." Granted, the regent in Szatmar-Nemeti had only gone so far because Jervais had gently encouraged his first tentative slanders, but Karolus hardly needed to know that.

"No immediate use!" Karolus spluttered. His lips, the last trace of color left in his vampire face, went livid. He picked up a silver bell from a little rack of bells and rang it vigorously. "No practical application! Why, if it weren't for my research both we *and* Szatmar would have been overrun decades ago, and he knows it!"

A Cainite of rather Turkish-looking features, tall and well built but carrying himself with the slight stoop of a devoted scribe, entered the room and made a hasty bow.

"Yes, master?"

"Master Jervais, this is Baghatur Kazharin. He is at your service for the scourging of the traitors in Livonia."

Baghatur ducked his head, probably more to cover his astonishment than to signal submission.

"Oh, no, this won't do, Master Karolus," Jervais protested. "I certainly don't wish to discomfit you at such an important juncture. There surely must be other chantries with Tremere to spare…"

"What good does it do me to have all my juniors here, if you return to Ceoris with nothing to contradict my treacherous brother's accounting of me?" Karolus cried. "No, I insist. I promise you, you will see with your own eyes the 'immediate' and 'practical' use of my work. Baghatur has been a most attentive apprentice, and he has recently attained the Fourth Circle, which I hope will suffice for your purposes. He won't disappoint. There, perhaps *that* will put an end to this nonsense once and for all! If so, I'll consider it well worth the hardship."

"Well, since you do insist. I thank you, Master Regent."

Jervais smiled slightly. As he turned, he noticed a large, wide parchment pasted flat upon the wall and secured with tiny nails along the edges, and moved closer to it. "Is this a ley-line survey?"

Karolus nodded and came to join him. "Yes, for a hundred leagues in either direction. Within the circle is the area surveyed in person, the rest done by scrying."

Jervais touched a little blue figure of a house, labeled in neat letters. "And these are the chantries?"

"Of course."

Jervais plucked his letter out of Karolus's hand and peered at it. Six names were listed on it for this portion of the route. He looked again at the map. Seven little blue houses.

Six names. Seven houses. Etrius had left one out. Etrius was not a forgetful sort.

Jervais chose a fine linen for Baghatur's thread. Over a few different conversations with the apprentice, he was able to glean a little about him: chiefly that he was a Khazar Jew (no doubt Hermann would be overjoyed), the chantry's resident copyist, a worshiper at the shrine of Avicenna and a fanatic for his teacher's theory of alchemy. The last, at least, seemed sufficiently heartfelt to serve as an anchor. And so after anointing the thread with a few drops of Baghatur's blood, he passed the thread through dirt, smoke, water and—*very* quickly afterward—fire. Then for good measure he recited the first verse of the *Shma*, the only Hebrew he knew aside from the few terms necessary to get through Ceoris's Latin translation of the *Sepher Yetzirah*.

Five...

"Yes, yes, plainly this is very important to the most reverend Councilor." Regent Laszlo glanced aimlessly at the letter. "And I won't dispute Ceoris's wise judgment in the matter of the Telyavs. But surely you've already noticed that it's we here in Hungary who must draw regular reinforcements from west and north...not vice versa. You'll have more luck with the chantries in Silesia and Poland."

"Do you really think so?" Jervais asked mildly.

"Well." Laszlo's lips gave an ironic twitch. "Perhaps not."

"You didn't finish reading."

"Did I need to? I think I've made myself clear." Laszlo must be very old, very entrenched or both. Of their whole band he seemed to think only Antal worthy of respect, though since Jervais was nominal head, he granted him the polite minimums at least.

"Look at the list," Jervais urged.

Laszlo did so. He frowned. "I'm not *on* the list."

"Precisely, Master Regent."

"Then why are you here?"

"*Because* you're not on it."

It took a moment, but the light dawned. "Ah."

"Perhaps if I explained that I am Malgorzata's eldest childe, that would dispel some of the mystery."

"Yes. Yes, it would. And he is sending *you* to take care of the Telyavs, is he?"

"He is indeed, but you see with what support."

"True. So, are you meant to fail outright, I wonder, or are you meant to die after having first battered the Telyavs to the point where a second assault will succeed?"

The latter possibility hadn't occurred to Jervais.

It was certainly perfectly likely.

"I don't know."

"I must assume that your gaining any sort of personal glory out of the affair would, in any case, annoy his lordship greatly."

"That is the safest of all assumptions, Master Laszlo."

Laszlo smiled a knife-thin smile. "In that case, you may have my youngest apprentice, Miklos. He's only Fifth Circle, alas, and I confess was brought in more for his skill at arms and tactics than his aptitude in the Art…"

"Fifth Circle will do quite well, Master Regent, and we'll need good tacticians." Jervais bowed low.

It didn't take much observation of Miklos—who despite his robes had about him the look of a squire just one advantageous ancestor short of knighthood—to determine that a thick sturdy hemp thread would suit him best. Jervais had Hermann cut the length of it with his sword. If the Saxon thought it an odd request that he should hack at a defenseless bit of fiber while shouting a lusty battle-cry, he didn't bother to say so. Jervais also noticed that Miklos proudly wore a necklace strung with several yellowed fangs, and that led him to dig out from a trunk one of two Tzimisce skulls he always carried about. He then temporarily dubbed the skull "Rustovitch," and used the hemp thread to jerk its fangs viciously from their sockets.

Six...

"Well, I'm always honored at his lordship's demonstrations of trust, and would normally hasten to do as he asks," Regent Albizellus said. "But this is the fourth time in a decade he's asked us to hand over one of our own. Surely it's someone else's turn. Apprentices don't just pop up in the chantry garden each spring."

"Believe me," Jervais assured him, "I have some idea what goes into the training of magi-to-be, Master Albizellus, and I do sympathize."

Albizellus looked rather surprised at this quick acquiescence, and indeed dismayed. So that was it—he was perfectly prepared to give up a student (perhaps he kept an unusually large crop of them about just for such occasions), but wanted it to be understood as a real favor. Jervais did not allow himself to smile.

"Is…is it really that dire?" The regent fumbled his way back onto the conversational path.

Jervais knew he'd already landed his fish, but he had no objection to providing the necessary diplomacies. He grimaced. "Master Albizellus, his lordship fears the very worst of these Telyavs. Not only have they almost completely cut themselves off from the clan's obedience, they may have thrown in their lot with our enemies. They may even be allied with the Fiends, or on the verge of doing so. We *must* act now, before all is lost."

"Ah, I see. Well, I suppose if our assistance is needed that badly, I can answer the call one more time."

"Ceoris thanks you, Master Albizellus, for your constancy."

"Not at all, Master Jervais. Zabor!"

To Jervais's astonishment, a head popped up from behind one of the library tables. It had a thatch of disheveled brown hair, and was attached to a youthful body whose left hand held a woebegone scrub cloth.

"Zabor." Albizellus didn't await a response or a bow. "You're going to Livonia."

"Of course," the apprentice said flatly.

"Forgive me, Master Regent," Jervais broke in. "But I must not have made myself fully clear. My recruits must be of at least the Fourth Circle in order to participate in the rituals I'll require."

"Zabor *is* Fourth Circle," Albizellus smiled.

And yet he's made to wash the floors still...not a good sign.

"You won't mind a bit of a trip, will you?" he asked the apprentice.

"No, master. It should be my honor to take part in something so important." He glanced ironically at the rag in his hand.

"Zabor isn't the most docile student I've ever had," Albizellus put in pleasantly, "but I don't doubt one of your experience can keep him in line easily enough. And perhaps this is just the sort of schooling the lad needs."

Albizellus also informed Jervais before he left that Zabor excelled in tearing apart the enchantments of others. And so Jervais selected for Zabor a length of nettle-yarn—stinging nettle, shirts of which the Slavs trusted to repel demons, dragons and lightning—and flicked it with drops of Zabor's blood and also a bit of solution of green vitriol. He then shielded the yarn by winding a thin wool yarn around it (the last thing he wanted was for Zabor's destructiveness to make naked contact with the threads of his fellows) and finished with the usual incantations.

Seven.

"Not to dispute his lordship's decisions, because that's the very *furthest* thing from my mind..." Regent Walenty frowned. "But were you really dispatched from Ceoris one Tremere short of a *sodalicium*? That hardly makes sense."

Jervais let his throat close over the gruel-thin draught of mortal blood he'd taken from the goblet Walenty handed him, then forced it down before replying. "Not one short, I'm afraid. My cohort was mostly assembled from the chantries along my route, from the regents whose names you see there."

"Ah. I see. But forgive me, I'm still confused. My understanding was that the Telyavs have done exactly as they pleased for well over a century now, and I hadn't thought the situation substantially changed. Why the sudden urgency? And if it is so urgent, then why must you go from chantry to chantry with cap in hand in order to fill out your ranks?"

"The ways of the Council are mysterious." Jervais was not, by now, feeling inclined to share the details of how precisely the situation with the Telyavs had changed.

There was a faint knock on the warded study door. Walenty looked irritated, but called, "Yes? What is it?"

A dark-eyed woman, modestly veiled, entered and curtsied low. Jervais's spirits rose slightly. Perhaps the goblet had been a stopgap while more appropriate refreshment was located. But then the regent gestured for her to rise. "Yes, Olena?"

"I'm afraid Pawel's just made a rather large mess of his exercise this evening, master."

His eyes widened. "*How* large a mess?"

"I...well, I think you'd better see, master..."

"Weren't you supposed to be supervising him?" he snapped. "Oh, very—forgive me, Master Jervais. I'll be back shortly, I hope." He stalked out, robes flapping behind.

Olena hurried up to Jervais. "Unorthodox, I know," she half whispered, "but there was no other way I could speak to you. He was determined to keep me busy all night."

"To speak to me?" Jervais returned, mystified.

"I've finished my Circles," she interrupted him. "I finished them more quickly than any other apprentice he's ever had. I finished them over twenty years ago, but he keeps saying no new regencies have opened up. That isn't true, is it?"

"I—" He stammered. "That is, I suppose it's unlikely that *no* new regencies have opened up in either Silesia or Poland, but I can't help you against your own regent."

"But you can. You're Master Jervais of Ceoris, and you're on a mission for the clan, aren't you? I need a chance to demonstrate my ability—to someone besides him. Otherwise I'll be teaching his apprentices until the Fiends *finally* turn him to ash..." From the way she gritted her teeth, he imagined that arranging for exactly that would soon be no more out of the question than arranging an accident for Pawel. "Just one chance, that's all I ask. Please." She threw a look over her shoulder, and then hurried over to the door. "*Please.*"

When Walenty returned a little while later, Jervais said casually, "I see that you don't have the aversion most of our colleagues profess for sharing the Art with the fair sex."

"I begin to wish I had," the regent sniffed. "I tell you, Master Jervais, the virtues of the Blood simply move too sluggishly through the female vessel. Nor are the powers of discipline and concentration what one should hope for, as you've just seen—our most sage and immortal Lady Councilor in England excepted, of course."

"And, of course, my own sire."

Walenty's jaw dropped, but he recovered fairly quickly. "Yes, yes, of course. An eminent exception."

"Well, in that case, perhaps it would be mutually beneficial if I were to take her off your hands? You would have the room to introduce another male apprentice, and all I really need now is one more Cainite body to fill out the last place in the *sodalicium*. She is Fourth Circle, at least?"

"Oh. Yes..." Jervais could fairly see the man's thoughts turning like a water wheel, as he tried and failed to think of some way he could contradict himself and not look like an utter fool. Jervais did not intend to permit him that luxury.

"Excellent! Then I shall be able to enter the pagan lands with everything in place. His august lordship will be so pleased."

For Olena, Jervais chose a worsted yarn, smooth and hard-twisted. Then he steeped it in a hot tincture of ivy—patient, tenacious, ambitious—and left it wrapped, seven times for each Circle she was so proud to have achieved, around a silver vial of mercury for a night and day before finishing the incantations.

He could remember being a very young boy, too young to recognize the difference between women's and men's work. Old Nurse—whose name he didn't know even though he still sometimes drank from her pillowy breast—was trying to braid his sister's hair and like any small child, he wanted to take part in whatever was being done. When her efforts to shove and slap him while holding onto the fraying strands only produced a screaming fit, she finally agreed to show him how if he would stand quiet and obedient. And so it was Nurse's hands that he thought of now, guiding him in spirit even though he doubted the woman had ever plaited more than three strands together, and he had to contend with seven.

Once he'd finished the broad band and gotten it loose from the stick the other end had been tied to, he began to knot it upon itself.

"With knot of one, I begin my charm in the name of Tremere.
With knot of two, I bind us in the blood of Tremere.
With knot of three, I bind us in the will of Tremere.
With knot of four, I bind us in the power of Tremere.
With knot of five, I bind us in the brotherhood of Tremere.
With knot of six, I bind us in the fate of Tremere.
With knot of seven, I seal my charm in the name of Tremere.
Though born to different natures and spun on different spindles, we weave our arts as one.
Our circle will be strong where theirs will be weak.
Our circle will labor where theirs will sit idle.
Our circle will know harmony while theirs will learn strife.
Our circle will prevail where theirs will fall.
Yes, amen, let it be so.
One House, One Clan, One Blood."
My blood.

As he finished this recitation, he took the braid—now looped into a circle secured by the seventh and final knot—and laid it in the little iron cauldron to steep in the dark red ichor.

It was a very simple, very old sort of magic, but things simple and old often had a power all their own, and he wouldn't shame to make use of it if it helped his newborn *sodalicium* hold together for even one night longer than it would have otherwise.

Or, to be more accurate: one night longer than the enemy did. That, after all, was the crucial thing, and despite his spell's hopeful demands, it was by no means a sure one.

Chapter Nine

Deverra did not generally stand for long on the hill where the sacred fire burned and the sacred *zaltys*-snake made its lair. As important as it was, the task was better suited to mortal priestesses, who saw warmth, home and food within the flame's red depths—not an end to immortality. But the smell from the wood and the sacred herbs that the priestesses threw upon it in handfuls drove away all other scents, good and bad. She wanted distraction from both sorts. Her eyes read the sky left to right, top to bottom, like a parchment page, and then restlessly began again.

"If you are really so desperate," Qarakh murmured beside her, "you could call to it—*make* it fly the other way. My people also believe in the messages of birds, but we are not above making our own fortune either."

She turned to look at him. Her lips wanted to smile at the welcome sight of him: the strange wind-weathered face still showing the ochre-brown of many years' sun even through the Cainite pallor, the little stub of rounded nose-tip emerging from a flattened bridge, dark narrow eyes that could be cruel as a winter storm or softly questioning, as they were now. She felt the smile but couldn't quite make it.

"No, Qarakh."

"No." He squinted, staring off into the sky. "But you will stand here night after night and watch for it to do as you hope."

"I won't succumb to self-delusion, but for hope I'll wait as long as necessary. It flew east, toward the flames of sunrise, three nights ago, shrieking all the way. It still has three more to fly west into the cool night and cancel out the omen. If it's there to be seen, I will see it."

"Will the omen not be the same whether you witness it or not?"

"What need would there be for a shaman, if it didn't matter what she saw or didn't see?"

"My shaman," he said, taking her arm. "I appreciate your devotion on behalf of the tribe, and I will not dissuade you from watching. But you have been up here for three nights and you have not drunk. You must drink."

"Purification," she said shortly.

"You must drink," he said just as shortly. "Three nights' purification is enough."

"Then have it brought to me, so I can continue to watch."

He didn't look pleased, but he nodded. "As you wish."

The wind sent her hair aloft, drifting on the currents of air. Since it had gone white, it had also become thin and light as flax-filaments. It was very responsive to weather and the passage of spirits.

"This has not been the only such omen in recent nights," he frowned.

"No, only the worst."

"Are they truly so bad? You had ill omens before Alexander came as well. Are these like they, or weaker? Stronger?" He added the last in a tone of great reluctance. "They are very bad...and also strange. I haven't seen such strange signs in a long while."

"Since when?" he pressed. She wondered whether now might be a good time to play the mysterious oracle and refuse to answer, but then she shook her head fondly.

"Since just before we met. That was a strange-fated evening indeed, you cannot deny."

"Yes, I remember. I thought at first you must be a *chotgor*..."

"A disease-spirit?"

"Yes. White, thin, fragile. Altogether ugly." Fortunately, she knew Qarakh well enough to let him finish before taking offense. "But you changed my mind quickly enough."

She answered his meaning, not his words. "I had a lot more to change your mind with, back then. But now..."

"Now we rule this people. Together." He caught her hand

and wouldn't let it go. She felt her blasted flesh protest, bits of it splitting and sloughing off. "Only together. That is our strength. Don't think I have forgotten it."

"Qarakh," she said, "you're hurting me."

He loosened his grip, but kept on pursuing his thought. "I also have not forgotten a certain sorcery you practiced a few times. When I slept at the foot of your tree, and you brought our spirits both out of their bodies. And we would seem to be mortal man and woman for a few hours…"

Again, she heard what he didn't say. *Not just alive, but alive and young.* The fact that he didn't look at her now made it all the more obvious. His pain moved her, and she wanted to comfort him by allowing him to try to comfort her. But the pain in her own soul when she even thought about it—escaping into false serenity for a few hours, and then having to return again to play the unbowed priestess, queen and avatar—decided her.

"My khan honors me. But I fear I find myself too weary lately to cast enchantments that are of no…direct benefit to anyone."

He nodded. "I will have the vessel brought up. But you must rest. I cannot have my witch weary."

"No, don't trouble yourself, my khan. I will go down and feed. It is long past the hour when such birds fly anyway."

He started to speak, but she gave him an abbreviated courtesy and brushed past. He watched her go down into the encampment. As she hobbled by one *ger* a furtive, shaggy figure stole out of it, going mostly on its legs but assisting itself with pushes of its taloned hands along the ground. Through the blur of hair and rags, Qarakh could still see the outlines of what had once been a woman, a proud warrior of his own Blood. The bestial figure mewled and brushed up against Deverra, who put out a gnarled hand to stroke the figure's head. His beautiful shaman and his northern Valkyrie. They at least still walked the night, unlike others.

"The gods…" He spoke in the vague plural, thus including all the many divinities held dear by his raiders, Deverra's priesthood and the Baltic peoples themselves. He had one god in particular in mind, but didn't wish to stir it with a particular mention. "The gods demand much of us in exchange for their gifts. We pay not only our own private prices, but each others' as well. Will there ever come a night when the price is finally paid in full? What will be left of us then?"

Feh. This sort of melancholic fit was not like him. But it had been happening a lot of late, and it unnerved him at least as much as anything Deverra had seen or said. He was finding that not even the blood of mortals drunk on mead or *qumis* could always shake him out of it. He heard the cry of a raven, and leapt, as though struck, back up the hill to see. It was flying east.

Chapter Ten

Tobiasz idly tapped the back of the neck of one captive, a youth, who glared up at Jervais with eyes hot with hatred. The lad flinched and put his head back down.

"These Balts haven't figured it out yet," he chuckled. "They'll sell each other to anybody. Pskovians, Hungarians—they don't understand they're already too few for their own good. I'm not about to tell them, of course. Well? What do you think?"

"What languages do they speak?" Jervais asked.

"Let's see. Not the Silesian speech. I have a couple of Esths, some Livs, some Letts, a Kur, a Semgall…"

"I don't need Silesian. One should speak the Samogitian tongue, or something like it. As for the rest, I'd prefer they not speak to anyone at all."

"Ah, you're continuing northeast. In that case, you're probably best off with the Esths. Their tongue is more like the Finns'. Or if you like, I could take some of the other Balts and cut out their tongues. But there's little need to worry. They all hate each other, as I already said."

"And the Samogitians?"

"They're wild, strong warriors. I don't have one right now. The Semgall might have some acquaintance with their language. Actually, now that I think of it, I seem to remember the Kur trying to talk to the Semgall in what was either Samogitian or the highland speech."

Jervais nodded. "The Kur, then. And I'll need a dozen others. Their nationality doesn't concern me so long as they're healthy."

"A dozen! A pleasure to do business with you, *mein Herr*. With or without tongues?" Tobiasz grinned.

"With. Mustn't run out of things to threaten them with too quickly."

"Indeed!" Tobiasz hesitated for a moment, then went on. "You're not familiar with these parts, are you, *mein Herr*?"

"Not at all, as I'm sure you can tell."

"Then if you will permit me, I wish to show you a spot of the local color." The slaver extended his hand. "I have a feeling you're the sort to appreciate it."

Jervais dipped his bare foot into the water of the spring. Even though a mist lay over it, he wasn't prepared for the warmth that enveloped his toes. He lowered himself the rest of the way in. It smelled a bit funny, and the water felt oddly slippery, but the sensation was quite pleasant.

"And mortals come here for leisure?" he whispered to Tobiasz.

"Not leisure," Tobiasz corrected him delightedly. "Witchcraft."

"I see."

"The people—the dissatisfied young peasants especially, but sometimes even the soldiers of Chojnik keep—they come here on nights of the new moon to ask the *vodyanoi* for aid. If they doubt you, just ask them to listen to your chest so they can hear that you have no heartbeat and are, in fact, a spirit."

For his part, Jervais thought it almost enough just to be warm and naked under the stars—after a little while, he could even pretend Tobiasz was not there—but presently there were signs of movement in the surrounding brush, and the dim outlines of a threesome of young maids, huddled fearfully together. They carried a loaf of bread for propitiation.

He understood precious little of what they said, but he nodded and answered *yes, yes of course* to everything that sounded like a question. Names were mentioned, of lovers, lovers-to-be, rivals, parents perhaps. Tobiasz spoke to the girls several times. Jervais didn't know whether he actually instructed them to disrobe or whether they already understood that to be the price, but in any case they too stripped bare of everything but their headkerchiefs. Jervais took one girl into his lap. She wrapped her arms around herself but didn't resist him. He caressed her a while, pleased with the slickness of her wet goose-pimpled skin—but there was something that bothered him as well. Not her fear so much (he'd long since become used to chantry prey being either terrified or abjectly obsessed with the Kiss), but the solemn pall that hung over the proceedings. Her submission had a ceremonial quality which should have been stimulating yet wasn't.

Quite suddenly he began to tickle her. She chuckled unwillingly, then cried out. An instant later, under his redoubled assault, she was shrieking peal after peal of laughter to the sky. Her friends gaped, doubtless convinced he was murdering her, but she turned and jabbed her fingers under his armpits, causing him to splash and mock-protest. Soon even Tobiasz had to chortle at them.

"This is meant to be a dire sorcerous rite," the slaver chided Jervais as the latter took advantage of the improved mood to bite into his vessel's wrist. She cried out again, this time in pain followed closely by lust. Tobiasz followed suit with one of the others.

Jervais finished his sip and sealed the wound shut with a touch of his tongue. Then he snapped his fingers at Tobiasz. "*That* for dire sorcerous rites!"

He examined the girl. He'd drunk very shallowly. She seemed little the worse for it, and indeed much the better. Her heart still beat strongly. Her buttocks, which had lain taut on his thighs before, had now softened and flattened against him. He put his hand into the triangle of hair at her belly's base. Extending his senses in the way Malgorzata had taught him so long ago, he could feel the pulse of her blood just underneath the skin—feel it and mystically draw it toward his fingertips, toward the surface of the tender flesh, engorging it. She drew in a shuddery breath. The scent of her sweat increased. He kissed the top of her neck, exulting in the knowledge that just beneath his lips, sharp and eager, waited her death if he so chose. The sheer dizzying joy of that power tempted him to hover there, between the resolution to either kill her or let her live. He held himself back, merely kissing her again.

There was a thrashing sound in the brush. Jervais started and looked up, expecting a deer to come blundering through.

But it was an armored figure, sword drawn, black cross starkly visible on his white tunic.

"So!" Hermann bellowed. "*This* is where you wandered off to!"

"What do you think you're doing, Hermann?" Jervais snarled back. The girls crowded away in a huddle.

"What do *you* think you're doing? We are taking the cross against the pagans, and here you are—"

"You are taking the cross, Brother! Not I! Look upon your chest, then look upon my chest. I don't recall ever swearing a pilgrim's vow."

"Go," Hermann shouted at the girls. "Go and save your skins, if not your virtue!" He shouted it in Saxon, but they took his meaning quite well enough. They splashed out, stepped into their shoes, slid their shifts down over their freezing bodies, wadded up the rest of their clothes and fled in terror.

"Believe me, it wasn't my intent to surprise you at your lewdness," the knight went on. "You disappeared and so did this... flesh-peddler, so against my better judgment, I decided to go out and make sure no ill had befallen you. Then I heard a woman's screams."

"Of course you heard woman's screams. This is vampire country," Tobiasz said lazily.

"And you..." Hermann's sword pointed in Tobiasz' direction. "Unless you so greatly enjoy sharing a warlock's water that you would dare my ire, you had better cover yourself and get out of my sight."

"A warlock's water?" the slaver exclaimed, his face falling. Then he turned to stare in dismay at Jervais. "You mean..."

"Yes. Now go."

"I'm going. You *niemczi*—always biting the hand that feeds." Tobiasz threw on his clothes.

"You cannot order *me* out," Jervais blurted, even though he no longer had the slightest wish to remain for any reason besides defying the Ventrue.

"No, I cannot order you out," Hermann agreed, irritated.

"Perhaps you should see to your own needs, *mein Herr*. Did you find any of the slaves suitable?"

"They'll do," the knight nodded. Jervais resolved once again to determine the secret of the Ventrue knight's finicky tastes. All through Hungary he'd refused to share the Tremere's vessels or allow any of them to procure for him, instead sending one of his mortal soldiers out to do it. Quite a few nights he'd simply done without, restraining his appetite with prayer-vigils. "I'll say this for your fellows, here and at Ceoris—they're a pasty, loathsome lot, but at least they don't luxuriate in it like brothellers at a stewhouse. They don't trick the mortals or toy with them, trying to turn it into a pleasure."

"Ah, you noticed that," Jervais said calmly.

Hermann stared at him a moment, saying nothing, then sheathed his sword and walked away. Jervais sat alone in the water for a long time. All contentment and ease had evaporated like the steam from the water's surface. He willed himself to let it go. They were in Tzimisce lands now. He couldn't afford to hate Hermann, or anyone else.

A new silhouette appeared quietly at the spring's edge. Jervais stared at it. An old bearded man stood there, stooped but unashamed, completely naked in the brisk winter air.

The man spoke. Jervais shook his head, then said, "I don't understand," in Saxon just to make himself perfectly clear. He was tired of playing spring-god for the night.

"So the devil speaks Saxon these days?" the man said. "Well, I should not be surprised. You look surprised. I have not come here for years. I asked you for many things in my youth. You took the salt of my blood, and I made many wishes, and none of them came true. Not one."

He came closer. His gaze was fixed and intense. Jervais could read it very clearly, could see the span of decades in it. He'd endured much bitterness, many disappointments, for which he was now deliberately choosing to hold Jervais solely responsible. At the moment, Jervais could find no fault in that.

"Now even to the one son I have left, I am like a dog at the door. There is no part of my body that does not pain me."

The man bent down to the ground, kissed it and whispered into it for a moment.

"I know that God will not forgive, because He will not forgive me even the crime of living, so I beg *matka ziemia*, Moist Mother Earth, for forgiveness," he explained, sitting up. "Perhaps she will be kind. Perhaps not. Of you, whatever you are, I make no more wishes. I ask only what I know you can give me. Spiteful spirit, I ask you to spite me unto my death."

Jervais sat there, awestruck, for several moments. Then he stood.

"That," he said hoarsely, "I can do. Come."

He held out his hand to help the old man into the pool.

Chapter Eleven

It wasn't so very different from the Christian country they had now left behind. Or at least Jervais didn't think so. Though he knew intellectually that Poland and Silesia were considered "settled" and Prussia was not, it had all felt more or less like forest primeval to him. At no point in the journey had he encountered a juncture where he could have said, "Here ends civilization; here begins savagery." Nations, churches and landscapes shaded into each other. None of it was Saxony, and certainly none of it was his France, where man and nature had long ago reached their eternal détente. Here, even in the places where fields and pastures stubbornly interspersed themselves between dense, looming tracts of forest or heath or marsh, they always seemed somehow tentative. It was as though they knew they would be swallowed up again at once should the slightest misfortune strike.

They came to a fork in the dirt road. Hermann pulled up short. The company of Black Cross knights, both Cainite and mortal, who had joined them at Stettin halted behind him in perfect formation. Even together with their squires and men-at-arms they weren't many, but their discipline at least was cheering to see.

"Which way now, Meister Tremere? It looks like we must choose between woodland and marsh. Are we still following the whim of your rock?"

Jervais snorted, but just to be sure his fatigued eyes weren't beginning to deceive him, he fished out his lodestone pendulum and let it swing until it found the ley line.

"We make for the trees."

They rode uphill toward the stately line of pine and fir. Just at the wood's edge Zabor, the lone Pole among the Tremere, shivered and held up his hand.

"Wait! We shouldn't be here."

Jervais turned quizzically. "What do you mean, 'shouldn't'?"

"It's an *alkas*."

"It's a grove," frowned Jervais.

"That's just what I mean, master," the apprentice said irritably. Jervais's brow wrinkled and he opened his mouth to reprove the lad for his rudeness, but Master Antal interrupted with one of his rare, typically blunt contributions.

"The Prus worship in certain groves, like the Tzimisce slaves in Hungary." He didn't look up from shaving his bit of hawthorn branch, carefully letting each strip fall into the open pouch at his waist.

Jervais dismounted, then bent down and touched the earth. His hand was greeted with warmth, pleasant and tingling now, but then it grew suddenly sharper, and he snatched his fingers away.

"Yes. Perhaps we'd best go around…" He brushed the dirt off. "But we must keep following the flow of the *vis*. It's our best chance of finding the Telyavs."

"You mean we don't know where they are?" Torgeir spoke up.

"They're like their Gangrel allies," Jervais snapped, "nomadic. We have a vague notion of their territory; within those bounds they might go anywhere. But I doubt they stray far from the wells of power. What magic-worker does?"

Torgeir's face seemed to wobble alarmingly in midair for a moment. Jervais started, then realized that something was rippling the ley line, plucking it like a lute-string.

"Someone's doing a working," he hissed at his murmuring brethren. They all immediately fell quiet and looked to him.

"We're *not* ready for witch-war, Master Jervais," Antal said definitively. "We haven't even trained properly yet. And we don't know this terrain."

Deciding that now was not the time to establish who would and wouldn't pronounce their troops battle-ready, Jervais nodded. "Right. I want everyone but Captain Hermann, Master Antal, Zabor and myself to withdraw behind the hill. We'll scout it out and see whether this is *koldun* conjuring or the Telyavs already or something else entirely."

"In there? But why me, master?" Zabor interrupted.

"Because you were the first to claim to know something about it," Jervais returned.

"Well, that will teach me, I suppose."

"Yes, I trust so." Jervais spurred his horse into the forest's cool dim depths.

Ah, I was mistaken, Jervais thought a little later. *The edge of this alkas, that was the line. Here ends civilization.*

The motley crowd seemed exclusively mortal, if their rosy soul-colors were any guide. Some rode at a stately pace through the trees, some walked, some were old, and some were children. All clustered together into a tight mass. Jervais poked his head a little further out from behind the massive tree that hid him and sharpened his eyesight to get a better look. In the midst of the crowd rode a thin man in a bloodied white robe covered over with a black scapular, his hands bound behind his back.

"A Dominican. One of the Teutons' missionaries?" he whispered to Hermann—then he turned and saw it was quite unnecessary. The knight had already caught that much, and he nodded grimly.

As they watched, the people gathered around the fire that burned in a stone-and-wood pillar set in the forest's clearing. The maid tending the fire had already been there when Jervais and his companions first arrived, a good while before the rest of the crowd made it in. It might even be that she or one just like her was always there, keeping it perpetually lit, though he saw no sign of a temple or even a shrine anywhere about. An old man in rather more fanciful garb than the rest—the priest, Jervais assumed— separated himself from the mob. He said something to their prisoner, who shook his head wearily in response. The priest drew out from among the people a pretty young girl of perhaps fifteen, her head crowned in a wreath of rue and dressed in a fine clean dress of new-spun linen. The priest gestured expressively at her. The friar shook his head again. The people murmured.

"Zabor, what are we looking at?" Jervais prodded.

The apprentice squinted toward the scene, but it was plain he couldn't make out the level of detail that Jervais could. "I—I don't know. She's dressed as a bride, but..."

Antal gave a contemptuous, gusting little noise. "They are offering him a wife."

"Why on earth would they do that?" Jervais murmured, fascinated.

"Because they're stupid superstitious savages, and they fear his ghost," the Hungarian answered. "They think if a man or woman dies unwed, and thus incomplete, then the vengeful spirit will haunt the earth forever."

"He must not have explained the Dominican vow to them properly," Jervais said with a wry glance at the fuming Saxon.

"Oh, I'm sure he explained it, they just couldn't believe it."

"If he said yes, would they kill the girl too?"

"Not sure. They might, or they might simply make her go through mourning."

"It doesn't matter," Hermann put in, aggravated. "He won't say yes."

"Now what, Zabor? Is he to be sacrificed in the fire?"

"He must be," Hermann rumbled, his hand already gripping his sword-hilt. Jervais plucked at his gauntlet to warn him to quiet.

"Well...he's mounted," Zabor frowned. "When their warriors die, they're cremated in the saddle along with their horses...so if he's a sacrifice, he's an honored one. That, or they're just afraid to murder him without the proper funeral rites. Superstition, like Master Antal said."

"If this were just murder, they'd kill him and then perform the rites, not burn him alive," Hermann protested. "This is demonolatry. They mean to feed their loathsome gods on his ashes."

"What is this business with the horse?" interrupted Jervais. "Looks like they're trying to spook it."

"No, they're trying to get it to lift a hoof," Zabor corrected.

"Either hoof."

"Yes, the horse chooses. It's a lottery."

All at once a great cheer rose up from the people in the glade. "Death," Jervais translated.

"I'd imagine so."

"This ends now." The knight glared at them all, as though they'd contradicted him already. "I won't stand here in the dark and permit this sacrilege. *You* hang back if you like—"

"No, *mein Herr*," Jervais implored him. "For all you know, one foot on that holy earth might destroy you."

"Unholy earth. I do not fear the demons of the savages!" Hermann hissed.

"Just look at the man. He's half dead already. Even if you did rescue him, what would you do then? Give him the blood and hope he doesn't wind up as one of us?"

The knight's face was a mask of unadulterated hatred. Jervais stared back blankly.

"Well? If you really must, then risk it. But why cheat any mortal's short life of a martyr's crown—to say nothing of one of the holy brothers of Dominic?"

"You have...the reason of it, warlock." Hermann cast his half-drawn sword fully back into the sheath and settled back down again. "It is a poor night when reason rules."

Not long thereafter, the thick stench of burning hair and flesh filled the glade. The vampires recoiled from it as from the sight of a sunbeam, leaving the magpie friar to his saint's end, melting back into the shadows that led out of the *alkas*.

Jervais contemplated the man as he sat unmoving on a little ledge of weathered rock. A noble mien, when it wasn't wreathed in choler as it was now.

In the short term, I need him. In the long term, we need his master.

He approached Hermann, allowing his quiet footsteps to make just enough noise for warning.

"I don't pretend to be a knight or a monk," Jervais said softly. "And God knows you would never make a wizard."

Hermann snorted, not looking at him. "You'll forgive me if I take that as a compliment."

"Of course. I forgive all our differences. I must, because our purposes are one. Be patient, *mein Herr*. Heathenism *will* fall here, just as it fell in Sweden and Denmark."

"Why do you say that?" he returned. "It makes no difference to you."

"But it does." He sat down on a fallen log. "You see, as the old ways crumble, the Tzimisce and their allies crumble also. The night will arrive when they can no longer play gods to their people, and then they will become our prey. Indeed, all vampires will have to grow more careful as the Church's power waxes, and that'll do us all, Tremere included, a great deal of good. It'll be a milieu where only the cleverest and subtlest survive."

Falco's ungainly gray body loped out from the shadows, toward them and up to Jervais. The gargoyle had a fox in his jaws, which he shyly dropped at Jervais's feet. Jervais lifted his toes away from the bloody carcass.

"Which of course suits you admirably." Hermann shook his head wearily. "Pious talk, master wizard. Sometimes I think the pagans we fight are more steadfast in their bastard faith than most so-called Christians are in theirs."

"Take heart," Jervais urged him. Then, to the gargoyle he said, "No, no, Falco. I mean, thank you, you have it." He put his hand briefly and gingerly on the monster's head. Falco removed his prize to a few yards' distance and began tearing into it with a good will.

"Take heart, Captain," he repeated. "That faith will be the Telyavs' downfall, and the Gangrel's, and the Tzimisce's."

"Will it?"

"Such complete trust won't bend," the Tremere explained. "It can only break. The Telyavs have made their fatal mistake in teaching their kine to regard them as holy. It will be only too easy to expose them, and then they'll lose everything in one great blow. The mortals will acknowledge the power of almighty God, and all will be just as you wish it."

"You seem to regard faith as a simple matter of bowing to the stronger of two parties."

"I think for most people, that's exactly what faith is," he allowed. "But since the one true God cannot be anything but victorious, isn't that enough?"

The silence yawned between them, and Jervais had to resist the urge to smile. Hermann was wrestling with the unavoidable limitations of both sword and sermon to truly change the hearts of men. Jervais would not be the one to tell him his entire purpose in existence was a futile lie, but if he reached that conclusion on his own, so be it. There was little danger of it, however. The Saxon was nothing if not stubborn.

"I suppose it is…a first step, as his Highness would say," Hermann murmured at last. "And what about you, Tremere? Is that your creed as well, always to bow to the stronger?"

"A true wizard…" There was a relish in saying these words, taking them out of Etrius's mouth and appropriating the right to change their meaning. "A true wizard's body may bow before the victor of the moment. His heart doesn't bow to anything or anyone, ever."

"Not even to God Himself?" Hermann replied, shocked.

"God chose to give me free will. That was His choice, His mistake perhaps. As for myself, I will honor the gift in the only way it deserves. I will exercise it. If there is a hell, here or in any other realm of being, I am sure it need consist of nothing more than that—the taking-away of choice."

"By those lights, servitude *is* hell, in and of itself."

"Yes," Jervais agreed. "Servitude is hell."

"And your masters at Ceoris," Hermann went on thoughtfully, "would they agree with that?"

"My teachers at Ceoris," Jervais answered. "Their wisdom justifies their position, not the reverse."

"I see." Hermann rose. "Well, it sounds like a very comfortable philosophy, Meister Tremere, up to a point."

"And which point would that be?"

"The point where death is with all certainty upon you, and all your power and free will can no longer help you." He smiled thinly, sketched a military bow and left.

And that is probably the very moment you pray hastens itself to you, Jervais thought.

"Servitude…is hell," Falco informed his mate Rixatrix and Master Antal's gargoyle, Cabo. He enunciated the words as carefully as he could through his crooked fence of teeth. His darling's answer was straightforward and to the point. She swatted him down off his branch to land face-flat in the dirt. "No," she said. He shook his head free of the filth and flapped up into another, slightly more distant tree.

"Master said it," he huffed, pushing out his chest.

"Mother says we must serve," Cabo pointed out reasonably. "Is honor."

"Master said is hell."

"Mother must be right."

"Master must be right."

They all pondered this for some time.

"Master has a Master," Falco went on. "If Master must serve his Master, but Master says servitude is hell…"

"Stop talking," Rixatrix rumbled. "You think like rock. Mother is right and Master is right. They are both right."

"How?"

For a moment she seemed stumped by this, but she soon recovered. "They are both right—in different ways," she pronounced.

"How?"

"I do not know," she said serenely.

"Perhaps," Falco said at last, "is hell for Masters, and honor for us."

"Perhaps," Cabo acknowledged. He scratched himself behind one of his curling ram-horns, shaking the branches and sending a drift of leaves falling to the ground.

"Then…we are luckier than Masters," Falco concluded, uncertainly.

"Of course," Rixatrix scolded him.

And that ended the argument.

Chapter Twelve

"This is ill country to stop in," Antal argued. "Too open. Too many birds overhead for so late in the year. The Telyavs might well speak with birds if their sorcery is as much like the Fiends' as you say."

"I understand that, but we can't get a really good survey on the move like this. At some point we're going to have to sit down and scry." Jervais shifted in his saddle. One thing he'd never thought quite just was that the horse should get a saddle blanket to prevent chafing, but no such comfort was extended to the rider. He threw an unfriendly glance in Hermann's direction. The knight looked as comfortable in the saddle as though he were under some enchantment to that effect. Now there was a thought.

"You can do some things on the move," the Hungarian said, an unusual (and worrisome) note of enthusiasm entering his voice. "Once a detachment of Brancoveanu's forces chased us for a solid week. I had a spell to drive them off, but only if we could find a well of *vis*. I soon discovered that one can briefly attune a gargoyle to the ley line, such that they instinctively fly along it…because they're very earth-heavy, you see."

Jervais restrained the urge to roll his eyes. Everyone thought he was a *vis* expert if he knew one trick. "Ah, clever. Still, I think we'll want to be able to make a chart. How familiar are you with that process?"

"Somewhat," Antal lied.

"Well, ideally we need at least two stable locations to scry from. That way there's something to compare against, and you also have a triangle of points, you see, from which you can use geometry to more accurately compute the distances."

"What makes you think we'll have the luxury of one stable location, much less two?" the other magus acidly interrupted. "It's certainly not a privilege I have often enjoyed."

"We may not," Jervais conceded, "which is part of why the most sage Councilor thought your services would be needed. Your ability to think on your feet."

"Not an ability I would have wished to have to acquire," Antal sighed.

"Come. I'm sure it's been an adventure, at least...and your name is famous among young Tremere from Ceoris to Aachen." Jervais was hoping yet to knock this conversation off track before it went where he feared, but no luck.

"And what good does that do me?" Antal lowered his voice. "Besides perhaps a slightly greater ease in luring the young out to the front to get themselves killed. Hardly rewarding. There's peril in being too good at something, Master Jervais."

"Yes, that's certainly true."

"Particularly, never being given the chance to prove one's skill at anything else. Anything less hazardous. Then again, I'm sure magi with more 'comfortable' posts also grow discontented with the sameness of things after many decades."

"Perhaps they do, sometimes. If you're referring to a specific rumor, Master Antal, you'll have to do me the favor of letting me know exactly which one—ahh!"

Jervais instinctively clutched at his horse's neck as the creature tripped and stumbled down onto one knee—nearly causing him to tilt off its back—and then rose limping. Jervais reined it in and dismounted at once.

"*Halt!* What's this?" Hermann wove through the apprentices up to the front. "Threw a shoe?"

"Probably, knowing my luck."

"Let me see." Hermann examined the bared hoof. "Easy, easy now, old fellow. Master wizard, how the hell have you been sitting this poor beast? Have you been leaning sinister all night or something? A man your size has to sit with *some* balance."

"Leaning sinister!" Jervais exclaimed indignantly, though he thought with a slight wince of pain that perhaps he had been a bit, given that his worst sores were on the right flank. A slight chuckle came from the knot of apprentices. Jervais looked murder at them, and whoever it was fell silent.

"See here, it looks like the tip of his back hoof caught the edge of the shoe and flung it off. Someone find it...ah, good, Fidus. Hm. We've got spare nails, but I don't know if our man can reset this. It's quite bent. We should find a smith."

"Out in this wilderness?"

"These Samogitians are supposed to be great riders. Surely they shoe their horses. There must be smiths. Have your Kur ask at the next mortal dwelling we pass."

Jervais privately doubted the slave was capable of such translations yet. He seemed to understand the natives in these parts far better than he had the Prus, but he was learning Saxon slowly. Still, he nodded. "Very well."

"So the farmer said this...what was the name..."

"Aukstakojis," Jervais said. The Kur timidly echoed the word, evidently correcting something in Jervais's pronunciation.

"Bonisagus, it's worse than Georgian. Anyway. He lives along *this* path?" Antal peered into the gloomy depths of the wide stand of trees. "In the opposite direction from the village? Looks like a bandit hideout to me."

"Well, smithies are rather noisy for most neighbors' tastes..." Jervais said noncommittally. "In fact, I think I'm hearing the ringing now. And look, there's a glow."

"Working awfully late," Hermann frowned.

"A commission for some impatient local potentate, perhaps. *Mein Herr*, you're the one insisting that my horse be seen to as soon as possible."

Leading their mounts single file along the narrow trail, they soon came up on a little lone shack from whose cracks orange furnace fire bled. They studied it a moment. An unmistakable clanging came from within.

"I'll go in," Master Antal said, "since I'm accustomed to being in close quarters with fire."

"No, I'll go," Jervais argued, "our Kur understands me best."

"We'll all three go in," Hermann said, determined not to

be out-couraged. "And that way we'll be prepared whatever happens."

Jervais knocked heavily on the open door's frame before walking in, for all the good it likely did. The two other Cainites and the Kur, whom he'd collected with an imperious glance, followed. Inside, Jervais's eyes tried unsuccessfully to adjust to the light, and his skin felt rimed in frost compared to the heat of the forge. Before the flames, a thin crooked silhouette undulated in the rhythmic motion of hammering.

"Smith," he called. "Smith!" Then he looked at the Kur, who translated. The smith looked up, gave his project—it looked like a knife-tang—one more whack and set it aside. He came forward. He was a small man (small everywhere except for his great shoulders, anyway) but wore a huge bristling beard and mustache.

He spoke. The Kur translated: "He say welcome fine sirs."

Jervais said, "Tell him we have a thrown shoe and will pay him well to fix it right now."

"Saxon merchants?" the smith spoke up, in that tongue. "Saxon merchants always pay well, sir. Always hurrying." He gave a funny little bow and smiled. "I fix shoe for you. Please give…"

Jervais handed it over. The little man examined it, running his fingers over it.

"You do quite a trade," Hermann remarked. "Look at all these stirrups. And they're not all built the same way. You have two different kinds."

"Every rider does not wish the same," the smith replied.

"True. But these are perfectly ordinary, and then these here are the sturdiest and heaviest I've ever seen. Look at the great flat plate on the bottom. You could stand all night in these."

"Save us from such a fate," Jervais exclaimed.

"I highly doubt they're for Saxon merchants…but I trust their purchasers pay well nonetheless?" Hermann stood and moved closer to the smith, who didn't seem to realize he was supposed to feel menaced.

"Those riders? They not pay at all," he answered cheerily. "They come at night on the backs of *tarpanas*, wild forest horse, and their eyes bright like moonlight, and they say if I give thin no-good wares then they will tear down my forge. So I think I should work."

Jervais and Hermann exchanged a look.

"Sounds frightful. These riders, what do they call themselves?" Jervais asked conversationally.

"The men call their leaders *darkhan*. I know no other word. But they are very strange. I know they are not of my people, because Samogitians only ride *zemaitukai*..." He gestured toward the assortment of more ordinary-looking stirrups. "And also some of them look very strange to me."

"Are they bandits? If we wanted to avoid them, how should we steer clear?"

"If they want you, they find you I think." The little man shrugged. "Twelve leagues north of here, they enslave whole village. Last week, that was. But Samogitians kill you too, if they see black cross of White Christ on you." He smirked at Hermann.

"Let them try," Hermann said imperturbably.

The smith put the horseshoe in to start heating and went back to working the bellows.

"Time to start looking for our first spot, I suppose," Jervais said quietly to Antal in Magyar.

"Yes," Antal murmured back. "Except now we've got to find a spot where they *aren't*."

"Well, these are real horsemen apparently. They're not going to go taking any long walks. We stay away from the churned-up ground, we should be able to stay away from them."

"Yes, but if they're that skilled, they'll see *our* tracks, and know right away that Herr Pious there has got a great hulking Friesian shod with the nail heads sticking out so as to kill people all the deader, and so on and so forth." The Hungarian chewed a bit on the end of his beard and then a thought seemed to seize him. "Tell the man he's got some more shoes to fix. My old master had a spell to lighten a man's tread. I think I can adapt it. One mark on each, and a bit of blood while the iron is hot."

"Re-shoe twenty horses? But that'll take a couple of nights, at least. Be practical—" Jervais protested.

"Yes, re-shoe them all," Antal interrupted. "Practical? Think about it. Do you really want them finding us first, or the reverse? Let's at least try it on Hermann's and see if it works."

"And what about the carts?"

"If the horseshoes work, I can figure out something with the carts."

"We've got more work for you," Jervais shouted to Aukstakojis, "and more coin."

"Work with coin much better than work without," the smith shouted back with a huge grin.

Chapter Thirteen

Hermann pushed into the tent. "Our scout's back from Riga," he announced.

Jervais and Antal looked up from the map they were making. "Ah? And did he bring word?"

"He did better than that." The knight stepped aside to let another Cainite in the Black Cross habit pass by. "This is Brother Wigand. He and a handful of survivors have been holding out up north."

"Qarakh and his tribe are no longer in Livonia," Wigand said. "They're much closer than you think. They've been driven south—not, alas, by our efforts but by sheer press of mortal conversion. But now they're among even wilder pagans than before. If they get a chance to recruit many Samogitians and Lithuanians, it will go very badly for you."

"A pleasure to meet you as well!" Jervais exclaimed. "You seem like exactly the sort of source we've been looking for. Come in, come in, my dear sir." Antal refused to give up his seat; Jervais scoffed at him and offered up his own chair instead. "Actually, we already know Qarakh's riders are here, but there's something else you might be able to tell us. Now I understand from the reports that made it back that Alexander and Qarakh faced each other alone."

The knight arranged himself in the chair. "Yes," he said. "That is true. But not by choice—not by our choice, that is. We were all trapped by a bog that suddenly opened up under our feet. All of us except for Qarakh and Alexander. Perhaps Qarakh did it using some beastly art, such as others of his kind use to sink themselves into the earth during the day. Myself, I think it was his witches. I was lucky. Only my legs were swallowed, and I managed to dig myself out with my sword, but…not in time to save anyone else."

"Yes, yes," Jervais said excitedly. "That is—it's very good to know that. It corroborates what our talebearers in Saxony said. But they escaped in the opposite manner—sank into the mire completely and so, alas, ended up missing the last of the single combat. Qarakh slew Alexander all alone, then?"

"Yes."

"And how was it done? The killing strike? Was it a sword blow?"

"No indeed," Wigand snorted as if the very notion were ridiculous. "That creature? He assumed the wolf's skin and devoured first our general's leg and then his throat, letting the gore stream from his maw like the animal he is."

"He drained him to the dregs, then."

Wigand looked him directly in the eye. "If you are asking me, sorcerer, whether Qarakh stole the ancient's soul, whether Qarakh committed that vileness known among our kind as diablerie, then the answer is yes."

Jervais's eyes lit so fiercely at that that everyone in the room drew back alarmed. "Then we have him!" he blurted, slamming the palm of his hand on the trestle table.

Several moments of stunned silence followed.

"What in our Savior's sweet name is the blackguard talking about?" Hermann directed this to Antal, who shrugged.

"Not sure," the Hungarian said. "Certainly, to commit the diablerie on one so powerful can have terrible consequences for the defiler. But *we* have no control over Qarakh's pains. That is, lacking something of the ancient himself…and surely Alexander must long since be scattered to the four winds."

"Not all of him, Master Antal," Jervais said grandly. "Look…"

He reached into his purse and set a coin out on the table, ringing it like a banker upon a banker's counter. It sang like metal but appeared black as a lump of coal. Antal left off his drawing, set his pen in its well and came over to examine it.

"Malgorzata's coin."

"Malgorzata's spell," Jervais corrected for the benefit of their bemused audience. "And certainly one of her handier ones. This particular coin I fashioned. It holds a small portion of the ancient's blood, locked up in the prison of the metal, but I should be able to extract it again."

"We could mix it with molten wax and form a figure. Inscribe it with his name in Greek."

"Yes, and dress it with this." Jervais went over to one of his chests, touched his tongue to the lock and whispered into the keyhole, then unlocked it. He brought forth a tiny strip of white bloodstained cloth and laid it next to the coin.

"Fashion it into a tabard, yes."

"With his arms embroidered on. *Vair, on a pale purpure, a laurel wreath or.*" Jervais mocked a herald's pompous tone. "I daresay Olena can embroider, can't she?"

"Pardon me, scholars," Hermann interrupted. "I hate to break up your plotting since you seem so eager to get about it. But I'm not sure I understand just what you mean to do. Alexander is *dead*—his soul devoured."

"Exactly," Jervais said triumphantly. "And where did that soul go? Into the belly of the beast."

"Into Qarakh."

"Who," the warlock finished, "is due for a terrible bout of indigestion."

"Here, Fidus," Olena said, tossing him the scrap. "Master Jervais said to embroider it like a tabard. *Vair, on a pale purpure, a laurel wreath or.*"

"But…but I don't embroider," he stammered.

"Neither do I," she said curtly. "But don't worry. I'll let you know if you've made a mistake."

Master Antal went about calling the quarters as though it were a life-or-death business, which, to be fair, it could be often enough. He started in the North and invoked the power of Uriel, archangel of death and the realm of Earth, drawing the proper sigil in the bowl of dirt with the tip of his wand and then bringing its power up to form its portion of the warding circle. He then moved Miklos into position there and again traced the same sigil on Miklos's chest, naming him the watchman of the North. Then he moved to the West, where Gabriel ruled, again "drawing" in the bowl of water that lay in that quarter and raising its power. He placed Baghatur in the West. In the South lay Michael, archangel of Fire, and a cone of incense in whose smoke Antal traced the necessary sign; Zabor assumed his appointed place there. Then Antal finished by consecrating himself to Air, to the East and to Raphael, and took up that position. Olena, Torgeir and Jervais stood in the circle's center.

"The creature of wax," Jervais murmured.

Miklos brought it forth from a fold of his ritual robe. "Molded by my hands," he said. He passed the poppet to Torgeir, who took it to Baghatur.

Baghatur took a little silver implement and carefully pricked tiny dots for eyes and gouged out a gaping mouth, then articulated a suggestion of fingers and toes. "Carved by my hands," he said.

Torgeir now handed the poppet to Zabor, who just as carefully inscribed ALEXANDROS into the poppet's chest. "Marked by name by my hands," he said.

Torgeir gave the poppet to Antal, who took two tiny snake-fangs and inserted them into the poppet's open mouth. "Marked by Caine by my hands," he said.

Torgeir then passed the poppet to Olena, who slid the little white tabard over its head and belted a tiny leather cinch around its waist. "Clad by my hands," she said.

Now Jervais took the poppet. "Creature of wax," he intoned, "I anoint thee and name thee Alexander, sometime of Paris, childe of the Ventrue patriarch and great-grandchilde of Caine who was cast out." He dabbed blots of dark blood onto its forehead, hands, feet, heart and groin.

"Alexander thou art."

"Alexander thou art," the other six repeated.

"Alexander thou shalt remain."

"Alexander thou shalt remain."

In his hands, the poppet seemed to grow ice-cold, leaching the vital force from his skin wherever it touched. To his mystical sight, it grew a thin, guttering halo of colors, shifting randomly for want of a guiding intelligence. There was no mind there, only essence, and even that was fragmentary.

"Not much of him left," he said softly to Torgeir. "But you'll make him stronger. Take him now and feed him. Three drops to make him yours."

Torgeir shuddered a little as the thing touched him, but he did as instructed. Biting into the pad of his thumb, he dropped one drop after another into the poppet's wide, hungry mouth.

"I bind thee once, Alexander, in my blood and will. I bind thee twice, Alexander, in my blood and will. Thrice I bind thee now, Alexander, in my blood and will, and thou art mine to command."

Let's hope so, a distant and unwizardly corner of Jervais's mind whispered, but he pushed the thought aside. It could only hurt the working. He guided Torgeir (whose awareness was already gone elsewhere) to a seat cross-legged on the floor. Olena took up the ritual sword that marked her as guardian of his body and anchor of his soul for the duration of the spell, holding it before her in an attitude of utmost vigilance.

"Can you see him?" he whispered to Torgeir. "Where are you?"

"I...I'm following the thread. Things are blurry...I'm flying over the ground."

"Which way is the moon?"

"That...that way."

"North-northwest," Jervais muttered, committing the direction to memory.

"And now I see odd little tents. No, they aren't little. They grow as I approach." Suddenly he hissed and flung one hand up over his face. The other hand nearly let go of the poppet it clutched. Jervais stiffened and moved in.

"What is it?"

"The twin fires...I may not pass through. I am not of the *ordu*."

A sorcerous warding, placed by the Telyavs? Or just a native superstition fueled only by the power of collective will? "You can pass through," he encouraged the Dane. "They cannot stop you. You carry a piece of the chief himself."

"No," he moaned.

"You *shall* pass through."

"He shall pass through," the other Tremere chanted as one. It was more than merely verbal support. As they said it, they were also focusing every ounce of their souls upon making the words reality. They needed no prompting as to when to add their strength. That was good Eastern training for you. Excellent.

"Do you hear that, Torgeir? We're with you." He bent down. "It's fine. Our wills are joined. You wield the might of Seven. Now hold Alexander's echo close to you, and walk through."

Torgeir nodded and gathered the poppet to his chest. "I hold a portion of your chief," he intoned to his invisible enemy. "You must let me pass."

There was a long, tense moment. Suddenly Torgeir began to gasp like a landed fish, and Jervais feared the ward had attacked him after all. But then he managed to say through his gasps, "I'm through," and a tingle of relief passed through the circle. Jervais took the Dane's shoulders and steadied him until the whistling breaths calmed and died.

"Good, Torgeir. Come. We may not have much time now, hurry. Find Qarakh."

"I see him. He shines. By God, I've never seen a man so strangely made…"

"Yes." Jervais gritted his teeth and silently cursed Etrius for not doing as other Tremere masters did and drubbing the use of *God* out of his pupils, particularly when in circle. "Go to him. You must enter in and find that sliver that was Alexander's. That is your link and your rudder. You must take hold of his heart."

"Take hold of his heart," the other Tremere echoed.

"Show me, my prince." Torgeir addressed this to the deceased, in student's Greek. "You must be here. One so ancient never disappears completely into his conqueror. Hiding, perhaps? Mourning?" He licked his lips, cracked and withered from three nights' fast to ease his spirit's release. "Or waiting… Waiting for revenge?"

The built-up head of power within the circle changed tenor in less than the space of a mortal heartbeat. Before, it had felt like an unseen mist, drifting easily between them except when driven forward by the workings. Now it crystallized, condensed, sharpened. Olena gripped the sword more tightly. The guardians of the quarters steeled themselves against the onslaught, containing it.

Jervais struggled not to let himself be paralyzed by the unexpected strength of the response. "I... You've got it all right, Torgeir. Easy, now. Direct it."

"Yes." Torgeir held the poppet forth. Beads of blood appeared on his forehead. "Let me guide you, my prince. Let me lend you the power of my mind, so that I may show you... how much easier it is to destroy from within..."

Qarakh set down his bowl, which a moment before had been full of the blood of mortals drunk on *qumis*, and wobbled up from his seat in the square of logs and stumps that stood in the middle of his cluster of personal *gers*. Deverra waited until he had blundered wordlessly away, then picked up the bowl and took it to be washed. Hopefully if he had to call for it again to get more, he wouldn't bother.

As she handed it to one of the scullions in the kitchen-tents, she felt a stirring at her back. She knew what it was, but said nothing until she was at the threshold of her own *ger*, where she turned.

"*Boyar* Osobei. Why do you follow me?"

The slim, elfin-faced Cainite bowed. "I pray that I have not given offense with my clumsiness, madam. But I was hoping to have a word with the great khan tonight."

"Then you should have followed the great khan," she said dully.

"The khan, alas, does not seem to be, ah, in the mood to conduct official business."

"The khan is in the only state he will consent to conduct official business in."

"Indeed?" Osobei was a diplomat, and as a diplomat disguised both his surprise and his disgust well—but not well enough.

"It's his way. He says the heart more truly sees the hearts of others when the mind is lulled out of interfering."

"I see. Then I have erred. Forgive me." One thing she had to say for Osobei, and indeed all the Tzimisce she'd met—they submitted to the demands of courtly etiquette with uncommon grace. Though she looked old enough to be his grandmother, he might well be her elder in actuality, yet he readily lowered his eyes to her in formalized shame.

"You haven't erred," she corrected him. "You can speak to me. The Telyavs and Qarakh's riders are as one."

He kept his eyes downward. "Yes, so the khan himself has said, madam."

"Then why do you hesitate? I'm not ignorant of what your Rustovitch feels toward us. We're thieves of the Blood, are we not? Has he not sworn to take back what he believes to have been stolen from his clan?"

"In his eyes," Osobei answered, now raising his glance once more, "you are still Tremere. Yes."

If he was hoping for some guilty reaction, she wasn't about to oblige him. "You've seen enough of us now to know how we fashion our existence, *boyar*. We've not been Tremere for over a century."

He shrugged elegantly. "A century is but a day's sleep to the *voivode*, madam."

"Then perhaps the *voivode* should sleep now, and hope things will be more to his liking when he wakes," the old woman said archly. "If that is all, *boyar*, I must tend to the needs of my people."

"Madam, it is my hope that the *voivode* will soon be prevailed upon to make the alliance that serves our best interests." His smooth words stopped her retreat.

"And you believe that this alliance is in his best interests?" she asked him.

"With whom else should he join?" Osobei replied. "With one of Jürgen's Germanic rivals? They hunger for our land no less than Jürgen himself. With the Arpad? They are constitutionally unreliable. They betrayed Jürgen when he most needed them and would gladly do the same to my *voivode*. As for the other *voivodes*, they're already theoretically our allies, and we've seen how well they hold up to their obligations."

"And what about the Obertus? They are Tzimisce, are they not?"

"We are not yet precisely sure of that, madam," he said dryly. "What I do know is that their goals are not our goals. But *your* people and ours do share a common agenda. To keep the White Christ out of those few remaining lands where he does not yet rule, and to crush the Saxon Ventrue before they have time to think of formally banding with Ceoris."

"Ah, but if you truly believed that, *boyar*, then you wouldn't begrudge speaking with me. If you really want to know what I think…"

"I am indeed most eager for your opinions, madam."

"I think you're hoping that we are only allies of convenience for the khan, and that if you offer him the services of the Tzimisce *koldun*-priests, he'll decide that one magic-worker is as good as another and break faith with us. Then Rustovitch would be spared the embarrassment of finding himself sharing ranks with those he considers Usurpers, and the Telyavs could more easily be crushed alongside the spawn of Ceoris."

Evidently he was not at all used to being so accused to his face. It took him a moment to recover enough to speak.

"You talk," he said at last, "like a woman who believes she does not need any allies at all."

"No, I talk like a woman who knows better than to believe I can have any." She smiled bitterly. Tiny crystals of snow landed on her face and did not melt. "Many will parley with us, cajole us, but no one will truly stand with us in the end, because what we have become is an abomination in the eyes of the whole world. Do you pretend that my khan will be received joyously as a brother-king in the halls of the *voivodes*? To you he's fit only to be a loyal war-hound. Many of his own blood reject him simply for being Mongol, or for aspiring to create something larger and more enduring than anything they've made. Ceoris hates me, yet your master regards me as one of its talons nevertheless. The Christians would wipe us out because we are pagan, and many mortals would exterminate us because we are *vampyri*. I am under no illusions."

"And if the great khan should feel differently, and wish to ally with us?"

"Then I will not fight him. I may permit you to use us, *boyar*, but never to divide us..."

She trailed off to a halt.

"Do you smell that?"

He glanced around. "What?"

"Fire—"

A vast dread lodged itself in her, shook her frail bones. Somewhere a boundary had been trespassed. The sense of alien intrusion was no less immediate and absolute than it would have been if Osobei had put his hand between her legs. But which boundary? She began making her way through the encampment, rising slightly on her toes as though that would really help her see better. Osobei fell into step beside her, his expression more curious than concerned.

Then they heard the first scream.

She broke into a stumbling run. The scream was immediately joined by others. They came from near the warriors' *gers*. She smelled plenty of roasting meat, horse-sweat and *qumis*, but the rising scent of vampire blood quickly threatened to overwhelm them all.

From the campfire protruded the lower half of someone Deverra was sure she should recognize. Qarakh stood in the center of a knot of his Cainite soldiers. Long earth-colored claws extended from the tips of his hands and also from his feet, shredding through his soft leather boots. As she watched, he bodily picked one Cainite up and threw him a good ten yards. Another he seized by the throat, then he snapped the man's spine over his knee and began to drink lustily from the outstretched neck.

In the intimacy of the circle, it was impossible not to know the moment something had gone wrong. Jervais felt it before he saw the change in Torgeir's faraway gaze. The others did too.

"We have to get him out," he said quickly. "Olena, help me bring him out."

Olena laid a long-nailed hand on the Dane's shoulder and

began to chant in Latin, calling Torgeir's name and bidding him return to her, his anchor, and also to his flesh. Jervais added his own words to hers. At once the young magus's inert body leaped into animation. He was on his feet, white teeth flashing, curling his lips in a wild snarl.

"Ho!" cried Master Antal. A military note came into his voice at once. "Dismiss the circle now! East, South, West, North!" Rapidly he began speaking his quarter's words of revocation.

Jervais fumbled for the wooden dagger at his belt. Olena crouched as Torgeir bore down upon her, thrusting up the ritual sword so that its length was buried deep in his belly. He howled but couldn't pull himself off the blade. Jervais, trying to measure Torgeir's back for his blow, found himself splattered with a shower of Cainite blood, which woke his senses like a trumpet blast. The blade protruding from Torgeir's back waved hazardously as he and Olena struggled. Then Torgeir pushed past Olena, the sword still in him, and charged toward Zabor—who chose the better part of valor and dodged aside, breaking his quarter prematurely and scattering the circle's energy into a hundred wounded, wasted fragments. Antal shouted at him, too late. The beast was on the loose.

They all stood there for several moments, dazed from the wrenching blow of the spell's sudden end, then Antal lurched away to follow Torgeir, and the others fell in behind him. There was no need to ask where he would go.

"Qarakh!" Deverra shouted, but the Mongol didn't hear. One of the soldiers, no doubt shocked beyond reason, grasped his lolling comrade and tried vainly to pull him out of Qarakh's raptor grip.

"*No!*" she shouted again. "Don't touch him, you're only provoking him! Back away slowly!"

They understood her tone, if not her logic, and obeyed. Qarakh clutched his prey and would not lift his lips from the streaming throat, but he lifted his eyes at least. In his stare she could see no recognition, no human thought at all, only the awareness of a threat nearby.

"Qarakh." Many times, as witch-priestess, she'd had to bury

her fear so that a sullen spirit would not taste it. This was no different. "Qarakh, you must put him down now. You are tired, you are sad—you need to rest, my khan."

He gazed blankly at her. His mouth opened and dribbled gibberish. She could make nothing of it at first. Then one word went by that she understood. The phrases themselves were disjointed nonsense—as though he realized he was being addressed and should respond, yet had forgotten how. But the language was one her old master had long ago made her study.

Greek. Holy gods...

What was the word? "Softly," she whispered to him in the best Greek she possessed. "Softly. It will be all right." She moved closer to him. He watched her warily, suckling the wound once more, as she took one step, two, three. Four was evidently one too many. He lunged for her, throwing the crumbling body of his clansman aside. She screamed. The other soldiers catapulted themselves onto him, weighing him down. He gave a roar and began flinging them off.

She muttered and drew herself into herself, calling for spirits of the air. She didn't have time to sweet-talk. She simply promised to summon them a storm, a storm of great violence in which they could dance for hours, if they would come to her now and do as she bid. Eagerly they brushed past her and seized hold of Qarakh, then lifted him from the ground until he was hovering in midair like a bee. Some of the fight went out of him as his feet left the ground, but he continued to writhe and spit and struggle against those who were still latched onto him. His face had begun to stretch, change shape. If he moved to wolf-shape now, in the grip of such rage, there was no telling when he would come back. She hurriedly fetched an arrow out of one of the soldiers' quivers.

"Hold him still if you can!" She opened up his coat and, with a prayer to Dievas, struck with every ounce of strength blood could give her. Her prayer was heard. The shaft slid through, splintering in her hand as it went, but at least one shard must have pierced his heart since he shuddered once and then went completely stiff.

Imploring the spirits to bear him down gently, she and the

soldiers laid him on the ground. His face was frozen in a rictus of hatred that she could hardly bear to look at.

"What happened?" she asked quietly, glancing toward the half-corpse at the fire.

"He came at us with an evil gleam in his eyes, and didn't seem to understand a word we said to him. Kasim tried to fend him off with a burning brand, but that only made him angry."

"Yes…" It was worthless to point out the folly of such a course to them—they'd now seen it with their own eyes. Fire was a fine tool for driving off Cainites who were still in their right minds, but once the Beast had already emerged, there was no telling how it might respond to a flame thrust in its face.

I don't understand it. He was drunk, yes, but not to any extraordinary degree. And now the Greek…

There was one way she might gain some understanding, if there was still anything of Qarakh to be reached right now. She gazed deep into his eyes—he had no choice, couldn't turn his head or even shut his eyelids.

Qarakh? Her thoughts reached out tentatively for his. *My khan?*

There. An echo, heartbreakingly weak. *My shaman,* his eyes answered. *Who is dead? Are there dead?*

Yes, there are dead. She felt tears threatening to start, and ordered them angrily back. His own riders whom he loved as kin. *I don't yet know who. I will find out, but do you truly wish to be told now?*

Perhaps not.

I will release you in a moment, I promise.

No! He couldn't move, but she thought she felt the barest shiver through his clothes. *No, you must not—it's not safe, my witch. I don't have the mastery of it.*

What is happening? Is he—

Shh. I do not know. There is…something, that is sure. And it draws not only on my own strength, but on the power of the god. It wakes the wolf in my soul and bids it raven.

Do you think you can master it, my khan?

I must. I will try. I do not think I can kill it, but perhaps I make it… understand, given time.

Time?

You must give me time. The voice had grown paper-thin. *You must be father as well as mother to the tribe.*

No, no. Don't do this to me. The last two words of this desperate thought were out before she could stop them. *Something's coming still. There's danger. We'll need you.*

You do not need one more thing to worry about. And now, sharing company mind to mind, she could feel the accumulated pain that she'd guessed at, but not seen, in these recent months. *Let us face facts, my shaman. Neither of us has been the same since Alexander, and since the god's burning touch. My change has simply been less obvious. I will return when I can be a help to you, and not a burden.*

She wanted to plead with him, but he was the wrong one to importune. She wanted to plead with Telyavel, but if the god hadn't stretched out his hand to help Qarakh yet, he must have decided by whatever mysterious reasoning gods employed that it wasn't right to do so. In that moment she would even have pleaded with their dead enemy Alexander, if there'd been anything there to plead with besides a mad, mindless fragment.

She held him close. *I will guard you,* she thought fiercely, *as faithfully as you guarded your blood-brother those many years. You will rise again, my khan.*

But he had descended too completely to respond, perhaps even to hear.

"No," Jervais said brusquely to the babbling, gesticulating slave. "Yes, I know what you want. You want to burn your friend's body. I'm telling you *no*. No fire. What you may do is dig. Dig, you know, dig?" Something caught at the hem of his robe. He looked down. The Esth woman who held the corpse and keened over it had reached out to wrap her free hand around his leg, leaving a red streak on his ritual robe. He stepped back. "Zabor! See if you can make these people understand that I realize perfectly well what they're asking, I just haven't the first intention of giving it to them."

"They don't seem to understand my Polish any better than your Saxon, master," Zabor pointed out.

"Well, find out what it is they do understand, or I'm going to take all the dead ones and one of the live ones just for instructional purposes, and crack the stream ice open with their thick heads."

"That sounds like it might work, master."

"Do you wish instruction from me as well tonight, whelp?" Jervais rounded on him, snarling.

"Master Jervais, if you will permit me..." Master Antal interrupted, holding up a hand. "I must borrow Zabor instead. There are words that should be had about the importance of remaining *in position* in ritual until instructed to take leave of it."

"Ah, true." Jervais was gratified to see an authentic look of fear pass across Zabor's face. "Feel free, Master Antal."

Jervais then made his way out of the campsite, to the tree where Torgeir was bound in a length of stout chain Miklos had packed in his trunk "just in case." The young magus's head was drooping now. Jervais thought he must have passed out, so he began to steal away again.

"Leave me be." The Dane's accent was far stronger than usual.

"I'm not here to hurt you," Jervais said soothingly.

He sniffed at the air. "Are you still bleeding, lad?"

"No."

"It smells like you are. If you need more..."

"*No.*"

Ah, so that was it. But of course. How could it be otherwise? He studied the albino's soul-colors carefully. It was hard to say which predominated, the dank gray-brown of shame or the licking scarlet of hatred. He looked slack and barely conscious, but it might be far too soon to consider unbinding him. It wasn't even the chain itself Jervais placed his trust in so much as the spell laid on it.

"If you need more," he said firmly, "then you need more."

"I'm fine."

Jervais walked up to the tree, put his fingers into the hair at the Dane's brow, and lifted his head up until his face came into view. Here was the source of the blood he'd smelt, tracking out of the odd eyes and down the white cheeks. There was an old dried set of tracks as well as a fresh one dripping sweet red. Torgeir wrested his head out of Jervais's grasp and shook it until his long fine white hair had fallen down over his countenance again, shrouding it.

"Yes. I see how fine you are." The scarlet in Torgeir's halo flared. Jervais pretended not to notice. "I know it's hard in that position, but you must try to rest and calm yourself. I can't unbind you until you do. Besides, there's no reason to be anything but calm. You've done very well."

He didn't answer, and that was answer enough.

"You don't believe me, but think about it. Whatever you suffered, Qarakh himself must have suffered threefold. Not all we hoped for, perhaps—still, at the very least, we surely sowed a great deal of fear and chaos in very close quarters."

"He...killed some of his own," Torgeir said quietly, not looking up. "I saw it."

Jervais brightened at that. "Did he? Excellent!"

The praise fell into dead air. Jervais studied the young magus again. He all but radiated sullen defiance. His slump on the tree had become rather irritatingly and stoically Christ-like. There were many things Jervais might have been inclined to say here. *This is war, what did you expect?* perhaps, or *Qarakh killed his own kin, you killed a few flea-ridden slaves. As far as I can see that leaves us ahead.* But no, he would have to be more subtle than that. He sat down at the foot of the tree but made no effort to peer up into Torgeir's face.

"I know what you're thinking," he murmured, "because I know what your master has taught you. I know how he thinks. You have sinned, and now you intend to torture yourself for it. Perhaps you've already planned how." He paused. "Let me ask you this. All this suffering you make yourself endure, has it ever lessened the thirst one iota? Or restored the dead to life? Do you honestly feel, in this moment, chained to a tree, unbreathing, belly full of blood, the slightest bit more human than I?"

Torgeir shuddered and said nothing.

"Let me tell you a clan story," he went on. "The Council of

Seven, of course, were the first Tremere to become vampires. As logic would suggest, at a certain point they were also the *only* vampires in the House, and had to decide whether or not they would remain so."

"I've heard this story."

"I daresay you have. No doubt Etrius further told you that he argued against the crime of dragging fellow magi into undeath without their consent, while Goratrix argued for the necessity of it. In the end, Great Tremere decreed in Goratrix's favor. Being obedient students, both Etrius and Goratrix brought magi across the threshold, and in roughly equal numbers. Finally, one night, there were no mortal Tremere left. No mortal House. Your master had as great a hand in that as anyone. Now that it's all finished, he repents of what he did. And he would have you believe that because he repents, he can now enjoy the benefit of his sin without having to pay for it. Doesn't that strike you as a bit…convenient?"

He paused for a moment. "After all, do you suppose it made the first difference to those who were transformed against their will whether Etrius or Goratrix did it, and whether either of them repents? Do you think those who are dead tonight care how you feel? And if it is God whom you think will see your agony and take pity…how much pity has He had on you to date? You didn't *want* to kill those mortals. Well, did you? Would you not have stopped yourself if you'd had the slightest power to do so? Tell the truth, Torgeir. We all know what a sin it is to lie."

"Leave me alone, devil," the Dane moaned, struggling for the first time against his bonds. "Go away. I tried to stop it. Oh Jesu…I tried, but I was so far away, I couldn't, I couldn't."

"Exactly. Now you're thinking more clearly. It *was not you*. Your conscience, such as it is, is clear. It was the Beast, to whom we all lose now and again. Or one could just as easily say it was Alexander. He was a poisonous old monster, and his rage against his conqueror burned out of all control. There you are. Hate Alexander. Or…" He shrugged. "Perhaps it was my fault. I selected you for the task. I knew you might not be able to hold on. Possibly none of us would have been able. Still, I chose you to take the risk. Hate me, then. Or hate the Telyavs, for rebelling against your master and making this all necessary. Hate your sire for making you what you are. There are so many choices available. Just pick one. Or hate us all."

"You...invite me to hate you?" A slight, disbelieving chuckle.

"It's a service I excel at providing," said Jervais. "I'm under no illusions in that regard. Between your hating me and your hating yourself, I'd far rather the former. It sharpens you, makes you keen—that I know from experience—and we must be keen here. You don't have the luxury of despair, lad. We've only begun the bloody tasks that fulfilling our mission will require."

He got up. Torgeir chuckled again. Disturbed, Jervais turned back. The albino's eyes rested squarely on him now, the red lines streaking down from them making them look somehow heraldic, like war-banners.

"No, master. I meant...what makes you think I need an invitation?"

Jervais considered this, then nodded and put a hand on Torgeir's shoulder. "Point taken, lad."

He went back to his tent, calling for one of the slaves as he went. All this smell of vampire blood in the air was making him thirsty again, damn it.

Chapter Fourteen

Zabor stood, wan and plainly underfed, in a guard's attitude of vigilance exactly four feet south of the cold fire pit. As Jervais watched, Olena and Miklos walked up to him. Miklos kicked Zabor hard in the belly. The Pole bent and had to cough his way back up to standing, but he didn't move his feet. Olena reached out with her hands and took hold of Zabor's arm. He cried out in pain and wavered as whatever enchantment she held passed into him. She quirked a satisfied smile and walked away. Torgeir came out of a tent and started to pass by. Then he seemed to change his mind, picked up a clod of mud and hurled it at Zabor's face. It pelted him, splattering, and dropped down onto his shoe.

"He's made quick improvement indeed," Jervais remarked. "With so many avid teachers, it's to be expected. Still, you must have done something impressive to him to begin with. Perhaps he's had enough punishment for now? Wouldn't want to wear him down to uselessness."

Antal shrugged. "If they don't fear us more than they fear the enemy, then what hope is there of obedience?"

"Admirable sentiment," Hermann said over their shoulders, "but it's time to stop admiring your handiwork now and come into council."

"Now the whole premise of this little adventure is that you shall succeed where Alexander failed because you have wizards. Is it not?" Wigand stood. "That being the case, I think it meet to ask just what the wizards plan to do, and why it's going to make a difference."

"Well, let's start with what we've already done and what we know from it," Jervais said amiably. He unrolled a large parchment. The soldiers bent over it.

"It's not a letter, it's not a map..." Hermann scowled. "What the devil is it?"

"Oh, it's a map all right. Just not such as any of you gentlemen have ever seen."

"It's accurate, for one thing," Antal snorted. Jervais gave him a quick warning glance.

"It's to true scale, that is," Jervais smoothed over, "and these blots of color show rivers and lakes, bogs, stretches of forest, hills. These are *alkai*, holy groves like the one back in Prussia where the friar was burnt. And these are areas we couldn't get to, because of either local natural disturbances or occult protections. All these sites are of potential significance to magical workings. If the Telyavs think to call up powerful spirits of air or earth or water, these are the places they'll have to go. This is their main camp, and here are the paths of the two patrols we witnessed. Now we've ranged out as far as we can. Up to this boundary, the ley lines are recorded from direct scrying. Beyond, I've charted out their likely courses according to the best calculations I can make. Now unfortunately, while we're here we'll be drawing on the same *vis*-flows as our enemy."

"I'm not sure I understand the first thing you're talking about," Wigand said, "but if you and the other Tremere must draw on the same...flows as the Telyavs, does that mean that you could draw more heavily and deprive them of what they need to work their witchery?"

"Not that simply, I'm afraid. Samogitia seems to be unusually bounteous. I don't know if we and the Telyavs put together could drain it."

"What if you simply cut down an *alkas*?" Hermann muttered, fingering one of the spots drawn in red. "I admit I'm tempted to do it in any case, but would it hurt the Telyavs?"

"It might," Jervais conceded. "But it would anger the local folk as well, and we have our hands full enough as it is." *And why destroy the treasure when we might yet seize it for our own?*

"Well," Wigand said. "So you have been doing something

all this time we've been sitting like birds in the bush—you've made a map. You've also tried to remove Qarakh, and you have very little idea of what *that* accomplished besides killing a few raiders. And of course alerting them to an enemy presence."

"Rubbish. Deverra certainly knows about the ill effects of diablerie. Most likely she'll put it down to that," Antal argued.

"Oh? And you're that familiar with what Deverra does and doesn't know?" Hermann challenged him.

"Well, she has to know about it. Who besides a rank neonate doesn't?" the Hungarian retorted quickly. Too quickly. Damn.

"That won't suffice." Hermann now stood to roll up the chart. He stared at Jervais. "Both of you seem to know a lot more about this woman than you've let on so far. Let's have it out."

"Don't…don't damage that," Jervais said a bit faintly. "It's very important. To all of us." It was also three weeks' starvation work, but he wouldn't demean himself by complaining of that to Hermann.

"Is it now? That would depend on what you mean to use it for, wouldn't it?"

A flush of outrage mounted Jervais's pale cheeks. "What else would we use it for besides what we all came out here to do?"

"That's just what I'm asking. No more evasions, warlocks. What are you omitting?" He held up the chart now, letting it unfurl, poised to rip it down the middle.

"You don't dare do that," Jervais growled.

"You don't dare stop me," Hermann said loftily. "Oh?" Jervais raised his arms. Antal hurriedly put a hand on his wrist.

"Brother, brother…easy, it's not worth it. He's bluffing."

Hermann smiled and very deliberately tore the chart in half.

"*He's not bluffing!*" Jervais lunged forward, teeth elongated and bared. Hermann was surprised, but not unprepared. His sword flashed out and nearly caught Jervais's chin. Antal restrained his fellow magus—barely.

"Quite a temper on our soft courtier after all," the knight remarked. "If you really want to try me, Meister Tremere, go ahead. You'd better not imagine that the thought of his Highness will stay my hand. He's already suffered a great betrayal from one ally who kept one secret too many, and he never trusted *you* to begin with. I assure you, he's not of a mind to become your tool, and neither am I."

"You prate to *me* about making *Jürgen* a tool?" Jervais shouted. "Let me tell you what I've no more mind to be, you cross-waving—"

"Please! We're all being very hasty here." Diplomacy was not a garment Antal wore well, but desperation seemed to impel him. "Please, Brother Hermann, I implore you, set the parchment down. You have no idea how Master Jervais and the rest of us have sweated over it, and all for the sake of our mutual mission."

"There's more to this mission for you than simply doing milord a service." Hermann did not budge.

"Yes, there is," Antal hastily agreed. "Please, Master Jervais. No, no, it is time. We cannot afford such distrust between ourselves and the knights. If the captain has guessed, then he must be told. I will take responsibility for it to Ceoris."

Jervais allowed himself to be guided back down to his seat. He was still furious at having this morsel that he'd been carefully saving up for the moment of best advantage so rudely swept off his plate. But Antal was taking blame, at least—the great war-mage willingly coming down a peg. That was worth a little something.

"The Telyavs," Antal explained, "are renegades of the House and Clan. Deverra was born a daughter of these lands, so we sent her here to found new chantries in our name. But she has turned her back on us. Thus she and her followers have been condemned to die."

The two knights held a moment's silent conference.

"I see," Hermann said at last. "Well, that would explain it."

"Are the Telyavs *aware* of this interdict from Ceoris?" Wigand asked.

"May we have our chart back?" Jervais returned. Hermann handed each half across the table to him with a twitch of the lip. "They're about to be made aware," he said once the pieces were safe in his hand once more.

"Ah, but why be in such a rush?" Wigand looked thoughtful now. "This changes things significantly. Since relations haven't been formally severed yet, you could visit as an official of Ceoris, and she would have to receive you or else admit her treachery, wouldn't she?"

"She could also," Jervais said, quite evenly he thought, "get suspicious, draw the natural conclusion that I was responsible for the business with Qarakh, kill me, deprive you of your chief wizard and doom the entire effort to failure."

"You mean the business with Qarakh that she surely attributed to the ill effects of diablerie?" Wigand quipped. "Come, Meister Tremere. You were eager enough to risk yourselves with what you freely claimed to be a most perilous spell. Have you no courage in any other area of endeavor? Brother Hermann had given me to understand that you were a skilled negotiator. Think of what you might learn under a flag of false truce. Qarakh's fate, the camp layout, the warriors' readiness."

"That is true." Antal rubbed his beard. Jervais glared at him. "Master Jervais, I'm not sure how much more scrying the children have left in them. They are tired, their concentration wanes, and the vessels are fatigued as well. Until we can get some fresh ones…perhaps we *should* make a more direct move. One that could gain us much knowledge without beginning the fight too soon."

"So you wish me to walk straight into the lion's mouth, with no guarantee of even an attempt at rescue should I be captured." Jervais cogitated on this. "Very well. I'll do it, on one condition. There's been an awful lot of talk of trust and the lack thereof tonight, and I do agree that we should do what we can to foster trust among us all. To that end, I will grant this as a personal boon to Herr Hermann."

"A boon?" Hermann cooled immediately. Jervais was invoking a tradition that far predated the entry of the Tremere into the Cainite race—one the Ventrue in particular held sacred.

"I'll gladly specify if that will assist you in making your half of the leap of trust, *mein Herr*. At some future point, I shall request your assistance in a spell. I promise that it will not deprive you of your existence or bring you to any permanent harm of any sort. You will give me that assistance freely when I ask it."

"It's not enough you ensorcelled my horse, now you want me to befoul myself with nigromancy," the knight protested.

"Do you want to remove this obstacle to your master's ambitions or not? We've now told you the truth about the Telyavs, and I'm further offering to take immense personal danger upon myself for all your sakes. I don't think his Highness will be nearly as forgiving of your reticence to accept one simple boon in these changed circumstances. Let us again revisit the key words of the discussion: Trust? Courage? May I add a third: Honor? Not a coin, of course, that dastardly sorcerers must usually trade in, but what about knights? I put it to you, *mein Herr*, that your honor and the honor of the faith you carry forward are worth a small promise to a wizard. You are, of course, free to disagree."

Hermann seemed literally unable to speak for a moment. Then, stiffly, he nodded. "Very well, warlock. I acknowledge the boon in the terms you have stated."

"Then I should start preparing for my journey. Excuse me, *meine Herren*." Jervais bowed his way out of Hermann's tent. As he made for his own tent, he saw Zabor once again, miserable but vigilant still at his "post." Some of the slaves had crowded up near him to stare. Jervais went up to Zabor and gave him a pitying smile.

Then he ripped the young Pole's robe open down the front and continued on his way.

Chapter Fifteen

If this was, indeed, the village the smith had meant, then he'd spoken true—it was well and thoroughly plundered. Not a soul stirred in the silent half ring of houses. Even whatever had once sat on top of the wooden post at the mouth of the semicircle (a horse's skull, the Kur guessed) was ripped away.

Jervais noted, however, that although the huts' deep thatched roofs nearly reached the ground, not a single bundle of straw had been burned. Unusual behavior for pillagers. And many of the bodies littered about—mostly of elderly folk and children who would have been too small to keep up—bore twin teeth marks eerily clean of blood as well as the more familiar gnawings of scavenger animals. Each body was also missing an ear. In the West no one dared leave such obvious unnatural traces anymore. The dead must disappear, as must the killer, unless he liked the idea of being thrown to the vigilants of the Church as a propitiating sacrifice. Vampiric power must be invisible, the vampires themselves never more than rumors and ghosts. The *voivodes* of the East were traditionally more blatant, but Qarakh's raiders had to be making even them uneasy.

"They'll come," he said benevolently to Torgeir.

"Maybe." The Dane rubbed fitfully at his forearms. If Jervais had been in a computational mood, he might have easily calculated where Torgeir would end up halting his mount as some function of maximum distance from maximum number of corpses.

"Their patrol should run right across our tracks," Jervais continued, gesturing. Since they'd certainly had no wish to inform the Telyavs that they were camped less than a night's ride away, they'd gone out quite some distance before removing Master Antal's enchanted horseshoes and doubling back northward. Finding this village had been an accident, not at all a happy one for Torgeir. Still, it seemed an appropriate place to wait. "But if they take too long about it, I'll send up a witch-light."

"Perhaps they've moved on. You said they were nomads."

"Even nomads don't move constantly."

"Unless they're suspicious. Perhaps we waited too long."

"I highly doubt any such luck will be ours. Besides, we needed a few nights to bleach out your robes."

"Of course."

"Well, you can hardly fault me. Look at you. You're bound to make an impression. They'll more likely forbear killing me to please you than the other way 'round."

"Or they might decide to regard me as my fellow Christians always have," the young magus said icily.

"So long as it's fear of one sort or another, boy, I'm satisfied."

A new scent on the breeze caught at Jervais's sensitive nostrils. A little later, it was followed by a distant thundering and spots of movement on the horizon. The riders came with uncanny speed. As though of one mind, they ranged out across the plain and circled the village, then drew in toward the Tremere. There were eight of them. Jervais's horse tried to shy; he calmed it as best he could, letting it smell of his wrist in an unspoken promise to feed it later if it would behave now.

That these were Qarakh's raiders there could be no question. He saw the whites of their vampire eyes glistening under the moonlight, and he heard that their short, slender-legged, bristle-maned and brush-tailed horses went unshod. Their faces weren't Tartar, or didn't match the description he'd been given in any case, but their armor was curious. Instead of mail rings, it consisted of many overlapping plates of what looked like hard leather, giving them, to Jervais's eyes, a certain reptilian cast.

The Kur, who stood with the Tremere, trembled and crowded unwisely close to Jervais's mount. Jervais toed the slave with his boot. "Tell them we come in peace. Shout it."

The man shouted out something. The riders might or might not have understood it, but at any rate they paid attention. One of them, who wore a fine metal-fitted belt and a bright-colored hat, shouted back.

"Well?" Jervais prodded the Kur.

"He say if you come in peace you can leave in peace. You go or you die."

"Tell them this. 'I am unarmed, so you can kill me if you like, though that would be very foolish. I am kin to wise Deverra, and I wish only to bring her word from afar.'"

"No Tremere is ever unarmed," called a voice in good Latin. A second head appeared behind that of the chief rider; then the rest of the body, which slid down off the horse and came forward. It was a slim, pale, young-looking man. He didn't wear the strange leather armor borne by the rest, only a simple cloak of weathered green. "But at least I only see two of you. Why have you come really?"

"As I said." Jervais deliberately loosened his grip on the reins to show himself unafraid. "It's been a long time since we've had word of Mistress Deverra, and I daresay the reverse is true as well."

"Indeed," the other replied with a smile. "Nor has Ceoris ever sent us an emissary to visit in person. I must wonder what prompted them to extend us this honor at last."

"Perhaps it is simply long overdue. But come, your mistress, is she well? May I see her?"

The young Cainite grinned. "I assure you, master, at this point you will see her whether you wish to or not."

After a long winter night's ride north and a day's rest in an abandoned wooden fort, Jervais awoke to find to his very great relief that he and Torgeir hadn't been murdered in their sleep after all. Indeed, their Telyav guide greeted them with a smile and a cold swig from a silver flask. A second small company of mortal horsemen had joined them during the day, however, two of whom were leading along light gray beasts a hand or two taller than the *tarpanas*.

"You must change horses now," the Telyav directed them.

"We must?"

"In this country, master, wizards ride only pale mounts."

"I see. Well, I certainly wouldn't want to be one to erode wizardly dignities," Jervais said amiably, although he gave the horses a good hard sorcerer's gaze before slinging himself up. The cloaked vampire helped Torgeir up, casting a curious eye upon him in the process but saying nothing.

Some hours later they rode into the pagan camp, preceded by flute and drum. Their guide passed through the twin fires marking the border of the settlement and formally welcomed them in with a bow and a recitation. Jervais felt the ward part uneasily as he rode through, but his attention was immediately drawn away to the odd tents. They were cylindrical up to a certain height and then peaked in a pointed roof, many with spiraling smoke-columns rising from the center. Every tent was oriented exactly the same, the felt-bracketed door always facing due south. They proceeded along an open south-north lane running down the camp's middle, the one clear area in what otherwise seemed a confusion of clutter.

As they moved inward, the tents also grew wider and grander, until at last they reached such a size that Jervais had no idea at all how they might be moved. From every tent poured mortals, old and young. They crowded around—a sea of heads upon which Jervais felt buoyed forward. He noted with satisfaction that Torgeir (who'd evidently resigned himself to playing the part) elicited many awed gasps as he rode impassively through their midst. True, he also saw several fists raised with thumb between index and middle finger in what had to be some sort of evil-eye gesture, but those were furtive, covert movements.

At the very center of the camp stood the grandest tent of all, festooned with trophies from years of plunder. A large cluster of figures had gathered there. Foremost among them was a wizened little woman with bent shoulders, dressed like the other women in the camp, but more elaborately so: a white shift and a red-orange linen overdress, caught with horseshoe-shaped brooches at the shoulders and sides. From her waist hung a multitude of draped beaded strings and woven bands. Her headdress was somewhat like a wimple, but decorated with medallions pinned on it to the left and right of her seamed white face. She carried a long branch-staff that was either freshly cut or else enchanted to remain perpetually green with leaves. Jervais dismounted and came forward to meet her. Torgeir followed suit.

"Master Jervais. Ceoris honors us beyond all expectation," the crone said, bowing low. She extended her hand. He took it and allowed her to lead him inside, holding open the tent flap for him. Two of the armored riders took up guard posts at the door. Low felt-covered cushions, arranged in a long rectangle, awaited them within the tent. The woman seated herself and her guests on the north side.

Jervais studied those around him. But for their cloaks, dyed in various woodsman's shades from green to rust, the Telyavs looked much like the mortals of the region. Jervais saw one face, but only one, that looked foreign to him, a dark-haired Cainite man of indeterminate age. He read among them colors of uncertainty, fear, resentment perhaps. Nothing he wasn't perfectly used to seeing during any visit of an official nature.

"May we offer you refreshment, Master Jervais?" the old woman asked.

"Of course. We'd be delighted."

She stood again and waved over one of the mortal servants who stood waiting around the tent's perimeter. The man engaged in a moment's anxious consultation with her, then hurried off. She smiled at Torgeir. "He asks me if you are the beloved of *Giltine*, Mother Death; or a *slogutis*, a nightmare; or perhaps the love-child of *Ausrine* and *Menulis*—Evening Star and Moon. I thought *Giltine* the most appropriate answer, but please don't take it as an aspersion on your character, my friend."

He simply bowed in reply. Jervais frowned but did not reprove him.

"I regret that this may take a little longer than expected. He won't wish to choose wrongly." She turned back to Jervais with a coolly arched eyebrow. "But of course we won't make his lordship wait for that…"

"No, no," Jervais said hastily. "We should all dine together as brothers and sisters, it's only right."

"Indeed."

"Forgive my rudeness, milady, but—will Mistress Deverra be joining us this evening?"

"Mistress Deverra has already joined you, milord," she answered with another dignified if labored courtesy. "But perhaps she has disappointed expectations. If so, I fear I can offer little remedy."

Jervais took a moment to realize what she was saying, then another moment to absorb it. "Not a single disappointment thus far, milady. However, if you're saying that *you* are she, then the description I was given was...not quite correct."

"Correct it might well have been, but alas, likely outdated." She arranged herself once more on the cushion. "Sometimes our Art is not only demanding, but cruel."

"It seems so," Jervais murmured. "I would certainly call any Art cruel that demanded of a woman her youthful beauty. My apologies if I've unwittingly pained you, mistress."

"There's no need, milord. For my part, I call it a bargain to pay heavily for that which is priceless. And now the age of my face more closely matches the age of my heart, at least. A lesson in truth."

"Ah, one of those. I've never liked those."

She chuckled. "Nor have I. But this land would teach me wisdom in spite of myself. And the land of Hungary, how does it treat our brethren?"

"I actually haven't been spending much time in Hungary of late, but from what I can tell, the usual climate prevails."

"Ah, then you're not here to recruit for the front."

"Recruit?" Jervais surveyed the assemblage with amusement. Most of them were staring at him now. He could just imagine what they'd been told to expect, and here was this round, jovial character trading dry witticisms with their matriarch. "Bonisagus's beard, no. It seems Ceoris feels it's become rather out of touch with your efforts here, that's all. I understand a few letters were sent which never received an answer... but perhaps they went astray."

"Yes, they must have. I should certainly never wish to worry Ceoris. We're probably not as easy to reach as other branches of the House and Clan."

"Quite true. An interesting mode of existence," Jervais nodded. "I can't help feeling a bit surprised by it, however. I hadn't thought the tribes of the Baltic *were* nomads."

"They aren't," she said simply.

"Indeed, the style of the tents, and the armor of your riders," he went on, feigning knowledge he didn't begin to possess, "actually reminds me more of reports of the Tartars."

Her face fell into more severe lines. "Well, there's good enough reason for that, Master Jervais. Much of this region is traditionally claimed by the *voivodes*, as you know, and any who would resist them find it necessary to make common cause. Some time ago we did exactly that with a group of Gangrel who wandered here from the Orient. It's not easy, but I do find that being migratory has its advantages. It's safer to stay on the move, and there are so few towns of any size in these parts. In this way, we avoid taxing any one area for too long."

But you do seem to make the most of the time you've got, Jervais thought, recalling the depopulated village. "Fascinating, milady. And these Eastern Gangrel, do they have a leader of their own, or do they call you mistress as the mortals do?"

"They have a leader, but I regret you've missed him for this visit. Nor am I precisely sure when he will return. He's close about his comings and goings, like most of his blood."

"Ah. A pity my timing proves so ill," Jervais said, scouring his voice clean of every trace of delight. He hoped she wasn't watching his halo, although he was doing his best to keep it suppressed in any case. "But perhaps there's a second-in-command to whom your ladyship would be kind enough to introduce me?"

"I am the second-in-command, so to speak. Just as my magi and apprentices are instructed to obey Qarakh in my absence, so the riders look to me when he is gone."

"Then the alliance must be a very close one."

"It pleases the mortals to have both a high priestess and a war-chief. Orb and scepter. It encourages their trust."

"Their trust or their worship?"

"I see the most august Lord Councilor has been preaching to you," she said imperturbably. "He doesn't distinguish between Cainites demanding worship *as* gods, and Cainites *leading* the worship of the gods. But he is a Christian, and he distrusts all other faiths. I have always understood that. Still, I hope you can explain to him that we haven't forced upon the mortals a cult of ourselves. They believe as they always have."

"That may be the part that the august Councilor has the most trouble with," Jervais pointed out. He was very glad the knights weren't with him. He glanced quickly at Torgeir; the boy didn't *look* offended, at least. Good. He would likely uncover more information if they could avoid insulting her bizarre religion for at least a little while.

"Well, as an official of Ceoris, you must surely know his mind on the subject," she said with a tiny, keen smile.

"Oh, I wouldn't dare pretend to that particular expertise. But you're saying, then, that this god of yours…"

"Telyavel."

"Yes, Telyavel. That he was always a god of these parts."

"He has always been exactly as he is, milord, which is to say, he's many things. He is a god of cunning, who brought the secret of metalcraft from the Underworld and used it to forge the sun-crown. He thus straddles the worlds of man, god and devil, death, darkness and secrets, hope and light."

"A most excellent deity for Tremere, then."

"Indeed. If you credit such superstitions," she said. He decided to change the subject.

"Since you move around so much, how can you be establishing chantries, which is, I'm given to understand, the task you were originally charged with?"

"If I may be forgiven the audacity of correcting milord…" He had to envy her. Even buckled under the weight of sudden unnatural age, she sat like a queen. Her dignity seemed completely unstudied, and she'd mastered the art of asking pardon without seeming timid. "It was primarily to research certain unplumbed aspects of the new Art that we were sent to Livonia. We were also asked to establish chantries as seemed fit. But what is a chantry, milord? Is it wood and stone? Or is it the souls that dwell within those walls, and the common purpose they share?"

"Then you're saying there are other groups of your…branch, elsewhere in these lands."

"Yes, there are. However, where precisely they are at any time, even I cannot say."

"Then how do you reach each other in times of need?"

"With difficulty, sometimes. This is strange country, Master Jervais. You'll find that what would be considered wisdom elsewhere is foolishness here, and the reverse."

A likely story. Well, she was suspicious, clearly. She was shading truths in a way that contradicted what he'd learned elsewhere. His informants, for instance, had been quite sure that Qarakh was the only Tartar (Gangrel or otherwise) to be found anywhere in Livonia, but here was Deverra, implying that there'd been a whole band of them. She was trying to minimize the idea that Qarakh and Qarakh alone had had such a profound effect on the culture of his tribe—that so much depended on him. And now she claimed that any number of Telyavs was lurking out there but she had no way of knowing exactly where, which was quite simply nonsense. No maga her age would lack such means.

"But now that you've found us, Master Jervais…what are Ceoris's instructions?"

"Instructions, milady?" he repeated.

"Come, milord." Perhaps he was imagining it, but her voice seemed to have steeled suddenly. "Ceoris always has instructions."

"Ah. Well, there were instructions for me, naturally—I was charged to find you if I could, to see how you fared and report back."

"But there is nothing in particular that Ceoris wants us to do? That seems highly…unusual."

This was going very bad very quickly. Jervais wished with all his might that he had the power some elders had, to speak mind to mind. He would have reached out to Torgeir and shaken the look of half-panic off the boy's face. Nor was the young magus's consternation escaping Deverra, though she pretended not to heed.

"Now that we know you're all right, I'm sure instructions will be forthcoming soon. It seemed folly to issue orders to a branch of the House and Clan that might have fallen into some calamity and been unable to obey in any case," Jervais answered.

"We could always fall into calamity after you leave," she pointed out.

"Oh! Heaven forfend," he exclaimed.

"It is not Heaven we look to in these tenuous nights, milord. The servants of Heaven who come here have shown themselves to be anything but friends. And they don't stop coming. The Sword-Brothers, the German knights with the black crosses, the Danes, the friars…"

He frowned, his thoughts racing to try to get ahead of hers. "The cross extends its reach across the face of the earth, milady, as it's always done. I understand that your lands have seen more than their share of bloodshed and tragedy lately, and that must surely interfere with your research—but it can't be helped. The Church does as it likes. Even Ceoris can't defy it. You simply must find some way to work around it. The paganism hereabouts is doomed, in the long term, anyway; perhaps even in the short. Surely you see that."

She actually closed her eyes for a moment, and he wondered whether she was nursing a great sadness or a great hatred. He dared not let his sight shift to look at her soul. But when she opened them again, she seemed still to have full command of herself.

"There must…there must be Cainites of the ruling bloods who support the knights and the friars." Deverra shook her head. "When I left Ceoris, already our Council was laboring to acquire the ears and favor of the mighty among the dead. Has there been no success in that, milord? Have they not proved useful to anyone important? Are we still utterly friendless in the world?"

She meant it as a diplomatic needling, but the question caught him in the throat. He found he had to recover himself to answer.

"We *have* proved our usefulness to dozens of princes hundreds of times over, milady. And there are now many princes who take our counsel, and grant us chantry rights, but…"

"But no friends."

He waved a defeated hand. "I had been going to say that I'm not sure how much influence they even have over these mortals, to say nothing of how much of it they'd exert on our behalf."

"Ah, you see. Nothing ever changes really." She smiled bitterly and smoothed her overdress. "You said, Master Jervais, that you've not dwelled at Ceoris recently. Where then have you been?"

"I go on many errands for the House and Clan, milady."

"You must be one of those whose business it is to make himself useful, then."

"I suppose that's a fair enough description."

"It sounds like frustrating work to me. I'm afraid I make a much better master than servant. One thing I can say for my situation is that at least there are none here to command me."

"Except for the Lord Councilor Etrius, of course," Jervais demurred.

"Of course. But he is not here. He has interfered very little to date, and I conduct myself and my endeavors as I see fit. There, looked at that way, I can't really complain, can I?" She stood and came forward, her watery hazel eyes now alight with that mirror-shine that Cainite eyes often showed in moments of hunger. "Perhaps you're right, Master Jervais, and soon we'll all be coming to German castles to pay tax and tribute, and kneeling to take penitential ash on our brows, and every sacred grove will be nothing more than some Saxon count's deer run. And men like you won't weep. You'll say, 'This is the world,' and you'll kiss the ring no matter whose hand it's on and hope that the boot treads on someone else's head. Or perhaps someone will order *you* to put on the boot."

He rose as she came up to him. It was quite clear now that they were no longer speaking of Saxon princes or Teutonic Knights. "Madame, we friendless wizards, as you've so rightly pointed out, must do without a lot of luxuries others take for granted. Pride, ambition, discontent, must all be hidden from those who would crush us as the threat we truly are. But above all, what we can't afford is to break apart within. To be divided against ourselves."

"How right you are, Master Jervais. Shall we make that the

toast, then? It is the guest's duty to think one up, after all."

She beckoned with one gnarled, braceleted hand. A group of mortals filed in, dressed in fresh garments and neatly coifed, carrying bowls. A fair, plump, light-haired girl of betrothal age walked proudly at their head, garbed in white and adorned with what was probably a chieftain's ransom in these parts. She came directly up to Torgeir without a word and got down on both knees before him.

He gazed upon her—astounded, appreciative, or most likely both—for a long moment before seeming to realize that a response was required of him. He looked up at Jervais.

"Well, go on," Jervais encouraged him, not without a tinge of jealousy. "Not your standard chantry fare, eh? Obviously you didn't realize there was a bright side to this..."

He nodded, then laid a hand on her shoulder and gave her a self-conscious smile. The mortals were so well behaved that Jervais hadn't noticed any tension in their frames, but they all seemed to soften in relief. The girl smiled in return and stood, taking his hand. He began to rise as well, uncertainly.

"Master, I think...should I..."

"*Yes*, Torgeir, go with her, off, off. Mustn't insult our hosts."

He could just imagine what Etrius would have said. At least the boy could claim later that diplomacy forced him.

"Now I trust you see that our land is not without its beauties," Deverra said dryly as the other mortals assembled themselves in a group and began bleeding each other in turn. Bowls were passed to all the company, the largest two to Jervais and Deverra.

"Not at all without," he agreed. He took the bowl, a fine bronze implement cast in curious patterns. At least the blood within was quite fresh, but it would not remain warm or perfectly liquefied for long. Divorced from its source, it was already beginning to die. He turned to his hostess and raised the bowl to her in salute.

She took hers, but before raising it to him, she went to the north side of the tent where a bench holding a collection of little felt and wooden figures stood. She daubed the mouth of each with a bit of blood and then further poured a splash of it onto the ground before them. Then she returned to the center of the tent and flicked a few drops into the cold fire pit.

"Gabija, be satisfied," she murmured.

"You serve your gods before yourself," Jervais commented.

"Of course. They are greater than myself."

But nothing is supposed to be greater than the House and Clan, Jervais thought grimly. *It's for that you die, not for being pagan. If only you had realized that…*

This thought needed chasing out. "The toast."

"Of course, Master Jervais."

"To the eternal unity of House and Clan. May it never falter in a thousand centuries."

She nodded, "Indeed," and drank readily. Jervais noticed, however, that she cast a quick look around to be sure her followers did likewise. "And may none of us here find ourselves divided against ourselves. Especially you, Master Jervais. For such a fate is not to be wished even on one's enemy, to say nothing of our ranking Tremere upon whom the fate of us all depends."

He raised the bowl again, accepting her toast both as it was said and as it was meant.

Chapter Sixteen

"How very interesting," Osobei said the next evening, swinging elegantly down from the saddle. "I'd assumed that it was *me* she wanted to keep out of trouble with this little trip away. But it seems she has other company...important company, if the music is any guide. Perhaps I'm not actually the one she's worried about?"

He turned to smile at the raider, who shrugged stonily. He didn't even stop to take the packs off his mount, although he did study himself in a little mirror he kept in his sleeve before walking into the center of the camp.

A mortal woman was dancing before the communal fire in front of the great *ger*, robed in a gown with sleeves that fell down well past her hands. She moved them like streamers, in circles and sinuous waves. A man played on a knee-fiddle with a carved horse's head for a pegbox—an instrument that, if Osobei recalled correctly, had been reconstructed from the great khan's memory at his special request. Bells and gongs struck at intervals. Sitting before the woman, bemused, were a pair of *nemci* in long heavy Western robes. He had to squint through the heat haze to get a better look at them.

Deverra, who sat beside them, turned and glared at Osobei as he came closer, but she said nothing. The stouter of the two *nemci* clapped his hands as the woman finished.

"*Pulchra, pulchra*," he said.

"The speech of the Western church, in this camp?" Osobei commented, also in Latin. "I am shocked."

"As am I," Deverra returned. "That is, to see you back again so soon. Alas, I must assume our countryside did not beguile you."

"On the contrary," he said easily. "I found it most charming. And I paid my respects to the lake, but I'm not *koldun*, milady. My devotions are simple. Rude, I am sure some of them would say."

He had the satisfaction of seeing the *nemci* stiffen at that.

"I am sure they would," Deverra agreed.

"But I see, alas, that I should have remained beguiled a little longer regardless. Evidently my presence is an embarrassment."

"Not an embarrassment, *boyar*," she said wearily. "I simply thought it would be best for all concerned."

"So your ladyship entertains emissaries of the *voivodes*," the stout one exclaimed.

"Yes. I entertain any emissary who approaches in peace," Deverra said.

"Not just any *voivode*, sir," Osobei corrected. "The *voivode* of *voivodes*, Vladimir Rustovitch himself. As for me, I am Osobei Vasilevitch vnuk Vladimirov pravnuk Kosczecsykev prapravnuk Triglavlev praprapravnuk Tzimiscev. And you? Do you intend to remain nameless all night?"

"Jervais bani Tremere," the *nemci* said. He did not get up. "However, as Mistress Deverra says, we've both come in peace, so I don't see why we shouldn't be able to overlook it for now."

"Don't you?" Osobei returned with a smirk. "For one thing, it wouldn't be consistent with any of our mutual history that I'm aware of."

"No, his difficulty is with me now," Deverra put in. "Is that not so, Master Jervais?"

"Well," said Master Jervais. "I'm sure you can understand my surprise, milady."

"So I could, if I thought there were any. But you seem remarkably unsurprised to me."

"Now I don't know quite what you're getting at. I wouldn't think that the Telyavs would see any need to receive envoys from Rustovitch—who has, after all, spent the last several decades making a brutal effort to wipe Ceoris off the face of the earth. Not an insult, *boyar*, but a fact."

"None taken, master sorcerer," the Tzimisce assured him.

"But perhaps you have your reasons. If so, then it is for you to justify them to Ceoris. It's not a matter for my judgment. I am but a messenger. I will merely convey what I have seen."

"Ah, but you're not *going* back to Ceoris, are you?" A new voice. One of the Telyavs, a dark-haired warlock whom Osobei had often seen in Deverra's company, rose to his feet. "For if you were, surely you'd rest here for longer than a single day. It's a long way to Hungary, and hospitality is rare and dear for Tremere in the east. That being the case, why do you shun us?"

"Bernalt, please." Deverra cut him off, and added something else in one of the Baltic tongues.

"I can't sit here and listen to these lies. What's the use?"

"Bernalt?" Master Jervais said. "Now I know I've heard that name. Doesn't sound Livonian. And your face…"

"Yes. We've met," the Telyav said. He came forward. There was something in his manner that pleased Osobei, an air of violence barely suppressed. "Long ago, before I came out here. Before there was any reason for me to come out here."

That seemed to take Master Jervais aback a bit, but then he recovered. "Ah. When you were mortal."

"Yes. I was going to stay at Ceoris for a month or so, do some research on optics, then return home to my own chantry. I remember you were very kind to me while I was there. Most helpful in the library. Very generous with the *vis*."

"Ah, yes. Well, that was my job."

"And I did indeed leave Ceoris the following month, but I never got to go home again." The man's lip trembled. "And you *knew*. You knew the entire time. And you said *nothing*. Never once did the smile leave your face!"

"Bernalt!" Deverra blurted again. Her voice cracked, a dry old woman's voice.

"You shall never deceive us again, Jervais," he barreled on. "We know you now. We know you'll smile right up until the ax comes down, and even if the Devil himself was holding your soul in the palm of his hand, you could not tell the truth to save it!"

"Bernalt, this helps nothing." Deverra's voice quickly

regained its strength, but it went unheeded.

"And just what in *hell* would you have wanted me to say?" Master Jervais exclaimed, bewildered.

"I was happy in Castile! I had work, good companions and the magic—the magic. Your masters destroyed all that, and you helped them do it to each and every one of us, and now even that's not enough. What's the use? Why do we sit here pretending that what's happening is not happening? Aren't we too old for this? Don't we know each other too well? I won't let you finish off what little we've salvaged of ourselves." Bernalt stopped then, as if astounded at himself. There was dead silence. He seemed to realize he had gone too far to recall things then, and took a deep breath. "I call certámen. To the death."

"No," said Master Jervais. Osobei felt a sting of mixed disgust and envy, that this warlock could dismiss a challenge to honor so easily.

"Naturally!" Bernalt shot back. "You shrink from justice in any form."

"This has nothing to do with *justice*," the other Tremere returned irritably. "You have a quarrel with me. Perhaps unfortunately from your point of view, I have none with you. You've done me no harm. Why should I want a duel?"

"Coward."

Jervais's square face creased in a smile. "Come, there must be better words to fling at me than that—"

Bernalt's fist cut him short with a cracking blow to the jaw.

Half the assembled company, mortal and immortal, shot to their feet with noises of dismay, including Deverra. Osobei could barely contain his delight.

"There. Now I have done you harm!"

Jervais stared at him silently, wiping away with a fingertip the trickle of blood that appeared on his lip.

"It is...legitimate grounds for a certámen challenge, on both sides," Deverra said at last. She picked her way carefully through the sentence, already weighing benefits and detriments. "Even Ceoris would agree."

"Ah," said Osobei, "but I'm afraid that if Master Jervais does not wish to fight—"

Telyavs and Tremere alike turned to glare at him. He gave Master Jervais the special light of his most gracious smile. "If Master Jervais does not accept the challenge, then Master Bernalt has broken hospitality."

"Hospitality!" Bernalt retorted. "For this serpent, this poisonous slug…"

"Who is nevertheless Mistress Deverra's guest," Osobei pointed out coolly. "And to whom you owe the customary forbearance. Perhaps you forget where you are, Master Bernalt, or perhaps the youth and…innocence of your bloodline serves you ill. But east of the Danube, we still take Tradition seriously—not only in the *voivodate* but in all the Cainite courts and dwellings of these lands. If it gets out that the Telyavs no longer honor this most ancient and sacred bond, then their word will be worth even less than that of Ceoris."

At once the look of loathing on Jervais's face became one of calculation. *Yes, stupid Usurper, think.*

Osobei then gestured toward the young albino who sat aghast in the place beside Master Jervais, and lowered his voice—even though he still spoke Latin. "Besides, I daresay your kine won't want to see one so clearly god-touched made angry. Will they?"

Deverra raised a hand to her throat, as though to keep the rage that showed in her eyes from getting past her voice box.

"Then I suppose the question is whether Master Jervais accepts or not," she managed.

"I do not accept," Jervais said. "As you can surely see, I asked for none of this."

"Then… Then we have wronged you." She faltered, then resolved herself. She held up her hands like a queen about to make a proclamation and spoke in one of the Baltic tongues. There was murmuring, but people sat down again. She then spoke again in Latin.

"Let it be known here tonight that my *sodalis* Bernalt has trespassed against the hospitality I offered Master Jervais of Ceoris, and that I as hostess most deeply lament this trespass." She got down onto one arthritic knee. Osobei felt an odd little twinge of mortal regret at that, something to do with the respect for the aged that had been drummed into him practically from infancy, but the etiquette demanded this gesture of her.

"I thank you for your apology, milady hostess," Master Jervais said.

She rose. "Bernalt. Come. You must crave Master Jervais's pardon."

Bernalt certainly looked as though the only thing he might possibly crave from Jervais was his heart's blood spilling out onto the ground, but he forced himself forward and down onto one knee.

"Forgive me, milord," he said.

The other Tremere paused and let a long silent moment go by. Again, the etiquette required it. If he gave in too quickly, he undermined his own position, and Osobei knew quite well that would never do.

"For the sake of the brotherhood of blood and the peace of House and Clan Tremere," he said at last, "I will bear you no ill will."

"Thank you, milord Jervais. You are most generous." Deverra turned and spoke to one of her Telyav women, who scurried off. "Please allow me also to offer you a token of my regrets and apologies."

"Ah, no tokens are necessary, madam, I assure you," he answered richly. "Your contrition and Bernalt's are more than sufficient." Osobei shifted, deliberately making a slight noise, and grimaced in mock-concern.

"Botheration. What is it now, *boyar*?" Jervais turned on him.

"Alas, master sorcerer, the same sacred traditions that forbid Deverra's kin to threaten her guest likewise forbid you to refuse any gift she may offer you—particularly one offered so humbly in apology." Osobei glanced at the Telyav who returned now with something hidden under a rich cloth. No doubt Deverra had planned to present whatever it was anyway, as a going-away present, but making it part of the process of amends certainly made sense. "Perhaps your brothers and sisters would be willing for family's sake to overlook such matters, but I wouldn't promise anything similar of all these kine. They know the ancient laws just as well as I do. If you were to break hospitality, Mistress Deverra would no longer be in a position to protect you from them. Or from me. I really think a man in your numerically unfortunate position should make it clear that you've reconciled with her ladyship before you leave, don't you?"

Master Jervais scowled for half an instant, then remembered himself and schooled his face into something more suitable. Deverra, however, cheered considerably. Idiot Tremere. Was it possible the sorcerers were so wrapped up in their own squabble that they had forgotten their true enemies?

The Telyav woman uncovered the gift and bowed. It was a lovely if rustic little box of some sort, painted in bright vegetal colors.

"A trifle, of course," said Deverra. "But I hope it will remind your lordship and all at Ceoris of the deep bond which we all share, and the esteem in which we poor wanderers hold our mighty brethren."

Jervais nodded. "Beautiful, your ladyship. I accept your gift with my deepest thanks." He hesitated. "In fact, it appears so finely crafted that I fear it could get damaged in the trip. Could I persuade your sister to wrap it up again?"

Deverra smiled. Of course her fellow sorcerer didn't want to handle her gift without a protective layer of cloth in between. "Of course, Master Jervais. Jurate, wrap it securely."

The woman bowed again and obeyed, then presented the lump to Jervais, who motioned for Torgeir to take it. Torgeir turned as though to hand it in turn to the slave but then seemed to realize what a grave *faux pas* that would be.

"And now we must unfortunately part," Jervais said to Deverra, offering his hand. She took it. "But I will bring the joyous news of your survival to our brethren."

"And I will see you to our perimeter fires," she returned easily. "Then our horsemen will escort you to our border."

"Most kind of you."

"Not at all, Master Jervais. It is you who have been too kind and indulgent."

"Oh, not at all, not at all," he answered quickly, with a chuckle. Osobei fell into place near the head of the crowd that followed behind them as they walked hand in hand toward the *ordu* perimeter fires.

Truer words were never spoken, the old Tzimisce thought gleefully to himself.

"I would rather have died than apologized to him," Bernalt said quietly later. He knelt before her. The funny thing was that he was actually slightly older than Deverra, but he'd never been the master of his passions that she was. When he and his compatriots had come from the Curonian Spit and the lake country to replenish her forces (which had been devastated in the battle with Alexander), he'd made a far better impression on Qarakh than most Telyavs before or since. Kindred spirits. "But you, old friend, I would rather die than offend. Forgive me, if you can."

"It's just as well," she said restively. "We didn't tell them we'd all but broken with them long ago. They didn't tell us they'd decided to destroy us. Evidently we've been at war with them for months. Somebody was going to have to mention it eventually."

"Are we going to mention it?" His eyes fastened on hers, and she took his meaning at once.

"No," she said. "Not to *him*. If he wanted to help us, he would have warned us by now."

"Do you think he knew?"

"His dearest childe dwells at Ceoris itself, and unless my memory fails me, this Jervais you're such friends with is that childe's childe. Besides, the omens say nothing of rescue, I'm afraid."

"I know." He sighed. "Well?"

"Well," she murmured, "there's my present to Master Jervais."

"Yes. The first of many, I hope."

"Indeed. Did you order the faithful to gather in my grove, Bernalt?"

"Yes, they're waiting for you at the place of sacrifice."

"Good. Our priests and priestesses must be well sated before the work begins. We have a long night ahead of us, Bernalt…no doubt, also the first of many."

Chapter Seventeen

They had ridden a couple of hours in complete silence. Literally complete, for with Master Antal's horseshoes in place once more, not even hoof beats sounded as they slipped through the trees. But at last Torgeir spoke. "How far out of the way are you taking us, master?"

"Not much. We should still make it back to camp by sunup, if that's what worries you."

"I'm not worried. I'm just assuming there's some good reason..."

"Yes." Jervais reined up and looked around. "You haven't seen any funny birds?"

"Birds?"

"Master Antal and his avian suspicions, he's got me going now," the older Tremere grumbled. He dismounted, then took out the bundle of cloth containing the Telyavs' "gift."

"Ah. I wondered if you were really going to keep that."

"Certainly not. The only question is how to get rid of it."

"She probably expects you to try to destroy it. Burn it. Break it. Disenchant it."

"Probably. Or to try to charm it to reveal its purpose, or to put it under ward and save it for later study. If we have a flaw, it's over-curiosity..." He examined the box, letting his vision shift. It was very definitely enchanted, though not through any method immediately familiar. The enchantment looked a good deal smaller than it felt, which generally indicated a spell held in abeyance awaiting some appointed time or event. But what event, exactly? The box itself seemed unremarkable, painted over with figures of trees and flowers and some sort of bird—a hawk, he thought. He had to admit the temptation was indeed strong to put some sort of hasty binding upon it and bring it back to camp. If they all put their heads together, they could learn quite a bit about Deverra's craft from it. But no.

"Well, what wouldn't they expect?" Torgeir mused.

"For us to just walk away from it."

"Ah, true. That would be odd behavior for wizards."

"Worth a try, you think?"

The young albino considered. "Yes, master. Well—there's really no way to logic it "out, is there? It all depends on what she thinks that we would think that she expects."

"Right. It's one of those nasty second-guessing exercises. But it seems the best of the several choices. At least this way, whatever it does, it'll do it far away from us."

"Better leave it in the cloth, just in case."

"Yes indeed." Jervais set it down with great care, nestling it between the roots of a tree so that passing deer or whatnot would be less likely to overturn it. They both watched it for a few moments.

"Well, then. Shall we?" Jervais said cheerfully.

"Yes, the quicker home the better."

"Yes. Wait." The sudden deadening of his tone warned Torgeir at once, and they both stopped in mid-turn. The cloth wrapping the box had begun to wrinkle and go brown, like a turning leaf. Then it deepened to an earthier shade and crumbled away completely. The box beneath trembled on its stubby little legs and expanded.

"Tremere's pizzle," he muttered. It had only been waiting to be set down, nothing more—perhaps on ground, perhaps on wood, perhaps on anything at all. Jervais set his hands in shape for a charm, but before he could finish even deciding what principle to invoke, the box shot straight up into the air and burst into pieces, belching smoke on him and spraying something sticky across his chest as well. From within the smoke a blurry shape took form, which looked momentarily like a raptor bird but then contorted into something more man-like. Skeleton-like, really, or at least the head very quickly came to resemble a skull with wide, empty pockets for eyes. Its teeth were like a vampire's, two slender fangs that descended as it grinned.

Jervais tried his countercharm on it—words of life to oppose death and words of water to damp down smoke—but was unsurprised when nothing happened. If this was a real bound spirit and not some figment of dweomer, it would take more than that to destroy it. It opened its sooty jaws and descended, grasping at him with talons that passed through his flesh, causing wracking pains. He drew out his ritual dagger, the only thing of his that might make a dent in such a thing, and plunged it into the shade's billowing middle with a whispered curse. It howled and turned away from him, then yawned toward Torgeir instead.

Torgeir had brought out from somewhere within his robes a brass cross with a Seal of Solomon set into its middle, and clutched it in his pale fingers as the smoke-creature enveloped him like a burial shroud. Jervais despaired: one instant to react, and the boy did nothing but reach for one of his pharisaic master's pious trinkets. He had chosen very ill to bring him—

And then the thing roared and broke away from its embrace of Torgeir's frame. It tried to compose itself again, reforming its ghostly claws.

"Torgeir, hold it up!" Jervais shouted. "Hold it up! What is it, *in nomine Patris...*"

"*I—in nomine Patris, et Filii...*" Torgeir stammered.

"*Et Filii...*"

"*Et Spiritus Sancti. O mi Jesu, dimitte nobis debita nostra, libera nos ab igne inferni, conduc in cælum omnes animas, præsertim illas, quæ maxime indigent misericordia tua.*" Torgeir's voice had quickly gained confidence, and now he thrust his cross almost into the creature's face. It gave a terrible shriek that quickly choked off into a sort of death-rattle. The smoke would not hold shape any longer, and it dispersed on the breeze.

They stood there, amazed, for several long silent moments.

"Well," Jervais said at last, "Hermann will be proud."

"The Prus say that the soul takes bird-form upon death and flies out of the mouth of the deceased," Zabor said. He squirmed through the huddle of gathered Tremere and reached out to tap the spot on the wood where the head of a hawk was still visible. "I'll bet it was a ghost. Isn't their god a sort of death-god?"

"Perhaps it was the ghost of one of her own Telyavs," Antal observed gloomily. "I have known necromancers among the Fiends who did not shame to call up the souls of their own childer slain the previous night, and make them run errands from beyond the grave."

"Well, let's try to remember that Telyavs and Fiends are not *precisely* the same thing, but…" Jervais frowned. "Even if it was a vampire ghost, I don't know why it would have feared Torgeir's cross so. Not that all wicked things shouldn't fear the cross," he added hastily, seeing the unfriendly look that Hermann and Torgeir simultaneously threw him.

Antal went over the pieces that remained of the box, running his keen fingers across them. "She bespelled it, yes. I can feel her touch on it. I can see her chanting and raising the shade. We could use these pieces for a ritual link to her—not a strong one, with the magic all dispersed, but better than nothing. Not much more could be told about it now."

"Actually, there may be one or two things more." Baghatur, the young Khazar, stepped forward with a slight bow. "May I see it?"

"I suppose so." Jervais nodded to Antal, who handed a piece to Baghatur, who took a ground-glass lens out of his pouch and examined it.

"Yes, you see? This was fashioned from living wood. Usually joiners dry out the wood first, so that it won't shrink, but this was put together with the sap still running."

"Oh, the sap, it blew sap all over my damned *bliaut*. It may never come out." Jervais brushed at it irritably.

"Then that must have been the idea, for the sap to run freely," Baghatur went on excitedly. "The blood of the wood. The blood of the wood…" He frowned and turned it over, then broke the piece in half again and sniffed at the fresh edge. "Yes, this tree was watered with it! With blood, that is. You can still smell it in the sap."

"Is it her blood, I wonder?"

"I don't know, it's hard to—no, it smells more like mortal blood."

Antal looked positively alarmed. "Either way, Master

Jervais, we've got to get it under ward at once! And you'd better change clothes too…"

Jervais gave a guilty start. Antal was right; if Deverra held a portion of blood from the same mortal who had (willingly or no) fed the tree, then that was a connection that she could use like Ariadne's thread, following it to her creation wherever it rested.

"Right! I've got a chest with a good ward." He snatched the fragments back and ran into his tent. Licking the key to let it taste just a hint of his blood, he unlocked and opened the chest and shoved the bits of wood inside. Gracelessly he squirmed out of the soiled *bliaut*, wadded it up and stuffed it in as well, slammed and locked the chest, then threw on one of his Magyar coats instead. He stood back, squinting to see whether any aura or glint of Deverra's magic bled through the cracks or the keyhole, but it seemed his ward held firm.

"We should post watch, just in case," he announced as he reemerged. "Cainite watch, through the night."

"We do post Cainite watch through the night, every night," Hermann said dryly. "You've all just been too busy with your conjuring to notice. But if you're worried you were followed, perhaps some of you sorcerers should lend us your impressive senses. Why don't you take first watch yourself, Master Jervais? You seem to have the best eyes of anyone in the camp."

"Best and worst, I daresay," Jervais muttered, then added, at the knight's puzzled glance, "Never mind. Very well, I'll stand watch. Where do I go?"

"I'll show you. Come."

They rode up along the little rise that bordered the camp's southern edge. The ground climbed steadily for several hundred feet and then leveled off into a nice little observation platform, as perfect as if it had been built to purpose. The knights or their men had chopped down a few stout birches that otherwise would have obscured the view. A low wind rustled through the leaves, making it sound as though the trees were whispering to each other. That thought started out as private poetry, but a moment later caused Jervais to shiver. It had been so long since he'd actually dwelt in Tzimisce country, but he could remember what it was like, fearing every bird noise, not trusting even the ground under one's feet to keep silence before the listening ears of the *koldun*-priests.

He stared down into the forest depths.

"What?" whispered Hermann.

"Something moving. There."

Hermann frowned. "Shadows...moonlight."

"No."

"I still see nothing. Is it an apparition, a spirit? Something invisible to all but wizards?" Hermann's horse whinnied. "Easy, Magog. Wait...there's..."

"Shh!"

They were silent for a moment.

"Well?" Hermann said at last. "Do you see what it is?"

"Yes, I see it."

"And?"

"Everyone needs to get out of the camp. *Now*."

Jervais didn't wait for further stupid questions. He galloped pell-mell back down the rise and into the camp, yelling. Hermann followed along, adding his far more authoritative voice.

"Evacuate! Evacuate!"

Jervais hurriedly dismounted outside his tent, ran in for his little casket of very small, very expensive and hard-to-repair ritual items, stuffed it into his saddlebags, then swung back up into the saddle.

"Evacuate! Move, for the love of Tremere! No, don't strike the tents! Just get your horses!"

The pounding grew steadily louder, until even Ventrue ears could not fail to hear it, and was soon joined by the tearing and thrashing of trampled underbrush; but because of the thickness of the trees and the darkness of their hides the herd still seemed to come out of nowhere. They poured forth between the trunks, great bulls and cows with massive black withers and long horns wickedly curved at the point, their nostrils wide and snorting. In all his years, Jervais had never seen such beasts—the word "cattle" would have been an insult as much as an inaccuracy. They fell in a furious stampede on the tents and also on the wagons, splintering wood and tearing cloth. Some actually jumped and bucked madly atop the piles of debris. Knights, Tremere and slaves alike scattered before them, screaming. He saw a couple of the mortals gored and tossed in the air like arrows.

"Move! Move!" he shouted. "Just run! Let them through!" Then he heard a burst of noise over his shoulder. Antal's hands were enveloped in a white glow, his sleeves pushed back and whipping wildly in the wind as he rose in his stirrups. Jervais got out of his path just in time. The white light waxed for a moment and then discharged with a thunderclap, crooking out like a beckoning finger and catching one enormous rearing bull right in the chest. It fell on its side, convulsing, amid the reek of burning hide. Auburn-haired Miklos, too, had ridden toward the animals instead of away. He held a long spear in his powerful hands and drove it down into the haunches of any beast that strayed out of the main mass. Jervais saw him take down two of them in this way, each time with a wild thirsty yell of triumph, but with the third, his spear became stuck and he had to break off, circling round. The knights and men-at-arms were also mounted now and bearing whatever weapons they'd had time to seize—a few lances and spears, but swords mostly. The three gargoyles swooped in from wherever they'd been napping. Between them, Falco and Cabo seized one of the cows and carried her off. Rixatrix landed on the back of one of the bulls, snapped its neck and split the flesh of it open with one great wrench of her talons. Then she lifted it, sinking her enormous teeth into the bloody wound.

"Get on either side!" Hermann shouted. "Let's herd them off west!"

"No, these beasts won't be driven!" Antal shouted back at the top of his lungs. "They're bewitched! Kill them!"

Jervais repaired to enough distance to get a good view of the scene. It looked as though Antal were right. Surely it wasn't in the nature even of these fearsome creatures to destroy with such determination. And while the mass of gleaming black bodies did flow and change shape under the assaults of the camp's fighting men, the beasts didn't seem at all inclined to take fright, which went against Jervais's admittedly vague ideas about bovine behavior. As he watched, Miklos was borne down to the ground and trampled.

"Bonisagus," he muttered. "I'm not going to see my *sodalicium* broken by a bunch of *cows*..." Spurring his horse over the little rise, he rode down to the stream and leapt down onto the ice, which was thin and cracked at once under his falling weight. He plunged thigh-deep into frigid, fast-flowing water. A moment later a rush of warmth spread through his veins as he drew out his ash-wand and called upon the Blood to steep his incantation with the authority of the element that ruled all others.

"*Ourior amen im tar chob klamphob phrephror ptar ousiri saiob telo kabe manatathor asiorikor beeinor amoun om menichtha machtha chthara amachtha aou alakambot besinor aphesior phreph amei our lamasir cheriob pitrem pheoph nirin allannathath cherioch one bousiri ninouno amanal gagosarier meniam tler O A etne ousiri ousiri ousiri ousiri menemb mnem brabel tnekaiob.* Hear me, Thou who drowned and thus mastered the Nile and all the waters of chaos, for I conjure Thee by Thy secret names, and if Thou do not my Will, then I shall no longer guard Thy names from profanation or defilement. As I raise my arms, so raise these waters, and follow me! *Nun, nun! Êdê, êdê!*"

The response was immediate. With a roar, the water of the stream reared up in a great sheet, bursting through its crust, bearing him like a chariot back to the shore and then taking up its battle-position behind him as he remounted his horse. He led it back over the rise, rousing it to greater speed with shouts and imprecations in two or three different tongues. It seemed quite willing enough, at least—perhaps even eager.

"Move!" he shouted down into the camp. "Out of the way!" He was pleased to see that the other apprentices seemed to have recovered their wits a little and now stood just yards removed from the battle with hands joined, presumably readying some spell or other. Even Fidus stood chanting along with them. But Antal, the knights and soldiers, and the gargoyles were still interspersed among the thronging herd, slaughtering them one and two at a time with lightning, iron and claw. Miklos was nowhere to be seen.

"Antal, *hold your fire!* Stop, damn you!" The Hungarian at once looked up and his eyes widened in comprehension. The unnatural radiance in his palms guttered and died. Jervais lost no more time. "*Exede armentum,*" he muttered. The water-wall rushed down past him. As it did, it rolled into several huge beads, like mercury skating along metal, which each swallowed up a portion of the herd and held them suspended, floating like motes of dust in air, feebly kicking as their lungs filled up. Jervais then rode down to meet the bewildered knights and Antal, who reined up beside him.

"Good!" Antal puffed.

"Yes, good," he repeated. "But where the hell's Miklos?"

"He must be caught up in one of the globes." With that, they scattered to peer into the gloomy depths of each one. Jervais saw the shadow of a human form, reached in, pulled it out and was irritated to see it was only one of the Esths, who had already died anyway.

"No, here, this is him! Jervais, tell it to let me in."

"*Antalo licet.*"

Antal tugged Miklos's muscular frame free of the water's grasp. The Czech vomited out the contents of his sodden lungs and struggled up to his feet, leaning on Antal's elbow. The plentiful gashes on his face and arms began to close up, and he put his dangling leg down to try his weight on it.

"That's it, use the blood," Antal urged him. "That's a lad."

"How long can you hold them in there?" Brother Wigand asked, rather awed despite himself. He dismounted and examined one of the water-globes but didn't dare touch its curious surface.

"Long enough," Jervais answered. He looked for further signs of movement within the water and found none. Then he made a gesture. At once the globes lost their form and dropped to the ground, leaving the vampires up to their calves in water that slowly began to drain downhill. The bodies of the cattle, too, collapsed limply.

"*Abi! Abi!*" he snapped, and the water began to flow away more quickly. "Let's see what we can salvage out of this mess."

"No!" Hermann called. He rode over toward them, sword

still out. "Back on your horses. Master Antal, back at it! They're coming."

"*Who's* coming?" Jervais asked in annoyance, but Antal was already leaping to obey, and Miklos was waving off Jervais's reaching hands. The apprentice took hold of his own upper arm and, with a wet crack and a grimace, reset a bone that had come out of joint. Then he limped away, stopping to pick up a lance that someone had dropped.

Jervais grabbed the reins of his horse—which seemed distinctly annoyed to find its hooves suddenly wet—and got back up in the saddle just in time. Some ten or twelve of Qarakh's raiders splashed into the camp, shrieking warcries, standing in the stirrups with bows raised high. Hermann called a charge and his warriors rushed to obey.

The other apprentices had already run up beside Jervais and Antal, with Olena at their head. "Command us, masters!" she exclaimed. "What should we do?"

"Stay out of the way," Jervais returned. An arrow flew past his cheek.

She scowled at him and turned her hands palms-up. As she did, she floated up several feet into the air.

"Ah," said Antal. "Don't do that. Stay on the ground or in a tree, and knock their arrows out of the air instead. That'll help."

"Yes, master." She turned and shot up into the dark canopy of leaves.

"All right, the *rest* of you out of the way," Jervais snarled. A rider charged directly at them then, but Miklos thrust his lance between the horse's forelegs and tripped it, sending the rider crashing to the ground. A tang of vampire blood began to scent the air. Hermann and Wigand were doing well. Antal knocked a rider off his mount and then jumped down himself. An instant later they were fighting hand-to-hand, their movements so unnaturally rapid that they were nigh impossible to follow. Suddenly his opponent screamed in pain and began to shiver. Antal thrust one of the hawthorn stakes he'd spent the past weeks carving into the rider's chest. The vampire's entire body decayed into dirt in the span of a mortal breath. Antal stowed the stake, now blood red and glistening all over, somewhere in his robe, then rose heavily to his feet.

While Jervais sat desperately trying to think what else he could do that might be helpful (he didn't think he had any more water-witching in him tonight), a pair of the riders converged on him with swords drawn. He spurred away from them, but they easily changed direction and closed. He drew out the dagger at his belt and caught one of their sword-strokes. The other dealt him a glancing slice to the back. He roared and turned, catching his assailant by the wrist. Years of training were channeled into the instinct of the moment: he felt the other Cainite's blood lying fallow in the veins just beneath the white skin and willed a portion of it to rouse, to diffuse through the tissue. The rider gave a shout, his rage stoked by the sudden unnatural engorgement of blood. He bared his fangs and sprang out of his saddle to land on Jervais. Jervais thrust his blade up through the rider's belly toward the heart, then pushed him away with the strength of panic, letting him fall. He heard the other rider shout and turned again to see a blade whistling toward his neck, but then it suddenly flew up into the air, tumbling end over end, and returned to cut its owner's flabbergasted head off. Olena, no doubt, but there was scarcely time to thank her. Jervais hastily got down. These Cainites were so much better horsemen than he was that he might as well stay on foot and have one less thing to think about.

"Master!" Zabor caught him by the arm.

"Get away!"

"But master, look!" The Pole pointed frantically.

"What, Hermann?"

"No, right beside him! Look. See it coming up out of the water?"

He'd let his vision slip back to its usual, slightly blurred state at some prior point in the chaos. Now he focused it once again. If it hadn't been shiny he still might have missed it, but there it was: what looked like a silver ritual mirror. It rose from the water, surrounded by a slight shimmering in the air rather like a heat haze. A moment later it, too, shimmered and disappeared.

"Whore's bastards—" Jervais gasped. He stretched out his hand, but the apprentice beat him to it. With a short, sharp invocation to the forces of Light and Truth and a precise hand gesture, Zabor sent a gust of wind into the center of the haze, which blew away to reveal a slight, green-robed Cainite girl who hissed at them. Hermann wheeled around.

"Witch," the Saxon cried out in his battle-passion, "to hell with all sorcerers…" He raised his sword high and turned his cross-emblazoned shield toward her. She cursed and flung her arm before her face, then fled in a blur.

"There must be more of them," Jervais said to Zabor. "Find them! Stop them!"

"Right!" For once, not a word of argument. He and the apprentice fanned out, all but ignoring the deadly fights going on around and above them. Jervais caught another Telyav almost at once and barreled headlong into him to prevent his escape. The next moment he had nothing in his hands but a slim green snake that wriggled out of his grasp and swam away from him, its body whipping sinuously in the water.

"*Verdammt!*"

"I did not think that was a word Christians uttered lightly," came an accented sneer from above his head. He looked up. It was a fierce-looking rider with a beard that actually grew up over his cheekbones and cat-yellow eyes. The rider's bow thrummed. An arrow plunged into Jervais's chest, piercing his ribcage through.

Jervais had taken sword blows before, but never an arrow. He was unprepared for the scope and depth of the pain. The entire left side of his chest throbbed and his veins seemed to have caught fire, the flames of which licked hungrily at the edges of his heart. The look of triumph on the rider's face (perhaps he thought at first he'd struck his target) soured as he saw Jervais's own expression change. He snapped his reins and his horse sprang away with a swiftness only blood could impart.

Jervais twisted his arms in a strangling gesture, and an eel-like column of water rose and snagged the rider around the neck, dashing him to the ground. The rider came up again, trying to pull free of the tendril's grasp. Jervais was already bearing down on him with fangs stretched taut. He literally sat on the man as he drank down the sweet, thick ichor in his throat.

All at once hands were on his shoulders. "Easy." Antal recoiled as Jervais turned toward him bloody-mouthed. "No, no, take him, keep him. But I think you have plumbed that well, brother."

Jervais looked at the body in his hands. It had begun wasting already, caving in on itself. In moments it would be ash. He dropped it in sudden disgust, then wobbled to his feet and looked around.

"Where...where are..."

"They turned tail," Antal answered. "Gone, just like that. We have two—rather, three dead raiders, or at least their armor. No Telyav remains, alas."

"And it's not even worth chasing after them, we know exactly where they're going," came Hermann's disgruntled voice. "And their horses are faster."

"But we must...Master Antal." Jervais shook his head, trying to clear it of bloodlust. "They were taking things. The Telyavs. She tricked us. The riders, just there to keep us busy. The ghost to distract from the sap. And the cows, the damned cows."

Baghatur coughed politely at that. "Not 'cows,' master. Julius Caesar spoke of beasts like these long ago. Great black forest oxen that only the bravest warriors dared face, that couldn't be made to submit to man." He gestured at the massed carcasses, still majestic even in waterlogged death.

"Though obviously they submit to *woman*, or to one woman in particular, at least," Jervais muttered. "But the Telyavs—"

"No, Master Jervais. We cannot chase them now," Master Antal decreed. "No profit in catching witches if we have no place to hide from the sun's face afterward. Come here. I will take out your arrow."

"Tremere's gory fangs!" Jervais stepped back just in time. Rixatrix bent over Falco, determinedly licking her mate's belly with an enormous pebbled tongue. A brackish flood of blood and vomit spewed out of the little gargoyle's maw a moment later, and he gave a doglike whimper.

"Now there's a pleasant oath—" Hermann began, but he immediately trailed off into something rather close to a retching noise. "Faugh."

Fidus looked distraught, twisting the front of his robe. "Lady Virstania *said* no large herbivores," he lamented. "She said it, I just—didn't think about it 'til too late."

Jervais glanced at him. Truth be told, he had no idea how little Fidus would have stopped any gargoyle from doing exactly as it liked, and he'd forgotten too, but if the boy *wished* to take blame…"Well, that's why you get to clean this up, Fidus. And make sure the other two can carry him all right. I'd hate to have to kill him just because he's got a tummy ache and can't keep up." Rixatrix looked up at him and whimpered a little herself.

"Is everyone fed, at least?" he asked, turning away.

"Yes, that's why we're down to six slaves," Torgeir said gloomily. "And they look faint."

"Well, that won't do, we've got to find more vessels. At least there's no lack of raiders hereabouts to blame it on. Captain, you're still cut up."

"I can manage," Hermann said.

"I'd rather have you better off than that," Jervais demurred. "Perhaps one or two of your troops could, ah, fill a cup on their commander's behalf…"

"I can manage," the knight repeated.

"Right." Jervais straightened up and raised his voice. "This is what we're going to do. The Cainites are going to take the horses with the good shoes and get as far away from here as we can before dawn."

"Taking into account that we're going to have to dig some holes once we get there," Hermann interrupted. "None of these tents are going back up tonight, and unless I'm mistaken, that means you can't work your charm to keep the sun out, doesn't it?"

"I'm afraid so. That means the Kur had better come with us. Meanwhile, the other mortals are going to take the rest of the horses, the carts and the gargoyles, and go in the opposite direction. Tomorrow night, assuming we all survived, we'll meet back up and figure out what to do next."

"*Schnell!*" Hermann beat his gloved hands together, and his men moved even faster to get things loaded up.

"Heirs of the Seven," Jervais said in a warm tone as the

knights busied themselves. The Tremere drew in uneasily about him. "It's clear what the Telyavs were really after with this raid. Our things. Ritual links. Now. Who lost what? Master Antal?"

"Everything I had is accounted for, Master Jervais," Antal said coolly. "What about you?"

"Well, I seem to be all right. But obviously someone wasn't so lucky. Children?"

They all blinked back at him. All their colors were a muddle of fear and fatigue. No help there.

"Oh, spare me! Nothing tries my patience worse than a bunch of blood-wizards trying to look innocent. Now I distinctly saw one of them make off with a ritual mirror. Whose was it? Come, I'm not going to get angry. This is important for all of us. Well?"

No one spoke.

"Is everyone finished *looking*?" he asked at last.

"Not, not quite, master," Fidus said very quietly. This was followed by an immediate chorus of "not finished yet, haven't had a chance yet" and what-not.

"Well, *get* finished!" he roared, and they literally jumped to obey.

Chapter Eighteen

He trudges down the Via Dolorosa. He carries no cross, but his body is bent all the same, wracked with thirst pains that have long since spread from his slack belly into his limbs and head. It is a cold night. He can't remember Jerusalem ever being so cold when he was there, long ago, in mortal nights. His belt hangs loose around his thighs and threatens to slide down his legs. The tip of his scabbard scrapes on the paving stones. His sword, too, droops in his hand, rusted away, useless. Church bells ring from every direction. The streets are empty, lay folk and clergy alike all gathered in the safety of the altar's glow for night prayers. There is no one left to fight.

Desperate now, he turns off the road and seeks out the Jewish quarter, but he can't find it anywhere. Where are the rabbis and scholars in their neat robes, the merchants in their striped cloth? Where are the synagogues?

Ah, yes. Burned. He'd carried one of the torches himself. He recalls this and with that recollection, he realizes in the odd way of dreams that there is one—and only one—infidel left in the whole world. He turns on his heel and begins limping in the other direction, his shriveled abdomen protesting with every step. He lifts his sword as best he can and summons a parched war cry as he struggles up the church steps. Tumbling into the heavy wooden doors, he busts them open.

There is the man he seeks, a nut-brown, bearded Saracen in a robe of gleaming white, kneeling humbly before a fat priest and receiving the waters of baptism.

"No!" he cries hoarsely. The priest turns. It is Jervais, who smiles in greeting.

"Brother Hermann. Our savior!" Then he clucks and waggles a reproving finger. "Ah, but you don't look well, dear pilgrim. It's not healthy even for the pious to fast too much."

Hermann ignores him. He addresses himself to the last infidel in the world, falling down upon knees so bony that the skin splits open immediately as it knocks upon the hard floor. "Please," he begs the man. "Don't. You are the only one left. I need you. Without you, I starve."

The man simply stares back at him, dark eyes lambent with the Holy Spirit. "But I must, brother," he answers. "You are right…you have always been right, all along. I see it now. We all see it now."

"Yes, everyone agrees," Jervais-priest puts in with another oily smile. "Even I. You have labored hard, brother. Now your work is done. It's time to rest…"

Hermann sees to his horror that his outstretched hand is decaying further with every word, fingers collapsing into ash. His wrist follows, then his forearm.

"My God, my God!" he calls, but he is unable to finish the sentiment. His teeth and jaw crumble from the mere act of making contact. He falls forward onto the cold flagstones. He can hear no reply. There will be no reward.

"Let us practice our mathematics," Leduc says. Antal hates when the man takes that smooth tone. He also hates mathematics. Every sunrise when he snuggles into his apprentice cot, he says his prayers and his curses. Pythagoras often figures prominently in the latter category.

The Frenchman smiles cruelly and flicks his finger in a silent command for Antal to bring out his stylus and begin making notes.

"Now in your battle at Szeged, you killed six Tzimisce, did you not? Take it down. Item: six Tzimisce. And you lost…let me see, nine Tremere. Four magi, five apprentices. Difference?"

"Three, their favor," Antal says numbly.

"Ah. But if you were to accord to Stilbon's strategic formulae, and consider that one Tzimisce is worth three apprentices, and one magus is worth five apprentices, now what is the difference?"

"Seven, their favor still."

"Seven. But you did hold the chantry, and Bonisagus knows that's what counts. Then at Osijek, it was ten Tzimisce, wasn't it? Good score. They were probably planning to break the truce anyway. A pity about the farmers and their families, but only five Tremere lost: one magus, four apprentices. Old Emerik didn't want to release his childer to you. You had to appeal to the Lord to get them, and a week later they were dead."

This is really unfair. He knows they are talking about battles that took place long after he'd finished his Circles and gotten out from under Leduc's fierce blue all-seeing eyes, and yet he distinctly feels himself as his younger self—his apprentice self. Everything he has since learned of stoicism, of control has deserted him. His hands begin to tremble as he digs the numbers into the wax of the tablet.

"Guti Forest. Eight Tzimisce, four Gangrel and one you never did figure out. Five magi; and twelve apprentices. Twelve! That was the one where the only question was which magi were going to die, because someone had to stay and close off the spell. They insisted on a lottery, but you fixed it, because it was quite clear whose loss would least hurt the House and Clan. Quick thinking. Truth be told, I think you liked Cornelius much better than Tiborc. Still, you didn't allow that to cloud your judgment. And the apprentices slowed down the war-ghouls' advance just long enough. Good thing you didn't warn them, because they would have deserted for certain. On the whole, a success. On the banks of the Medvestak: four Tzimisce and an entire brood of their infernal Bratovitches. For only two magi, quite a trade. You didn't think you could ever lose Rebeka, she'd come through so many scrapes all right, but eventually her lot was bound to be cast. How's it totting up, Antal?"

"I'm... I'm running out of room, master..."

"Well, that's no good, we've hardly begun. You'll just have to write smaller. You wouldn't want to forget any of this. How else are you going to know whether you've won or lost in the end?"

The stylus scrapes through to the wood, skidding across the tablet and out of his hand. He sets it down and rises on unsteady feet.

"I'm going," he says thickly. "I don't know who you are."

Leduc—or whatever it is—is beside him in an instant, seizing his wrist. "What a dull-witted pupil you always were, Antal," he hisses gleefully. "No head for figures. I remember you could use the abacus well enough, though. Perhaps you need to be able to see it and feel it. Perhaps that would be of help to you."

"No. No, I don't need to see." He protests and pulls away, but it's no good. His master drags him over to a great archway with tombstones for doors, and throws them open. Within the next chamber is a wall of skulls strung like beads on hanging ropes. Hundreds of them, some gaping with jagged fangs, some monstrous altogether, others showing only the blunt teeth of humankind. Some are large, some small, and some still pierced through with arrow or blade. They strike against each other as though alive, or stirred by an unseen breeze, clacking musically.

"Now," said Leduc, whose hand has begun to burn in a most unvampirelike way, "we're going to do this again, my lad. By hand, one at a time, name by name. Until you can decide who wins."

Jervais shouts at his laggard apprentice. "Fidus! More onions! More cloves, and mind they be ground fine! We've a pottage to get in the oven. You keep chopping, I'll serve forth the broth and rolls."

He hurries out with the platters and lays them out with a bow before the three diners. Etrius casually snatches a roll and rips it open. Malgorzata waits daintily as he ladles her out some broth. Goratrix smiles at him and spears a bit of cheese. He wipes his sweating hands on his apron and retreats behind the screen to fetch more wine.

"I thought he was yours," Etrius says conversationally.

"Oh no, I rather think he's yours. I think I lost him some time ago," Goratrix replies just as amiably. Jervais is amazed; he's never heard either of them sound so friendly. He also hadn't thought Goratrix the sort to talk with his mouth full.

"I certainly haven't got much use out of him of late," Malgorzata comments. "Either of you have him if you want."

"I don't know," Etrius says, "I've never been much for leftovers."

Jervais scurries out and pours the wine for them.

"How's that pottage coming?" Etrius asks him.

"It's coming, but I still haven't found the pork."

"I wouldn't worry about that. You always think of something," the Swede assures him.

He ducks behind the screen again and starts to head back into the kitchen, but then Goratrix speaks, and something in the way he says it leads Jervais to linger, eavesdropping.

"Well, she went down stringy, didn't she? Told you she would."

"You're the one always complaining about told-you-so's," Etrius returns. "I'm sure it'd please you to see her disagree with me. I notice you didn't ask for a change of menu."

"Oh no. She was getting a bit past ripe anyway. Besides, I'm used to it now. One for you, one for me, that's the way it'll be for the next age I expect."

"And none for me, as usual," Malgorzata puts in.

"True enough," Etrius says through a mouthful, "but think of the alternative."

"True," she agrees reluctantly. "What about tonight?"

"Well, I don't know what's keeping that boy, I thought I'd made myself clear. NEXT COURSE!" comes the shout, and Jervais leaps as if struck and hastens into the kitchen.

"Fidus! What's taking so long? Why isn't that pottage in the oven yet?"

The apprentice gives him his usual rabbit-like stare. "But master—there's still no meat in it."

"Well, that hardly matters now, we've got to get something out there!" Jervais bellows.

"No, master, I'm afraid that won't do. It's been made clear to me." Fidus is clearing off the counter, sharpening a large blade.

"What are you doing?"

"What you taught me. I'm making ready to carve."

"Who's *made* what *clear*, Fidus?"

"Everyone, master." The boy turns to him, looking a bit forlorn.

"Even you. I'm sorry, but you must admit you would do the same. You have done the same. Alexia à la broche. Raban au jus. Lucien émincé. To think I believed for a while you'd never serve up someone so much after your own heart, but then Alexander got hungry."

"I see. And you think you'll make a better chef than I did? No one, no one will ever be better than I was. If my turn has come, Fidus, then so will yours."

"I know," he returns with those same sad eyes, "but not tonight, and that's what's important. You taught me that, too. Now please don't be difficult."

"Difficult? I've never been difficult in all my days, why would I start now?" He lays himself down on the cutting board, slick with the juices of garlic and onion. "I will make a rich dish indeed, Fidus. You'll see."

"I know, master," the lad agrees as he studies Jervais for a starting place. "And you already know the sauce will be excellent."

Chapter Nineteen

Jervais awoke to utter darkness. That was nothing new; he always awoke to utter darkness. He hadn't been frightened of it since his first night after dying. True, that complete void held many things. There were terrible rituals that required absolute dark. Some of them required nakedness as well. He had been made, once, to—

No. What was this? One little bad dream—did a magus succumb to such things? He wriggled. They'd packed the dirt in very loosely. He should be able to make just a little bit of room and get leverage. Something felt odd, though. The texture was no longer the texture of soil—too lumpy. There hadn't been so many rocks, he was sure of it. He stretched out one finger of his hand. Something cold, wet, smooth and fibrous brushed against it.

Tree-root. He probed into it. It extended as far as he could reach.

It was all around him.

He struggled. The mass surrounding him seemed almost to squeeze back. Perhaps he was imagining it. He was seized with a sudden, awful terror that he had no idea what time it was or how deep he lay. These roots might have dragged him yards and yards lower in the soil as he slept.

He began to scream and thrash.

"Master! Master!" He was in such a state he didn't even notice the spot of moonlight that now shone into his living prison. But when he heard the voice he stared out through the gap in the roots. He could see part of Fidus's face and part of Antal's.

"The tree! Get me out!" he shouted at them.

"Patience," said Antal. "It seems both you and Hermann are swallowed."

"Don't say swallowed."

"Master Jervais, are you entirely sure the Telyavs got away with nothing of yours?"

"Nothing. I swear it." For once, it was true. Many of his things were wet or broken, but none missing.

"Some other means of reaching us, then." Antal frowned. "Perhaps the earth itself. No more underground sleeping in these thrice-cursed lands. We must dig you out. The mortals, alas, have our only ax."

"Well, use your fingernails, I don't care!"

"Master Jervais, you must calm yourself. You are safe. We have plenty of time."

Jervais felt something very large wrap tighter around his leg. "We haven't got any *fucking time*, Antal! The whoreson tree is trying to *eat me*! Oh *Jesu*—" Fidus's face went absolutely aghast at hearing his master utter that word. "I mean Tremere, Great Tremere—"

"No, no," Antal interrupted. "Master Jervais, shh. Look at me."

But the choler that he'd only partly quenched in the blood of his enemy last night was taking hold of Jervais again. He applied every ounce of strength blood could summon against his bonds. They seemed to slither and weave around him with a papery, chuckling sound. He would never get out. Never, and these bastards would give up and leave him, they'd go away laughing…he screamed again, this time in fury. He felt his consciousness taking leave of his body, removing itself to a safer distance. Heat flushed his face, his neck. Heaven and earth reversed themselves, wheeling round.

"Jervais of Ceoris! Listen to me, I'm using your name." Was that a hint of fear in the stoic voice? "Listen. Shh, shh. You are Jervais bani Tremere. You are a magus. You are a creature of Reason. Will. Wisdom. Will you look at me?"

Something cool touched against the small exposed spot on his forehead. He barely recognized the dark eyes that hovered very close to him now.

"Master Antal, Baghatur says he can take a sample of the wood and transmute it into its antithesis, whatever that means, with his alchemy..." A pearlescent face with palest-blue eyes took the place of Fidus's. It was Torgeir, who stared curiously down at Jervais. The Dane would surely enjoy seeing his erstwhile tormentor lost in terror and rage. He couldn't allow the sanctimonious little rat that pleasure.

"Yes, all right," Antal shushed him. "Tell him to do it, quickly. Master Jervais, don't mind them. Look at me." The Hungarian's gaze captured his own now. He realized that Antal was forcing his mind with blood-art, and some part of him was enraged even further by it. But a different corner of his soul heard his brother magus' plea and understood the necessity. "Look at me. Help me help you. Reason, will, wisdom... Yes, that's it. Please, Master Jervais."

He didn't know how long he let Antal talk soothing nonsense to him. Every so often he gave in to the ill-advised urge to flex his muscles uselessly against the entwining roots, which inspired a fresh bolt of panic. But eventually he heard another flurry of activity behind Antal.

"Hold still, Master Jervais," Baghatur's voice called.

"I can't very well do otherwise," he called back.

"I mean don't startle. This should hurt only the tree, not you."

At first nothing seemed to have changed. Then there was sort of a convulsion in the root-mass, and a shiver, and over the next several minutes it softened and crumbled. A mighty stench arose, but at last the tendrils loosened their grip and, with the other Tremere's help, he worked his way out of the decaying pod.

"'Antithesis of wood,' you say?" he asked as he emerged. He examined the rest of the tree. It was not only dead but foully dead. "Well done, boy. A most practical application. Your master will be so relieved."

"Honored to be of service, milord." The young Khazar bowed and presented him with a half-full flagon of alchemical muck. A little ways off, a very irritated-looking Hermann shook stinking mulch from his hair, and the other Tremere and knights milled about untying horses. Wigand went over to the Kur slave (who sat, drowsy from the day's guard duty, inside a circle he'd drawn on the ground with his knife—an "iron fence to keep out ghosts and *velniai*," or so the heathen insisted) and pulled him to his feet.

"Are you quite all right, Master Jervais?" Antal asked cautiously.

"Don't fuss, Master Antal, I'm fine. We've got to decide where to go now. My thinking, currently, is what is the matter with Zabor."

That hadn't been at all how he'd meant to finish the sentence. But now he frowned over Master Antal's shoulder at the Pole, who stood slightly separate from the group and trembling. Miklos, too, had wandered off. He sat on a fragment of rotten log, huddled with his head in his knees.

"I don't know." Antal shook Zabor's shoulder, then slapped his cheek. "Zabor. Speak, lad. Bonisagus, he's searing to the touch."

Zabor suddenly cried out and bent over, twisting. His skin began to look oddly lit from within, glowing with a pink-orange light. Jervais dashed over and seized hold of the apprentice's wrist, already painfully hot. He chanted the names of principles of ice and winter, tracing signs in the air with stabbing motions of his finger. "*Ill working, I charge you begone from this flesh of my brother!* I think I know a certain little Tremere who should have confessed to missing something." He bodily sat the now-shivering Zabor down on the ground, then went to see to Miklos. Hermann stood helpless beside the brawny lad. Evidently he now had tender feelings for one of the eight Tremere, at least, since last night's battle.

"He's like stone," the Ventrue said hoarsely.

"Must be a stone-spell, then. Stand aside."

With a second exertion of will and sorcery, the curse was repelled from Miklos as well. But, as Jervais pointed out, "Only temporarily, I assure you. These devils will keep flinging their maledictions, and our nights of hiding from them are over now. We need to make camp at a nice well of *vis*, so our *sodalicium* can cast a good strong ward to protect us all. Fidus! My chart! Hand it to me and I'll plot out a likely spot."

"Yes, let us see the chart," Antal chimed in.

Bonisagus, save us from the journeymen, Jervais thought, shaking his head, but he said nothing.

"The mortals are here at last," Fidus said, trying to rouse Torgeir. The Dane only mumbled in reply. He and the rest of the *sodalicium* sat stupefied in the same exact spots where they'd stood to enact the large, complex ward that now ringed the hill-top.

"Come. You can feed, at least a little."

"No..." Torgeir stood. He stumbled, dizzy. Fidus held him up. "No, the slaves can't be recovered yet. I'm all right. God, is everyone drowsing? That's no good. Let's wake Jervais and Antal."

But Hermann had already beaten them to it. In dribs and drabs the Cainites gathered in the middle of the ward-circle, while the mortals around them labored to cut new tent-poles to replace the broken ones.

"The crucial thing," Olena was saying, one finger held up for emphasis, "the crucial thing is that what Baghatur describes— wood infused with blood for sap—can't have been made overnight. Perhaps she built the box, or had it built, and trapped the ghost all in the one night between learning of Master Jervais's approach and his arrival. But the tree itself she must have been feeding for weeks."

"I'd say more likely months or years," Baghatur put in, nodding.

"There's a lovely thought," Torgeir shuddered as he sat down.

She snorted in reply. "My point is that she'd never expend that kind of effort unless it were good for more than just making the occasional spirit-box. These trees, they must be important to her magic."

"Yes, she seems to have a real predilection for trees," Jervais said sourly.

"And if they're important, she must have more than one. Perhaps next to this one? In an *alkas*?"

"Perhaps, perhaps." Jervais felt that some part of his intellect was slowly getting at her meaning, but not the part that was on speaking terms with him at the moment. He busied himself with grating the mushrooms he'd found on the hilltop. As a mortal, he could have simply eaten them to ingest the *vis* they contained by virtue of having grown at the exact confluence of ley lines. As things were, the process would have to be far more roundabout.

"The box isn't a very good link to Deverra, as you've said, but it's got to be a marvelous link to the stump it came from, doesn't it? So we could scry that out instead," Olena went on impatiently. "Find her sacred grove and *do* something to it."

"Ahh. Yes. You're right. We should find it and hit it hard and fast. They're certainly doing their best to keep us busy. It's time we returned the favor."

"But master," Zabor stammered, "we'll have to leave the ward's protection if we're to inflict anything really worthwhile on some faraway *alkas*. And we're already half starved just from setting it."

"The former can't be helped, my boy," Jervais said, not unsympathetically. "The latter can."

"But the slaves," Torgeir protested.

"Were purchased for a single purpose." He glanced at Hermann, who stiffened. Well, perhaps they'd better leave at least a couple of slaves alive, until the Ventrue could acquire more vessels. He smiled. "Or we might prevail on Herr Hermann to let a few of his men donate. They can make themselves handy for something besides killing cows."

The Saxon scowled, but then nodded. "If it'll accomplish anything concrete, master wizard, then do what you must."

Once again the four quarters of the directions were called and the guardians standing in place. This time, however, it was Torgeir who stood in the East, while Master Antal and Jervais stood in the middle holding the fragments of Deverra's box—foci and conduits for the combined will of the *sodalicium*. Antal was adept at raising fire, which had been the initial plan, but he and Jervais both could conjure lightning, so they'd decided in the end to cooperate in that and thus amplify the magic all the more. Olena's role was to hold and bind in a netting of gold wire the ax that symbolized Perun, Slavic thunder-god, whom Zabor had sworn and the Kur had confirmed was dear to Balts as well. The Tremere would brook no interference from any self-important local deities, particularly any that might be in congress with the Telyavs.

"Perun, Pargnus, Perkunas," she crooned over and over as she knotted the wire, "warrior and judge, be bound and bearded by our will, arms slackened, eyes drooping, go to sleep and leave the sky masterless..."

"You must rouse, Grandmother," Jurate whispered. Deverra looked as if she'd slumbered a century and could do so for another. Her recumbent face made Jurate think of a craggy outcropping of rock, not so much defiant of weather as ignorant. And surely she deserved her rest, for she'd been wakeful much of the previous two days readying and casting charms against the invaders. But Jurate couldn't let her.

"Grandmother, please. There's an ill cloud."

The crone opened one eye, then summoned the effort for the second. "Ill cloud?" She waited for a moment, smelling, feeling. "Yes, something's not right." She hobbled over to the bench of votive deities that sat along the north of the *ger*. "Why is everyone clamoring for libation except for you, Perkunas? What's this? The eye of heaven closed?" She raised her hand, restraining an urge to knock the little idol off its perch in most disrespectful fashion. "Telyavel, father, I beg you, don't drowse alongside the ax man. Rise, take your hammer and come with me. Zvoruna, bitch of the woods, sniff and bay. Call the hunters." She hurriedly poured out a bowl of mixed mead and beer before them, then added a sprinkle of blood from her fingertip. "Jurate, daughter, help me to the hilltop. Show me this cloud."

The younger Telyav did as she was bid. From amid the tall grasses, waving in a wind that blew the wrong way, they could clearly see a blackness gathering several miles away—directly over the *alkas* that held Deverra's own *zaltys*-snake, her shrine and shrine-maiden, her trees and seedlings. Rumbles and flashes milled deep within the mass of thunderheads. Blue-white fingers of light streaked down into the leaf-canopy.

"Grandmother!" Jurate exclaimed, afraid that the old woman's eyes were closing from weariness.

"They came here so much more ignorant of our ways than we were of theirs," the high priestess murmured. "I was hoping they'd remain so, just a little longer. But perhaps they're beginning to see."

"Grandmother, you mustn't despair!" Jurate pleaded.

Deverra turned to her and stroked her hair. "Despair? Child, I despaired over a hundred years ago. But I will never give up, for our god is with us. Come, help me back down again."

When they got back into the *ger*, Deverra said, "We must start a fire and consecrate the *ger*. And the mirror, that little mirror you were playing with last night, we need it again. Jurate, don't fear. The power of Seven is a terrible thing indeed when wielded by our old blood. But fortunately, it's a good deal easier to break than to build."

Jervais was a little astonished that he and Antal could share an armful of pure lightning between them so easily. Clearly, what Jervais had always regarded as a useful but slightly discomfiting art was a source of outright ecstasy for the Hungarian. He fearlessly let the tiny sparks of illumination play among his teeth, allowed it to set his long dark hair on end until it floated about him like some sort of unholy halo. He must have been one of those damned born weather-witches in life. Jervais refused to let himself be cowed.

"Once again. On my word!" Antal commanded with a wide grin. "*Unus, duo, tres, verbum!*"

Squeezing their right hands closer to each other, they forced the sphere of blue-white chaos they'd raised together down into the fragments of wood in their left hands. Jervais felt the discharge leave him with a bracing, stinging snap. Exciting as it was to build up, it was always a relief to be rid of it.

"Good!" the Hungarian boomed. "Good! Now another."

It pained Deverra's eyes to watch the reflection, but the curse required it. In the polished silver of the ritual mirror, the flames of her hearth-fire leaped high. The one who'd sat out in the moonlight for hours on end chanting, who'd so painstakingly carved his name and sigil into the rim, who'd no doubt spilt blood only recently stolen from another over the metal's limitless depths, could hardly help but feel those flames. Such ties could no more be denied than could one's ownership of one's own body.

Jurate came back into the *ger*, bowing first to request passage from the felt gods of happiness and fortune that guarded the door-flap. "Fire," she said.

"Yes, fire," Deverra said, not moving her gaze.

"I mean your trees. Grandmother, the lightning must have struck them, the grove is afire."

It was hard not to let the fear in the younger Telyav's voice affect her. One step at a time. No tripping over oneself. That was how Deverra had survived this long. "Only if I can take the sky back I can put out the fire," she said calmly. "Only if I can break the circle can I take the sky back."

Flames in the mirror.

Zabor felt it at once. It was as though the globe of lightning in the magi's hands expanded, flattened and dispersed. Then he could *see* the flames, and Deverra's eyes, watery and rheumy but full of malice. She knew exactly what she was doing and exactly how much it hurt. The worst part was that the burning started from within and moved outward, rather than the other way around. It raged in his bones, smoldering and blasting like the cracks of heat in a half-burned log. He half-expected to collapse into a puddle of skin and tallow right there, but somehow he stayed upright.

There are words that should be had about the importance of remaining in position *in ritual until instructed to take leave of it.*

"Right. That was good, but let's send off one more to be sure." Jervais's voice seemed to float in from far away. Zabor thought of saying something, but between the effort of holding the South and the effort of enduring the pain, his mouth wouldn't open. One more, he could hold through for one more.

Your sire had the wrong idea, didn't he? Scrubbing floors and dumping corpses, those aren't humiliations. You're a bright lad. You know when you've **truly failed**. There are spells, Zabor, where a broken quarter will kill everyone participating. Entities who can steal your soul if you break eye contact. What did you think it would be like to become magus? All power, no pain? This is why you're still Fourth Circle after all these years, not because of your smart mouth. Everyone else stood fast. Everyone else did their duty. And they know it. They know now that you're the weak link, that you are more dangerous to them than the enemy. They'll kill you themselves before they let you lose us this war. And I shall not stop them.*

He clamped his jaw shut, but a groan escaped nonetheless. He was melting, running like wax. Something dripped onto his cheeks.

"Very good. On my word...make ready. On my word. *Unus.*"

"Master Antal, something's wrong with Fire—with the South, Zabor."

"I know. Hold your quarters, all of you. Zabor, we *can't lose* Fire. Not with this spell. Hold them! On my word now. *Unus.*"

An odd, frightening calm settled over him. He would hold, yes.

"*Duo. Tres.*"

The mirror-flames hissed as they devoured his innards, his heart. One especially bright and beautiful flame appeared before him. No, this was his hand, aflame in truth. Now they would all see he was worthy.

"*Verbum!*"

"Done!"

"Torgeir, the quarters! Now!"

Zabor thought he said the words for South as soon as Torgeir had finished East, but he wasn't sure. He was thinking them, anyway. Syllables he knew as well as his own name. He had no idea how he came to be looking at the stars, no idea whether it was someone's cloak or simply the end of all earthly sense that blotted those stars out almost immediately afterward. But he heard voices for a few moments more, most shouting or dithering, only one close by and intelligible.

"Good lad," it said. The voice was Antal's, and it was hoarse.

"Good soldier."

It was not the benediction he needed where he was going, but as it was the only one he had, he clutched it to his soul and rose on his own ashes into the new dark.

"I can choose another *alkas* and make it mine. I could do it tomorrow, if I weren't promised to other tasks." Deverra handed Bernalt a cup of blood that steamed in the cold air. "It's the Samogitians who must grieve. Those trees won't grow back for many years. Each holy place that dies leaves behind an empty space for the Cross to fill."

Bernalt nodded, but said nothing. He had to concentrate. He'd offered to spare her the exhausting task of taking the winds back one by one, turning them around so that the fire that now raged through her *alkas* would not spread down to the camp or the rest of the plain.

Tears streamed down Jurate's face. She was new in the blood and had never met her southern cousins before. She was shocked at how casually they could blaspheme.

"And all this time I thought they coveted our lands, our power," she said.

"No," Deverra said ruefully. "Once, they might have. When they were living men with living magic, and pure self-interest forced them to husband the *vis*-flows. But now they take what they need from human blood, and everything else is secondary."

"But humankind itself cannot survive without the holy places…" The young Telyav blinked. "Surely they know that."

"You seek reason where there is none, daughter. These," she gestured toward the horizon, "are the fruits of fear and desperation. It no longer matters to them what they do or don't know. They forgot wisdom once, long ago, and may never remember it again."

"We must kill them, Grandmother," she said. "Kill them all, now. This cannot be allowed."

"Don't lose your head, Jurate. Hate tonight, call down the god's curses on them, then put it aside. Tomorrow we'll need your cunning, not your passion. But their *sodalicium* is broken, at least." Bernalt glanced over at that. "Yes. Seven have become six. Now we can go to them, and nothing they erect will be able to stand against our assault."

"At least we've crippled her power by ruining the *alkas*," Jervais reminded them. He opened up a little leather folder, set it on the ground, took out the tiny brush and the vial and began carefully to sweep a bit of Zabor's ash into it.

"For the love of God, warlock, what are you doing?" Wigand cried out. Jervais squinted up at his and Hermann's scandalized faces, then he turned to look at the other Tremere, who stood no less aghast. "What any war-commander does," he answered, returning to his work. "Conserving armaments."

"Carrion-vulture!"

"What is done with the sainted bodies of dead Christian knights in the Holy Land, *meine Herren*? That is, when they're not just left to rot."

"Well," Wigand began, frowning, "when possible, the remains are conveyed home—"

"What, a hundred stinking corpses on a great sailing cog?" Jervais looked up again.

"No. No, it is necessary, because of the long journey—"

"They're cut up and boiled, aren't they?" he interrupted dourly. "To extract the skeletons?"

Hermann snorted and turned away. Wigand didn't speak again.

"Surely you don't need all of him," Miklos said hesitantly. "We could save the rest and have…have a memorial when we get back."

"If we get back." Jervais got up. "Do as you wish, lad."

The apprentices hurried to gather up the rest of the remains in a box, as though afraid Jervais would change his mind.

"Quite a little family we've got going," Jervais murmured to Antal. The Hungarian sat sharpening his ritual dagger.

"Each of them is wondering who will mourn him if he falls." Antal glanced at him. "Have you never considered that?"

"No. I already know no one will mourn me." He paused. Something in Antal's eyes made him uneasy. "This time he held. He did as you taught. And we gained a victory. Brother, this is why you're here."

"I know why I'm here."

"But do you understand what's at stake?"

Antal pretended to be absorbed in studying his edge, but he was pondering a safe reply. Jervais knew that look intimately. "War is war," he said at last.

"No. It's not the Hungarian war. Do you understand why all our lives aren't too high a price for Ceoris to pay for this?"

"Am I your student now, Master Jervais—one you feel needs lessoning?"

"I do not want, at this late stage, to doubt your devotion to our enterprise."

Antal literally gritted his teeth for a moment, then he shook his head. "Our Art is all we have to survive on, all we have to barter with. No one else must possess it. No one who doesn't give sole allegiance to Ceoris. Rest assured, if I understand anything, I understand that."

Jervais reached into his robe, brought out a wine-dark band of disparate threads braided and knotted together, and showed it to Antal. One thread had been burned to a char. No trace of it remained but a black smudge upon its neighbors.

Antal shrugged. "Nothing to be done about it," he said.

"Not so. Fidus! Bring your skinny arse over here! My dear boy," Jervais said, putting a hand on his student's shoulder as he arrived. "The time's come at last."

"The time, master?" Fidus blinked at both of them.

"You've waited so long to make Fourth Circle. Well, here it is. Go purify yourself. We begin the ceremony first thing tomorrow night."

"But…but you said my geometry had to improve first, and my—"

"We all have to get through *this* first, my lad, or the only geometry that shall concern you is the concentric circles of the Inferno. What's the matter? I thought you'd be pleased. Off with you!"

"Ah, how stupid of me," Antal said as he watched the apprentice scamper away. "I forgot about Fidus. Of course. One thread's as good as another."

"The important thing is the weave," Jervais answered quietly. Antal chose his times and places abominably. And to think he fancied himself a potential *vis*-master.

"I daresay the one who holds your thread thinks so. Perhaps I shall be there to see if you still agree on the night it is cut."

"If you're lucky, I suppose." Jervais felt the pique rising in him. He admitted it to himself, allowed it to smolder. Antal might despise his own role in affairs, but plainly he, like everyone else, despised Jervais's even more: to say what must be said, to dispense with the unnecessary and to deal with realities as they presented themselves. The knights wanted an unstained holy cause. The apprentices wanted to believe in their own importance. Now Antal wanted permission to wallow in self-loathing. In a court setting, indulging such whims was Jervais's entire *modus operandi*, but here, it was a luxury he simply couldn't allow, and they would all hate him for it.

Well, what else could be expected, really?

Chapter Twenty

Since Deverra's grove was laid waste, the ceremony had to be held at a local cup-stone instead. In daytime, it served the mortal natives of the region, but doubtless they wouldn't mind too much if a throng of witches and devils borrowed it in the small hours. If they did, they would remember Qarakh's raiders and think better of interfering. The *alkas* in which the stone lay bristled with ancient congregations of oak and linden, betraying it as a resting-place for the *siela*-souls of men and women. The broad top surface of the slab was flat, and hundreds of indentations pockmarked it—tiny little mouths hungry for satiation. Some of the indentations were already filled with beer or mead or blood. Those Deverra did not disturb. Local lore also held that if you pressed a coin to a wound or boil and then deposited it in one of the cups, the stone would devour your disease as well. Clearly it wasn't a fussy eater.

The chosen mortal—a fine-boned Samogitian convert—stood before the stone, offering his final supplications. He prayed that Telyavel would find his blood nourishing, and he begged the god also to mediate with both Veliona and Dievas, and to guide him by way of the stars to the blessed abode of Dausos. Then he rose. Deverra nodded. Each of the other congregants, both mortal and Cainite, came forward one by one, carefully biting off the tips of their fingernails and placing them in baskets of oak-bark for burning. This was a gesture of profoundest gratitude for his gift. Every fraction of fingernail they donated would help his spirit hang on during its long climb to heaven. Other baskets contained cheese to nourish him for the journey.

At last he lay on his stomach across the stone. Deverra placed a sheaf of barley across his back, a reminder that like the grain, he too would rise again after death. She lifted his head and kissed him goodbye. Then she took her bone-knife and cut open his throat. The blood gushed forth, drenching the stone and welling up in each little hole. She let him bleed until the god was replete. Then the vampire priests and priestesses gathered in a close semicircle and drank of the remaining blood, which she drained into a large bowl for them to share. At her gesture, his livid body was removed, carefully washed, robed in white and adorned with jewelry, then set aside for later burning.

It was now time for the more earthly preparations. Razors and bowls were brought out, and paints and lengths of linen and nets of knotted hair. Deverra smiled at the young woman who came to her with a pot of lead white and sat down facing her.

Tremere were notoriously difficult to impress—although she hoped that her herd of aurochs had been unexpected, at the very least—but she was sure the effort would be well worth it in the end.

"And there we are." Jervais attached the little pendant to the chain that lay across Fidus's robe. Since there was no way to make a real Fourth Circle sigil-charm out here, Fidus had to content himself for now with the appropriate symbol drawn on a piece of parchment and folded into a sheet of lead. Jervais made a minor fuss of arranging the chain's drapery nonetheless. He remembered how much these little honors along the way meant to one who labored so long and hard between rewards. To deny such ornaments would be like denying a bride her wedding-finery—improper and unwise. "And now you have a war story of your own to tell, Fidus."

Fidus tried not to glow too brightly. "Yes, master."

"Hold out your hand."

The lad did so without question, nor did he seem surprised when Jervais brought out a shunt and extract a small vial's worth of blood from his fingertip. Jervais hadn't had near as many options open to him for choosing Fidus's thread, but he'd at last settled for a bit of linden bast from one of the slaves' bast shoes. Linden wood was easy to carve, another virtue Jervais hoped would transmit.

"One House, One Clan, One Bloo d. Our *sodalicium* is restored," he announced. "We mustn't falter now." Then he turned to Miklos. "What is it, my lad, that the Telyavs got of yours? No more games."

The Czech rubbed at the back of his neck. "A blood-stone, master. Forgive me. Honestly, I didn't realize at first. The bag spilled, and I just gathered them all up willy-nilly and didn't count them 'til later."

"Well, that's damned unfortunate, isn't it? Since you have matching stones, we *may* be able to reach the one they have and destroy it. That'll be risky..." He shook his head, thinking better of it. "Or perhaps we can craft a talisman instead. Not nearly so risky, but far more difficult...I don't know. We'll have to see."

"That's if we even *get* a chance to cast any more big spells," Torgeir said gloomily.

"Well, we got a chance to promote Fidus at least. Even they have to rest sometime."

"I don't know, master." The Dane shook his head. "There were something like thirty Telyavs at the camp. Plus Deverra. Thirty to our eight...seven."

"Ah, but our seven are bound in a *sodalicium* circle, whereas they've repudiated the House and Clan. Neither can they call upon the power of Seven nor benefit from the centuries of workings performed by Great Tremere himself on down to hallow that number to our use. They're little more than hedge-wizards now, Torgeir. Powerful examples of the breed, but hedge-wizards nonetheless. And they rely overmuch on their queen, who still remembers the true learning. If we can kill her...and that Bernalt as well, he's another relic of the old days...then the rest of them should be far easier to wipe out."

They looked rather skeptical; not that he blamed them. Certainly they'd all been lectured on the importance of Seven before, but the true intricacies of the numerology, the full scope of those centuries of workings, were hardly common knowledge among the young.

"Just trust me," he finished lamely.

"They also have more raiders than we do knights and men-at-arms," Olena pointed out.

"One of the captain's knights is worth four of those mangy bandits," Miklos said with feeling. Antal flinched.

Jervais raised an eyebrow. "Exactly. So we'll manage."

"They've also got a lot of vessels," she pursued. "We don't. We can't keep up like this. We don't want to go on using Hermann's men."

"Well, I think the captain was planning to go raiding tonight for that very reason."

"Wizards." Hermann came over.

"What is it?"

"This mist, is it natural?"

What mist? Jervais looked out across the camp. There was indeed some kind of haze, a bank of it rising up sheer like a fortress wall in every direction.

"Of course not," he retorted after a moment, "or else it'd be coming inside the ward, wouldn't it?"

"I can try to drive it off," said Antal.

"No, don't leave the ward."

"I'll do it from within."

Well, that was unlikely to work if anyone on the other side actively opposed him, but Jervais didn't argue. "Fine. What the deuce is your gargoyle's name again?" he called after Antal's retreating back. "Never mind. Rix! Falco! You other beast there! Get up there and scout! Tell me where the enemy is."

The gargoyles looked up quizzically from grooming each other, then lumbered up into the sky.

Hermann went to his knights and men. "No, don't mount," he ordered the ones who were already getting on horses. Instead, he made all of them but the handful who were good archers stand at intervals just inside the perimeter of the circle, where he assigned each soldier, man and Cainite, a number from one to fourteen. At his command, they marched forward out of the circle in a spreading ring, calling their numbers in sequence.

"What in hell is he doing?" Olena muttered.

"Trying to buy us a moment's warning," said Jervais. "Be sure to use it."

She nodded and started fishing through the purse at her belt.

"Twelve!" "Thirteen!" "Fourteen!"

The second round of calls ended; the third began. They were slightly further out now.

"One!" "Two!" "Three!" "Four!" "Five!" "Six!"

Silence.

"That way!" Jervais shouted. Except for Antal, who continued chanting, trying without much success to drive off the fog, the Tremere turned in the direction Jervais pointed. Olena had a globe of bale-fire readied in her hands, which she threw heedlessly outward. It hissed and dampened as it passed the ward's perimeter, but continued on until the mist obscured its light. Lightning poured forth from Jervais's fingers. He had no idea what or if it struck, but he thought he heard a groan. Torgeir had picked up a handful of dirt and molded it into something vaguely bat- or bird-shaped. At his whispered word, it flew out to do Tremere alone knew what. The archers, too, fired shot after shot into the unknown distance. Jervais could hear that some of the arrows were striking *something*, though it could be mostly trees.

Meanwhile, the other Black Cross soldiers had retreated back within the ward's confines and now pressed up against the edge where the attack seemed to be coming from, peering vainly to see the enemy.

"Bonisagus. They'll probably try for the ward," Jervais suddenly realized. "We should shore it up. No, not *you*, Miklos. The rest of you. And Torgeir, you lead them."

"But master," Miklos said rapidly.

"No arguments!" Jervais snarled.

"Then what do I do?"

"I'd recommend *hiding*," said Jervais. "And maybe drawing a circle in the ground with your knife."

The young war-wizard looked stricken, but he withdrew into a tent.

The others spread out to the perimeter of the ward. Torgeir

called out: "*Una Domus, Una Gens, Unus Sanguis,*" and then they sat and dug their fingers into the earth. To Jervais's wizard-sight, those streams of *vis* that welled up from within the heart of the hill at the ley lines' intersection and then flowed through the geometry of his beautiful ward design flickered momentarily, then brightened.

But there were other sorcerous energies out there as well, not belonging to the Tremere.

"Enemy everywhere," Falco reported proudly as he circled to land on one of the wagons by Jervais's head.

"Yes, I can *see* that now..." Jervais snapped. He ran over to Torgeir.

"My God," Torgeir said as he came up. "Look at them all."

The mist literally teemed. A hundred bizarre forms appeared and disappeared within it. There were skull-faces and beast-faces and glimpses of hood with no face visible at all. Here was a woman in a circlet of tubular gold beads and heavy neck-rings, garbed in white, blood tracked down the front of her gown. Here was a figure in wisps of torn gauze, carrying a scythe. Jervais sent a ball of lightning straight into its chest, but it only whirled unconcernedly and glided back into obscurity.

"Ghosts..." Torgeir shuddered. "Unhallowed dead."

You should talk. Jervais put a hand on his shoulder. "No. Keep your cross by your heart, my young friend. They can't get past the ward anyway. Hold on. It's coming."

"The attack?"

"Yes." Jervais cursed under his breath. He could see glowing motes, traces of spell-work moving suspiciously, weaving. But he couldn't see what they were attached to because of the mist. Where were the Telyavs? They had to be here. Someone had called up all these ghosts.

Antal ran to join them.

"There, there, there!" he shouted.

"What did you see?" Jervais shouted back. He let his vision retract into the natural.

"There!" Antal repeated frantically. With a grimace of supreme concentration he thrust his arms at the fog directly before them, his fingers curled in a clutching gesture. A small portion of the mist fled as though fanned away. Another eldritch figure stood there, decked from head to toe in medallions and figurines of amber and veiled in a long, trailing white length of linen.

Then Jervais saw the bare, wrinkled feet.

"*Deverra!*"

The figure raised its arms. The mist at its fingertips seemed to solidify into streaking lines of frost, which reached left and right to catch two of its fellow apparitions. They stretched out their hands in turn, joining in. A great thick ice fog rolled from them into the boundary of the ward. Jervais was safe behind it, but he could still feel the chill radiating hungrily toward him, could sense his design crystallizing and threatening to shatter under the assault. The four Tremere buttressing the ward cried out as one. Torgeir stiffened, his eyebrows and hair suddenly bristling with ice, but then his voice rose in the Hermetic cant. Jervais hurried away, to the tent where Miklos crouched, peering through the flap, sword drawn. From the look on the lad's face, he already felt the attack on the ward. At least Jervais hoped that was all it was.

"Miklos," he grated in Latin, "Torgeir calls the power of Seven. Join the chant. *Ambrath Abrasax sesengenbarpharangês. I am barbadônaiai barbadônai who conceals the stars, who preserves heaven, who establishes the cosmos in truth.*"

Miklos nodded. "*Ambrath Abrasax sesengenbarpharangês...*"

Jervais went back out again. Antal had already sat down at the ward-border and stuck his fingers into the earth, and Jervais did likewise. The ward, supported at least vocally now by the entire *sodalicium*, waxed in strength and drove off the probing frost tendrils of Telyav magic that sought to penetrate and crumble it as ice cracked stone.

We're doing well. She must have been expecting to find the sodalicium *broken...We could even push back.* Unfortunately, he couldn't tell Torgeir that without breaking the chant, but he let the notion steep in his consciousness, willed it to diffuse, hoping that in the intimacy of the circle Torgeir would pick up on it regardless.

He didn't have long to wait; or perhaps the Dane, who was certainly a bright boy as they went, thought of it on his own. Jervais's hands and the tip of his nose buzzed with a sensation rather like the tingling of a foot that had fallen asleep.

Deverra. Get Deverra, lad...

Torgeir's chant had changed slightly as well. Words of mere summoning and potency were now bolstered by harder sentiments. Jervais echoed as many of them as he caught. He could feel their working change tenor, then it flooded outward all at once, racing back through the conduits the Telyavs had created. Jervais saw two blossoms of bale-fire burst on either side of Deverra—her unfortunate compatriots—and a veritable pillar of it rise up where the high priestess herself had stood.

Keep going, keep going... They poured all their will and strength into the counterassault for several more long moments, and finally, as one, they released, spent.

There was a vast silence. Even the throng of ghosts momentarily faded.

Then suddenly a new apparition lunged forward from the mist toward Jervais. It was an iron face with iron fangs, to which bits of charred detritus clung, and its open maw glowed with red heat. The blackened remnants of the amber tunic clacked as it reached for him, but its talon stopped at the ward's edge. Then it sat back on its haunches.

"Deverra," he choked. He meant to shout it, to warn the others, but the air wouldn't come.

"*We are strong in the Lord and the power of His might,*" the Deverra-thing said. It hefted a hammer that it had in its iron hand and brought it down upon the earth. A boom of thunder rolled through the ground, pealing and echoing. Jervais felt nauseated. The iron cheeks bent, with the scream of a rusted hinge opening, into a smile. Then it drew backward, out of sight.

He leaped to his feet. Hermann was just behind him, his face lengthened into a rictus of dread. He grabbed the front of the knight's tunic. "Some of the ghosts are Telyavs."

"They're all demons!"

"You and Torgeir," Jervais hissed. "They're vampires, that's all. I'm telling you some of those ghosts are flesh, just attired to frighten and confuse us! Tell your men to shoot them, throw spears at them, throw rocks at them. All of them."

The Saxon nodded dazedly. "Yes...yes."

Jervais went for his tent and his chests. Deverra's *alkas* was ash. The old crone should be weakened, lost. Yet here she was, leading the charge and apparently still under the aegis of some vastly powerful witching.

"We are strong in the Lord," he muttered. He wished they'd all stop dragging religion into this. Only Deverra surely didn't mean *the* Lord. She must have meant her own god, Telyavel. Flesh into iron...well, there were other Tremere who could do such things, though only the mightiest of magi, and then there was that glow like hell-fire from her maw... No wonder the Saxons were spooked. He felt more than a little spooked himself.

Miklos peered out of the tent, but he couldn't see whether the working had ended because his brethren had finished it, or because something terrible had happened. It felt more like the former than the latter, but still...at last he could stand the uncertainty no more, and he stepped out. The knights and men-at-arms were running around shooting arrows and hurling spears into the fog, and it looked as though everyone but Jervais still guarded the ward. Where was the old scoundrel? Surely he hadn't gone out after the witches alone, while Miklos himself stayed hidden in the tent like womenfolk.

"*Miklos.*"

It was a woman's voice. For a moment he was sure it was his mother's, but she was long dead. He turned. His tent stood quite near the edge of the ward boundary, and the ridge of the fog was only a few feet away. He peered out into it.

"Miklos, look." The voice belonged to a young woman there, robed in a blue cloak embroidered and decorated in metal. A snake brooch clasped her garment shut. Twin chestnut braids, thick and glossy, descended almost down the length of her body. She was beautiful, but he didn't allow himself to notice that. Instead, all his attention was on what she had in her hand: a tiny red pebble.

"I brought it for you," she said, "They told me that we must kill the evil sorcerers, but they lied—you are fair and brave."

"But not stupid. Who are you trying to fool?" he returned.

"All you have to do is take it, Miklos." She stepped closer, holding up the stone. It was now only a foot or so away from him. He stepped up to the edge of the ward. She bent down on one knee and carefully placed it on the ground before him. "Will you not take it?"

"No."

"If you don't, you'll remain in Deverra's power," she said sadly. "You'll never be able to leave this hilltop."

He stared at the pebble. The girl couldn't trespass the ward, of course, nor could any spell she might cast, but physical objects could move over it easily.

Well, that's damned unfortunate, isn't it? Since you have matching stones, we may be able to reach the one they have and destroy it. That'll be risky...I don't know. We'll have to see...

He drew out his sword. "Hold still," he said. She did. He laid the tip of the blade against the top of her throat. She swallowed but didn't move.

Slowly, he knelt down. With his free hand he took out his dagger and flicked the pebble the two inches necessary to move it inside the bounds of the ward. Nothing happened.

He picked up the pebble and rolled it around in his palm, looking it over with both mundane and mystical sight, just in case it might have been tainted or booby-trapped somehow. But no, it seemed as it should. Inexpressible relief washed through him. He lowered his sword and looked up at the girl, who smiled shyly.

Then the pebble melted into a pool of cold blood in his hand.

"I did not say it was *your* blood-stone," she murmured. "You have kindly brought part of me over the threshold, fair one, of your own free will..."

She stepped across. The force of the ward blew her shawl back like a strong wind but offered no more resistance than that. He swung his blade at her with every ounce of strength he could muster. She caught it in her bare hands. He felt the shock of the impact all the way up his arm, but it didn't even seem to nick her. Brambles and leaves sprouted forth from her fingers and with unholy speed entwined both his sword and him, wrapping his legs together and throwing him off-balance so that he hung like a fruit suspended from her vine.

"And now I have seen to the rest," she finished.

"*Miklos!*" came a cry from across the camp. She glanced up and saw the round Tremere charging at her full tilt, arms raised.

With another smile—not quite so shy—she turned and fled on swift feet into the mist, dragging her hapless prize with her.

Jervais shouted. "Hermann! Wigand! They've got Miklos! Come on!"

One good thing about these Black Cross knights was that, once recovered from the initial shock of witnessing a strange sorcery, they fell right back into their usual mode of quick response without a lot of idiot questions. Hermann picked up a spear and nodded.

"Jervais...wait." Antal waved at them, then dashed into his tent. Jervais waited impatiently, using the free moment to get a willow branch out of his purse and break it in half. A white-yellow light bled out of the broken ends and collected into a ball that Jervais brought into his palm to hover.

Antal emerged carrying a sword. He pulled it partway out of its sheath to show Jervais. The blade had an odd green glint to it.

"Take this." He handed it over. Jervais wanted to say *Who do you think I am, Lancelot?*, but he simply nodded his thanks and set off.

Deverra shed her iron skin as she walked back down the hill. It was a useful thing, no question, but moving and witching were both far more difficult under its effects. Almost immediately after, she felt the slight thrill of a brush against her heart. Somewhere something of hers was being touched, focused upon. This didn't worry her too greatly. Before the battle she and several of her senior priests and priestesses had exchanged little talismans and keepsakes.

Deverra? Deverra...

It was Oluksna, to whom she'd given a few straws from her

ritual broom. Oluksna was one of the few Telyavs who didn't call Deverra Grandmother or mistress. Though not quite so old as Bernalt, she was close to it.

Yes, my friend?

I have the boy. Shall I kill him now?

No, put a stake in his heart and take him away. We shan't try the ward again tonight.

Very well, but the fat one, that Jervais, is chasing me. It will be hard to lose him dragging this deadweight.

So calm, Deverra marveled. *We must distract him, then. Where are you?*

The north side, I think.

Daine and Ako should be nearby. Their grove is just to the north of here. And Ako had certain blood-gifts bequeathed by an exlover among Qarakh's riders. Yes, they would do well. *I will send them.*

And you?

I am left to do those few things I can do with the ward intact. We shall withdraw soon.

A silent reverberation of understanding, and Oluksna's mind slipped away.

Jurate and Bernalt were still where she'd instructed them to stand, just to one side of the great oak that stood directly upon the main ley line axis. Jurate held the bag tightly.

"Open it up," Deverra directed her. She did as directed. Deverra lifted out one of the dark adders inside. Bernalt quickly followed suit. They spoke to the snakes in their own crude and ancient language. The beasts were rather more surly than Deverra ordinarily liked, and sluggish in the winter cold. But alas, for the present purpose they couldn't be soothed with any sweet draughts of vampire blood, and the Telyavs' wills soon overpowered their feeble minds in any case. They drew serpent after serpent out of the sack, something like twenty in all, and set them slithering through the snowy grass back uphill.

"Stay close," Jervais whispered to Hermann and Wigand as they entered the mists. Unfortunately, there was no question of running through this haze. Never mind Telyavs, one could knock oneself out crashing headlong into a tree or trip over a rock and go tumbling head over heels downhill. At least he was doubtless more used to wandering about half-blind than these two. Hints and echoes of movement surrounded them, and the knights kept themselves somewhat back-to-back, swords at the ready, occasionally slashing out at one of the shades that swooped down upon them and then immediately took off again, shrieking something between a laugh and a scream.

"*O tu zalty prakeiktas...*"

A mutter, just on the edge of Jervais's pricked-up senses. He frowned. It seemed to be coming off a little way to the left. He could hear nothing of Miklos, but it was quite possible the lad was unable to call out. He felt his way slowly toward it, holding the globe high. Its radiance burned off some of the mist, but only enough to illuminate nine yards or so in any direction. He steered well clear of hanging branches. Never again would trees be innocent in his sight.

Even knowing that any given vision might be a vampire rather than a spirit, Jervais still froze when the wild-haired woman with a face painted to look like a skull suddenly appeared. She growled, then half-cartwheeled onto her hands and kicked out at him like a disgruntled mare. Her shoes were iron, and they slammed into his jaw, sending flashes of light popping across his field of vision. He felt his knees crumple, but by some supreme exertion he managed to step one foot backward and set his legs akimbo, holding himself somewhat upright. He called upon the strength of blood to make the world stop spinning, then brought the blade Antal had given him up into the base of her ribcage. It slid into her like a hot knife into wax. She cried out. Then she said something in her own tongue. The ghosts emerged again and this time, though their touch remained insubstantial as ever, somehow it caught and plucked at him. They actually managed to raise him into the air a few inches before he fought out of their spectral grasp.

"Hermann!" he shouted as best he could through his cracked jaw, but there was no reply. He snapped his head around. The Ventrue were nowhere to be found. He thought he heard scuffling behind him, but he wasn't sure.

The woman darted away. He cursed and started to follow her, but a glimpse of two pinpoint flashes out of the corner of his vision startled him. They came swiftly toward him, and the next moment he was borne down to the ground with the great weight of an enormous bear on top of him. Its flesh was Cainite-cold. Its snout, flaring spit, closed on his wrist and tore. He couldn't raise his sword to use it. His globe, however, required only a thought to move, and so he sent it up into the creature's coal-red eyes. It shook its head wildly and let go. He laid hold of its fur and sent a levin bolt through its body. The creature screamed—a remarkably human sound—and fell over. Then it limped away, still in bear-form.

He sat up, feeling at his ribs, unable to believe none of them were broken. Hermann and Wigand gone, Miklos and that girl who'd grabbed him gone, his own two attackers fled... Then he smelled something and edged over toward it to be sure. Here were the woman's footprints in the damp ground, and a splatter of blood from her wound had dropped down into one of them.

He felt about for the subsequent footprints. There were more drips there. Vampire wounds didn't usually flow the way blood driven by human hearts did. If she were hunched over with pain, though, the blood's own weight would conduct it down to the ground. Groaning, he fished out one of his vials and scraped some of the bloody earth into it. Then he sharpened his sense of smell to as fine a sensitivity as it could command and crawled downhill on his hands and knees, gathering the globe under his chest so that it both illuminated the grass and snow he searched and, hopefully, became somewhat obscured by his own bulk.

"No, no more," Antal bellowed. "You just waste arrows..."

He flapped his hands wildly at the soldiers. They looked to one of their number, a young ice-blond Cainite who seemed to be the authority of resort when Hermann and Wigand were absent. The knight chopped his arm downward, and the bowmen brought their weapons down.

"They're not attacking anyway. Not attacking, but not leaving…" Antal added to Baghatur in Magyar, frowning. "The ghosts still haunt us, at least."

One appeared at the border of the ward then, its head growing to an enormous size, and roared deafeningly at them as though to prove his point.

"Shall we keep holding the ward, master?" the Khazar inquired stonily.

"No, save your strength. But be ready to go again at a moment's notice." Antal walked up to the blond knight. "Forgive me, what is your name?"

"Landric."

"Brother Landric, I mistrust this seeming calm."

"As do I."

"They're plotting something. I think perhaps I should leave the ward after all…truly get rid of this mist…" He scratched at his beard.

"Well, I hope you're not asking *me*," the knight said.

One of the men-at-arms gave a lusty scream. Antal and Landric rushed over at once. A great dark snake dangled from the mortal's leg, hanging on in what Antal suspected to be an entirely willful fashion despite the man's frantic shaking.

"Stop, stop," he said. "Don't excite yourself. Let me take it off…"

"No, let me take it off, master," Olena interrupted, hurrying up.

He nodded. With a wavelike motion of her hand, she caused the snake to fly off his leg, then bent its legless body in midair until the spine snapped.

The man's face had drained to white, and he breathed shallowly. "No fear," Antal assured him. "We don't wish you to die of fright. You'll be well, I promise. Will he not?" he added with a glance at Landric.

"Yes, of course," the knight nodded. "Come." He got the man to lean on his shoulder. Then he clapped his hands and addressed the other soldiers. "Men! Those of you with reason to fear a serpent's bite, I want you to get up on the horses and not come down 'til I give word—"

Just then another soldier cried out.

"There must be more," Antal told the other Tremere, who'd quickly gathered. "The ward can't keep common beasts out. You must find them. Search the grass. Crawl."

Meanwhile, Landric had sat the first victim down by the cold fire pit, and motioned for the other to be brought to him as well. He tore his arm open with his fangs and began to drip blood into the first man's waiting mouth.

The wizards dispersed through the campsite parting grasses and lifting branches, and most of the undead knights joined in as well. Antal and Torgeir each found a snake—the latter by suddenly having one attached to his hand—and the knights between them hacked the heads off several.

Baghatur stood up, made some little noise of dismay and then ran into a tent. Antal glanced over. Ah yes, the tents, they had to be checked as well.

"Master, come quickly!" came the yell from within.

They all did, and Antal had to shove them aside to get through. It was the tent where the slaves were kept—

"The slaves," Torgeir groaned. "We forgot about the slaves… dear God."

Easy to forget about the slaves, except of course at feeding time. But Antal cursed his slowness nonetheless as he knelt to examine the men and women who lay on the ground in their rope bindings. One was clearly dead already, or so close as to make no difference—most of his head had turned a puffy, bruisy purple and Antal could clearly see three sets of punctures on his neck. Two of the other men showed similar bruising on their hands, spread all the way down from bite marks that had actually pierced the shoulders and upper arms through their sleeves. Their fingers were swollen, and to Antal's ears, their heartbeats were dangerously off-rhythm and weak. The woman in the group actually had her hands over the serpent that still nestled on her chest where it had poisoned her, and her eyes were closed as though in blissful sleep. The Kur rolled to turn toward Antal as he approached. He too had an ugly bite on his face, but he struggled to speak through his greatly swollen lips and tongue.

"Master," he said.

"What happened?" Antal exclaimed. "Why did no one scream?"

"I woke...when snake bit me," the man managed. Antal hurriedly began to untie his bonds. "They just sit there...they say that *mürkmadu* has come to free them. I try to call out..."

Antal began to roll up his sleeve to administer the blood, but then hesitated. For these people it might be too late to do anything but make vampires of them. The Kur seemed best off of the lot, of course—he was far less often bled than the others, owing to his function as translator. Still, even his was a doubtful case. Anyway, if there was the slightest chance that undeath might result it had better be a knight giving the vitae. For Antal to sire a childe, even to exterminate it a moment later, was technically a violation of the Code that any of these young ones might report should the malicious whim take them.

"Baghatur." Antal glanced backward. "Your alchemy."

The apprentice shook his head. "They're dying, master. Multiple bites...and I can smell the venom from here. I can try."

"Well, try, try!" Antal snapped. The Khazar went off to get his things. "I want one of the brother-knights."

Landric shook his head. "We gladly shed Cainite blood to heal our fighting men, Master Antal. But not for these. Especially when it might not even save their bodies, to say nothing of their heathen souls."

Ah yes, bless Antal's Transylvanian blade. It had struck quite true. The snow, though half-melted from a turn in the weather, helped Jervais to find the indentations of her metal shoes and the occasional splats of dark blood. His clothes were soaked nearly through. The ground leveled out for a while—he was definitely off the hill—and then rose again. Unfortunately, he had very little idea which direction he was going in. Vaguely north, he thought. He could see neither moon nor stars. He was more or less following a ley line, but he didn't know which one. He also had very little idea of time's passage. He was absorbed in the trail of blood and footfall, and more peripherally in the growth structures of grasses and weeds, the traces of insectile life that remained even in the winter's bitterest cold.

The earth began to feel distinctly warmer under his hands, yet the slush and snow remained. At last the sensation reached the point where it penetrated his benumbed mind, and he stood, suddenly alarmed.

Wherever he was, he wasn't wanted. The trail continued determinedly on ahead of him, but he no longer trusted it to lead him anywhere he wished to go. He hadn't been attacked again yet. That wasn't right. Surely it was just a matter of time. Even if they were having as much trouble finding him as the reverse, one of them almost *had* to stumble across him at some point.

With a curse under his breath, he took his leather gloves out of his belt and threw them down on the ground. Then he took off his cloak and boots as well.

There are some *advantages to being dead already, Lord Councilor.*

He knelt and called the snow to him. It came in clumps rather than fluffy drifts, but obeyed him nonetheless, hastily forming into a pillar whose lower half he directed to split in two. Two tapering cylinders for the arms, and a roly-poly little head. There was very little need for accuracy here, as long as the overall shape and size were right. The movement was more the trick—if he were Etrius, he would simply have called up an elemental spirit to inhabit it—well, never mind what Etrius would have done. Resigning himself now to coming back to camp thoroughly drenched, he dressed the manikin in his robe, boots and gloves and set it into something like a walk with the globe hovering over it. Then he sheathed his blade so that its own uncanny radiance wouldn't give away his real position and followed along behind as quietly as he could. Keeping the globe aloft was near-instinctual—he knew the charm that well—but it did hamper his concentration on his snow-self. The going was rather slow, but that was all right. Every so often he wiggled the haft of the sword to make sure it hadn't stuck in the sheath.

Once again, he saw the red eyes just before their owner leaped. The "bear" seemed a bit startled to find that its headlong attack crumpled its opponent so quickly and completely, and it tumbled to the ground tangled up in Jervais's cloak. Jervais rushed in and brought the blade down onto its neck. His blow released a great deal of blood but stuck in the spine without severing it. Panicked, he put his bare foot against the struggling beast's shoulder to help pull it out. It reeled up to standing on its hind legs, head now lolling.

There were few things more dangerous than *almost* slaying a Cainite, and Jervais knew it. He sent a fork of lightning toward it before it could regain its balance, knocking it flat. The bear-form melted away then, hair drawing up and muscles rearranging themselves in the space of a blink, leaving behind the naked body of a young man. Jervais brought the sword down again. Before it even connected, the young man had vanished. Jervais looked around in a panic. He felt a tickle and saw a beetle land on his hand; in the next instant, a vicious hunting hound was hanging from his hand. It tore off a chunk of his flesh and sprang away. He screamed (and berated himself a moment later for making the noise, but too late).

"*Puteresse, lichieres pautonnier,*" he muttered savagely, clamping his good hand to the wound and finally recovering his ice-filled glove to put on over it. Then he ran after the dog. It was already invisible in the mist, but at least it had bled far more copiously than the woman.

"Yes, good…" Antal moved forward slowly, down from the hilltop, knights on all sides of him, the Tremere clustered behind and the gargoyles gliding along above. "Clear all this rubbish out. Then we can see what we are dealing with, whether they're even still here." As he moved his arms in a sort of swimming and scooping gesture, the mists separated and rose.

"Dear heaven," Torgeir said. He looked up. "Is that the time? Master Antal—"

Antal looked up too, noting the height of the moon. "Yes, young Master Torgeir, I see it now."

"Master Jervais and the *Herren* may not be able to. Hadn't we better…"

"Yes, we'd better. Cabo! Rixatrix! Falco!"

The gargoyles descended, floating down like autumn leaves in spite of their stony bodies.

"Now let me think. Falco is the sharp-eyed one? Falco, go look for your master."

"His mate should—" Fidus began to volunteer, then stopped. Antal stared at him, as did everyone. Evidently Fourth Circle lent one new airs.

"Yes, Fidus?" Antal prompted.

"His mate should go with him," the apprentice gulped. "Master Antal. She's the fighter of the pair...ah, as you can see... and Lady Virstania said they almost think in concert. If Master Jervais and the knights are in trouble, then..."

Antal blinked at him.

"Of course," he said after a moment. "Cabo should be enough for us. Rixatrix, go with Falco. Cabo, you stay with us."

"Rix go," the big female grunted. She and her mate took off, and Cabo returned to circling just overhead.

The dog's trail ended abruptly at a little brook of melt runoff. Jervais didn't know whether that meant that he'd splashed into the brook, or that he'd turned into a bird and flown away, or something else equally aggravating.

He sat down, pulled off the glove and examined his wound. It would take only a few nights to heal—that was if he could hope for regular meals in the meantime, which seemed a slim and uncertain hope just now. But it was a good-sized hunk of flesh, enough for some really malicious spell-work. He certainly hadn't set out to become the next risk to the *sodalicium*. Damn Miklos for a fool. If he'd only stayed in the tent. Evidently the boy would follow any order without question except the order to lay low...

He shook his head and took a little lodestone out of the purse at his belt. He dripped some of the blood from his wound into the finger of his glove, then dropped the lodestone in and settled in to wait. In this fog, there was no way to see an hour's passage, so he quietly recited a chant he knew took about that long to get through.

When it was done, he took the lodestone back out and suspended it on his purse-string. Naturally it pointed further in to what he had already determined was an *alkas* of some size. With a gusting sigh he got up again to follow it. Come what may, he had to recover his missing portion.

Not long afterward he found the stone slowly turning left, then whirling. Just in time he dodged out of the way as they both came at him from behind. He spun to face them. Having now seen the enchantment once before, he spotted the vines beginning to sprout from the woman's hands and caused them to wither with a gesture and a phrase invoking the forces of decay. The naked young man who had been a bear slashed at him with long clawlike fingernails. The woman flicked her hand and sent a rock flying up from the ground and dashing into Jervais's injured jaw. He roared and lunged at her, seizing her arm and twisting it as he pulled downward. She gasped.

He sent a good solid bolt into her while still holding onto her arm and threw her aside. Then he did the same to the man and straddled across him, pressing his blade into the Telyav's neck.

"What did you do with it?" he hissed.

"With what?"

"My flesh."

"I ate it," the young man grinned through a bleeding mouth.

"Unwise." Jervais lifted the blade and made to plunge it into his abdomen. The young man laughed at him. "Son of a whore..."

Something he could only have described as a sensation of pure malevolence brushed across Jervais's back. He stumbled to his feet. The Telyav was still laughing, pulling himself up unhurriedly. The woman had also begun to rise, but she made no move to attack. Jervais peered up to see what was diving at him now. Another ghost?

Then it happened again—this time to his face, a much sharper pain. As it did, a faint patch of brightness showed through the roiling mist above him.

The first fingers of dawn, seeking to reach down and touch them.

All thought of battle was abandoned. Jervais looked wildly around. It was still difficult to see much on the ground, but there was no sign of any hole or hollow he could jump into. For one dazed moment he thought of simply covering himself in a mound of slush, but no, that might well melt away completely if the day turned warm.

The Telyavs slowly backed away from him, no longer laughing but eerily silent and smiling in the purple light. Jervais ran toward the young man with a cry, thinking he would take *one* with him, anyway, and drove him up against the bole of a great tree.

A moment later he had hold of nothing. The young man's maddeningly serene face grayed, softened and flowed backward into the very wood, soon followed by the rest of him. Jervais turned. The last of the woman's arm was fading into the bark of a slim linden.

"Trees. Double-damned *trees*..."

This had been the plan all along, he realized. Or it had been the plan ever since he'd undertaken the supreme idiocy of charging out of the ward. He deserved this fate every bit as much as Miklos. More.

Purple took on roseate hues, and the mist rose like bread. The pain began in earnest now, and the fear. He ran back and forth. There was nothing but snow. Surely he could do better than snow. There must be some charm, some incantation... It dimly occurred to him that these were his final moments and he should do something, say something. Now was the time to pray or curse or utter some deathless sentiment, if there were anyone here to hear it. He offered up all he had to offer to the burning face of Heaven: a cry of cheated hate.

And Heaven answered. He thought at first the darkness that fell upon him was Judgment, wings of demons come to drag his soul to hell, but then he put out his hands and touched a familiar, pebbly texture. The smell, too, of niter caves and butcher's stalls.

"Falco?"

"Shh. Master must be still..."

"Sleep now," came Rixatrix's rumble. They were embracing him between them, arcing their wings until their bodies met at every seam, blotting out every last bit of the horrible light.

"Master is safe."

He could feel their skin calcifying around him, entombing him immovably in the mountain-rock of Carpathia. Yes, he remembered now, Goratrix had had to invent the spell, gargoyles weren't always bright enough to get themselves out of the sun in time—of course, given the circumstances perhaps he shouldn't disparage... The danger now over, the lethargy of daytime took him with unaccustomed speed. So, then. He would owe the next night, and every night thereafter, to the luck of fools and gargoyles.

It was certainly better than the alternative.

Chapter Twenty-One

"No sign yet?" Torgeir called up to Antal, who had actually climbed a tree just outside the ward circle in order to get a better vantage.

"No sign," the Hungarian called back.

"There you are," Torgeir said, clapping a hand on Fidus's shoulder. "Now next time you can just ask him yourself."

"Aren't you at all worried?" Fidus entreated him as he walked away again.

"Why, what would be the point of worrying?"

"Well—" Fidus stopped in the middle of what he'd been going to say, realizing that none of the reasons it personally worried him mattered nearly as much to Torgeir. "Well, Master Jervais was the only one who really knew what we're supposed to be doing, and why."

"We're out here to kill Telyavs because the Lord Councilor told us to," the young magus replied easily. "What else is there to know? Peace, Fidus. Either he's all right or he isn't. But knowing Master Jervais, I'd wager the former. If there's one thing the man excels at, it's taking care of himself."

Jervais doubled over in pain and fell to his knees, clawing at the stake in his belly to dig it out before the buds on it had a chance to sprout. It wouldn't come loose, though, until he choked out a formula of revocation. Right away the broad-set one was charging again. Evidently all the savage had to do was slather himself with a bit of mud to heal his wounds, or at least he didn't seem to feel them anymore. Rixatrix picked the man up and hurled him away.

Five. He'd fully expected to awaken to two, but not five. Evidently he'd walked into a damned *orchard* of Telyavs. At least the naked young man was still looking worse for wear, and the iron-shod woman's wound didn't seem to have healed either. They hung to the rear. The new three, however, were considerably fitter and haler for battle than Jervais himself.

Jervais stayed where he was for a few moments, hunched over, pretending to be grievously wounded. Sure enough, the little blond girl with the bone-tipped spear decided to press her advantage and ran at him with a battle-yell. He knocked the spear away with his sword. She raised her arm to strike again. With his other hand he drove the stake into her foot. Its magic had fled, but it could still cause terrible pain. Falco swept down and knocked her on the head with a thick fallen branch—a choice of weapon Jervais found most gratifying.

Jervais got up then and, with a sweeping motion, sent a clump of dirty snow-slush into her face. That bought him some time to get out of the way. All of a sudden the smell of Cainite blood completely suffused the air. Rixatrix had taken the naked young man's head the rest of the way off. She shot up into the air, carrying the head aloft with a triumphant shriek. The iron-shod woman screamed and ran up directly underneath her. Rixatrix snuffled—it wasn't a laugh exactly, but it was as close as most gargoyles got—and dropped her prize at the woman's feet.

The broad-set man was back from wherever Rix had thrown him. Now he stood aghast at seeing his comrade's body so used. Jervais tried to run him through, but he overbalanced. The man easily caught him, wrapping his powerful arms around Jervais's own, turning him toward the iron-shod woman.

"Daine!" he called hoarsely. "Daine!"

The woman turned to stare, but then seemed to understand. Once again the vines and thorns shot out of her fingers with deadly speed, and this time Jervais couldn't make the sign necessary to stop it. As they enveloped his head, the man who held him hastily stepped back. Jervais flailed at the vines with his sword, but it became entangled as well.

Something yanked on the vines, and he fell facedown on the ground. Wriggling to raise his head, he saw that Falco had barreled into the woman and was now worrying at her flesh. Leaves and coils of green twined around him as well, locking him and his opponent together.

And now the third one, the sharp-faced old man, was chanting in Jervais's direction.

"Rix!" Jervais shouted. The big gargoyle landed beside him and caught up the vines in her mouth. She put her front talons down on them, pulling and shearing with all her might until they tore just above his head. Then she seized hold of him and struggled clumsily up into the air. A burst of orange and a flash of heat exploded under Jervais as they rose.

A rock flew up and battered against Rixatrix's wing, laying open a gash. The spear flew at them and the old man sent another blossom of fire toward them, but she managed to dodge them and stay aloft. They spiraled upward. Jervais stared down at the battle that continued on in his absence. The Telyavs descended on Falco now. The poor creature tried to break his wings free of the strands that bound them, and he put great rakes of gore across any Cainite flesh that was unlucky enough to come within range. Then the bone-spear plunged into his chest, and he gave a piercing cry that echoed across the canopy of the *alkas*.

Rixatrix gathered Jervais up into her vast arms now, so that he no longer dangled like an overripe fruit.

"Master is safe," she said for the second time in as many nights.

"I hope so," he answered, "though I fear the same can't be said of Falco." Virstania would be most displeased. Then again, the old harridan had never quite managed to get it through her skull that the whole purpose of her charges' existence was to die in their owners' stead.

"Is true," she rumbled.

He glanced up at the gargoyle's grim, knobby face. For him, at least, it was impossible to read feeling in it. "Don't you care?" he asked curiously. "He was your mate."

"He dies for Master. Is great honor. My great honor come another time."

"Ah yes. The kind and noble masters..." He didn't expect her to catch his irony, but to his surprise she made a little demurring noise.

"Some Master is cruel. No matter."

He wondered where he fell by the gargoyle reckoning. "No?"

"For Mother's children, is honor to serve whether Master is kind or not. Master do as he wish. If I serve well, then honor is mine in any case."

"I see." He'd never thought to see a moment when he would envy one of these creatures, especially knowing the existences they led, but here it was. "Then your Mother has taught you well." *Better than I was ever taught, certainly.*

"Yes," she said, and banked left to catch a favorable wind. Rixatrix delivered him to the center of the Tremere campsite like war booty, and he once again had to endure the indignity of being pried free of greenery.

"Master! Thank Great Tremere!" Fidus exclaimed with evident relief.

"Here, boy. Take this vial and put it away safely," Jervais gasped, squirming to get his arm out. "Herr Hermann, Herr Wigand. You made it back in before dawn?"

"Just barely. But for Miklos," Hermann said solemnly, "you are the tardiest of us, master wizard. I'd hoped you would recover him."

"I wish any of us had—" Jervais retorted, stung. Hermann bared his teeth, and only then did Jervais see the great wound in the knight's chest. He hastily added, "Not for lack of trying, I'm sure. For that matter, I wish we'd managed to stick together. I could have used you."

"Forgive us. Something ran in a circle around us, and suddenly there were two witch-lights, and we didn't know which one was you anymore. Obviously we guessed wrongly."

"Well, I got a little distracted myself, so I suppose fair's fair."

"Open up your hand," Hermann said. Jervais did so warily. The knight deposited a pair of fangs into his palm.

"It isn't just their ghosts that fear the cross," he went on. "They do themselves. They recoil at the sight of it. I thought I saw it during that last battle, but I wasn't sure. This time there was no doubt. Brother Wigand made the sign of the cross and invoked the name of Our Lord, and the witch screeched and fled straight into my arms."

"My vigor and hope are restored," Wigand agreed heartily. "This time God blesses our endeavors. Jürgen was right—sorcerers to kill sorcerers, it's all in His plan."

"Is that so?" Jervais pondered. "Well, it certainly helps *my* plans, anyway."

"Why? What are you going to do?" Hermann asked.

"Learn by imitation, like any good scholar."

The Saxon nodded heavily, despite having not the slightest idea what Jervais meant, and made for the slaves' tent. Antal started and ran after him. Seeing the look on the Hungarian's face, Jervais shook off the last of the clinging vines and hurried along as well.

"Captain," the Hungarian was saying. "Captain, I must warn you—"

Hermann stopped short in the doorway in the tent. The two magi crowded up behind him.

"There is but one left. And he's ill."

Hermann stared at the Kur, who sat up from his rags of bedding with wide eyes.

"So he is," the knight murmured. And came forward.

"No. No, no," the mortal man begged. Hermann paid him no heed. "No, please—I can tell you things." He looked pleadingly at Jervais. "I can tell you useful thing!"

Hermann stopped again then, but his mouth was partway open already.

"If you can do that, why haven't you done it before?" Jervais asked.

"About Telyavel. About his shrines."

"Stay...stay out of this, wizards," Hermann said huskily.

"You're right." Jervais held up his hands in a pretense of apology. "It's your decision. After all, he's the only one left for you, isn't he? The only infidel."

"About his shrines, please. If your enemy is high priestess of Telyavel, one thing she must have, one promise she must keep. I tell you—if you promise no to bite me!"

The knight drew up his knees and sat. He raised his hand to push his metal coif back off of his head, revealing the linen arming-cap beneath.

"So you guessed," he muttered to Jervais.

"Finally, yes I did. Casts a much more interesting light on your religious fervor, which, as you know, I'd been finding rather tiresome. But I won't stop you. You need your strength. Whatever he thinks he knows, it's quite possible someone else out here knows too, and we've got to get more of them anyway..." Jervais shrugged.

"You. You must have a name, don' t you?" Hermann grated at the terrified slave.

"Kalju," the man gasped.

"How about this, Kalju? You tell me this 'useful thing'..." He actually mimicked the man's accent. Apparently hunger brought out the spite in Hermann. "If it really is useful, then I promise I won't bite you. And if it isn't, then I promise I'll make you *wish* I had done so."

Kalju told them. A little later, Jervais burst out of the tent with Hermann and Antal following.

"My chart!"

"Yes, master." Fidus fetched it out of his master's tent.

"Let me see." Jervais ran his finger over the tracks of the ley lines.

Antal was at once peering over his shoulder. "Looking at the spots we couldn't reach in scrying?"

"Yes. Because if our Kur speaks truly, then we should have found the place already, except if it was in one of these spots... hm. How odd. How very, very odd. Look at this one, in the south here." He tapped a spot.

"What?"

"Well, this was our travel route, wasn't it? Something like this?"

"Slightly more west, because we crossed this stream I think, but yes."

"We went right by it. Right past it."

Comprehension dawned on Antal's saturnine features. "So we did."

"I know exactly what we're going to do now. Exactly. And as long as we're doing that...Fidus, get me that vial. And some thread."

"Which vial, master?"

"The one I handed you not a moment ago!" Jervais snapped. Antal laid a hand on his arm.

"Stop shouting," the Hungarian warned. "We're all hungry."

Jervais rounded on him as well—but then he caught sight of the other Tremere. Exhaustion and over-vigilance warred in their faces. Even Antal's fingers gripped him a little too tightly. With an effort, he nodded.

Fidus brought the vial out again. Jervais took it from him, suspended it from the thread and said an incantation over it, then swung it out over the chart until it began to spin rapidly.

"So this is where I must have been last night, the northern *alkas*. It's attuned to that iron-shoed bitch... probably not her alone, either. That one we destroy for certain. And this other *alkas* and this—what did Zabor call it, *pannean*, the sacred bog—they're also within a half a night's journey from the Telyav camp, so we should hit all three. Olena, can you carry a man while you fly?"

Olena blinked. "Well, I haven't tried, but I think so..."

"Good. Then you're with Master Antal."

"What for?" Antal exclaimed.

"Baghatur," Jervais said over the other magus's huffing. "You're with me."

The Khazar looked just as baffled as everyone else, but he said, "Yes, master," and gave one of his little bows.

"Torgeir, Fidus, you're together, and take one of Herr Hermann's mortal soldiers with you. You two leave tonight, since you've got the furthest to go."

"The furthest to go *where*?" Torgeir broke in.

"Back south." Jervais tapped the blank spot that he and Antal had been mulling over. "Fidus, go saddle the horses. Sit down, Torgeir, and practice patience. You'll get all the explanation you need in a moment." The Dane went rigid, and for a moment Jervais honestly thought he might lunge forward, but then he obeyed. "The rest of us will set out tomorrow. But we must prepare. Above all, we must feed."

"Then that means raiding a village tonight," Hermann said.

"Yes, indeed. Order a raid. And make sure to tell your men to take all the axes they can find, because tomorrow they're paying a visit to the northern *alkas*."

"Axes. Good." The Saxon's eyes glinted.

"But five knights of the Blood have to stay here, both tonight and tomorrow night. And you as well. Remember that boon you owe me, *mein Herr*," he added when he saw Hermann's scowl. The scowl turned to a momentary look of what Jervais was gratified to label terror, but then smoothed out again.

"I see." Hermann bowed from the neck. "My word is my bond, Master Jervais. My services are at your disposal. Call me when you require them." Then he walked away, Wigand at his side conferring with him.

"Say what you want about the Cainite traditions, they certainly do simplify certain transactions," Jervais remarked to the others. "My brethren, and sister, with Miklos in Telyav hands, I think you all understand that our ward is doomed to fall and that we will lose our safe haven once more. Now I don't know about you, but I haven't the first intention of letting that happen without a retaliation in kind."

Hermann knelt grudgingly in the circle of salt that Jervais and Antal had constructed.

"Both knees," Jervais instructed.

"A man only goes on both knees before God," the monk-knight said stiffly.

"That's exactly the idea. Pray to God. It's your devotion that we require for the spell. Just don't pray for protection from us, or from sorcery, mind. That'd be rather counterproductive."

Hermann looked greatly surprised, but he folded his hands and began intoning under his breath. Jervais took the six Black Cross surcoats, folded them so that their blazon showed uppermost, and then laid them out on the ground along the inner perimeter of the circle. Antal picked up the bowl and used the brush to stir up the mixture of paste, gold dust and ground lily petals.

Jervais touched Hermann gently on the shoulder to interrupt him, then proffered him a different bowl. "Drink," he said. "Replenish yourself. You'll need it for this."

"But I cannot..." Hermann began. Then he sniffed, and cautiously took the bowl from Jervais's hand. He tasted of it, then glanced up at Jervais.

"I *promised* him he wouldn't be harmed," he said. A low, dangerous note entered his voice.

"You promised him no such thing," Jervais returned comfortably. "You said you wouldn't bite him. You didn't. I have saved you that labor, and your honor as well. Now drink."

There was a curse all but spoken in the Ventrue's eyes, but he drank.

Jervais gazed out over the plain, toward where the Telyav camp lay, but it was useless. Too far away to detect any but the most gargantuan working. Whatever they might be up to, he hadn't the resources to stop it. A dark bird streaked across the sky from that direction. He followed its flight with interest. It circled once overhead, then it fluttered down to land before him. It was a great, graceless black raven. Something light-colored was wrapped around its leg and secured with a knotted thread. He stepped toward it. It croaked at him and lifted its leg, looking up at him with what he thought a rather supplicating air, as if to say *I was told you'd help me out with this infernal thing.*

He carefully untied the knot and extracted the long tape of parchment, first looking it over carefully, even though no spell should have been able to pass over the ward anyway.

The letters were learned, but cramped and a bit wobbly. *As you know, we have Miklos. We are willing to parley for his safe return. Send reply by bird. Yours.*

Antal came up beside him. "What's this? More beastly couriers?"

"Rather more innocuous this time, but yes." Jervais withdrew from the raven a bit, motioning for Antal to follow. "Have the others fed from the new prisoners?" he asked quietly.

"I assume so. We were all famished."

"Then we should gather them. I'm afraid there's more work to do."

"The sun dawns in a few hours," the Hungarian cautioned him. "Not enough time to purify for a major working."

"Then we'll do without. Not sure this is the sort of working for which purifications are really appropriate, anyway."

He showed Antal the parchment.

"They haven't killed him, then?" Antal murmured.

"No. And this—" Jervais held up the braid-band. "This shows that they're telling the truth."

"You are right," Antal said heavily. "There is no other choice. The boy is part of the *sodalicium*—as long as it stands, they can get at the rest of us through him. We must break the circle."

"We can't break it in the proper manner. All of us would have to be present for that."

They were both well aware of the things they told each other now. The essential conversation was already had. Yet, to the faint amusement of some disconnected corner of Jervais's mind, they kept talking, sharing not information but resolve.

"This will not please the children."

"No, it won't."

"He said he had other bloodstones. We'll use those."

"Yes. Have Fidus bring me my pen and ink, I need to write a reply."

"You'll say yes, we shall parley." Antal nodded his head toward the bird.

"Of course."

"You'll say anything, won't you?"

Jervais gave Antal a churlish glance, but for once the Hungarian seemed more curious than disparaging.

"I'll say anything required, yes," he answered.

"That must be why you are sent to woo princes, and I am sent to feed *vozhd*," Antal ruminated.

"I would imagine so."

Jurate felt awkward doing chores in front of the big auburn-haired Christian, even though he was laid out flat, his heart spitted on a shaft of ash-wood, unable to even turn his head to watch her. But at last, shortly before dawn, she finished her work. Then a perverse curiosity seized her. Deverra had firmly instructed Jurate not to speak to him; she'd said nothing about touching. Jurate went over to his still form and with her fingers closed his staring eyes. Then she sat beside him, studying the things he wore around his neck—a handful of teeth strung on a chain, a funny little charm with Western writing on it. In his purse she found a quaint assortment of things, some of them reminding her of the odds and ends curious children might pick up. There was a bit of thread wound on a spool, several smooth stones, a ball of wax, some fragrant anise seed, coins from various mortal mints, a bit of willow twig and the skull of a mouse. Then there was a little pair of wooden boards hinged together with silk thread. She opened them. Here, set into one of the panels, was what looked like it had once been a portion of eggshell, brightly painted with a colorful design. It had been crushed flat, giving it rather the look of a mosaic, and then shellacked into the shallow hollow of the board.

It certainly didn't look like a tool for any fearsome sorcery. What was it? She turned it this way and that, trying to make sense of the broken design. Someone had labored over this, bent over it with a tiny brush. Part of it looked as though it had been rendered with a wax-resist technique or something similar. And he had carefully saved it, found a way to preserve the fragile surface and yet carry it with him. She glanced pensively at his slack face. He doubtless wouldn't tell her anyway. What was the mystery of these Tremere? They had two eyes, two ears, and their blood was the blood that ran in Telyav veins. How could it be that they'd wandered so far from the life of the world, while they still went about with old lovers' tokens hidden away in their purses?

He made a noise then. She started like a rabbit and shot to her feet. Vampires on stakes were not supposed to be able to make noise. His eyelids fluttered. Then he moaned again. His body began to shiver. It was the minutest possible movement, impossibly fast, visible only as a blurring at the tips of his fingers and nose and the edges of his clothes.

"Grandmother," she murmured, and then raised her voice, backing away, still holding the little wooden token. "*Grandmother! Grandmother!*"

"What in the name of Moist Mother Earth is it, girl?" Deverra hurried in, pushing open the tent flap.

"Look!"

"Yes, I see…" Deverra laid a hand on Jurate's arm. "Step back. Back."

A moment later the Christian's head burst into flame, the auburn of his hair supplanted by a blazing corona of candle-light-yellow. Jurate felt the blood-terror enter her bones, urging her to flee, but Deverra held her fast. The rest of the body caught fire and began to blacken.

"I thought they said they wanted to meet," blurted Jurate.

"This is their true answer," Deverra returned with a gesture at the charring corpse. "Daughter, I want you to stay here with him until he is ash. Then you must gather every speck of him up and open the tent to air it out. We'll stay in Bernalt's *ger* until we have time to purify this one. Perhaps tomorrow."

"Perhaps?" she echoed. "Where are you going, Grandmother?"

"I must find the *darkhan*."

Jurate sat uncertainly down, clutching the token now, to keep watch over the dead as requested. Deverra went and sought out the current head of the raider band, who stood conversing with the one person she had no desire to look at right now.

"*Darkhan* Alessandro. *Boyar* Osobei."

They both bowed to her, the latter rather more floridly. "Mistress Deverra. How may I be of service?" the Tzimisce inquired.

"I was seeking the *darkhan, boyar*, but I'm glad that I find you as well, because the news is the same either way."

"Oh?"

"Yes." She turned to Alessandro. "Tell the mortals they move camp tomorrow. I want everyone gone by sundown except for my own priests and acolytes. Obviously that means your riders won't be sleeping in the *gers* tonight. I trust they can manage."

"Yes, milady." He frowned. "Which way are the mortals to go?"

"Any way that's far away. I would say east."

"And the riders?"

"You will join the mortals after sundown, to lead them."

"I see. It will not please the great khan that we left you…"

"The great khan is not here," she replied grimly. "Nor can I concern myself with what would please him. Instead I must do as I know he would do in my stead."

"True." Then to her surprise, Alessandro got down on one knee and took her hand.

"We will guard the tribe, and pray Father Tengri that you rejoin us in triumph." He paused. "And Father Telyavel."

She laid her other hand over his. "May the wind bear you up, *darkhan*."

Then she looked to Osobei. "We have enjoyed the honor of your company, *boyar*," she said, "but it is time for you to go now."

The emissary bowed again. To his credit, at least he didn't smile.

"It would seem so, milady," he agreed.

Antal set down the platter upon which the blood-stones had rested. It was blasted and cracked now with the remnants of the heat.

He spoke quietly. "Dismiss the quarters."

Torgeir was East, Olena South, Baghatur West, and Fidus North. The last recited his words with rather more care than strictly necessary. Everyone else waited patiently, even though the sun lay in wait just under the horizon.

Jervais put out the incense. "Get some rest, everyone."

They stirred like dreamers just awakened. Antal remained where he was, standing bent over the platter.

"Everyone comes upon death by and by," he said. The others looked at him. "Not everyone has the—privilege of serving others by that death."

The futility of the sentiment hung there in the air of the disbanded circle. Jervais sheathed the ritual sword and stood. *Antal, you idiot, this isn't helping them. Keep your own demons out of this.*

"Or of being remembered." Torgeir cleared his throat by way of preface. "I have an idea. A pact."

That drew their attention sharply.

"A pact?" Jervais echoed.

"A promise. I don't know if anyone would be interested. A

promise that…whoever falls and has fallen, those who survive will remember." He met Jervais's eyes then. "Not in prayer, necessarily. In whatever way each one chooses to honor them. Once a year. Forever."

He bit into his fingertip and let the blood run. Olena did likewise and stepped forward, touching her finger to his. Then Baghatur joined them, and then—not without a nervous, permission-seeking glance at his master—Fidus.

"Why not?" Jervais came forward as well. "Master Antal. Come."

But Antal stood as if rooted to the spot. He had a rather odd look on his face, and twisted the end of his beard.

"A promise so much more easily made than kept," he said.

"Bring your arse over here, Antal!" Jervais blared. The Hungarian obeyed.

"Zabor and Miklos."

"Zabor and Miklos."

They held all their fingertips together in somber silence for a few moments, then parted.

"Perhaps a *sodalicium* can endure even as six," Jervais murmured to Torgeir as they made their way back to the tents, putting a hand on his shoulder. "Well done. Your master could take a lesson from you."

Torgeir pulled away disgustedly. "Don't talk to me now. You don't understand anything."

Jervais raised his hands and let him go. He watched the young albino slog determinedly across the muddy grass. He had, at one time, drawn great distinctions of character between the Black Cross knights and his fellow Tremere, and also distinctions among the Tremere themselves. No more. One essential characteristic united them all, outweighing every difference.

"I do understand some things, at least," he told himself. "I understand what a promise is, and is not, good for."

Chapter Twenty-Two

"Know any good songs to sing?" Ditmar asked Werner with a grin.

"No, I'm used to swinging a sword, not an ax," Werner retorted, grimacing, as he laid another stroke into the foot of the alder beside him. All around them the sunlit grove echoed with the sounds of chopping.

"It would pass the time, anyway. I hope they don't expect us to have this whole grove down today."

"God save us, no. I think the idea is just to—desecrate—" He yanked the blade out from where it had stuck for a moment. "Trespass the pagan law, render it unfit for their blasphemous use."

"A pity a man should have to break his back for hours on end just for that..." Ditmar returned to his task, selecting a new tree, a slightly smaller one this time. He sank his ax deep into its bole. An instant later he cried out as dark liquid gushed forth from the slit he'd made.

"Werner, look!"

Werner came over at once, crossing himself. "Blood!"

"There's godless filth for you—" Ditmar attacked it with fervor now, all complaints forgotten. Werner joined him. Between them, they soon had it crashing down. The blood continued to flow from it, brighter red now.

"*Deo gratias!*" Werner exclaimed as it fell. Ditmar echoed him. The fallen trunk before them shivered, all its leaves shaking as though in a breeze. Then a section of it softened and shifted. A moment later the cloaked body of a slim youth lay before them, its right foot severed off. The youth half-rose and lifted his trembling hand toward them. As they watched, it reddened with sunburn and exploded into a fiery mass that soon consumed him completely.

They crossed themselves again, breathing heavily. Then all at once Ditmar broke into some lusty song about the baron's daughter and went to find another tree.

"Brothers!" Werner shouted to his compatriots. "Brothers, look sharp! We must try them all, and find the ones that *bleed*!"

As it turned out, they could find only four in the entire grove, but even that gave them great satisfaction. It was a victory they could report to the senior brothers (whose Devil-inflicted daytime infirmity regrettably kept them from joining in) and claim as their very own. Better yet, several hours into the work a band of pagan worshipers wandered unwittingly into their midst, seeking the cup-stone that had already been turned over and pissed on. The men among them had spears, but that would help them precious little.

"Now there's something I know bleeds, and my favorite sort of tree to fell moreover," Ditmar smiled as he hefted the ax and went toward them.

"Couldn't you just give me one of those stones, like you gave to Torgeir?" Hermann grumbled that evening. Jervais restrained a smirk. One night the man was terrified at the prospect of even entering a ritual circle, the next he wanted playthings. Granted, the signal-stones *would* have been simple enough for even a Ventrue to use, since all one had to do was trace the *alpha* on the sending-stone with one's finger to set the *omega* on the herald-stone alight.

"I'm afraid that was Master Antal's only pair, and Torgeir's going to be a good deal further away from me than you are. Now Baghatur wrapped these up very nicely for you in the proper color cloths. The blue bags will send up blue plumes when you throw them on the fire, and the red bags will send up red plumes. The blue plumes are to make anyone that's watching think the Tremere are up here on the hill working sorcery, so just throw one on every so often. Then if you do get attacked, throw on a red bag."

"And the other red bag?"

"Is to signal your victory, or at least your survival. I trust you won't ask me for one to signal defeat."

Now it was Hermann's turn to smirk. "No, Master Jervais." He rearranged Jervais's sigil-embroidered ceremonial cloak around his shoulders and glanced at Landric and the other four knights, who were likewise doing their best to make Tremere cloaks fit comfortably over knightly mail. "Well. It's a good thing we won't need to pass for sorcerers at *close* range…"

Jervais chuckled and went to check on the young Khazar, who was working furiously in his tent.

"Ready to go yet?"

"Er…" Baghatur held up one flagon. "Here's the remnant of the antithesis I made to get you out of those roots, it should still be good. And here's another batch."

"This won't do, my lad. It's a good-sized bog. We'll need at least one more of these."

"But I can't, I'm out of ingredients."

"What would you need more of?"

"Well." Baghatur started to speak, then stopped and blinked. When he spoke again, it was more subdued. "I would need some of…Zabor, actually."

"Ah. For the filtration?" Jervais took out the vial of ash and passed it over.

The Khazar took it uncertainly. "Yes. Thank you, master." He bowed.

"It's not me you should thank," Jervais said. "Hurry. We need to be gone."

"I give up," Antal shouted over the wind. "Take me somewhere else."

Olena shook her head. When they first took off, her hair had been well braided in a thick rope, but that was long gone. One could take her for the wild *vila* of so many peasant tales now, with locks black as midnight whipping about in the chill air and her skin chalk white under the moon's radiance. They'd quickly found that the best course was for Olena to hold Antal's left hand. If she let him go entirely, he was too afraid to concentrate; if she carried him, he couldn't conjure the bale-fire properly.

"You've dried it out now," she shouted back. "One more, master."

He spread his hands, and another ball of flame appeared between them, expanding into an amber-bright bead. Then he sent it down into the forest canopy. This time it caught. Nothing could be seen of it other than a tiny trail of smoke, but if it or one of its siblings would only blossom a little over the next hour or two, then a conflagration would start that only weather-witching of the highest order could put out. And if several of them caught and endured, then perhaps not even weather-witching would save the eastern *alkas*.

They flew back over to another spot where they'd been working before so that Antal could try to fan it with a friendly wind. Olena gave a cry of satisfaction as a glow of orange sprang up from within the tree crowns.

"There, you see? It's begun."

"Yes, it has." Antal cast his gaze across the wide, shadowy blanket of foliage. Who knew how long it had stood here, how long the people had come? And that other billow of ash coming out of the very edge of the forest there, was he mistaken in thinking that was not one of his fires, but hearth-smoke? "Just as in Hungary, no one will be able to mistake where the Tremere have been."

"Don't look down. Don't look down. Don't look down..."

"You can open your eyes, Baghatur, we *are d*own," Jervais called out heartily as the gargoyles rotated their wings and slowed to a stop just short of the ground. The Khazar's feet fumbled a bit in the soft heaped peat and spongy moss of the bog-floor. Then he recovered himself.

"Now you've a good idea of the strength of your concoction, don't you?" the older Tremere asked.

"Yes—yes, master."

"Good. Your job is to portion it out as evenly as you can. Dig little holes and bury it."

"Yes, master. And you..."

"My job is to spread it. Put your hand down on the soil here. Push on it. Feel that? It's more water than anything else."

"I see. That's why it's you and me here instead of the others." He peered around. "Interesting. I'll be curious to see if the moss affects the rate of absorption or—"

"Exactly. Now you understand what you need to do?"

"Oh. Oh, yes." He padded here and there among the dense stands of pine trees, pouring out a little from the flagon each place he stopped. Jervais chose a puddle to start from and knelt down before it, thrusting his arms elbow-deep into the acrid muck. This would have to begin very small and grow gradually, with careful attention to the rhythm of the miniature tides he was generating in the mass of peat-soil. Even so, it might not be possible to kill the whole mire. But if he'd chosen his spot as well as he hoped, then it would be enough to cripple the *vis* well, and perhaps even the flow of the ley line itself.

"Master!"

"What?"

"There's a...ugh. How, er, singular."

"There's a *what*?" Jervais called irritably.

"Well, look." Baghatur reached into the weeds at the edge of a pond and dragged up a bloated arm. Its black-nailed fingers flopped back. "She's weighed down with gold jewelry."

"Hedge-wizards," Jervais scoffed.

"I don't suppose you—want it?"

"No. You have it if you like. Go ahead and drag her out, anyway, if it's one less ghost serving the Telyavs that's all to the good."

He bent to his work again.

Five ravens and a hawk touched gently down upon the grass at the hill's foot. A moment later there were no birds at all, but a hunched old woman, a young woman with brambles in her hair and four men who immediately lifted their spears and began to search the brush around them.

"What a horrible stink," Daine whispered.

"Yes. I know I've smelled it before, but..." Deverra frowned and stared up at the billows of blue-gray smoke. "All the ingredients. It's been too many years."

"Now, at least, there must be only six." Valdur was one of the Curonian group. None of the old magi were left among them except for Bernalt, but at least they took this business of numbers seriously once it was explained to them.

Yes, now they're six. Alas, we here are only six as well, but only six could come swiftly enough. The mortal Saxons, at least, must die before they could chop down more trees and send more of her children to shameful, helpless deaths in the sun. And whatever the Tremere themselves were doing up there, all hunched and huddled together in a tight circle, could be nothing good.

"First, the ward," she said. "But then, be ready to attack swiftly. The one thing you cannot allow them is time to *think*. And remember, it's better to concentrate and kill one of them than to wound them all, so if you see one beginning to falter, show no mercy."

They nodded.

Suddenly Valdur fell to the ground, moaning. "My priestess—"

They bent over him. He coughed, and a black foulness splashed out of his mouth and fell upon the ground. Where it touched, the grass withered.

"My priestess, they're poisoning me... fouling the *pannean*..."

So that was the nature of the *maleficium*—mortals by day and vampires by night, nonstop blasphemy. "Stay here, and hold on," she told him. She took out a *zaltys* snakeskin from her pouch. "Here, eat this. It'll help you purge the curse. I promise you, we won't let them finish. Will we?" She looked up at the others.

Daine nodded. "For Ako," she whispered fiercely. "For all our fallen."

They climbed up with souls and minds girded and hands linked, already speaking the prayers that would call upon the favor of the Maker-Unmaker and enlist his aid in this particular unmaking. The Tremere rose as their attackers crested the hilltop, startled, but they couldn't react quickly enough. This time the Telyavs' combined will surged up against their weakened ward and dissolved it like *aqua fortis*.

"Forward!" Deverra cried. Her voice wasn't what it once had been, but passion carried it. Determined to remind her kin that they did not have exclusive purview over the flames of the Underworld, she sent a barrage of bale-fire directly into the head of the nearest. He fell flat on his back, dead almost in that instant. But as he fell, the cloak opened. Underneath was the bone-white flash of a surcoat with a great black cross emblazoned across it.

And now the other "Tremere" ran forward, throwing their cloaks back to reveal the warrior-garb underneath. Worse, each cross was alight, outlined in a golden glow that both mocked and invoked the memory of the sun. As one, her Telyavs recoiled from the sight. They didn't flee, but the advance that had been perfectly unified and resolute suddenly became a confusion. The knights closed in with swords upraised, screaming something in that barbaric tongue of theirs. It was all the Telyavs could do to raise their spears and their most instinctive charms as the Saxons fell upon them.

Jervais got up, or tried to. He felt as though his legs had been bought new that evening, and only just now attached.

"I wonder if anyone lives around this little stain of pestilence," he said vaguely as Baghatur came to help him.

"Someone must, master. Shall we find them?"

"Master." Rixatrix had tried once to land in the soft soil here, and just as rapidly abandoned the idea. Instead, she coasted over to the trunk of one of the sturdier pines and clung to it. "Tower of red rise up."

"Good, good..." Jervais looked in his purse and took out the signal-stone. Nothing yet. "Theoretically, that means at least *some* of the Telyavs are busy. But we've still got to wait for Torgeir. Yes, Baghatur, let's look for a house. Some lone farmstead. Hellfire, a herd of cattle would suit at this point." The gargoyle brightened alarmingly at that and gave an eager little whine. "No, no. A farmstead. That'll do."

Chapter Twenty-Three

"Master wizards, please…"

Fidus straightened his sigils—all seven of them—and turned to follow his new-minted brother magi out of the ritual chamber. He couldn't help a quick peek at the spectators as he did. There was Jervais, smiling broadly, and his old grammar teacher from Compostela, and his mother, and even Aristotle. And Lucien serving as usher, dressed finely as ever but now bowing. He bowed to Fidus, all the contempt in his princely face transmuted to affectionate respect at last. Yes, it was true what his teachers had said. Knowledge could open the gates of the kingdom to a man regardless of his state or station. "Come, master wizards," Lucien repeated politely…

But no. Lucien was ash, and this wasn't his voice anyway. It was the voice of the young mortal knight who'd been sent along with them. The heavy tent-cloths they'd wrapped themselves in for day-sleep tugged, and the leaves on top rustled. Fidus rolled counterclockwise and wriggled to free himself.

"What did you say?" he asked as he emerged. He just wanted to hear it again.

The knight sat back. "I said please wake up, master wizards."

"I'm up. Torgeir…"

"I'm—I'm getting up." The other pile of leaves rustled, and the albino's head and torso emerged. He blinked at the mortal. "All right, what have you seen?"

"The hammering never stopped, not for more than the space of a *Pater Noster*."

"It was the same last night…not even to make water."

They all exchanged looks. Torgeir shook off the last of his

cover, and the knight loosened his sword in its sheath.

"Well, that settles it," Torgeir said. He laid a hand on Fidus's arm. "Look out. It's going to be fiery in there, you know."

"How many corpses have I had to incinerate over the past decade?" Fidus retorted. Then he belatedly remembered he was in mixed company, and gave the knight a sheepish glance.

"Nevertheless…" the Dane pondered. "I think we'd better see to at least a few protections first. Even leaving the fire aside, we have no idea what we're in for." He stood. "Keep watching, sir knight. We won't be more than an hour or two. If anything changes, tell us immediately."

"Saxons!" Aukstakojis said brightly in that tongue when they entered the shack. "Saxon merchants always pay well!"

But Torgeir answered in Latin, calling over the noise. "We're not here for ironmongery this time, I'm afraid. And you understand everything I'm saying, don't you?"

The smith's face fell slightly. He stopped hammering, set down his tools and turned to them.

"Even the busiest of tradesmen can usually find time to take a piss," the Dane went on. He collected his companions with a glance. "Come on—"

They pinned the wiry little man against the wall. Torgeir brought out his cross and held it up where Aukstakojis could clearly see it. At the sight of it the smith's eyes went wide with terror, and any fight that had been in him drained out.

"Look!" Fidus exclaimed. "Brother, look!"

He forced down Aukstakojis's bushy mustache with his hand and pulled back on his hair to force his head upward. Without the thick garland of whiskers, they could all see that the smith's nose had no nostrils.

"Yes, I don't suppose imps strictly *need* to breathe. Neither do we, but at least we have the souvenirs of humanity." Torgeir smiled, allowing his fangs to descend. "No more playacting, smith. I've drunk a great deal of ungodly blood here already, and I'm hungry for more. So if you can kill us, then try. If not, speak." He forced the cross in closer. "Where is it?"

"Where is what?" the smith cried in Latin.

"The fire that must never go out. The fire dedicated to Telyavel the Smith, by which his covenant with his high priests is always sealed. She never even told the raiders that *you* were its guardian, did she? Now is it the forge itself, or only a single coal within? Probably a coal, since she had to move it when she came down from Livonia. Isn't that right?"

Aukstakojis said nothing. Torgeir nodded at Fidus, who rather joyously knocked his head a sharp blow on the wall. The knight dug his sword's tip into the smith's chest.

"Yes, I carried it in a bucket!"

"Fidus, get the tongs and get it out. You're probably looking for something more like a glowing piece of jet than a true coal."

"All right…" Fidus's dark-accustomed eyes watered, but he did as he was bid, poking and grasping gingerly. "Here, this one I think. It's harder than the rest."

Torgeir squinted at it too. It was hard to tell in the heated air, but to his sorcerer's sight the thing did seem to radiate.

"Right. Now how to destroy it?"

"Water?" Fidus shrugged.

"I doubt it," said Torgeir, but he saved a corner of his eye for Aukstakojis's reactions, looking for something telltale.

"You can't destroy it," the smith insisted. "It is eternal."

"I'll just bet. Not much of an oath for Deverra to take, is it, to protect something that's eternal anyway?"

But Fidus hefted the tongs, considering. Master Jervais had always said the funny thing about conjured devils—assuming that's what this really was—was that they never outright lied, only by omission. "Well, maybe it's not destruction she has to protect it from."

"What then?" Torgeir paused a moment. "Sacrilege?"

"Perhaps…"

"Sacrilege, Dane?" the smith spat. His kindly face had contorted beyond human limits now, twisted with immortal pain and fear. "You are a walking sacrilege. And that piece of brass you hold, to you it is nothing but a talisman to ward off what troubles you."

"Shut up," Torgeir snarled in return. "This talisman is going to send you back to whatever black underworld vomited you up."

"Well, if you're going to do that *anyway*—" Fidus interrupted. Torgeir glared at him. It was a hard glare, rather like one of Jervais's, and all the more frightening for the reddish tinge his eyes took on in the reflected firelight.

"If you're...I mean," stammered Fidus, "why not just send it back with him?"

The look on the smith's face decided Torgeir at once. "Right! Hold him!" As the two of them struggled to keep Aukstakojis's head still and stood on his feet, Fidus tried to pry his mouth open. When that didn't work, he brought the handle-end of the tongs down onto the gritted teeth, smashing them in. The smith gave a gurgling scream and dark blood gushed from his lips as Fidus forced the pincer end of the hot tongs down into his throat, then pulled apart the handles so as to drop the coal down into his belly. Meanwhile, Torgeir pushed the cross against the smith's taut-stretched cheek.

"*Adjuro te, serpens antique, in nomine Patris, et Filii, et Spiritus Sancti...*"

The knight quickly joined the chant, and even Fidus picked it up in a moment. The smith's body shook and smoked, giving forth a horrible boggy odor, and then it began to deliquesce in their very hands, first blackening and bloating like an old corpse and then transmuting into a sludge that splashed across them.

"Ugh! No sign of the coal?"

"No." Fidus felt hurriedly around for it in the muck. "No, it's gone."

As he said it, an enormous groan and crack sounded throughout the shed. They turned to gape at the forge. The very earth was giving underneath it, tipping it in, swallowing it up. As it turned over, Torgeir caught sight of the marks that had been etched into it, ancient glyphs of concealment and promises of retribution on the would-be defiler...

"Out!" he shouted. His companions needed no further urging. They pelted out of the shack just as walls began to fold in on themselves and the fault in the ground parted beneath their very feet. Before they'd even reached the edge of the clearing, the whole thing was already gone as though it had never been.

Only a stinking pit remained.

Telyavel had reclaimed his own.

Once, as an apprentice, Deverra had been sent to gather the dew of the alchemilla plant and had ended up clinging to the side of an outcropping of rock whence a small growth sprang. Halfway through the preparatory prayer, a section of it collapsed out from under her and she was swung out, fingers desperately entwined in the herb-stems. She made the mistake of looking down in that moment. Her heart fell into the chasm, and for several hours afterward, she wasn't sure it meant ever to return.

This felt much the same, except that the chasm was bottomless. And in that one simple, irreversible moment, a battle that was unpleasantly pitched but winnable became a lost cause.

"Retreat." She couldn't make it sound above a croak. Ako had been laid out nearby, a spear stuck in her shoulder, but she was getting up already. Deverra stumbled over to her.

"Ako. Ako, call retreat."

Ako stared at her, aghast. One of the three surviving knights, a big blond, came charging at them. Deverra swiped her arm sideways almost distractedly and a gust of violent wind sent him flying.

"Call retreat," she croaked again.

"Retreat!" The younger vampire's voice rang out damnably clear. "Retreat!"

The Saxons heard but didn't understand the Livonian version of the word. They cried out in astonished fury as their opponents suddenly halved, quartered and then dwindled even further in size, sprouting feathers and rising up into the air.

Jervais poured a cup of mead into the little cauldron that hung over the hearth fire. He also put in a little mistletoe that he found in a pot. Baghatur watched him with interest.

"Is it a *ritus aquam,* master?"

"Hm?" Jervais looked up. The blood of the farmer's wife was reviving him, putting a fine warmth in his cheeks, but sharpness of mind hadn't returned just yet. "No, I just enjoy the smell. Most of the foods that pleased me in life sicken me with their scent, but not mead."

"I see," Baghatur said, though it was plain he didn't really. He went to the window. "We're not going back to camp tonight, I take it?"

"No. We're meeting the knights at the lake, just west of the Telyav camp."

"Not Herr Hermann," the Khazar frowned, confused.

"No, he and those with him stay at our camp. They could never join us in time anyway. It may be that they'll have the privilege of meeting the fresh edge of Deverra's wrath when she learns what we've done. Or possibly poor little Fidus and Torgeir will actually earn that honor. But I think it more likely she'll run to ground among her mortals and plot something we mustn't let her finish plotting. Therefore, we march on them tonight with Herr Wigand and the rest. Never give Tremere time to think, my boy."

"You've said they're not Tremere, master."

"True. Nevertheless."

"Is that our hill, way over there?"

Jervais pushed himself out of the chair and came to look out of the window across the broad marshy plain. "Yes, indeed. And a new flare of red from atop it. Good."

"Now we leave?"

"Well, let me see." He took out the signal-stone again. Much of him was hoping (even though it would be bad news indeed) that it wouldn't light anytime soon. As he held it, however, the etched lines of the Greek letter upon it came to life, glittering. Out at the forge Torgeir was tracing *alpha*, which was quite appropriate considering that the forge-fire had been the start of a covenant. How much more appropriate, then, that Jervais should be here shepherding the quickening of *omega*.

"Yes. Now we leave."

It took their demoralized little flock what seemed like forever to make it back to the *ordu*, flying against the wind. Deverra was glad to see that the very last of Qarakh's riders was now gone at least, vanished into the deep, welcoming night of Samogitia. Perhaps it would be kind to them.

Bernalt and Jurate were already running to her even as she shook off the bird shape.

"Grandmother! Back already? What happened?" They pressed around her. The closeness nauseated her unaccountably. She waved them off. Ako began to keen over Valdur, whom she'd had to carry all the way back. He was still in his hawk body, and did not move. Deverra shushed her by placing a shaking hand on her head.

"Everyone," Deverra managed. "Mortal and vampire. I need everyone together. Call everyone."

"At the place of sacrifice? Deverra?" Bernalt took hold of her and lifted up her chin. At the sight of the blood tears tracking down the seamed channels of her aged face, his own face went slack with shock.

"No. No, just here."

"Are they coming?" he asked her.

"Yes, they're coming."

There was a moment's pregnant silence.

"Very well," he said. He helped her to the door of her tent, then went to obey.

But Jurate tagged alongside her, stricken. "Grandmother. Something is very wrong! Tell me what it is!"

Deverra said nothing. She went to one of her chests and opened it.

"We're going to fight, aren't we?" the younger Telyav pursued. "We're going to stop them at last?"

"They'll never stop." She pinned on her white apron, then brought out her bracelets and slid them onto her arms. "They stop at nothing."

"You said that *you'd* never stop, not while Telyavel was with us."

"Yes," she said, "exactly. I have endured through these long years of hardship only because I trusted in him, in the land that bore me, in the gods of this good earth... I knew they at least would never betray me, no matter what I'd become. Jurate, the last time I called upon Father Telyavel, he gave Qarakh the very power of the moist black earth, so that Alexander would fall to his fangs. He asked my beauty of me in return for the miracle, but he did it, and the enemy army was confounded. Nothing they did availed them. This time—well, there is nothing I haven't offered him these past few weeks—"

"Then we'll pray with you! All together, our voices as one! Let us spill the sweetest blood before him! He can't ignore us then."

"Yes, he can. He can do as he likes. He is a god." She cast the rising bitterness out of her voice as best she could. "And the Tremere have blasphemed against him in every way possible, and I could not stop them, and he did not. Or perhaps he cannot. It's over, my daughter."

Jurate was fighting her own tears now. "We should have called the others here. From Prussia and Estonia."

"No. I'm more glad than ever that we didn't."

"And what about…him?" She almost said his name, but wisely decided against it at the last.

One of Deverra's tears fell onto her apron, sullying it with red. She made no move to wipe it away. "They won't find him, because I alone know where he rests."

Bernalt entered. He was already changed into his ceremonial robe. "They're coming," he said quietly. "All of them. Living and unliving."

Deverra picked up her ax and followed him back out, with Jurate on her heels. The crowd was indeed gathering. There in the center of what had so recently been a large, rowdy encampment, they looked few and meager indeed. "What did you tell them?" she murmured to Bernalt.

"Nothing. It would only be an insult."

"Grandmother, you can't do this!" Jurate turned to her fellow priest. "Bernalt, make her see."

"She does see," the Frank said heavily. "I see too, Jurate. You don't, only because you've never been to Ceoris."

"And she shall never go to Ceoris," Deverra said.

"No. As fascinating a subject for study as I'm sure they'd find her…" Bernalt laid a hand on Jurate's shoulder. She shuddered. She'd never seen him look so sad before. Then he let her go again.

"You're going to wait for them, I presume?" he asked Deverra. She nodded. "Promise me that you'll kill Jervais bani Tremere."

"I'll kill as many of them as I can," she said. "If no others, though, then Jervais bani Tremere for certain."

He nodded and got down on his knees before her. "Then I will be first to offer my strength."

She nodded again, kissed him on the forehead and either cheek, and then bit into his neck.

Jurate tottered back on deadened feet, but she couldn't tear her gaze away from the spectacle of Deverra, drinking down the salt of her oldest surviving compatriot. As she watched, the old woman dropped Bernalt's unconscious body to the ground, hefted her ax and chopped his neck through. Oluksna came forward next. Then Ako, still cradling Valdurhawk in her hands, and then a sad-faced mortal youth...

Jurate's nerve snapped completely then. She bolted. Deverra didn't move to stop her, didn't even look up from her work. One of the priests of Bernalt's group seized her arm as she ran by, though, holding her fast with his undead strength. Their gazes met and they had the entire argument with their eyes: life and death, honor and hope. Then, just as suddenly, he let her go.

She knew she was committing a sacrilege, but she didn't care. Let Telyavel strike her down if it was not his will that one, at least, should escape to give warning. Let his hammer fall.

Chapter Twenty-Four

Wigand reined in his horse. "You said there were dozens of tents in the enemy camp, Master Tremere," he exclaimed, frowning.

"Hush," Jervais said desperately. There *had* been dozens. Now he could see only a handful, and the perimeter fires were out, but that wasn't the trouble.

"What?"

"Smell," Antal hissed.

"Smell what?" Then the wind changed, and even Ventrue noses couldn't miss it. Wigand grimaced. "Almighty God... what's going on over there?"

Jervais whirled on him. "I don't know. Shut up, idiot!"

Wigand gripped his sword, but something in the warlock's face warned him.

"I can't see," Antal whispered.

"Nor I. The tents are in the way. Herr Wigand, if your mortals *must* carry torches, can they at least stay back?" Jervais pondered. "Perhaps... perhaps if we circle 'round, quietly..."

"We've got to go in sometime," the Hungarian reminded him grimly.

"I know, but..." The protest died on his lips. Antal was right. Whatever it was that froze the air and set it ringing at a shrill, nigh-inaudible pitch—whatever drowned them in the reek of blood, whatever sent the vermin running and slithering through the grass past their mounts' pawing feet—it was his bounden duty on pain of treason to meet it. "Well, let's circle round as we go."

"Children." Antal gathered Olena and Baghatur with a

glance. "Our horses will do us no further good, I think."

The four Tremere dismounted. Antal joined hands with the apprentices, then looked at Jervais. "Together, Master Jervais. Always together."

Jervais nodded and added his own hand. He and Antal murmured words of protection, words to unweave enemy curses. The others repeated them as best they could. If only Zabor were here to add his strength in this particular art—well, never mind that. Wigand and the other knights looked uneasy, but they too had little choice but to do their duty by God and Jürgen. They followed along, still mounted, as the wizards crept through the abandoned grounds toward the remaining tents. Jervais had positioned himself on the left so as to keep one hand free for calling lightning; Antal was on the right, a flickering tongue of bale-fire readied in his free hand.

The only tiny stir of sound seemed to come from behind the tents rather than within them. All else was silent. There were no clamoring voices, no horse-skulls on pikes, no rows upon rows of dwellings perfectly aligned with the four winds now. Some signs of habitation remained, and nature wouldn't erase them for months: holes from tent-poles, worn patches of ground marking traffic, flat yellowed grass where floor-planking had lain, remnants of fire pits. A people's unintentional memorial to itself, Jervais thought. Then he came upon the gap between the tents at last and saw how apt that description was.

There were dozens of them. An almost visible miasma of blood-stench hung above them—a thing that should have roused the newcomers' hunger in an instant, but for the sheer magnitude of the atrocity. Mortal bodies and moldering Cainite frames lay beside each other, sometimes on top of each other, equal at least in death.

Deverra looked up. She pulled the ax, with some difficulty, from the head of the man it was buried in.

"Getting dull, the blade," she said. She staggered a little. The old woman and her visitors regarded each other.

"They're gone. Qarakh's riders," Jervais managed at last.

She brushed a red-matted lock of hair out of her eyes. "I told them to flee. Your fight is not with them."

"Not yet."

"Not yet is good enough for most these nights. As for the children of Telyavel, we have no wish to outlive either our faith or our covenant with our god. But perhaps he will grant me this one last kindness: that I will have the honor of ending my own existence, after having first sent your souls to him in apology..."

"Now!" Antal shouted hoarsely. He threw his handful of bale-fire at her. It hissed and died yards short, as did the levin bolt Jervais tried to fling. And suddenly the miasma around Deverra *was* visible. It turned smoky, then began to bubble and seethe. Faces appeared within it, moaning and shouting—faces with tiny pinpricks of light for eyes and gnashing, ghostly teeth. Jervais realized a moment later that he'd seen some of these faces before.

They belonged to the corpses that lay right in front of him. Deverra's Telyavs were dead, but not departed. They surrounded her now, cloaking her in the very stuff of Hades. As many as they were, they moved in perfect unity, as though one mind had absolute command of them—which, given the circumstances, was very likely the case. She lifted her hands and brought them together in a gathering gesture. They churned around her, through her, cycling from ground to sky like a waterwheel.

Jervais barely had time to gasp out the first phrase of the *Pater Noster* before the stream of unhallowed souls descended on him. He was no Hermann, nor even a Torgeir. The words in Latin couldn't quite stop the languor of the grave from stealing through his flesh, thickening his tongue and numbing his limbs. Shreds of thought and passion that didn't belong to him brushed against the edges of his awareness and would have intruded, if he weren't a magus of experience and skilled at defending his mind from just such assaults.

And then it had passed through. His drooping eyelids snapped back open. He realized that he no longer had Olena's hand, and he reached for it, but too late. The younger Tremere's eyes had gone distant. She turned back toward the knights, her hands full of eldritch flame.

Jervais yelled and grabbed her legs, knocking her down.

Even as she fell her bale-fire streaked out like an arrow. Herr Wigand, foremost among the knights as usual, caught it full in the chest. He screamed and half fell, half leaped out of the saddle. Antal was beside Jervais in that instant. In the next instant, the Hungarian had the wooden dagger off Jervais's belt. He plunged it into Olena's back. She roared hideously and tried to struggle up to standing. Antal clung to her, swearing. Almost too quickly to see, he jerked out the dagger and tried again. This time he struck true. Olena collapsed.

"Back! Back!" Jervais gasped to Baghatur. Baghatur stood agape, and for a moment Jervais feared the ghosts had him too, but no, the lad was simply horrified. He came around enough after a moment to let Jervais drag him away from Deverra, Jervais gamely praying all the while just in case it helped.

The throng of bodiless faces swept forward now. They seemed to shrink from most of the knights, but not from Wigand, whose cross-emblazoned surcoat was now burning to black. They swarmed over him. Still afire, he lumbered over to the brother-knight beside him and fell against his leg, kindling the Cainite flesh as easily as tinder. The knight's horse cried out and reared. The knight himself fell to the ground. He rose up in a mindless terror and fled, sending the ranks about him into a panic.

Antal ran over to Jervais, Olena in his arms. Jervais took out his ritual knife and stuck it into the ground, cutting a hasty circle around them. Who knew—heathen customs might always ward off heathen ghosts. The wraiths seemed satisfied with the havoc they'd wreaked among the knights, at least for the moment, and flew toward the Tremere once again. They met the boundary Jervais had just drawn, then fell back, but they were soon straining against it, against the membrane of Jervais's failing will. He could hear Deverra's throaty, bitter laugh rising through the babble of spirit-voices.

"We've got to pull out. She's devoured her whole damned cult, we can't fight her like this," Jervais blurted.

"You're right," Antal said calmly. "We can't." He put a steadying hand on Jervais's shoulder. Jervais turned to him with a frown. He opened his mouth to tell Antal that if they both agreed with this assessment then perhaps they should consider acting on it in the near future.

And then it began.

The Hungarian's touch sent stabbing lances of pain down through Jervais's chest, threads of ill sensation that sought out his blood in the channel and inflamed it, riled it into a raging tide. Muscle and sinew were suddenly engorged in strength that must be spent, thoughts suddenly abuzz and scattered. The ten thousand petty injuries he'd sustained ever since he'd first rode back into Magdeburg rose up and cried out for retribution. He was in the grip of his Beast. He knew this charm, he'd used it countless times himself—on enemies...

Antal stepped back. "Forgive me, brother. It was necessary. The witch's powers so exceed our own…you've just admitted that yourself."

Jervais didn't have to ask what he meant. He could feel it now, what Antal had wakened in him: a strange contagion that rose within him alongside the fury, first mirroring and then outstripping it. It was some insatiable, indescribable evil that battened on his blood and anger and pressed ever harder against the walls of his soul. It cared nothing for its container. When it outgrew him, it would simply explode. Even Deverra's ghost-mass seemed to sense the presence of something that matched its own malice. It left off its frantic milling and pushing and subsided into a sort of uneasy ground fog. Deverra herself watched the two Tremere with keen puzzlement now, her hands frozen in midair. As for Baghatur, he was thunderstruck, plainly completely unsure where his obedience now lay.

"I hope you don't think you're actually going to be *rewarded* for this." Jervais closed the distance the other magus tried to put between them. He could barely put two words together through the haze of boiling humors, but it was that important to say something devastating to the Hungarian, that important to tear his throat out. "That they're ever actually going to let you *rest*. It will never happen, Antal."

An unexpected voice—but not an unfamiliar one—sounded in Jervais's ears then.

Now, now, Jervais. Not Antal. Leave him alone. He's not the one I sent you to kill.

Jervais froze. As he watched in horror, the bulky shadow of Etrius stepped out from behind a tent and passed around Deverra toward the Tremere, navigating the heap of fallen bodies and the sea of ghost-faces with suspicious ease.

"You..." Jervais forced his voice to solidify. "You're not really here. You can't be."

No, of course I'm not, the Councilor replied wearily. *I'm at Ceoris, just as always. You see me because of the spell. What—surely you didn't think I was going to leave it all up to you?* He smiled nastily, but for all that he looked even more saggy and jowly than usual. *You are both my courier and my message. You're the ritual link.*

"Etrius." It was clearly something Deverra felt rather than actually heard. She bent her wrinkled head to and fro, peering about. Then she hissed. With astonishing speed she snatched up the branch-staff of one of her fallen Telyavs and also drew a bone-knife from her belt. "*Kuradi munn...värdjas raisk...*

Snake poison and snake blood," Jervais growled suddenly. "Spiders and scorpions, essences of venom." *I see your colors, Jervais, not a pretty sight. Keep at it. This is exactly what the charm needs.* He'd known from the ingredients that it must be unpleasant, but this was worse than even he could have imagined—that the old toad could so callously steal the very things that were most precious to him in all the world, that were his alone, his private hatreds, the vengeance he secretly nursed, and turn them into the vehicle of yet another damned *spell*.

That's true, the Etrius-shadow acknowledged. *It was all yours to begin with, Jervais. I put nothing into you that wasn't there already. But you know you haven't got the skill to direct this safely, and I do. Now let me in before it kills you.*

Never. He'd conceded so much already, playing jester to court ladies, groveling before contemptuous princes, lying, smiling, the vehicle for everyone's intrigues, slogging from one corner of the earth to another, finally abandoning even his sire and grandsire; all for the sake of hanging on one more night, of surviving long enough to prove Tremere alone knew what.

There had to be an end at last. There had to be a limit. Didn't there?

Pressing. Squeezing. The Councilor's voice was directly in his head now. It chuckled. *Sign of the scorpion. And scorpion in truth: hard, venomous, cringing, willing to lie in wait under a rock for however long it takes. The lore also holds that sometimes the scorpion will sting itself to death to spite a surrounding enemy. Is that how you'd have it, Jervais? Like Deverra? Or will you try for me? You could. Make up your mind. You've got to sting* someone. *Ah, how well I chose. In fact, you're almost too good a subject. Master Antal tells me he's had to calm you down several times for fear you'd accidentally set yourself off.*

Antal doubtless wasn't hearing this mental converse, but he threw Jervais a half-anxious, half-guilty look. Deverra brought her staff and knife together with a clack, and her ghosts flocked to her once more, muttering, humming. Once again she seemed far larger than her wracked frame should have permitted, full to bursting with injured pride.

No wonder Etrius found Jervais to be the perfect counter.

The Councilor, or the thought of the Councilor, had come to stand behind him. *Yes. Comfort your shriveled soul with that if you like. Loathsome as you are, I needed you. In fact, I find myself needing your ilk more and more all the time.*

"Perhaps I *am* the cloth out of which Tremere are now cut, then," Jervais murmured in a kind of bitter triumph.

Yes, perhaps you are. Lo, how the mighty have fallen.

The old sorcerer reached out again, and this time Jervais opened the portals of his will and mind to him. Once again, that masterful touch invaded him, gently pushing aside the various instinctive resistances that rose to meet it. It found the painfully burgeoning gland of *maleficium* and began to squeeze. For a moment he felt more pure malevolence than he could ever remember feeling in over a century and a half of existence. Then, on their own, his arms lifted and glided in gestures of summoning and conduction. He was astonished at how effortlessly his muscles and joints could move, how mathematically perfect the dimensions of each shape. One exceedingly unwelcome revelation that came to him as a result of this was that Etrius could have done Jervais's job at Ceoris at least three times as well as Jervais himself.

And then it all came pouring out of him in a flood of black bile. It came through his mouth and ears and nose, from the tear-ducts of his eyes (which promptly swelled almost shut in protest); through his fingertips and his toe-tips. So much of it, and so virulent. He felt perversely proud of his output. He'd been holding back for such a very long time, and so few had realized it. Well, Etrius had, obviously.

Deverra chanted rapidly. Her ghosts rushed forward to meet the onslaught and drove it backward, causing a massive roiling between them like the collision of storm fronts. His poison-muck threw out spits and gobbets. Wherever they touched, a voice shrieked in agony and a face withered down to a skull and then faded. Yet some of the shades fought their way through. One opened its mouth and latched onto Jervais's wrist with its spectral fangs. He cried out, but hadn't enough mastery of his body to do anything further; a moment later his other hand reached over and squeezed the thing, sending gout after gout into it until it was well and truly dissolved. Then it forced the other interlopers back into the mass and began pushing the whole thing outward, moving the border of the contest slowly but surely back in Deverra's direction. She shouted and redoubled her gesticulations, but the tide had turned against her for good now.

She doesn't know when she's beaten. She never concedes...the bitch. The spark of loathing that this thought touched off in him seemed to give sudden amplification to his magic *(Etrius's magic)*. The bilious wave was suddenly twice as large, dwarfing everything, blotting out his sight. He heard and felt, but did not see, it surround and engulf the Telyav priestess, snuffing out her power like a candlewick and then falling upon her flesh. He heard her scream.

He heard the final curse of her lips, as well, two words in Latin: "*Sicut fecisti.*" *As you have done.*

He did not know whether she meant himself, Etrius, Jürgen or possibly the whole world.

And then the blackness evaporated. He had sovereignty over his legs again an instant later, and they buckled. Deverra lay before him, sprawled across the bodies of her devotees. The knights stood behind him, dismounted now. Herr Wigand and the other wounded knight had vanished, probably for all eternity, but at least it seemed no others of the Black Cross had died while his attention was elsewhere.

And his brother Tremere were at his side.

"I know you'll hate me forever," the Hungarian said. He spoke quickly, seemingly knowing how unwise it was to speak at all. "But I will not hate you. I can't. Not after—"

"Shut up, for the love of God." Oh, to have had a drop of venom left for Antal. Jervais tried to get up, groaned, then shook his head. "Hurry. Take this packet…it must be sprinkled on her, or she'll rot away completely. After all this, we *will* have something to take back to Ceoris."

"Yes." Antal rose and took the parchment envelope from Jervais's trembling fingers, beckoning for Baghatur to follow. "Yes, we will, by Tremere."

Epilogue

The smoke was all the more acrid for the remnants of curing powder that clung to the wasted corpse's skin. A pole and rope had been required to make her sit up properly on the horse's back, and her face had been nearly unrecognizable even before the torch was lowered. Still, Jervais had taken the precaution of lopping off her left hand and presenting it to Etrius as evidence, so that the suspicious old Swede could analyze it to his heart's content. And she was dressed well for the occasion. All her queenly heathen ornaments would doubtless outlast her, but not, alas, the fine linen.

The three Councilors sat where he had directed them, at one end of the courtyard in their places of honor. Etrius stone-faced; Meerlinda, Lady Councilor of the British Isles, outwardly calm and serene; Goratrix had put his sleeve over his nose to block out the fumes. Malgorzata and Curaferrum stood attendance on their respective masters.

"Novel, Master Jervais," Meerlinda remarked questioningly.

"It's a Baltic custom, madame," Jervais said with a bow. "She would have wanted it so, I'm sure." Gazing at the climbing bonfire, he added silently, *She'd have appreciated the irony, at least. She sacrificed to her gods, now I sacrifice to mine.*

"My grandchilde has always been a sentimental sort," Goratrix said from behind his sleeve.

"Not too sentimental to get the job done," Etrius remarked grudgingly. "Or mostly done, anyway. There might yet be survivors lurking out in that wilderness, mightn't there?"

"I'd be surprised if there weren't, milord," Jervais replied. "But their queen is dead, their sacred pact with their god violated. They shan't regain his favor before the crusade annihilates the last of them."

"And of course Prince Jürgen plans to renew the crusade fully, now that Qarakh is crippled."

"Of course. And your lordship willing, I and Brother Hermann and Brother Landric will all be there to ensure that it remains a priority of his."

"Beg pardon?" Goratrix's eyes lit at that and moved from his archrival's face back to Jervais's. He lowered the sleeve. Malgorzata stirred too, but thank Bonisagus it wasn't her place to add to this particular conversation. Jervais did not look at her.

"Master Jervais has asked for a transfer to Magdeburg, to head up the new chantry there." Etrius shrugged his round shoulders. "But..."

"Magdeburg?" Goratrix gave Jervais what was evidently meant to be a friendly, teasing smile. "Not *la belle France*? Speaking that gravel-mouthed tongue all night every night, and not a decent woman in view?"

"Since I've spent all these years working to establish a relationship between our clan and his Highness of Magdeburg, milord," Jervais answered stoically, "it would seem folly not to pursue it now that it's finally achieved. I truly believe it to be the best service I could presently render to House and Clan."

"And fairer words than that could hardly be spoken," Meerlinda said kindly.

"Well, you've certainly spent long enough *trying* , I suppose." Goratrix squinted as the wind changed and sent flecks of Deverra's ash winging into all their eyes. Jervais hadn't yet learned how to read minds, but there were times he thought he nearly had it, such as right now. He could decipher his grandsire perfectly. The old rascal was furiously thinking it through and nearing the realization that he had no way to stop this. He had nothing left to threaten or bargain with, nothing left to fetter Jervais with, not even his daughter-in-Blood Malgorzata. The dawning look of disbelief on both their faces was the dawn of a moment's utter, transcendent joy in Jervais's starved little heart.

"Still," Etrius said dourly, "I'm not sure we can do without our *vis*-master."

"Oh, there must be others in the clan who could fulfill those duties, milord," Meerlinda pointed out. Out of the corner of his eye, Jervais couldn't help noticing Antal's back straighten and lengthen another couple of inches. "It's clear to me that your *vis*-master possesses the soul of an adventurer. If his ambitions have outgrown Ceoris, then so be it. To keep him here when he yearns to be elsewhere would accomplish nothing more than to make of our illustrious High Chantry a cage…and we all know how dangerous caged beasts can become. Do we not?"

From the way Etrius shifted, Jervais had no doubt that she was giving him some deadly serious advice despite her light, courtly tone.

"Yes, milady, we do," he acknowledged. "Very well. It's not an unreasonable request. And in so doing, as Master Jervais points out, he'll certainly be helping to secure the more western portions of my region." He laid no particular stress on the word *my*, but Goratrix snorted regardless.

Meerlinda nodded. "Exactly. Congratulations, Master Jervais." Her Ladyship looked directly at Jervais then, blue English eyes locking with his for just one instant.

Careful, those eyes said. *You are away, but not free.* They darted upward, toward the pillar of flame and soot behind him. *Even she was not quite patient enough. And she waited a century.*

I can be patient, he answered.

Can you? The lower lids, caught forever in the only barely marred smoothness of not-quite middle age, puckered in a hint of a smile. *I shall be watching to see.*

Very well, milady. At least he didn't have to ask her to leave his mind; her whisper-touch departed on its own. He glanced down now, wincing, at his wrist where Deverra's ghost had seized it. The tracery of dark green that colored the vein there had still not faded, nor had the pain. In fact, he might not be imagining that it had spread. He could always ask her ladyship to take a look at it. Or even Etrius. Doubtless they could help, although it would mean giving up his hard-won, all-too-fleeting leverage before he'd even had a decent chance to enjoy it.

No, not free, never free. The game never ended, did it? *Very well.*

"You certainly have a way with the dramatic," Torgeir remarked. One by one, the albino carefully took his travel-beaten books out of the chest and put them back onto the shelf.

"My dear young friend," Jervais said, "a thaumaturge who is not also a dramaturge is more than half a fool. There, one nugget of wisdom, gratis."

"Nothing's gratis with you. You must want something. Perhaps you're here to gloat over how after all this, you're still going to declare that I didn't perform my ordeal to satisfaction."

"Oh, nonsense," the older Tremere exclaimed. "There's no possible reason why I would do any such thing. Well. Only one possible reason."

Torgeir stopped unpacking. "Yes, and?"

"You see, Master Antal seems determined to hook my old post, despite the fact that he isn't even remotely qualified for it. Actually, I'd planned to nominate Olena."

"Who's no more qualified." The pale eyes did not blink.

"Nor less qualified."

"I see. A personal matter."

Jervais shrugged. "Unfortunately, I've reason to believe his lordship is hardly going to take any criticism of Master Antal that I might offer seriously. You, however, are one of his favored students."

"And if I refuse to disparage Master Antal in my report, and he winds up *vis*-master, then you'll declare my ordeal null. In front of Lord Councilors Goratrix and Meerlinda, and Malgorzata too."

"I'm pleased our close association has brought us to understand each other so well." Jervais stretched out his shoulders and leaned against the doorframe.

"I could try to outwait you.

You could."

"Oh, for *God's* sake," the Dane blurted. He took a wad of clothes out of the trunk and fairly hurled it onto the bed.

"That's my boy," Jervais grinned.

"Hurry *up*, Fidus." Jervais indulged in a nice satisfying shove of the boot upon his apprentice's skinny backside. That was the trouble with war, one always had to be coddling the morale of even the most insignificant foot soldier. It was good to have the luxury of a little unrestrained lording it over again. Fidus stumbled headlong but managed from long practice not to drop his burden. The last saddle-pack was bundled on in short order and Jervais got up on his mount. His rear immediately complained of insufficient convalescence, but he ignored it. Plenty of time for rest in Magdeburg.

"Why the third horse?" Jervais asked the groomsman who stood beside them, gesturing at it. "Ceoris is being unusually generous."

"Don't ask the *grog*," the mortal man replied. "I'm just told how many to saddle up."

"It is because I told them that even the Fiends haven't bred the beast that would take my weight along with yours." Master Antal stepped down into the courtyard, his ever-meager possessions slung across his shoulder.

Jervais tamped down a bolt of pure dread. "Master Antal! Headed back out to the front?"

"No," he said, "Brandenburg. To found a chantry, since I am told that now that Jürgen has one, all the Holy Roman princes will be wanting one next. I'm also told it is not twenty leagues distant from Magdeburg."

"No, no it isn't…"

"And no Tzimisce. Not sure what I shall do with myself out there. Still, it is an improvement on Bistritz, and I imagine I have you to thank for it. Well?" He secured his pack. "Lead on, Master Jervais. Surely the man with the vastly superior geographical skills should take point. Don't worry, I'm right behind you."

"And I'm coming too," Fidus piped up, scurrying to adjust a stirrup strap. "One moment, master. I'll be right there."

"Oh, I know you will," Jervais said, snapping his reins. "I know you both will."

Etrius, Master of Ceoris, First among Equals, Guardian of the Sleeper, Councilor of Hungary, Silesia, Bohemia, Poland and the Holy Roman Empire for House and Clan Tremere, awoke gasping and sobbing. He sat up slowly, piercing the gloom with his sorcerer's gaze as though seeking out some hidden enemy. Then he rose and threw on a battered old robe and went to his desk, where an unfinished manuscript sat awaiting him. His pen floated down from its silver inkwell and into his hand. He stared at the diagram he'd been making, wishing there were some further detail he could add, but no, it was done. Now he had to comment upon it, say something wise for the generations of blood-wizards to come. A drop of red enchanted ink fell onto the page as he sat there unmoving. With an irritated noise he touched the nib to the blotch and it sucked the pigment back up, leaving not a smear.

Something wise.

His ward shivered. He grimaced, but then identified the touch and with a silent wave turned the battlement wall of the spell into a curtain light as silk and easier to part. She came in and sat down.

"You sleep no better, do you?" she said at last. She sounded tired. It felt like daylight still outside. He was sorry to have roused her, but she'd always been sensitive to such things.

"No," he admitted. "No better.

The same dream?"

"The same. I have no other dreams, not anymore. It's just this one, always expanding and expanding. Now it chases me through the Doissetep library too. I could never find my way out of Doissetep when I was alive."

"Yes, I remember." She gave the tiniest of smiles. He liked her to smile, but it wasn't her old smile. That he hadn't seen in literally ages. "Still, it never catches you, does it?"

"Never yet."

A long, almost processional silence.

"You did what had to be done," she said. "I know that doesn't help. And she knew what path she was choosing. I suppose that doesn't help either—"

He set his pen down and put his head between his hands. "And next year something else will have to be done, and the year after that."

"Ingvar." He winced to hear the pagan name of his birth, but he raised his head.

"Forgive me, Molle."

"What do you want me to say, Ingvar? I'll say anything that will help you."

Another silence. "Except for that."

"You don' t have to say anything. Unless perhaps…you're in the mood to critique my diagram of the World-Soul."

She nodded. "Since we're both awake, nothing would please me more."

He started to bring his work over to where she could see it, but then stopped midway across the room. His heavy eyelids drooped with sorrow and fatigue. The book sank in his arms, lower and lower, until it threatened to slip through his fingers entirely.

"Keep moving," she murmured, letting just a hint of maternal firmness enter her tone.

"Keep moving," he echoed mournfully.

"Yes. It's all you can do, my brother. Unless you wish our fates to catch up with us at last?"

He sighed. "No. God knows we can't have that."

Meerlinda smiled again, or tried to, and reached for the book.

About the Author

Sarah Roark is a professional writer, violinist, teacher and (as should be obvious from the foregoing) masochist. She has worked on a number of White Wolf's roleplaying products, including various supplements for *Vampire: The Masquerade, Dark Ages: Vampire, Dark Ages: Inquisitor* and *Mummy: The Resurrection*. She has also authored the novel *Dark Ages: Ravnos* and two short stories: "The Prodigal Son" in *Penance by Firelight*, companion volume to the Dark Ages: Vampire core book, and "What Shelters Them" in *Demon: Lucifer's Shadow*. Some of her personal projects can be viewed at the *World Lit Only by Fire* website (http://www.wyrdsisters.org/), which she co-authors with fellow White Wolf freelancers Myranda Kalis and Janet Trautvetter.

She lives in Sammamish, Washington—beautiful lakeside community and former hunting grounds of Ted Bundy—along with her husband Brett and the world's two coolest cats.

Acknowledgments

The author would like to thank her friends, Janet and Myranda, for enduring faithfully as the other two-thirds of the Wyrd Sisters trio; her husband Brett for his patience, love, encouragement and willingness to fetch food; her editor Philippe for his kind words and his criticisms, both equally welcome and valuable; and Guido, Vincent and (again) Myranda, for help with German and Latin (any remaining errors are, of course, the author's fault and not theirs).

Curious about other Crossroad Press books?
Stop by our site:
http://www.crossroadpress.com
We offer quality writing
in digital, audio, and print formats.

CPSIA information can be obtained
at www.ICGtesting.com
Printed in the USA
LVHW051811020221
678152LV00017B/2267

9 781950 565610